TWICETIME

CAROL CARMAN

TWICETIME

First published in 2022 by McCaw Press

978-1-9998523-2-0

Printed and bound in Great Britain by
Impressions Print and Label, Cambs PE28 3EE

McCaw Press
mccawmedia.co.uk

By the same author

Gingerbread Children

'Every page sizzles with fun. Carman's deliciously dark storytelling
paints a fantastical world that's a work of art, with sublime
characters… a world you'll love to read about, and will have you
coming back for more. Hugely recommended!'
Paul Kerensa
Comedian and writer (Not Going Out, Miranda)

'Very funny… crisp one-liners,
surprising allusions, original perceptions'
Christopher South
Broadcaster and author

'A startling re-telling of Hansel and Gretel'
David V Barrett, Fortean Times

For Tony
the best big brother anyone could have
and the funniest man I know

A boy cartwheeled expertly across the grass and came to rest near the pond. He crouched and watched the water closely before gently scooping out a frog, which was stolen from his hand by a second boy.

The second boy dangled the frog by one leg and shook it backwards and forwards until a third boy gripped his wrist and carefully took charge of the frog. Leaving the first boy laughing and the second boy whining, the third took the frog over to a girl, who put it under glass and studied it.

But that was many years ago, when things were easy to take.

In the castle...

Seven years. Seven years since her father's henchmen had held her down while he forced her hand into a signature on the marriage contract, and Lady Rosalind Dibkiss had never given her husband, Lord Rudolf, what he really wanted. Never.

So he usually paid for it elsewhere, but temporary financial embarrassment had called for a different approach, one which had propelled him up the spiral stone staircase to the room at the top of the West Wing Tower of Castle Stein, Rosa's ancestral home and the place where she and Rudolf lived in a wedded bliss that depended on them seeing each other as little as possible.

The room – Rosa's laboratory – was strictly off-limits to Rudolf, but if the ancient stone walls looked down on him with disapproval, he didn't notice and wouldn't have cared. Rudolf only noticed what mattered to him, and what had mattered to him from birth was himself. From greedy baby to moody child to petulant adolescent to grasping adult, he had whined, tantrummed, kicked and snatched his way through life, demanding much and taking all.

1

Few people resisted him; it was generally accepted in Maund that that's what aristocrats do, and if you gave him what he wanted, he shut up and went away a lot quicker than if you didn't. And in the castle the servants gave him what he wanted because it was their job to.

But then there was Rosa. If she caught him in her laboratory, his life could be entirely different – much shorter for a start. However, she was in the library getting a quarterly report from the Chief Alchemist, so Rudolf had a good couple of hours yet, but better not risk it. He locked the door.

On a scarred and stained wooden table lay open a small book so old it only held itself together out of force of habit. The serif-littered handwriting caused eye-strain, particularly where the black ink had bled into rainbows under the splash of chemicals. Holes in the ragged pages indicated the power of acids, and brown rings and grease marks showed that those pushing back the frontiers of knowledge still have to eat and drink. Alongside the book, various spoons and spatulas had been thrown onto the table; an assortment of phials, bottles, waxed paper sachets and round ceramic dishes had been assembled; a large glass beaker stood at the ready.

Rudolf rubbed his hands together.

'Now for Great Grandpa Stein's Love Potion.'

He started filling the beaker.

'*Two drops of...* this one; one, two – oh, never mind. *Six ounces of...* this; there, that must be about six ounces... bit more for luck. *Half an inch of...* that'll be the blue one... *then fill ye glass up to...* there... with this.'

He held the beaker up to the light and shook it slightly; the ingredients jostled around each other momentarily before reasserting themselves into separate entities.

'Hmm.'

He put the beaker back down, wiped his sweaty palms on his britches and ploughed on.

'*One of...* those... *two tbsps of...* this... is that *tbsps* or *tsps?* Too late now... *stir ye mixture with a glass rod...* oh, a teaspoon'll do... *and when it doth cease to bubble, it be fit for use.*'

After impatiently whisking the concoction, he banged the teaspoon twice on the side of the beaker before throwing it back into the pile of assorted implements.

In the swirling mix, thousands of tiny bubbles laughed.

'Come on, come on,' urged Rudolf.

Tiny bubbles, massive energy.

'When it stops fizzing, it's ready,' he said sternly.

Energy that wanted to be out and about.

'Are you going to stop, or what?'

Out and about playing havoc and making noise.

'You're not going to stop, are you?'

Playing havoc and making noise on an epic scale.

'Oh-oh.'

There were two doors in the room, and no time to unlock one of them. Rudolf pushed open the other one, ran through and let the wind slam it after him. It was a doorway that was rarely used, given its close proximity to the sky and the fact that it only had floor on one side. A long scream echoed and fell away, as did Rudolf and – shortly after the explosion – variously sized fragments of laboratory and castle.

In the cottage...

The witch opened the closet, instinctively catching the broomstick as it fell towards her. She put it to one side, as she did a wicker washing basket, a garden fork, spade, sieve and trowel, a small wooden stepladder and another wicker basket full of empty glass jars.

Finally, she reached into the closet and pulled out a folded pasting table which she carried into the garden. The noise of the cottage door opening and closing caused the head of a miniature lion to pop up from the tall grass to see what was happening.

'Get changed,' said the witch. 'It'll put folk off if they see a lion hanging about the place.'

'Folk?' said the lion. 'What folk?'

The witch unfolded the table. 'Folk coming for the sale.'

'Today?!' said the lion, suddenly blurring into a shimmering cloud which shrank rapidly until it formed a domestic cat, pure white from nose to tail and all points south.

The witch pushed the table legs into place. 'Yes, today.'

'But you— you only found out yesterday.'

4

She stood the table upright. 'Nowt gets past you, does it?'

'But—'

'But what? I got the news; we're having the sale. I'm not hanging about.'

When somebody doesn't want to talk about something, talk about something else. The cat sat down and thought.

'Are you—' he began, turning to look at the witch, but she had already gone.

He padded into the cottage. As he stuck his nose round the bedroom door, the witch said, 'You'd best sort out what you're taking. And not a lot, mind. We're travelling light.'

He leapt onto the bed where she was sorting through a meagre pile of clothes next to a small carved wooden box, three well-used books and something that made his heart sink even further.

'Oh, no,' he said. 'Not the cat-box. You know I hate the cat-box.'

'You have to use it if we're going away.'

'You haven't said where we're going.'

The witch took a haversack from the back of the bedroom door.

'Home,' she said gently. 'We're going home.'

'But this is our home.'

'No, this is just where we've lived and worked – but not for much longer.'

'Are you going to stop working?' the cat asked.

The witch packed the books in the haversack.

'Don't see why not.'

'What? Stop being a witch?'

5

'Ah, now that's a different thing altogether,' she said, wrapping the carved wooden box in the clothes she had chosen. 'A witch is what I *am*, and work is what I *do*.' She put the bundle into the haversack. 'I can't stop being what I am.'

NOTES ON

Castle Stein

Castle Stein is the second oldest thing in Maund. The oldest thing is The University of Nature – the seat of learning, witchcraft and natural sciences popularly known as The Union – and nobody knows how old that is; the best guess is that The Union was already ancient when time immemorial was born.

The ancestral fortress of a family so long established that their history isn't so much recorded as fossilised, Castle Stein stands proud and unapologetic on a moat-surrounded mound, a magnificent showpiece of the rock which gives the Steins – quarrymasters, aristocrats, eccentrics – their fortune.

Those who built the castle intended it to be a bastion against weather, armed insurrection, personal grudge and drawbridge-to-drawbridge merchants. Hewn limestone blocks were shaped not only into walls and floors, but also into tables, chests, cupboards, shelves and anything else it would have been quicker, easier and cheaper to have made out of wood.

A double-thickness drawbridge spans the moat and, when raised, completely covers the castle's portcullis gate, although centuries of peace have rusted the portcullis mechanism and it no longer drops down to impale invaders or frustrate their swordplay.

Immediately behind the portcullis gate – unlike many other castles – is Castle Stein's front door, which opens directly into the Great Hall. The first Stein reasoned that if marauders did get across the drawbridge and past the portcullis, they'd have to turn and leave because there'd be no large open courtyard to stable the horses and camp out in while they ransack the place, and even the most savage barbarian doesn't want the living quarters carpeted by horse manure, especially when he's gone to so much trouble to obtain them in the first place. But that kind of logic was to be expected from a man who'd have put stone doors and shutters on the place except he couldn't find any hinges strong enough.

When he placed the original cornerstone centuries ago, the first Stein thought he was laying the foundations of a dynasty which would fill this castle and others like it all over the world for many generations to come. Alas, what the Steins were blessed with in tenacity they failed to match in number, and if the Stein line had soaked deep into history's pages, it had been drawn with a very fine nib.

And so numerous empty rooms line long, draughty corridors, and everyday life takes place mostly within a stone's throw of the Great Hall, which is much the same as entrance halls the world over, except for the huge stone fireplace, the sweeping stone staircase with its carved stone balustrade and the life-size stone reindeer that are used as cloak-stands.

~✦~

In the moat, the oldest and most revered inhabitant was Great Grampus, who was the nearest thing the fish had to a founding flounder. He was their history and geography, oracle and encyclopaedia, entertaining countless generations of silver-scaled youngsters with his lurid historical tales, even though he was many ancestors away from the actual events.

He instructed them in the origins of their waterworld and why it encircles the Ancient Mound of Stones. He warned of the dangers to hot-headed little fish who try to swim all the way round: the writhing weeds that grasp, the poisonous brown water that chokes the gills and the bright colourful flies that can lift a fish out of the water, never to be seen again.

He taught them not to fear the Great Trapdoor that sends ripples through the world and darkens part of their skies, and told them legends of the olden times when all was war above, and how men dressed in metal and their four-legged beasts had rained into the water, crushing those too slow to swim away.

He prophesied that all would be death and disaster should the Ancient Mound of Stones ever tumble.

The parents of the enthralled audiences had themselves grown up with such tales and so considered them to be the harmless ramblings of an old codger, until one day they saw the legends of Great Grampus come alive as into their world dropped a man, swiftly followed by a rain of shattered stones.

Great Grampus was not one to gloat. Great Grampus wasn't one to do anything any more, as one of the tumbling Stones of the Ancient Mound had assured him a place in a legend of his own.

Small shards of splintered limestone still skittered down the castle walls and plopped into the moat as Rudolf emerged gasping from the depths.

He shook the water from his head. 'Beaton! Drawbridge!'

~✦~

NOTES ON

Witches' Cottages

Where you live depends on how: how much money you have, how many people will be living with you, and how far it is to the nearest water and sewerage connections.

Some individuals live alone in vast mansions which could garrison two opposing armies whose paths would never cross; equally, in some houses the occupants are so closely packed that when they go out they can't keep their balance unless there's someone holding them up at each side.

Accepted wisdom is that witches live in cottages. And the problem with accepted wisdom is that it's far more accepted than it is wisdom. Witches live wherever they like. Nobody's going to tell them they can't.

Many witches do live in cottages, normally because they inherit them from another witch. This means the cottages are generally old, although the increasing number of witches graduating from The Union means it's inevitable that new ones are built. These are often in the traditional style for the benefit of those who call upon the Systers of the Black Cauldron: people feel reassured by the sight of a witch in a cottage, and reassurance is a large percentage of healing, just as perception is everything in business.

When a witch takes her final leave of her dwelling, she must nail a silver coin somewhere indoors before she goes, thus ensuring the next occupant starts her tenancy in credit; she must also leave a bed, a chair, a table, a stove and a kettle, so the new occupant can at least come in and have a cup of tea, a sit down and a bed for the night.

Beyond that, she may dispose of everything else as she pleases, and this is detailed in the Last Will and Returning Wishes that a witch writes to stop the family squabbling over the candlesticks and cutlery. Usually a witch will sell any or all of her personal possessions to raise money for her Returning Journey, funeral or burial, but it's not compulsory. After all, to quote former Matriarch Imelda McGinty, 'They've never left anybody on the top yet.'

~•~

On the pasting table in the garden, an assortment of non-matching cups was heavily outnumbered by a wobbly pile of non-matching plates and saucers. Beside them stood a set of stacking saucepans, three stewpots, a clattering of cutlery from the kitchen drawer and an empty tea-tray.

The witch knew this was the calm before the storm, so she savoured the peace and quiet of the open space. Would she ever know such peace again? Maybe one day. Maybe in a twelvemonth, give or take.

She took the empty tray back into the cottage and reloaded it with the remainder of her books and clothing plus a badly painted ornament proclaiming itself *A Present from Scrubble.*

When she stepped back outside, at least twenty people were already reaching, stretching and pointing in all directions as they tried to match up the crockery.

She put the tray on the table and eager hands snapped at its contents.

Laying open a long, thin, felt-lined wooden cashbox, she pushed away reaching fingers.

'That's not for sale.'

She clapped her hands, rubbed them together and smiled at the jostling crowd.

'Right,' she said. 'Who's first?'

Despite the number of people in the garden – and their desperation to buy anything that might contain even a trace of residue magic to bring them good luck – the dealing was swift and without rancour.

Soon the table was cleared except for the felt-lined box which now contained an assortment of coins, mostly copper and silver. However, there were two gold pieces, thanks to the Countess of Chayley's manservant who had been given leave to use them to pay for whatever he could get his hands on, which turned out to be two badly-stained teaspoons and a rolling pin.

Thick hawsers lowered huge beams and before long Rudolf's wet feet were slapping across the drawbridge and onto the stone flags of the Great Hall.

'Fetch a towel, Beaton, then run me a bath.'

'Very good, milord.'

Beaton bowed and headed for a pair of double doors that were flung open as a distraught Rosa ran into the hall. She stopped when she saw the bedraggled Rudolf, britches torn, sloshing over to the fireplace.

'Ye gods!' she cried. 'You're still alive!'

'So I am.'

He started to wring out his waistcoat, and small rivulets ran into the fire, sizzling and spitting.

Rosa paced back and forth behind him.

'That's bloody typical of you. You blow up the castle and don't even have the decency to die in the explosion.'

'Must be my lucky day.'

'Lucky day?'

'Nothing wrong with your hearing, then.'

'The only thing wrong with me is that I didn't stab you with the cake-knife at the wedding.'

'I wish I'd stabbed your father.'

'You bastard,' Rosa began. 'That man—'

'That man,' Rudolf shouted her down, 'ruined my life.'

She stopped pacing and put her hands on her hips.

'As I recall it was *your* father who ruined *my* life by selling *you* into marriage for more money to gamble away.'

Rudolf spun round to face her. Drops of moat-water lashed from his shirt flaps and britches onto the fire, where they hissed and raged.

'Your father promised me half his fortune!'

'And you've already had half of it!'

'Those pitiful bits you give me? Don't make me laugh.'

'I won't,' she said. 'I'm going to make you cry. Beaton!'

'Stop whining, woman. It was only your laboratory.'

'*Only* my laboratory? *Only* my life's work?'

The double doors opened and Beaton entered carrying a large towel. Rudolf took it from him.

'I don't know why you're making such a fuss, Rosa.'

'No, you don't, do you? Because you haven't even got

enough brains to be a half-wit.'

He waved at her dismissively. 'Just—'

'You have absolutely no conception of the enormity of what you've done, have you?'

'Get the—'

'So I'll give you a clue. Beaton, set fire to the Games Room.'

When everyone else had gone, a tall, skeletal figure walked sombrely along the cottage path. His flowing grey hair and beard were recently combed and his pink face looked as if it had been the victim of a surprise vigorous washing in the not-too-distant past. His full-length coat and pointed hat were fashioned from sumptuous red brocade covered in gold-embroidered mystical symbols, and he bore not only a long wooden staff with a golden screw sticking out of the top but also a strong smell of mothballs.

The witch and the wizard stared at each other silently for a few moments then the witch lifted a small red cloth from the centre of the table, revealing a clear glass sphere standing on a short silver shaft.

The man shivered momentarily.

'How much?' he said.

She folded her arms.

'That's up to you.'

Resting his wooden staff in the crook of his elbow, he put a hand inside his robe and retrieved a leather drawstring pouch hanging on a cord around his neck. He opened the pouch, took out five gold pieces and slowly laid them on the table.

The witch glanced at the coins, then at the pouch, then back at the man. 'I've got a long way to go.'

He laid another two gold pieces on the table.

'And I'm not coming back,' she added.

That was worth another three.

'Ever.'

Five more.

She nodded.

The man gulped. His trembling, spindly fingers closed around the glass orb, and he rotated it until he saw a tiny hole in the end of the silver shaft. He took a quivering breath, put the tip of the golden screw into the hole and turned the staff, watching the screw bite into the silver until it could go no further. He let go of the glass gingerly, lest it fall to the ground and splinter into thousands of irreparable shards, but to his obvious relief the crystal was securely fixed. He held it up to the sunlight, and his knees sagged slightly as he pressed his lips together and whimpered.

He breathed deeply, bowed to the witch and then walked, a little unsteadily, back up the path and out of sight.

'Silly old fool,' muttered the witch, unfolding her arms and brushing the coins into the felt-lined box which went into her pocket. She folded the pasting table and carried it indoors.

The cat was in a fireside chair, pressing into the cushion as if trying to imprint on himself a tangible reminder of a fast-disappearing time of his life.

The witch emptied the money onto the kitchen table.

'Sounds like thar's gold in that thar till,' said the cat.

'Go on then, smarty-paws, how much have we got?'

He closed his eyes. 'Stack 'em into piles.'

She did as he wished, trying to throw him off the trail by chinking the coins a lot more than was necessary.

'Well?' she said eventually.

There was no reply, so she looked towards him. He screwed his nose up and moved his head to one side, paused, then moved it back. He sat up and rubbed his paws against his ears.

'I thought I counted seventeen gold pieces, nine silver and four coppers,' he said, 'but that can't be right.'

'Bang on.'

'What? Seventeen nine and four for that load of tat you took out there? Have they got more money than sense?'

'That damfool wizard has.'

'A wizard? Parting with money? Is he not well?'

The witch chuckled. 'He'll be a sick as a pig once he realises he's given me fifteen gold pieces for a glass doorknob.'

Beaton stooped to juggle a couple of burning coals onto the fireside shovel.

'You touch that Games Room, Beaton, and you're a dead butler,' said Rudolf, drying his face and hair with the towel.

Beaton straightened up again. 'Milord.'

Rosa adopted that reasonable, smiling tone of voice used by those wishing to gently illustrate a foregone conclusion.

'Beaton, who pays your wages?'

'Milady, milady.'

'And who will drink and gamble us into bankruptcy?'

'Milord, milady.'

Rudolf stopped rubbing his hair and draped the towel around his neck. He sighed. 'All right, all right.' He looked at her with the air of one about to undergo some waste of time in order to placate those in charge. 'I'm sorry about the lab,' he said with a practised false sincerity, 'but if you get the builders in, you can carry on your little hobby in no time.'

'Little hobby?' Rosa snarled. '*Little hobby*?'

She clenched her teeth and growled, bending and flexing her fingers as she moved towards Rudolf.

He started to back away.

'Now, now, Rosa, you're just a bit wound up. You know how tense you get around this time of the month.'

'How *dare* you!'

She lunged, grabbed his waistcoat and pulled it down over his shoulders, trapping his arms, then barrelled him against the wall, knocking the wind out of him. As he buckled, she gripped the towel and kicked his feet from under him; as he fell, she went with him, slamming his aristocratic features into the stone flags. She sat on his back and twisted the towel tighter.

'Now listen to me, you inbred imbecile,' she hissed. 'You may have ruined my life's work, but no more will you ruin my life. Beaton, fetch the Chief Alchemist and some rope.'

The cat dropped two items onto the bed.

'You're not taking very much,' said the witch.

'Only my bargain-token and Cecil.'

The bargain-token was a lock of the witch's hair set in a silver clasp. When cat and witch had first been matched after her graduation from The Union so many years ago, the cat had been given it as the symbol of the lifelong bond between them. Similarly, the witch had been given a lock of the cat's fur in a silver clasp. In accordance with the rules of The Union, '*These shall they keep until they be separated by proven Misfaith or Death.*'

The witch put her fingers in her collar and teased out a silver chain, onto which she threaded his bargain-token. It slid down to the lowest point of the chain and collided with hers. A working lifetime lay in the bargain-tokens: after all their years together the cat's fur was still white, but the witch's black strands bore no resemblance to her now steel-grey topknot.

From the bed she picked up a small, honey-coloured teddy bear who wore a fading red ribbon around his neck and had one ear raggy from countless carryings and chewings.

'Is Cecil going in the haversack or in the cat-box with you?'

The cat groaned. 'Do I *have* to go in the box?'

'No, no, it's entirely up to you – if you want to fly there yourself, be my guest. But if you're anything bigger than a sparrow, everybody in Maund'll be shooting at you for the pot.'

'Can't I become human-shaped and sit behind you on the broom like I used to?'

'No. Being a human's exhausting and your concentration's not what it was and I'm not having you spontaneously rearranging yourself to a massively different shape and weight when I'm at cloud level.'

The cat sighed.

'I'll go in the box. But I want Cecil with me.'

'I'll get you for this, Rosa!'

This seemed an empty threat from Rudolf since he was spreadeagled on his back on a billiard table, hands and feet securely anchored at the corner pockets courtesy of the rope-tying skills of Beaton – founder and life-president of Maund Knottologists – and the iron grip of Redvers Millicole, Chief Alchemist, whose day had taken a distinctly more exciting turn.

Rosa smiled at her marital millstone.

'Will you? Oh dear, how tiresome.'

'You'll pay for this!'

'I did pay for it. I paid for everything in this castle, which means I can dispose of it as I please – and that includes you.'

'At least untie my hands!'

'Are you uncomfortable?'

'Of course I'm uncomfortable, you hell-hag! It's a bloody billiard table, not a bed!'

Rosa feigned surprise. 'But you spent so many nights sprawled across this thing in a drunken stupid – sorry, stupor – I thought you'd feel right at home.'

'You crazy cow! You're mad!'

Rosa slapped her hand over his mouth and put her face closer to his than it had ever been.

'Rudolf, for once in your miserable little life' – her eyes narrowed and glittered as she patted his cheek – 'you're right. Beaton, would you ask Mrs B for a jug of water and a slice of bread, please? Oh, and a knife, a bowl of dripping, and a cake-icing syringe.'

The cottage kitchen sink was a deep stone rectangle designed to accommodate anything from peeling a grape to bathing a goat. It stood on two small brick walls, left and right, and covering the gap between them a gaily patterned piece of cloth hung on a string.

The witch pushed the cloth aside and grasped a hammer which was lying next to a jam jar containing nails of varying sizes. She stuck two fingers in the jar to pick up a nail then took a silver coin from her pocket. She held the nail against the coin on the back of the cottage door.

'Once it's up, there's no going back,' said the cat.

'No,' she said, hefting the hammer. 'No going back.'

She took a deep breath and stuck her tongue out against her top lip.

Tap, tap, bang.

She replaced the hammer under the sink and straightened the cloth.

Both she and the cat looked around as if seeing the room properly for the first time; they'd spent every day living in it but not actually taking much notice of it.

'Ready?' she asked.

'If you are.'

'Let's get off, then.'

She took her pointy hat from its hook beside the cottage door, went outside and placed it over the stick end of the broomstick and interlaced its strings through the leather straps holding the cat-box.

The cat took one last look at the cottage, then his head drooped and he sidled morosely into the box and slumped with his front paws wrapped around Cecil.

She bent down and smiled at him.

'It won't be for too long.'

'I know,' he said gloomily.

She fastened the cat-box door. Straightening up, she walked

21

back into the cottage, donned her shawl and put on the haversack, tucking the ends of her shawl under its straps. She went outside for the last time, turned and faced the open doorway.

'Goodbye to roof and walls and hearth,
My time is now to let thee be,
With thanks for shelter, safety, warmth;
Do this for them here after me.'

She closed the cottage door for the last time, patting its wooden frame like the shoulder of an old friend, and climbed aboard her broomstick.

'Nnnn-nnnnnn! Nnnn-nnnnnn!'

It was difficult to tell exactly what the bound and prone Rudolf was saying because his speech was hampered by the thick woollen sock stuffed in his mouth and kept there by Rosa's hand.

'Splendid,' she said, as Beaton put the tray on a side table in the Games Room. 'Redvers – fill the syringe for me, please.'

The Chief Alchemist hurried to the tray and dipped the steel cake-icing syringe in the jug of water.

'No, no,' said Rosa. 'From the bowl.'

The Chief Alchemist emptied the water from the syringe.

'How much?' he asked, slathering and scraping Mrs B's finest beef dripping into the syringe.

'As much as you can get in. Then bring it over here, please.'

The Chief Alchemist's face had a look of rapture as he handed Rosa the full syringe. He and the members of his collective usually spent their days staring at disappointing test results so to see a person getting what they wanted out of life was something of a departure for him.

Rosa held the syringe over Rudolf's face, which wavered between defiance and puzzlement. She pressed the plunger until soft, glistening fat curled out of the nozzle and dropped onto his forehead.

'Any ideas what I'm going to do with this?' she asked.

Rudolf's eyes widened, as did those of the Chief Alchemist.

'Trust me,' Rosa said. 'This won't hurt a bit.'

She plonked the Chief Alchemist's hand firmly on the sock in Rudolf's mouth. 'Keep him quiet, would you, Redvers?'

Rudolf's scream was deadened to a fierce bleat by the sock and the Chief Alchemist's grip.

However, when no further injury befell him he quietened, mystified. From his prone position on the table he couldn't see what his wife was doing but he was greatly relieved she wasn't doing it to him.

What Rosa was doing was squeezing Mrs B's dripping lavishly onto the bearings of each wheel on the billiard table.

When the greasing was complete, she spread the last of the dripping on the slice of bread and folded it in half to make a sandwich. She placed this on the billiard table cushion along with the jug of water and a full moneybag which she took from her pocket.

'Open the doors please, Beaton.'

'Milady.'

'This,' said Rosa, moving the Chief Alchemist's hand out of the way and pouring the entire jug of water over Rudolf's face, 'is the last drink you will ever get from me.'

He writhed and jerked but the restraints held him fast.

She pulled the sock out of his mouth, and as he gasped for air she jammed the sandwich in its place.

'This is the last food you will ever get from me.'

She lifted the moneybag high above the table.

'And this is the last money you will ever get from me.'

As the bagful of coins crashed into Rudolf's main source of satisfaction, the Chief Alchemist sucked in air, half-turned away and lifted one knee.

Rudolf screamed and tried doubling up but his bonds were too tight. He bit the sandwich fiercely and breathed heavily through his nose as his eyes watered to overflowing. He shook his head and half the sandwich fell away; he tried spitting the other half out but couldn't summon enough puff. He started chewing furiously.

Rosa smiled at him. 'And here is my last wish for you.'

'Wish?!' he flubbered through the bread and dripping.

'Yes. I wish that one day you'll feel such complete and utter joy as I do now.'

~✦~

NOTES ON

Flying a Broomstick

Flying is like walking, only faster and not as good for you. It gets you from where you are to where you want to be, provided you have enough power and not too much luggage.

However, there is a misconception about flying which must be laid to rest, and that is: flying is easy. Not at all.

Firstly, it needs intense concentration, as a broomstick pilot has to constantly monitor direction, distance travelled, energy reserves and weather, as well as looking out for landmarks, startled hawks and drunken farmers taking a pot-shot.

Secondly, it's very uncomfortable. Having to grip the shaft with some part of your lower anatomy and continually adjust your balance means that witches who are regular flyers tend to have handlebars, saddles and footrests fitted to the broomstick, otherwise they end up not only with knock knees but also with corns in very peculiar places.

Thirdly, flying is frequently cold. The wind in your face may be refreshing in high summer, but at more than twenty feet off the ground, the temperature loss and wind chill directly correlate to your flying height and speed, and the number of garments needed to compensate for it is exponential.

Lastly, flying is always draining. Constant mental and physical adjustment allied with the danger of icing-up mean that non-stop flights of any great distance are only attempted by only those with the strongest of constitutions or largest of thermal underwear collections.

So, flying a broomstick is not easy. Generally, the older you get, the more technically adept you become but the less inclined to actually fly unless it's absolutely necessary.

It's a skill that's taught in The Union Flying School, situated to the south of Maund, a short walk from the main Union campus. It's a vast sweep of grassy fields surrounded by an invisible rebound barrier which stops any trainee flyers coming to grief with either The Union's Main Tower or Magic Pool, and also prevents any accidental airborne interference with the runners and riders at the Horse Course just across the road. Those people whose business takes them to that area of town have long learnt to ignore the sight of an assortment of figures on varying-sized broomsticks taking off, circling, hovering, landing, looping the loop and crashing into hedges.

Practical flying instruction starts with intensive pogo training in a huge wooden barn. The cavernous emptiness resounds to the pounding thuds of little girls on pogo sticks energetically getting in each other's way, taking evasive action and bounding as high as they can before dropping back to earth and springing off in a different direction. This education through play prepares them for buffeting from air turbulence, and sharpens their reactions for the times when short-sighted migrating geese may cause them to veer sharply.

Once pogo-proficient, the girls advance to two-seater training brooms in an even bigger barn – an expanse of flying space that on the inside looks as if it's made mostly from cushions. The floor is covered with such deep layers of softness that it's difficult to walk on, and witches who fall off their training brooms find that the best way to get back to the start is to roll over or somersault. The walls, too, are thickly padded from top to bottom, and a safe distance below the glass roof an extremely strong net is strung to halt any witch who finds herself on an upward trajectory with no means of control.

The trainee sits on the broom in front of the tutor, who teaches her to grip the shaft correctly, to balance, wheel, bank, soar and dive, to take off and fly efficiently and to land safely.

From the padded barn, it's out into the open air, where a witch soon learns the power of the elements to help or hinder flights, the unpredictability of the others who inhabit the skies, the dangers of flying too close to trees and the inadvisability of attempting to fly back from a Walpurgis Night party.

In the classroom the novice flyer learns about power-to-distance ratios under different climatic conditions, cargo loading, how to compensate for the extra weight of passengers and how to keep a broomstick in good working order by regular applications of home-made flying ointment.

A witch has to put in a hundred hours of flying time before she's awarded her flying proficiency badge, and it has to be said that some witches take to flying like a duck to water, whereas others take to it like a duck to a broomstick.

~✦~

The witch circled high over the village, bidding a silent farewell to the people to whom she had ministered for so many years. Far below her, a thin old man with a long grey beard was steeped in concentration, focusing every last one of his mental and physical powers trying to unravel the ancient mystical art of future sight by staring at a glass doorknob.

She headed south, and the high Stylten Hills in whose shadow she had lived gave way to gentler slopes, bleak moors and primeval woodland punctuated here and there by clearings for farms, where sheep and cattle grazed lazily in the pastures and paid no attention to the overhead traveller.

She passed small groups of houses huddled together, communities just starting the inevitable transition from hamlet to village, and she flew over ragged-edged towns asserting their identity by eating into the surrounding countryside.

Eventually the landscape flattened out further and in the distance the witch saw the landmark that set her destination town apart from every other place in the country: punching through the low clouds like a giant steeple hat, its crystal tip glinting in the sunlight, was the conical Main Tower of the University of Nature, the high point of the town of Maund.

She eased down into the valley that cradled the River Maur until she reached the sprawling town, landing close to the huge limestone gateway that marked its northern entrance, Bog Bar.

She dismounted and opened the door on the cat-box.

'Come on, stretch your legs.'

The cat yawned and shook himself. 'Are we there yet?'

'Just outside town. I thought we'd walk the rest of the way – see what's changed since our last visit.'

Under the arch of Bog Bar ran the Great North Road, the busy thoroughfare that pushed from one end of the country to the other, bisecting Maund and many other towns on the way. Carts and coaches trundled along it, wheel-rumbles and hoof-clops blending with the calls of draymen, the creak of basket-ware and the knocking of seg-studded clogs on the causeway.

The cat winced at the assault on his ears as he and the witch passed sawmills, timber yards and iron foundries. The road bridged a spur of the river before heading off past the rozzer shop and on through Maund, its pavements lined with shops of variable status and viability, cramped houses, crowded courtyards and innumerable coaching inns. Fifteen minutes and three changes of street name later they arrived at another massive gateway, Stone Bar, once the southern entrance to Maund. Now it stood as a historical curiosity and well-used meeting place, as enterprising builders had expanded the town way beyond its original boundaries leaving the imposing barbican marooned in the middle of the town.

They walked under Stone Bar and up a gentle slope, at the top of which they turned right, leaving the Great North Road to its own devices. The noise level dropped as they moved away from the bustling trade route and into an area that could be called 'residential' only by virtue of the fact that people lived there, not from any pretensions to gentility. Residents of the broad section of the street known as The Horse Fair were envied their views over the stabling paddocks and the consequent bumper crops of roses, but further along, the road narrowed, housing encroached on both sides and the occupants had nothing to look at but each other.

The travelling companions drank from the hand-pump at one end of The Horse Fair, then rested on a stone bench on which auctioneers, grooms, squires and dealers would stand to survey the horseflesh on trading days.

'Not far now,' said the witch.

Rosa braced herself against the billiard table.

'Push, Beaton. You too, Redvers. Come on.'

The wheels on the table began to roll across the floor, aided in no small part by Mrs B's beef dripping. Tied to the top, Rudolf ranted all the way across the Great Hall.

'You won't get away with this, you viper! Once the townspeople find out what you've done to me, they'll—'

'They'll be eternally grateful. How many times have you said that the Lamb and Werewolf could do with a new billiard table? Well, now it's going to get one.'

'What?!'

'It's a straight run down. I've calculated it – you'll be fine.'

'You crazy, mad bitch! You'll die for this! I will kill you!'

'When you're big enough, you'll be too old.'

Dockside invective spouted from Rudolf as the table rolled across the drawbridge and gathered momentum down the hill. Discernible words gave way to a broken, juddering scream as the wheels rattled over the cobblestones.

'Yes!' shouted the Chief Alchemist, punching the air.

Beaton coughed politely. 'Should I send some washing soda to the tavern, milady? Perhaps the landlord could use it to get the stains out of the green baize.'

The cat pressed his paws to his head, his face pinched in puzzlement. 'I think the flying's affected my ears,' he said unhappily. 'I've got this noise... like a man screaming... on a... billiard table?... and not hanging about by the sound of it...'

The witch looked at him with less than total belief.

He shrugged his shoulders and pointed a paw towards the

encroaching housing. 'Coming from over there.'

She followed his gaze, and they watched in silent surprise as a billiard table shot out of the narrow end of the street. They turned their heads to follow its progress as it passed them, the screams of its tied-on passenger echoing across The Horse Fair as the table hurtled towards a local hostelry.

The witch prodded the cat.

'See? There's nowt up wi' your ears at all.'

'Seems not.' His nose twitched. 'Can you smell roast beef?'

It had never occurred to Rudolf that the billiard table could be a mode of transport. Over the years he'd used it not only for its intended purpose, but as a dining table, a bar, a beetle-racing circuit and a bed – something he usually discovered the following morning when he woke up stiff-necked and foul-tempered – but not once had it been a substitute carriage.

He'd certainly never wondered just exactly how deep the pile was on green baize, and as his head bounced up and down with every stone in the road, he'd never have to wonder again.

In the empty taproom at the Lamb and Werewolf (house rule: *No Swordfighting Near The Upholstery*), the landlord, Rigton, polished the counter, leant back on a barrel, folded his arms and contemplated much. How much to charge for the new imported light beer, for one thing, and how much he could dilute the ale before anybody noticed that it was only marginally stronger than the water they could pass themselves. And what was he going to do with that box of citrus fruit that his wife had bought? And why was that scream getting louder?

Just as Rigton glanced out of the window expecting to see someone running past, probably on fire, his previously gleaming surfaces were covered in shards of glass, lath and plaster. The bar-wench shrieked and ducked behind the counter as a billiard table with an unwilling passenger burst through the wall of the inn, scattering tables and benches, coming to rest in a swirling cloud of dust directly in front of Rigton on the public side of the bar.

Rigton mentally counted to five before he spoke to the bound figure, which still had its eyes closed.

'Ah, Lord Rudolf. A pint of the usual, is it?'

'Does this look like a half-pint situation?'

Rigton took a tankard from a hook, wiped it on his apron and started to fill it from one of the barrels.

Rudolf spat out tiny shards of plaster. 'Are the others here?'

'In the parlour, my lord. Shall I tell them you've arrived?'

'Unless you want to push me through that wall as well.'

'My lord has been kind enough to make one extra doorway; I fear another would be structurally undesirable.'

Rigton prodded the bar-wench with his foot.

'Wench, tell Lords Yedder and Guildman that Lord Rudolf has brought them a new diversion.'

'New diversion?' asked Rudolf.

Rigton turned off the barrel tap and placed the foaming tankard by the centre pocket. 'My lord's new billiard table.'

'Oh, *this*. This is for you, from my late wife.'

The landlord's eyebrows rose. 'What? Is my lady dead?'

'Not yet.'

On the mantelshelf over the fireplace in the Great Hall stood a large portrait of Rudolf. When he'd first placed it there, he'd lolled smugly against the chimney breast, silently goading Rosa to comment, and had been genuinely surprised when she'd said it was perfect. He didn't realise that what she'd seen leaning on the chimney was a pale imitation of a real man, its face covering a large, thick-walled cavity full of hot air and impurities.

Rudolf's painted gaze was impassive as Beaton walked around a pile of sporting goods threatening to engulf the Great Hall and gave Rosa a shotgun. 'Behind a secret panel, milady.'

'Ah, yes. His favourite toy.' She gave it a cursory inspection and pulled the trigger. Click. She tutted. 'Typical. Something else more show than use.' She threw it onto the pile and was startled by the ensuing boom and subsequent hole in Rudolf's portrait. 'Hm. Might save that after all. Are we done?'

'The Games Room is completely clear, milady.'

'Good.' Rosa picked a jemmy from the pile and prised the Games Room nameplate from its door. 'That's that.' She threw the nameplate and the jemmy onto the mountain of tackle, some of which was hardly used, some battered to death, some unfathomable, all expensive. 'Chuck this lot in the dungeon.'

'Might I suggest somewhere a little less damp, milady? One never knows when any of this... equipment... may be of use.'

'As long as Rudolf doesn't get his filthy hands on it, I don't care. It's all yours.' She rubbed her hands together. 'Now I can have my new laboratory. Get me the carpenter, the instrument maker, the glassblower and the silversmith. They can start work straight away. And get a builder too. The sooner the West Wing Tower's rebuilt, the better. I refuse to let my ancestral home be scarred by that loathsome lothario.'

Straining wires screeched through pulleys and a metallic jangling echoed somewhere deep in the castle.

'I'll get it,' said Rosa. 'You carry on dumping this stuff.'

She crossed the hall and opened the front door.

'Looks like you need a bit of building work doing,' said a mischievous voice.

Rosa threw her arms round the old woman with the steel-grey topknot who stood on the doorstep.

'Aunty Fran! How lovely to see you! And Sooty!'

She bent down and welcomed into her arms a body of fur so white that it looked as if someone had painted a cat's face on a snowdrift. She kissed him. 'Hello, Sootbags!'

He squirmed with pleasure. 'Hello, Rosa.'

She giggled, the cares of the past hours dropping away from her as she ushered the visitors in. She put Sooty on the floor then hugged and kissed her aunt again.

'Oh, I'm so glad to see you, Aunty Fran.'

The old lady pointed to the pile of sporting goods. 'I've not come to do the tidying up, if that's what you're after.'

Rosa laughed and helped Fran take off her haversack.

Fran looked around. 'Where's the idiot?'

'Thrown out,' said Rosa, with more than a hint of pride.

'Would that be about twenty minutes since?' said Fran. 'Tied to a billiard table?'

'You've seen him?'

'Oh, aye. Passed him in The Horse Fair. Well, he passed us, actually. We heard a crash not long afterwards. And then we saw a really excited-looking feller on a horse.'

'Oh, that'll be the Chief Alchemist galloping home with a tale to tell.'

A discreet cough came from the double doorway.

'Beaton,' beamed Rosa. 'Look who's here!'

The butler smiled and bowed.

'Good day, Miss Frances, Master Sooty.'

'Hello, Mr B!' said Sooty gleefully.

'Still not got a proper job then, Beaton?' Fran teased.

'Miss Frances, it would be a dereliction of my duty to yourself were I not to stay here and look after your niece.'

'A charge which could never be laid against you, Beaton,' said Rosa. 'Ask Mrs B to rustle up some tea for us, would you?'

'Already on the go, milady. And for Master Sooty?'

Sooty's eyes sparkled. 'A Beaton Special?'

'No,' said Fran. 'It's too early.'

'It's never too early,' said Rosa, and the cat laughed.

Beaton winked at him. 'If Master Sooty would accompany me to the kitchen, I will ensure that he is suitably refreshed.'

'I don't want him as refreshed as a newt,' Fran warned.

Mock shock filled the cat's voice as he lifted his head high.

'Oh, Mr B, what a terrible awful slur upon your character! I think we'd better go see Mrs B before anything else is said.'

'Shall Mrs B prepare Miss Frances's room, milady?'

'Yes, please. You are staying, aren't you, Aunty?'

'Oh, yes,' said Fran. 'We're staying.'

The parlour of the Lamb and Werewolf was home to a few rickety tables, one of which held three tankards of ale, each decorated with a slice of orange. Rudolf massaged his wrists, red weals illustrating his recent ride into town, and looked disbelievingly at one of his companions.

'What do you mean, you can't put me up, Yedder?'

Somewhere along Yedder's family line there must have been a dalliance with a troupe of clowns, because Yedder was irrepressibly cheerful, extraordinarily resilient and possessed cheekbones that could support a monocle the size of a fist.

'Sorry, old boy. In-laws staying. Doing the Grand Tour and decided to call in.'

'But you've got umpteen bedrooms in your castle!'

'Married a large fortune but also a large family, old sport. All bedrooms fully occupied, plus marquees on the back lawn.'

Rudolf scowled. 'Then I'll have to stay with Guildman. Beggars can't be choosers.'

'They can't be lodgers either,' smiled the long-limbed, immaculately bearded Guildman. He lifted the fruit from his drink, shook it and hooked it over the rim of Yedder's tankard. 'Yedder and his delightful lady are our guests.'

'Oh, Yedder and his delightful lady,' mocked Rudolf. 'Are they taking up every available room in your castle?'

'No, but the overspill of relatives from Castle Yedder is.'

'Besides, Lady Guildman won't have you near the place, old thing,' Yedder added. 'Wasn't that what she said at dinner, Gil?'

'Her very words, Yedder.'

Ale leapt out of the tankards as Rudolf slammed his hand on the rickety table. 'You let those women walk all over you, you pair of doormats! You might as well have "Welcome" tattooed across your forehead and lie down behind the drawbridge! You're a disgrace to the lording profession!'

'That's only one way of looking at it, old boy,' said Yedder.

'Oh really? Pray tell, what's the other way?'

'The other way,' obliged Guildman, 'is that I've still got a roof over my head. And Yedder's, for that matter.'

'So have I,' snapped Rudolf. 'And I'll just stay here for a week until that cow in the castle comes to her senses.'

In the drawing room at Castle Stein, the only eavesdroppers on the tea-fuelled conversation were the huntsmen and wood-nymphs on the fading tapestries hanging sullenly on the walls.

'How long are you here for, Aunty?' asked Rosa. 'You know you can stay as long as you like.'

'I only wish I could.'

A stranger wouldn't have noticed the change in Fran's voice, but Rosa was family.

'Are you in some kind of trouble?' she asked.

'Only the kind that comes to us all, sooner or later.'

Rosa put her teacup down abruptly. 'Oh, Aunty Fran, no.'

'I'm afraid so,' said Fran gently. 'Now what are you looking at me like that for? We've all got to go one day. You're a scientist – you know about death.'

'Not from personal experience. It happens to other people.'

'I am other people.'

'No you're not, you're...'

Fran put her hand on Rosa's arm. 'Listen, love. It's going to happen and there's nowt anybody can do about it.' She saw Rosa's eyes starting to glisten with sadness. 'And don't get all mushy on me. You'll only set me off and I don't want that.'

Rosa looked into the old lady's face and saw a request that

she couldn't ignore. She sniffed back the tears.

'No, no, you're right, you're right.' She covered Fran's hand with her own. 'You don't want that. There'll be time enough for that... erm... oh, Aunty, I don't know what to say.'

'Nowt you *can* say, as far as I can see – which is about a twelvemonth, give or take.'

Rosa breathed deeply. 'A twelvemonth. Right.' She sighed and patted her aunt's hand. 'In that case, we'd better make the most of you while you're... here.'

'Good lass.'

There was a pause more substantial than the castle walls.

'I hope you don't mind me coming back here to die, Rosa,' said Fran.

For a brief moment, Rosa was lost to the world.

'Er... What? No, no, of course not. I will mind you dying, but I don't mind you coming back.'

'It's just... I was born in this town. I grew up here, and it's where I became what I am. Other places have taken their toll on the outside of me, but this is the place of my heart.'

Rosa smiled ruefully. 'I understand.'

'And besides,' said Fran, clasping Rosa's hand, 'everybody should die holding hands with somebody who loves them.'

Rosa tightened her grip. 'Yes, they should. And you will.'

Rudolf's residency at the Lamb and Werewolf proved substantially longer than he'd predicted. At first, he was unperturbed; the summer's sport was diverting and he enjoyed his new-found freedom, but as the weeks wore on and his money dwindled to nothing, the worm of discontent ate away at his soul. He attempted various forays to the castle, but the drawbridge remained resolutely raised against him. The first messenger he sent returned with the nameplate from the Games Room door, partly burnt; the second returned with a plan of Rosa's newly refurbished laboratory.

His original dream – of seeing her thrown onto the street, destitute and begging, wandering the town as a constant testament to his righteous superiority and victory over the wrong inflicted upon him – was souring. By the time the third messenger brought back his shotgun-blasted portrait, Rudolf's discontent had fermented into something much, much deeper.

Around a rickety table in the parlour of the Lamb and Werewolf sat three aristocrats: one elegant, calm and self-confident; one fashionably caped, cheerful and harmless; one well-worn, short-tempered and bitter.

'Wench! Three more beers!' commanded Rudolf.

'Relax, Rude,' said Yedder. 'Don't get so worked up. As far as I can see you're better off where you are. You've got a roof over your head, regular meals, easy access to both the bar and the landlord's wife... what more could you ask?'

'Yedder, do I seem happy with the roof over my head?'

'You seem happy with the landlord's wife! Ha! Ha!'

Yedder bent forward across the table as he laughed exaggeratedly. Rudolf smacked the back of Yedder's head, causing his forehead to thump on the table.

'Ow! Very unsporting, Rude.'

'Listen, stupid. I need that fortune. I need that castle. I need to give that tart in that castle a good seeing-to before I bind her hand and foot and chuck her in the moat with rocks round her ankles. And you two are going to help me. All right?'

'The fortune and the castle pose no problem,' said Guildman, 'but we draw the line at your last proposal. Rosalind is your wife, she is a lady and she deserves respect.'

'Respect?' choked Rudolf. 'Respect?!'

'A founding principle of the lording profession, I believe.'

'What the hell sort of lording is that? It wasn't like this in the olden days. Oh, no. People counted themselves lucky to be done over by a lord in the olden days.'

'But these aren't the olden days,' said Guildman, 'and Rosalind won't take kindly to being "done over", as you call it.'

Yedder nodded. 'She'd have your soft bits in a glass jar in her new lab before you'd gone two foot across the drawbridge.'

'You gutless wonders,' Rudolf sneered. 'Does the term "lord and master" mean nothing to you?'

'Roz might take you back if you ask nicely,' ventured Yedder, holding out a flame of possibility.

Unfortunately, Rudolf was a barrel of gunpowder.

'Ask? Ask?! A lord doesn't *ask* his enemy *nicely*!'

'Roz's hardly an enemy.'

'Not an enemy? That hysterical harpy's ruined my life, and I will have my revenge, I will have the castle and I will have my fortune. And I'll show you two worms what lording's all about. Master of your own castle and all *enemies*, Yedder, vanquished!'

'Hate to keep pointing out the obvious, old boy, but it's not your fortune, is it? It's Roz's.'

The bar-wench approached, carrying a tray supporting three full tankards, each adorned by a large slice of grapefruit.

'It's mine by right of marriage and I shall have it,' ranted Rudolf. 'And the castle. I'll throw her on the streets and—'

'And then you'll show us what lording's all about?' said Guildman with a smile as the wench set tankards in front of himself and Yedder.

'Don't push your luck, Guildman.'

Rudolf snatched violently at the last pot of ale, sending tray and tankard clattering and beer cascading onto his britches. He shot to his feet.

'You stupid tart! Look what you've done!'

'But sir, I didn't...'

'Oh, I'm imagining it, am I?' he snarled. 'Well, imagine this!'

He slapped her hard across the face.

Yedder and Guildman stood up.

'I say! Steady on, Rude,' said Yedder.

'See, Yedder?' Rudolf said. 'That's what lording's about.'

The bar-wench picked up Yedder's drink, threw it in Rudolf's face, walloped him round the ear with the tankard and booted him in the groin. Then she ran.

Once Rudolf's shock had subsided, the other patrons of the pub had to duck as the legs and top of the rickety table parted company when he heaved it across the room. With a battle cry of 'Bitch!' he hurled more furniture aside and wrenched open the inn door so hard it bounced back, thumping into his side. Roaring in pain and fury, he threw himself into the chase.

Castle Stein's large kitchen easily accommodated a round wooden table at which sat Rosa, Fran, Beaton, Mrs B, Sooty and a balding, dust-covered individual in overalls with a cement-spattered pencil stuck behind his ear.

'Tea for milady and Miss Frances...' said Mrs B, passing cups over, 'a saucer of...' – she looked at her husband and sniffed at the saucer before putting it down – 'milk for Sooty... a cuppa for Mr Beaton and myself... and an enormous chipped mug covered in dirty fingerprints for Mr Mason.'

'Beaton,' said Rosa, 'since Mason began work on the West Wing Tower three months ago, he's done precisely what?'

'In the first month he was "making safe", milady.'

''S got to have safe working conditions – it's the law,' said Mason firmly, reaching for a plate of shortbread on the table.

Fran smacked his hand away.

'A month to move sixteen loose stones and a pile of dust?' she said. 'I could have done it myself in five minutes.'

She took a shortbread and gave it to Sooty.

After glaring at the cat, Mason blew out his cheeks and blustered. 'Well, the weather was against me, wasn't it?'

'Oh, yes,' said Mrs B. 'It's been a terrible long hot summer.'

Mason wagged his forefinger at no-one in particular.

'Heatstroke's the curse of the building game, your ladyship. That and vertigo.'

Aristocratic noses are used to being looked down.

'Vertigo?' said Rosa. 'I've never seen you standing on your own two feet, let alone a ladder.'

'And,' Fran added, 'you don't move fast enough to qualify as game.'

Mason was adamant.

'Heat and high altitude, that's a recipe for disaster, that is.'

'Altitude?' said Rosa. 'Working from inside a fourth-floor

stone-built room, an integral part of a secure stone-built castle? Not exactly dangling from a rope over the battlements, is it?'

Townspeople staring after the fleeing bar-wench were thrust aside by a rage-fuelled aristocrat bellowing for revenge. Given his propensity for treating his body not as a temple but a pleasure palace, Rudolf should have been a shambling wreck crumpling into a heap after thirty seconds. However, a voracious sexual appetite didn't just drain his pocket; it provided plenty of exercise, both in the act and in the high-tailing it before the cuckolded husband discovered him.

Spurred on by personal injustice, a longer stride ensured that he steadily gained on the wench until he caught her.

'Not all the delays were my fault, your ladyship.'

Mason tried to look as honest as the day is long, but he was two months past the equinox and the nights were drawing in.

'Perish the thought,' said Rosa. 'The first month was wasted due to a combination of perfect weather conditions and a safe working environment, and the second month was spent...'

'Waiting for the architects,' supplied Beaton.

'Architects, that's right,' Mason nodded. 'An intricate, complicated, long-drawn-out process, architecting.'

'What's an architect?' asked Sooty.

Mason jumped at the chance to show off some knowledge.

'Well, if you wants a house built, an architect asks you what you wants, then he draws a picture of it and shows you the picture so's you can change your mind about it.'

'But I want a house built, not a picture drawn.'

'Ah,' said Mason, 'but the builder uses the picture as a plan to show him how to build the house.'

'Can't I just tell the builder what I want? Why do I have to have this middle man drawing a picture?'

'Plan. If you hasn't got a plan, you can't build from it.'

'All we want,' said Fran, 'is for this tower to match the East Wing Tower. How much more of a plan do you want than the East Wing Tower?'

Mason gave her a patronising look. 'Just 'cos you's got one of something already, it don't mean you wants another one. If we builds it like the East Wing Tower, you'd have an East Wing Tower on the west wing, whereas your ladyship wants an East Wing Tower *reversed* on the west wing. Now, reversing things – that's architecting.' He beamed in victory and utterly failed to see another army sneaking up behind him.

Rosa folded her arms. 'Rumour has it that the architect you waited a month for is called...'

'Mason,' said Beaton.

'Your nephew's doing really well with the architecting, isn't he?' said Mrs B brightly. Mason's smile vanished.

Rosa sucked on her teeth as she spread out on the table a scroll Mason had brought. 'Call me naïve, but I'd've thought keeping it in the family would've speeded things up a bit.'

'It did,' affirmed Mason.

'And it still took a month to produce this sketch?'

'Plan. Not sketch, your ladyship. Plan.'

'Eight pencil marks? A plan?'

She let go of the scroll, which bounced on the table as it re-rolled itself.

Mason smirked as he unrolled it again. 'Not *a* plan, your ladyship – you's actually got two plans there. One here...' – he tapped on the scroll, then turned it over – '...and one here.'

The original drawing had been done so heavily with a thick, blunt pencil that the back of the scroll was ridged with its imprint, and someone had drawn along the ridges in a different colour.

'In the building profession,' Mason said, 'we calls it "a mirror-image representation of the original blueprint".'

'In here,' said Fran, 'we calls it "the back of the drawing".'

By the time Yedder and Guildman came upon the body in the ditch, the perpetrator of the injuries was nowhere to be seen.

'Hell's teeth,' said Yedder, surveying the boot print across the victim's cheek.

Rosa leant on the table. 'Now don't think I'm being unreasonable, Mason – it's simply that while you've been having heatstroke, vertigo and rampant nepotism, other people have kitted out a complete new laboratory and re-done the kitchen to Mrs B's personal specification!'

Mason blew out his cheeks. 'All that in three months? Gimcrack builders, they are. It won't stand up to wear and tear, your ladyship. One good experiment or a particularly heavy chicken pie and it'll all come tumbling round your ears.'

'Rosa!' said Sooty urgently. 'Screaming. Cries for help. Heading this way.'

'Beaton, front door,' Rosa ordered. 'Mason, stay there. Mrs B, keep an eye on him. Aunty, come with me.'

Sooty, Fran and Rosa entered the Great Hall as Beaton opened the front door, shortly before the bar-wench streamed across the drawbridge and collapsed on the stone flags.

'Sanctuary... sanctuary!' she gasped.

Fran bent down to comfort her.

'Steady now, steady. Take your time.'

The girl's whole body heaved as she gulped air.

'Can't... no time... please help.' She looked at Rosa. 'Your husband... after me... for my life.'

'Rudolf? Why? Is it money? Sex? You haven't given him any deadly diseases, have you?'

The girl looked further distressed. 'Certainly not, ma'am!'

'Pity. Bolt the door, Beaton.'

'You're safe now,' said Fran. 'What's your name?'

The girl wiped sweat and tears from her crimson face.

'Igress, ma'am. Please hide me. He wants my life!'

Rosa helped her to her feet. 'Don't worry, he's not having it. Beaton, take Igress to the servants' quarters.'

'I'll take her,' said Fran. 'You might need Beaton. Come on, Igress. Let's get you some tea. Sooty, you come as well. I'll need you to keep an ear on what's happening.'

'The bitch,' groaned Rudolf, clutching at the half of his body that was submerged in ditch-water.

'Bit of a turn-up for the book, eh, Gil?' said Yedder.

Rudolf glared. 'Don't just stand there – get me out of here!'

They started to haul him up.

'Gently!' he yelled.

Rosa retrieved the shotgun from the laboratory.

'Beaton, you stay behind the double doors. If I have to kill him I'll need a witness to say it was self-defence.'

Beaton bowed and took up his appointed position.

'Aunty!' hissed Rosa. 'Can you hear me?'

A whispered reply from the servants' quarters arrived in Rosa's ear. 'Sooty's receiving you loud and clear.'

'Good. Now when I call you again, I want you to undo the front door quietly. Can you do that?'

'I should think so.'

The thump of feet on the drawbridge was followed by a hammering on the front door, a rattle of the iron ring handle and a muffled demand. 'Open up!'

'Who is it?' called Rosa sweetly.

'Cosmetics By Courier – who the hell do you think it is, you stupid sow? Open this door right now or I'll kick the damned thing in!'

'You? You couldn't kick your own shoes off.'

As the front door deadened Rudolf's howl of rage, Rosa crossed to the fireplace and stood with the shotgun concealed behind her back. A variety of noises told her that Rudolf tried kicking the door in, failed, and now one, two or possibly three members of the aristocracy were preparing to shoulder-charge.

'Ha-one!'

Thump.

'Ha-two!'

Thump.

'Ha-three!'

Thump.

'Owwwww!'

'Aunty!' said Rosa. The iron ring on the front door turned and the bolts slid back as noiselessly as fog. The door swung open, dropping Rudolf in a disorderly bundle on the floor. Yedder and Guildman, who had apparently shared Rudolf's enthusiasm for a broken shoulder right up until the point of impact, stepped over him and approached Rosa.

Yedder kissed the back of her hand.

'You're looking well, Roz. Doesn't she look well, Gil?'

'Magnificent, Yedder.' Guildman's eyes locked on hers as he gently brushed her hand across his bearded cheek before kissing her fingers. 'My lady grows more beautiful by the day.'

'Something's obviously agreeing with you, Roz.'

Rosa grinned slyly.

'What can I tell you? Getting rid of fifteen stone of ugly fat made a tremendous difference.'

The ugly fat staggered to his feet.

'I do not weigh fifteen stone! You vicious harridan – you've never even considered being nice to me, have you?'

She smiled sweetly. 'It wasn't in the contract, my darling.'

'Sarcastic sow. Come on, hand the serving-wench over. That's all I want this time.'

'Serving-wench? What serving-wench, my dear?'

Rudolf's jaw tightened. 'The one who ran in here about two minutes ago.' He tutted. 'We followed her, you dozy mare.'

Rosa's face was a mask of innocence.

'I don't know what you're talking about, or why you've brought Yedder and' – she shot a look at Guildman – 'Guildman, my love.'

'Beaton!' Rudolf called, glaring at Rosa, who simply smiled at him until Beaton entered through the double doors.

'Ah, Beaton,' Rudolf crowed, scenting victory. 'Where's the wench who ran in here a few minutes ago?'

'About twenty-three, five foot four, masses of raven curls, milord?'

'Sounds about right.'

'Midnight dress, sunrise socks, stout boots?'

'That's the one.'

'Skin like golden acorns, lips the russet of autumn leaves, cheeks like two robins?'

'Beaton...'

'Panting as if she'd fled for her life, milord?'

'I'm warning you, Beaton...'

'She left the hall a minute ago, sir.'

Rudolf rubbed his hands together with renewed vigour.

'Yedder, Guildman – look upstairs. I'll search down here.'

'I wouldn't if I were you,' said Rosa, stopping Rudolf before he even set off.

'And why not?'

'Remember what happened to your portrait? Well, life could very soon imitate art.' She revealed the shotgun.

Rudolf grabbed Yedder and used him as a human shield.

'My gun! But that was hidden...'

'Behind the secret panelling, yes, yes. Move out of the way Yedder, there's a good man. You don't want to go home with a bloodstained cape, do you?'

'Yedder, you stay where you are!' hissed Rudolf.

Yedder stepped smartly away.

'I always do what a lady tells me,' he said.

Rudolf put his hands on his hips.

'Just hand the girl over and there'll be no more trouble.'

'What girl? There's nobody here except me, Aunty Fran, Beaton and Mrs B, my assistant Igress and a builder who'll suffer the same fate as you if he doesn't get a move on.'

'Assistant? What assistant?' said Rudolf.

'Beaton, fetch Igress, please.'

'Milady,' said Beaton, setting off.

'Now don't frighten her, Rudolf. She's only just started as my assistant and I don't want her upset.'

'Upset? Upset? I'll give you upset, you barmy bint!'

He was about to lunge for Rosa when Yedder and Guildman came between them.

'Ah-ah,' said Guildman. 'Not to a lady.'

'Respect, Rude,' said Yedder.

Rudolf turned his back on them, muttering to himself.

Guildman looked at Rosa. 'How is your aunt, my lady?'

For the first time a shadow passed across Rosa's face.

'She is... fair, thank you, Guildman... fair.'

'Pray give her my regards.'

Rosa smiled. 'Thank you. I shall.'

'And mine, Roz,' said Yedder. 'Absolute hoot is Fran.'

The double doors opened and Beaton entered with Igress at his side. Her hair was scraped back into a voluminous bun, a pair of wire-rimmed spectacles sat on her nose and her once-russet lips were a deep plum colour. She wore a long blue dress, a white overall and no hint of recent exercise.

'That's her,' cried Rudolf. 'Hand her over!'

He started towards Igress.

Rosa stepped in front of her.

'Igress,' she said, 'this misbegotten misery seems to think that you are a serving-wench who has wronged him.'

'I don't think, Rosa,' said Rudolf. 'I know.'

'But I'm not a serving-wench, ma'am,' Igress protested. 'I'm your assistant.'

Rudolf snorted. 'Are you buggery!'

'I fear he is mistaken.'

'I don't fear him at all,' said Rosa, 'which is why I'm telling him to sod off before I do something he'll regret.' She lifted the shotgun. 'Mind you, *I* wouldn't regret it.'

'You wouldn't dare,' said Rudolf.

'Don't bet on it. You'll only end up losing – again.'

'I'm not scared of you. You're a terrible shot.'

'And you're something very similar. But let me remind you of something: this is a shotgun. It fires shot – loads of little pellets which, from this distance, will turn you into a human colander as long as I point it even vaguely in your direction, which I am quite happy to do.'

'Look – hand over the wench and we'll go.'

'And if I don't?'

'I'll stay here until you do.'

Rosa took aim at Rudolf.

'Not in my castle you won't. Take yourself back to whichever pit you crawled out of.'

'Right. I'm laying siege to this place until you give her up.'

'You? Camping out? In the open air? You're too soft.'

'Oh, am I? We'll see about that.' Rudolf strode off through

the doorway then turned. 'Come on, you two. We're going to blockade the front door. I'll show you what lording's all about.'

He turned away again and sat down on the drawbridge.

Yedder clicked his heels. 'Roz.' He bowed and left.

'Aren't you joining your playmates, Guildman?' Rosa asked.

He put his mouth close to her ear and murmured, 'The one with whom I would wish to play is here, my lady.'

She giggled.

'Guildman!' called Rudolf.

Guildman lifted Rosa's hand to his lips. He gazed steadily at her as he kissed her wrist and her palm, and his dark eyes dared her to melt as he slowly kissed her fingertips.

'My lord,' said Rosa softly.

'My love,' he said.

'Guildman!' shouted Rudolf.

With a final kiss to the back of her hand, Guildman walked through the doorway.

Rosa breathed deeply, closed the door and bolted it.

'Beaton,' she said dreamily, 'raise the drawbridge.'

Beaton did as he was bidden, prompting one scream, one laugh and three separate splashes.

Two aristocrats sat on the bank of the moat and faced Castle Stein. One was tall, bearded and relaxed; the other was shorter, clean-shaven and fidgety. Both were dripping wet.

'Roz looks well, don't you think?' said Yedder, squeezing his sleeves. 'Seems to have done her good, elbowing Rude.'

Guildman smiled a long, slow smile. 'Indeed.'

Yedder took off his velvet cape, wrung it out and shook it

open. 'Oh, I say! Look at this pattern I've made, Gil. Wouldn't that make a spectacular pair of britches?'

'You'd certainly turn heads, Yedder.'

Yedder chuckled and spread the cape on the grass.

Splashing and gasping came from the water's edge.

Guildman grinned. 'I fear our first lesson in lording didn't go quite as planned,' he said loudly as Rudolf hauled himself out of the water and flopped onto Yedder's cape, panting.

Yedder pouted. 'Hm. Bit of a shambles really.'

Rudolf growled.

'Still, Roz looks well,' Yedder continued. 'I was saying, wasn't I, Gil, how well— ow!'

Rudolf pulled Yedder towards him by the collar.

'I don't want her to look well, Yedder. I want her to look dead. I want her out of that castle and out of my life.'

'You'd be better off staying out of *her* life,' said Guildman.

'What?'

'Forget Rosalind. Give her up as a bad job. Leave town. Take Millie; marry her, like you always wanted, and be happy.'

'Happy,' croaked Yedder, still in Rudolf's grip.

Rudolf threw him back onto the grass.

'Oh, and you'd love that, wouldn't you?'

'We'd come and visit you, wouldn't we, Gil?'

'Indeed.'

Rudolf jabbed a finger at Guildman.

'Don't think I don't know what you're up to, Guildman. I know your game.'

Guildman leant on one elbow and arched an elegant eyebrow. 'My game?'

'You want to be one of these "new" aristocrats,' sneered Rudolf. 'A goody-goody throwing off the proud heritage of your ancestors who looted, pillaged and trampled on peasants just so's you could be where you are today. I live by all those old aristocratic values that you want to dump, and you want to dump me as well. That's your game, Guildman!'

Guildman lay back down again.

'No, no. That's not my game at all.'

Rudolf stood up.

'Oh yes it is. And I'll tell you something, mate. Firstly, I will see to it that Rosa dies. Secondly, I'm not leaving town. Somebody's got to keep the old traditions alive, so I'm staying here and teaching you two some proper lording if it's the last thing I do. Tomorrow morning. All right?'

'Is that for lesson two?' asked Yedder.

Rudolf stooped and slapped him across the head before snatching his cape and stomping off.

'I say, that was a bit uncalled-for,' said Yedder, rubbing his head. He received no sympathetic reply from Guildman, who lay on his back in the sunshine and laughed, from the depth of his soul, way up to the clear blue sky.

The street that Rudolf staggered along carrying a bottle and a half of cheap wine was at that stage where its oldest residents could still remember when it was *the* place to live. Long since fallen from the first rank of desirability, it had not yet gone so far that the latest generation of fashion-driven socialites had rediscovered charm in its quaint solidity and brought in tradesmen quite prepared to commit any decorating heresy for those with more money than taste.

The house that Rudolf swayed outside of gave the impression that it was the only one in the street jutting out its chin, straightening its tie and muttering that someone around here has to at least try to keep up certain standards in an increasingly unregulated world, damn it. Its air of gentility should, by now, have been fading, but the gleaming paintwork, polished doorknob and dazzling white net curtains were taking a stand against the ravages of social and moral decay.

Rudolf tugged at a bell-pull which displayed hidden strength by keeping him upright as he tottered backwards a few paces, dimly hearing a succession of bells tinkling out an old folk-tune. He let go of the bell-pull and it raced back into its socket, as if trying to put as much distance as it could between itself and this drunk who had the effrontery to disturb it.

Swigging from one of the bottles he carried, Rudolf missed the twitch of the net curtain. He was leaning forward, hand poised to tug at the bell-pull again when the front door opened rapidly and was stopped short by a security chain.

'What the hell are *you* doing here?' hissed someone as welcoming as a cornered cat.

Rudolf changed his direction of sway and beamed at the gap in the doorway. 'Millie! 'Sme, Rudi.'

'Push off, I'm busy.'

Rudolf's face started to crumple. 'Aw... come on, Mills, lemme in... I won't be any trouble,' he wheedled.

'Go away! Now!'

'We can have a little drinkie together or...' – he took another swig of wine and waved the bottle with a broad sweep of his arm – '...or I can sit out here with it.'

The door closed quietly, and Rudolf smiled broadly at the sliding sound of the security chain. His smile faded when the door reopened and he found himself face-to-chest with the most tattooed, burly, muscle-bound individual he'd ever seen. One massive hand grasped his lapel and hauled him into the house, while the other relieved him of the bottles of wine.

'Mills!' Rudolf shrieked as he was dragged past a small, neat lady in a dressing gown. 'What's happening?'

'I told you I don't work when Bill's here,' she said coldly.

'But Millie—'

'You heard the lady,' boomed Bill, continuing to drag Rudolf through the house and out of the kitchen door. 'She doesn't work when I'm here.' He heaved Rudolf into the back lane and pinned him to the ground with one foot.

'Millie!' screamed Rudolf.

Bill bit the top off the unopened bottle of wine and spat it out. 'And,' he said, emptying both bottles over Rudolf, 'she doesn't drink.'

In the drawing room, Fran poured more tea.

'Wine for forgetting, water for drinking, ale for memories, tea for thinking,' she recited. 'A good cuppa gets your brain warmed up ready for concentrating.'

'Yours must be permanently boiling with the amount you put away,' said Rosa. 'What takes that much thinking about?'

'Your happiness.'

Her niece poured the milk. 'Believe me, I'm a lot happier now than I have been for years.'

'Oh, I can see that, love. I just want it to stay that way.'

Rosa looked closely at her.

'Are you sure you and my father were related?'

'Your grandmother always said so. Why?'

'If he'd cared about my happiness at all, he wouldn't have forced me to marry Rudolf.'

Fran picked up her cup and saucer.

'He was more worried about your future than your happiness. He was dying, your brother had... gone... I wasn't here, and he didn't want to leave you unprotected in the world.'

'So he married me to the one person in the world I needed protecting from!'

'And you still do.' Fran stirred her tea rhythmically, looking at the swirling mixture as if it were the deepest well of thoughts. After a while she said, 'Your father only wanted what was best for you, you know. It's just a shame his perversity got the better of his good intentions.'

'Perversity?'

'Well don't you think it's perverse that he chose Rudolf rather than Guildman? I don't know – maybe he thought that you'd love Guildman too much and if Guildman got killed in battle somewhere you wouldn't be able to stand it, but if Rudolf got killed, you wouldn't give a monkey's.'

'Bloody hell, that *is* perverse.'

'Aye, but the world needs people who think differently.'

'Not *that* differently.'

'Yes it does. Visionaries. People with that bit extra imagination and... single-mindedness.' Fran surveyed the plate of biscuits that Rosa held out. 'How would the world progress without... free thinkers? Inventors? Scientists?'

Before Fran could take a biscuit, Rosa withdrew the plate and pulled a face. 'So now I'm perverse, am I?'

'You're swimming against the tide of tradition, aren't you, with all your experimenting and inventing and chucking your husband out tied to a billiard table?'

'I suppose so...'

One of Mrs B's home-baked digestives rose from the plate and drifted towards Fran's hand.

'Oi!' laughed Rosa. 'Cheat!'

Fran smirked and caught the biscuit. 'Look, all I'm saying is that there's a... a streak of unconventionality runs through you – through all the Steins. Always has done. Let's face it, the people who built this place – our ancestors – weren't exactly doling out soup from a full cauldron, if you get me. I mean, stone furniture? Easy to wash down but a swine to rearrange.'

'And what about you?' said Rosa. 'Do you have this streak of unconventionality? Perversity? You always struck me as the sensible one.'

Years of being invited into people's homes for a cuppa had honed Fran's ability to carry on a conversation while eating the crumbliest of biscuits without pebbledashing everything in sight. 'Oh, I've done stuff that was... out of the ordinary, let's say... and would do again, if pushed.'

'Like what?'

Fran sighed. 'Like... my going to the University of Nature wasn't exactly welcomed with champagne and bunting.'

'What? Why not?'

'The daughter of the aristocratic family? Supposed to marry

well, cement alliances between noble families and not have a mind or a life of my own? Stop me if you've heard this one.'

'I've heard it, I've heard it.'

'See? I was never going to conform and neither were you.'

'I must get it from you, then.'

Fran laughed. 'I hope you do. Embrace your heritage: be perverse, but not perverted. And don't be reckless with it, either. Know the facts, stand no nonsense and make decisions that are right, even if other folk think they're as wrong as a tash on a toddler.'

In a part of Maund where only the dead had nothing to fear, Rudolf hammered on a door. A panel behind a grille in the door slid back, revealing a face.

'Welcome to Top Chop,' it said. 'You ask, we axe. Demolition experts, undertakers or vets?'

'What?' said Rudolf.

'Property, person or pet?'

Rudolf put his face to the grille.

'I want the executioners.'

The face retreated from the second-hand wine fumes.

'Password?' it coughed.

Rudolf hefted his recent find in Yedder's cape – a large and very full moneybag.

'*This* is my password.'

Seventeen locks were released in quick succession and a section of the bottom half of the door swung open.

Rudolf ducked through, and as he stood up someone behind him said, 'Mind your head.' He turned to face a dwarf standing on a platform built onto the back of the door.

The dwarf held out his hand. 'Let's see the gold.'

Rudolf passed him the moneybag. The dwarf looked in it.

'Aren't you going to count it?' asked Rudolf.

'No need,' said the dwarf. 'I can tell there's enough to get somebody killed.'

Early the following morning, as Igress settled down to her new job as Rosa's assistant, Fran popped into the laboratory.

'Me and Sooty are off into town. Want anything?'

'No, thank you, Mistress Stein,' said Igress brightly.

'Ah, Aunty, yes.' Rosa pulled out a sheet from a pile of papers in front of her. 'I've been thinking about what you said and... are you going anywhere near the printers?'

'What I said?' asked Fran. 'What did I say?'

Rosa grinned as she handed her the paper.

'I thought I'd embrace my heritage, as you put it.'

Fran nodded in admiration as she read.

'So you have. How many copies do you want?'

'Let's say forty, and ask him to have them pasted up around town near the shops and pubs. That's if you don't mind.'

'Few things would give me greater pleasure.'

That same afternoon, in the parlour at the Lamb and Werewolf, Rigton was slicing pineapples ready for the evening trade when the door swung open, pushed by a tall, gangly youth wearing overalls that had clearly been made for him to grow into and subsequently out of again. Slung across his skinny chest was a canvas bag of rolled-up posters, and he carried a large bucket in which an emulsion brush appeared to be held upright by industrial-strength tapioca.

'A foreign and fruit, please,' he said cheerily.

'No,' replied Rigton. 'You're too young.'

'A fruit juice?'

'No overalls in the parlour.'

'I'll go in the taproom.'

'The taproom's shut for redecoration.'

'I'll take the overalls off.'

'No lewd or indecent behaviour in this establishment.'

'I won't be behaving – I'll be standing having me drink.'

'No lewd or indecent standing in this establishment.'

'Can I put one of these posters up, then?'

Rigton laid his knife on the bar and wiped his hands on a towel hung from his waist. 'Let's have a look.' The lad handed him a poster. Rigton unrolled it, read it, re-rolled it and tapped it on his fingers.

'Where else have you put these up?'

'All over town.'

Rigton looked around the parlour. Among the patrons was an aristocrat sitting alone at a rickety table. Rigton bent down and put the poster under the counter. When he straightened up, he gave the paste-boy a small glass of clear liquid, glowing with hazes of blue and purple. 'Drink that.'

'But you said I couldn't have a drink.'

'You'll need this one.'

'Why?'

'Putting up posters can be a dangerous business.'

The youth looked blank. The safety aspects of his trade had

never occurred to him; after all, it was a sloppy job with no sharp corners. 'I don't use ladders, mister.'

'Drink it.'

'How much?'

'All of it.'

'I mean how much is it?'

Rigton gritted his teeth. 'On the house.'

'Oh, thanks!'

The youth downed the drink in one go. There was no scouring of the tongue, no searing of the throat, no watering of the eyes. He looked quizzically at the empty glass.

'It'll take a minute to kick in,' Rigton said, taking the glass. 'Put a poster on the notice board over there.'

He pointed to a square of wall that bulged on account of successive layers of announcements having been pasted up. The events they told of had been forthcoming, come, gone, and passed into legend, their advertisements buried as deep on the wall as the events themselves were seared into memories.

The youth ambled over, put the bucket on the floor, withdrew the brush and casually slapped paste onto the wall, sending glutinous splashes perilously close to the rickety table. He smoothed a poster onto the wet surface and swished the brush over it, leaving it flattened and glistening with paste. He picked up the bucket, dropped the brush into it and ambled towards the bar again.

'What was that drink you gave me, mister?'

'A Spinning Bilious Gargoyle,' replied Rigton. 'Because that's what you'll think you are when you wake up.'

'Oh, right,' said the youth, and turned to leave. He found

himself staring into the wild eyes of an infuriated aristocrat holding a still-glistening poster.

Rudolf grabbed the paste-boy by the throat. Luckily the drink kicked in right on time and the lad's consciousness slid into his boots; unluckily, as it did so it opened his hand and dropped the paste bucket on Rudolf's foot. Rudolf yelped and released the youth who folded up onto the floor, sending posters from the canvas bag bobbling across the wooden boards. Rudolf yanked the paste bucket from his foot, emptied it over the oblivious body of its owner then sent it bouncing across the room, clanking out of all proportion to its size.

As Rudolf scrabbled around on the floor for the escaped posters, Rigton took two wax-coated paper straws from a tankard on a shelf, walked round the bar and carefully inserted one straw up each of the youth's nostrils. He was back behind the counter in time to greet Yedder and Guildman, who entered the parlour as Rudolf vehemently plastered the hapless paste-boy with the remaining posters.

A lump of dull brown residue dropped from the upturned crucible onto the laboratory workbench.

Rosa frowned. 'Not quite what I was expecting.'

'It does seem a boring thing to expect,' said Igress.

Rosa prodded it with a pencil, scarring its surface.

'Too soft to be stone, yet too solid to be liquid. Retains an impression, like wax, yet' – she rolled the pencil lengthways across the point marks – 'is easily smoothed again, without heat.' She picked up the substance, dug her fingers in and pulled it in two. It stretched in the middle before separating into thin tendrils which sagged and gave way. 'Tacky, but not elastic. Doesn't regain its original shape.' She handed one half to Igress, who pressed the tendrils back into the substance.

'It gets more pliable the more you work it,' Igress said. 'It's a bit like clay without the wetness.'

The door opened and into the discussion stepped Fran.

'Oh good, you're back,' said Rosa. 'Here, what do you make of this?'

She tore her lump of brown in two again and handed half to Fran, who weighed it in her hand, sniffed it, held it to her ear and squeezed it, then threw it at the wall. It stuck for a couple of seconds before dropping to the floor.

'No idea,' she said.

'Neither have we,' said Rosa.

Igress moulded her piece into a disc and stuck her finger through the middle. 'It reminds me of play pastry,' she said.

Fran picked up the brown residue from the floor and threw it onto the workbench, where it landed on Rosa's notebook.

'Oh, sorry. Any damage?'

Rosa gingerly pulled at the residue, which lifted the page of her notebook. She held the page down and tried again; this time the residue peeled off without tearing the paper, lifting the ink or any other mishap.

'No – good as new.' She pushed the peeled residue back onto her own lump. 'Any ideas?'

Both Fran and Igress shook their heads. The three of them studied the brown, tacky, pliable substance. Fran pulled another piece from it and rolled it between her palms.

'By the way,' she said, 'I got your posters done.'

'Oh, excellent. Thanks, Aunty.'

'The first creditors should be arriving any minute now.'

'Creditors?'

'You can't expect to put up a notice like that without some comeback,' said Fran, pressing the residue onto a sheet of paper then peeling it off again.

There was a knock on the door shortly before Beaton opened it and said, 'Milady, several tradespersons wish to speak with you.'

Rosa sighed and followed him out of the laboratory.

Fran rolled four small balls of residue, pressed one to each corner of a sheet of paper, held the paper up and pressed the corners onto the wall. The sheet of paper hung there.

'Why, Mistress Stein,' cried Igress, 'that's—'

The paper slid gently from its moorings and drifted to the floor, where it was soon joined by four balls of brown, not-tacky-enough residue.

'Not working,' said Fran. 'That's what that is.'

'Nearly,' said Igress. 'What do you think went wrong?'

Fran looked at the brown substance.

'It's the wrong colour. I bet it'd work if it was blue.'

'Afternoon, Rigsy! Three of your finest, please,' said Yedder as he and Guildman approached a non-sticky part of the bar. He picked up a slice of pineapple. 'You know, Gil, I've often thought about having a coat this colour. What do you think?'

Guildman looked at his companion.

'It may draw the eye away from your lime-green britches.'

Yedder held the fruit near his leg and considered it, then

took a bite out of the pineapple and waved his hand in the direction of Rudolf, still frenetically obliterating the youth with his own posters. 'I say, Rigsy, one doesn't like to pry, but...'

In reply, Rigton handed over the poster from under the counter and returned to pouring the drinks.

Yedder read the poster and squealed.

'Woo-hoo! Pin back your lugholes and listen to this, Gil! *To whom it may concern... Lady Rosalind Dibkiss... renounces all responsibility for Lord Rudolf Dibkiss... financial, legal, moral and matrimonial... will honour no debt, promissory note or other form of bond incurred by him... considers herself no longer bound or in any way connected to him... now reverts to own family name... Signed this day, etc., Lady Rosalind Stein.* I say!'

Guildman took the poster and read it. A long, slow smile spread across his face and through his entire body.

'Rigton, another round – with extra pineapple for Yedder. And one for yourself.' He rolled up the poster and tucked it inside his shirt. 'Who's the poor unfortunate on the floor?'

The landlord set down their first round of drinks.

'He's a paste-boy who's been sticking the posters up around town, milord. I took the precaution of giving him an SBG to deaden the pain.'

'Good show, Rigsy,' said Yedder. 'So, Gil, it looks like fairly final to me – she *considers herself no longer bound...*'

'Indeed.' Guildman took the fruit from his beer and dropped it in Yedder's tankard. 'And evidence would suggest that Rudolf isn't too happy at being considered unbound.'

'Evidence is right, old thing. Although this could be simply another of his lording lessons.'

'Really?'

Yedder grinned.

'Lesson Two: how to give someone a good pasting.'

Rosa sat behind the large stone desk in her study. On the floor to her left was a cashbox; on the desk was a large piece of paper with a pre-written paragraph at the top and an expanse of signing space at the bottom.

'Right, Beaton,' she said. 'Bring the first one in.'

The first one in was the large and greasy owner of a small and greasy but nonetheless expensive eating-house in Maund. He bowed exaggeratedly, flourishing a large handkerchief and brandishing a sheaf of papers. 'Lady Dibki— Lady Stein.'

Rosa took the papers. 'What are these?'

'Promissory notes written by Lord Dibkiss for meals taken in my fine-dining establishment – quality is our watchword.'

She looked through them.

'Why do you bring them to me?'

'To be honoured, your ladyship.'

'Well, I'm honoured that you brought them. Good day.'

'But am I not to be paid for providing your husband with three square meals a day to keep his body and soul together?'

Rosa put the papers down and looked him in the eye.

'One: why I should pay you for such a disservice? Two: for the size, content and price of the meals you serve, it would be more nutritious, tastier and cheaper to eat gold. Three: this' – she took one paper out of the sheaf – 'is a promissory note allegedly signed by Rudolf for a six-course banquet for fifteen people. I don't doubt his ability to consume such a meal, but if you were to trawl his life from start to finish you'd not find fourteen people willing to sit and eat it with him. Also, on the date in question he was otherwise occupied; in fact, he was tied to a billiard table.'

The large man quivered right down to his handkerchief and placed his hand across his chest as if physically wounded.

'Is her ladyship accusing me of forgery?' he said, rolling his eyes dramatically.

'Her ladyship is saying that either you are trying to get money out of her under false pretences, or some fool with fourteen friends is going around Maund pretending to be Rudolf and deceiving poor honest tradesmen like yourself. In either case, the debt is not her ladyship's and her ladyship will not pay.' Rosa ripped the papers in half. 'Good day to you, sir.'

'Her ladyship is cruel in the extreme,' he declared.

'Her ladyship can live with that. Next!'

Three aristocrats sat at a rickety table. One was tall, elegant and so self-composed that nobody would suspect he was revelling in the sensation of secret desire; one was shorter, cheerful and everybody would assume he was excitable; the third was glowering, prising his fingers apart and covered in so many little scraps of paper that anybody would think he had been the victim of a horrendous shaving accident.

'Nnnnnn,' moaned the papier-mâché body on the floor.

'Rigsy?' said Yedder. 'Another drink for the lad, please.'

Rigton poured another SBG and set it on the floor next to the paste-boy's face, which was thickly plastered with well-glued posters. He drew his paring knife lightly across the lip area and pulled open the mouth. Lifting the youth's head a little, Rigton poured the drink in and closed the mouth quickly, holding the jaws together until a dull gulp indicated that the boy had swallowed. He laid him back down again.

'I'd be grateful if my lord could move his victim,' he said.

'Only fair, Rude,' said Yedder. 'The lad's blocking the bar and people are having to step over him.'

Rudolf snorted. 'You haven't learnt a thing, have you? One of the basic principles of lording is: nobody ever brings a lord bad news. Not if they want to live.'

'But what a waste of energy,' said Guildman.

'How so, Gil?' asked Yedder. 'Rude got a right old result for his efforts.'

Guildman ignored Rudolf's smirk. 'Oh, yes, Yedder, undoubtedly he got *a* result, but was it *the* result?'

'Not with you, old boy.'

Guildman leant towards him. 'Rosalind...' he started, and Yedder saw his eyes sparkle and his lips twitch slightly as though the feel of her name in his mouth took on a particular frisson because of Rudolf's presence. 'Rosalind has made it very plain she's cutting Rudolf out of her life.'

'Yes...'

'The paste-boy knows Rudolf's not happy about it, and we know he's not happy about it, but Rosalind...'

'Roz doesn't know! We should go and tell her!'

'About time!' Rudolf exclaimed. 'Come on!'

He and Yedder leant forward as a prelude to rising from their seats.

'Or...' said Guildman.

Yedder and Rudolf slumped back again.

'Or?' snapped Rudolf.

'Yedder,' said Guildman, 'if I came to you and told you I'd cut Rudolf's throat, what would you say?'

'I'd probably say that I'm surprised nobody'd beaten you to it ha, ha, h—'

Yedder's laughter was curtailed by a slap on the head.

'Ow! All right, Rude, just a joke. I'd say that I didn't believe it, Gil.'

'But,' said Guildman, and in the space of that one syllable his dagger-point was dimpling the skin on Rudolf's throat, 'if you *saw* me cut it, you'd have to believe it, wouldn't you?'

Yedder's face said that his brain was trying to tie things together, but his mental string was too short. 'Well...'

'Yedder!' hissed Rudolf, his body stiffening like that of the rapidly drying paste-boy.

'I'd have to say...'

'Yedder!'

'Oh... hang it all, Gil, yes, I'd have to believe it. But I'm still not entirely sure what you're driving at, old thing.'

Guildman kept Rudolf on the dagger-point.

'Hard evidence, Yedder. You would have to see Rudolf's throat cut; Rosalind would have to see the boy.'

'Damn it, you're right!' said Yedder. 'She'd have to see the boy to see exactly how upset Rude is!'

'Nnghhh!' gurgled Rudolf.

Guildman withdrew his dagger.

Rudolf sagged and rubbed his throat.

'Sometimes, Guildman...'

'Oh, wasn't that your plan?'

Rudolf stuck his chin out.

'Yes, yes, of course it was. Now take the boy up to the castle.'

Yedder and Guildman stood up.

'Not coming with us?' asked Yedder.

Rudolf coughed.

'Er... no, no, I'll stay here and plan what to do next. You can manage. Just make sure that hell-hag knows exactly what the score is.'

'Don't worry,' said Guildman. 'I'll tell her.'

Beaton showed into the study a short, expensively dressed man. His oily hair was slicked back, revealing a widow's peak that pointed onto a pinched face carrying squinty eyes which, on any other person, would have been the result of making many finely-judged decisions or being out in the sun too long. This man's eyes were squinty from a permanent sneer which he'd adopted in his youth to make him seem frightening, something only achieved when he tried to smile, as he did now.

'Lady Stein,' he smarmed.

Rosa fought not only the urge to throw up but also the reflex action of squinting back at him, which would only lead to face ache after half a minute. 'Hand them over,' she said.

As he passed her the promissory notes, the gold-piece rings that he wore clashed together and a heavy gold bracelet dragged at his wrist. He licked his lips, and in a nasally whine said, 'Payment in full would be appreciated.'

'I'm sure it would,' Rosa replied. 'Why don't you ask the

person who owes you this money to pay you?'

'You misunderstand, my lady. Those notes are signed by Lord Dibkiss. For debts accumulated in my gentlemen's club.'

Rosa pushed the papers across the desk.

'Your gambling den, you mean.'

He pushed them back.

'A gentleman needs a little... relaxation.'

She pushed again.

'Then I suggest you take these back and unrelax him.'

He pushed once more. 'And I suggest that you pay me.'

Rosa lifted the papers and tore them up.

'I don't like that suggestion.'

The man stopped smiling, making him altogether more bearable. He cracked his knuckles.

'Don't be foolish, Lady Stein. I have influential friends in town.'

'And I have a dungeon under your feet,' said Rosa, 'so if you ever want to see the light of day again, I'd advise you to sign here and go.' She tapped the paper with the pre-written paragraph and the large signing-space.

The man leant forward. '*I hereby declare,*' he read, '*that I have been paid in full and will pursue no further claim on Lady Stein for debts incurred by Lord Rudolf Dibkiss?*'

'That's very kind of you,' said Rosa.

'You must be mad,' he spat.

'Beaton?'

Beaton locked the door. 'Milady?'

'Have you fed the dungeon rats lately?'

Yedder threw two silver pieces on the counter.

'I say, Rigsy – borrow your knife a minute? And we'll need the dray for a couple of hours. All right?'

'At your disposal, my lords,' Rigton said, chinking the coins and putting them in his trouser pocket, from where it would be a very brave thief indeed who tried to steal them. He gave Yedder his paring knife.

Yedder slid the blade under the prostrate youth and sliced all the way around the outline of the body. He and Guildman took hold of the paste-boy's wrists, the dried-out pasted posters crackling as they dragged him across the floor and out into the pub yard, where a large horse stood between the shafts of the dray. The horse eyed them suspiciously but said nothing as they loaded the stiffened body onto the flat cart and climbed on the driving board. Yedder took the reins, made the appropriate reassuring noises born of a lifetime in the saddle and the horse steadily pulled the dray out of the yard.

Beaton led into the study a petite, black-haired woman who stood very straight and walked as if she wanted to disturb the air as little as possible. Well-scrubbed, her unadorned face was framed by a severe haircut that had apparently been based on a helmet. Her long brown overcoat was button-through from neck to ankle, and her thick-soled flat shoes had been built for considerations of comfort rather than attraction.

She handed over her unpaid account.

The first page opened Rosa's eyes wide; the second sent a shiver down her spine; the third made her jaw drop.

'You do all this for Rudolf?'

The woman's voice strayed neither into pride nor shame. 'I do.'

Rosa waved her hand vaguely. 'Beaton – a seat for er...'

'Mildred,' the woman supplied. 'Or Millie. I don't mind.'

'Millie,' said Rosa absently, scanning the pages again. Then, as if she'd been stabbed in the back, she looked up. 'Millie? Are you *the* Millie? As in Rudolf's... erm... um...'

'Ex-fiancée? Yes, that Millie.'

'Oh... erm... I'm not sure what to say now, apart from I wish he'd married you instead of me.'

Millie's head twitched briefly. 'I understand it wasn't your choice,' she said, 'and with all due respect, Lady Stein, I came here to get paid, not to rake over old embers.'

'Right, yes, of course. Please... have a seat.'

Beaton brought a chair, and Millie sat down.

Rosa re-read Millie's account, incredulity growing with every page. Her natural curiosity was what made her a scientist, and here was a whole underworld that she knew nothing about. In under five minutes she learnt things about Rudolf it would take her a lifetime to forget.

She took a long, hard look at Millie.

'Please excuse me staring, but you don't er... you don't exactly look like um... er...'

'A lady of the night?'

'Um... yes.'

'It's my day off. And truth to tell, I'm more a lady of the afternoons, anyway. Things tend to get a bit too boisterous at night nowadays.'

'Forgive me – I thought you'd be wearing... erm...'

'Traditional costume?'

'Well, yes...'

'Only when I'm working,' said Millie. 'It's not what you might call practical.'

Rosa tried to imagine a situation in which that particular traditional costume would come anywhere remotely near practicality; she failed.

'High heels are no good for your feet,' Millie continued, 'and thigh-length boots can chafe something rotten. And corsets are very constricting – we've all got to breathe.'

Rosa found herself smiling until she looked down at the papers again. 'Some of these activities sound very... painful.'

'That's what they pay me for. And I do need to be paid, since I have no husband to keep me.'

Rosa swallowed.

'Yes... indeed. Er... this... er... work. Is it just you? Do you have a... bodyguard? In case of... trouble?'

Millie bristled.

'A pimp, you mean? No fear. I work hard, and I don't want some pasty-faced creep skimming money off me for sitting outside the door doing nothing. I take care of myself, and if someone cuts up rough, I take care of them.'

Rosa reached for the cash box.

'Millie,' she said, 'I like you. And you've saved me an awful lot of bother over the years.'

If one of the aristocrats on the front seat of the dray wanted the horse to go faster, he was too respectful of his companion to say it. If the other aristocrat on the front seat had something biting at his soul, then he was too well-trained a soldier to speak of it until the dray was clear of the houses in the Horse Fair and only trees framed the long, lonely approach road to Castle Stein.

Yedder leant towards the back of the dray.

'I say! Young feller! You all right back there?' he called.

Response came there none; the paste-boy was unconscious and oblivious to the world.

'Good, good,' said Yedder brightly, before straightening up again and clearing his throat. 'Gil?' he said, something in his tone indicating further questions to come.

'Yedder?'

'Gil. You and I and Rude have knocked around together all our lives.'

'We have.'

'Boys at school, brother officers in the military, fellow members of a small circle of aristos...'

'Indeed.'

'But chiefly the three of us go around together now because you and I want to keep an eye on him.'

'For a very good reason, Yedder.'

'Oh, for a *very* good reason, Gil. But in all that time, no matter how greedy, mean, unlikeable or just plain nasty Rude's been, you've never pulled a weapon on him as you did earlier.'

The noise of the horse and dray moving towards the castle was nowhere near big enough to fill Guildman's silence.

'You've fought him, certainly,' Yedder continued, 'but never drawn a blade against him in anger. Not once. Not in fencing class, not in military training, not even when you found out that Rosalind was being married off to him. Not even on the day of the wedding, even though you vowed that if he lifted a finger against her, you'd kill him.'

'And you vowed to help me.'

'I did. And yet in the years since their marriage – in all the years that you've known him – today's the first time that you've ever raised a weapon against him. It's as if... no, not as if; tonight, I've seen something in you give way.'

Guildman stroked his bearded chin as he considered his reply. At length he said, 'You've seen something give way in me; I've seen something give way in him. His threats no longer ring as hollow as they once did, as our friend in the back can testify. Rudolf has become... vengeful.'

'Do you believe that he will harm Rosalind?'

'Today – for the first time – I do.'

'In that case,' sighed Yedder, 'it seems I have two people to keep an eye on.' He paused. 'Could we buy him off?'

Guildman shook his head.

'Not this time. This time he wants the victory. I'd gladly give him all I possess if I thought she'd be safe, but he can't be trusted. He'd take the money with one hand and kill her with the other.'

'If he got the chance,' said Yedder.

'Which we're not going to give him,' Guildman smiled, 'are we, Yedder?'

Yedder chuckled.

'Absolutely not, old love. One way or another, the chance will not be his.'

Rosa paid the vintner what was owed, which was not a large amount. After all, Rudolf drank mostly at the Lamb and Werewolf, and only went into the wine shop when he couldn't go the distance between pubs. Besides, the vintner supplied Castle Stein, and there was no point Rosa cutting off her nose to spite Rudolf's face.

She also paid the tailor, because she knew the long hours that the tailor and his wife worked to make ends meet, plus the outfits they'd made were still hanging in Rudolf's wardrobe and would fetch a good price at the next summer fair.

Yedder backed Rigton's horse and dray onto the drawbridge with the minimum of fuss and no mirrors at all, then he and Guildman jumped down and walked to the front door.

'Think there's anybody home, Gil?' Yedder grinned, tugging at the bell-pull.

Guildman smiled his long, slow smile. 'I do hope so, Yedder. It'd be a shame to come all this way for nothing.'

As the door opened they could hear Rosa.

'If that's more creditors, they're too late. I'm not paying anybody after sunset.'

'My lords Yedder and Guildman,' announced Beaton as they strode in. He closed the door behind them.

'Hello, Roz!' beamed Yedder, bowing extravagantly.

Rosa tilted her head slightly in return.

'Good evening, Yedder. Hello, Guildman.'

Guildman interlaced his fingers with hers and gently kissed her hand. 'My lady.'

The doors at the back of the hall opened, and in walked

Sooty and Fran, who carried a steam-topped mug. 'And I'm telling you – oh, sorry, I didn't know we'd got company,' she said. 'I was just on my way to bed.'

Yedder beamed. 'Frances Stein, as I live and breathe!'

'As you live, breathe and dress ridiculously, Yedder. Lime-green britches? When are you going to grow up?'

Yedder advanced towards her with his arms outstretched.

'If I grow up I might be tempted to come and ravage you in your bed, you gorgeous creature.'

He cuddled her roughly and planted a kiss on her cheek.

She smiled and pushed him away. 'Get on with you, you fool. You've made me spill me sleeping draught now.'

He giggled and bent down to Sooty, who was lapping up the spilt tea. 'Hello, Sooty. Caught any good rats lately?'

'Only you, Yedder,' replied Sooty, and Yedder tweaked his tail before standing up.

Guildman walked over to Fran. 'Mistress Stein.' He bowed, kissing her hand and then her cheek. 'You are well, I trust?'

'Oh, you know me, Guildman. Mustn't grumble.'

'Doesn't usually stop you,' laughed Yedder, so Fran hit him, which made him laugh all the more.

'I hope that Spirit of Co-operation is looking after you,' Guildman continued. He and Fran looked at Sooty, who lay on his side, eyes closed, returning their enquiring look with a gentle snore.

'Oh, aye,' said Fran, flatly. 'He's a great companion, he is.' She sniffed dismissively. 'Anyway, what brings you two here? Not trying to sneak that misbegotten low-life back in, are you?'

'Perish the thought,' said Yedder. 'However, we do bring a

message from him. Open the door would you, Beaton? There's a good chap.'

Beaton did so. The two lords walked over to the dray, lowered the backboard and tilted the flat bed of the cart until it re-engaged the backboard and the whole thing became a slope, the bottom end of which touched the ground. As Rigton's penchant for polishing encompassed even the dray, it was without hindrance that an apparently papier-mâché body slid down the slope onto the smooth stone flags of the hall.

'A dummy?' asked Rosa.

'Oh, no, Roz,' said Yedder. 'The dummy sent it.'

'What?'

'My lady,' said Guildman, accompanying Yedder back into the hall, 'Rudolf – unlike some – does not approve of your latest decision.'

'Here,' said Fran, tilting her head and peering at the body, 'these are your posters, Rosa.'

'And underneath,' added Guildman, 'is a paste-boy.'

'A paste-boy?' cried Rosa.

'Don't worry,' said Yedder, 'he's had a couple of SBGs. He's out cold.'

Fran tested the air coming out of the straws in the paste-boy's nose. 'He's breathing – he'll be all right. Mind you, he'll have a hangover the size of the Town Field when he wakes up.'

'Rudolf did this?' Rosa gasped. 'To get back at me?'

'Very keen to see a return to old-style lording, isn't he, Gil?'

'Indeed.'

'Well, this time he's gone too far,' said Rosa. 'I will not have him terrorising the townspeople. If he's got something to say, he should be man enough to come up here and say it himself.'

'We fear that he intends to do that, my lady,' said Guildman.

Yedder leant towards her. 'A word to the wise, Roz. Be careful. He's not nice when he's angry.'

'He's not nice at all, Yedder. What are you getting at?'

He backed off. 'Said too much already, old girl.' He tapped the side of his nose, and there was a louder knocking noise than he expected. His face was overcome by curiosity until he saw Fran tapping on the stiffened paste-boy.

She looked up. 'Just trying to figure out how best to unset him,' she said. 'Carry on.'

'Yedder,' said Guildman, 'don't be secretive. Didn't Rudolf say that my lady should know exactly what the score is?'

'He did, Gil, he did. I'd forgotten that.' Yedder brightened considerably. 'So, Roz, it's like this. Rude wants your castle, your fortune, and preferably your death. Not necessarily in that order.' Rosa gaped at Yedder, who was warming to his subject. 'You are his sworn enemy, so prepare yourself for assault, siege, personal vilification... that sort of thing.'

'That sort of thing,' said Rosa.

Yedder nodded. 'And we're supposed to be helping.'

'Oh.'

'Which means we may be more frequent visitors to Castle Stein in future,' said Guildman.

'Oh,' Rosa repeated, in a completely different tone of voice.

'Well,' chirped Yedder, 'that's the message. Would madam like to send a reply?'

Rosa glanced at the paste-boy. Fran had found the slit left by Rigton's paring knife, and had reopened the boy's mouth to improve his air intake. He was starting to accompany Sooty in a gentle snore.

'Yes. Tell that maggot that if he's got any bones to pick with me, then instead of taking it out on innocent bystanders, he'd better drag his sorry little carcass up here. I'll be only too glad to pick his bones.'

Yedder rubbed his hands together and winked.

'That's the spirit, Roz. And don't forget – violent crime is the exception not the norm, so please don't have nightmares.'

'Oh, I don't,' she said. 'The landlord at the Lamb and Werewolf has mine now.'

Yedder laughed, bowed to Rosa and her aunt, and went to restore the cart to normal.

Guildman took Rosa's hand between his own and looked into her eyes.

'My lady, Rudolf is on the attack and you must be forever vigilant. But never forget that Yedder and I are at your service.' He kissed the back of her hand. 'My heart and my life are yours. I will be there.'

Rosa smiled. 'I had hoped it would be so.'

'Ahem,' coughed Fran.

Guildman bowed to her, formally kissed Rosa's hand again and left to join Yedder. Beaton closed the door after him and walked across the hall.

'Will the visitor be requiring a room, milady?'

Rosa shook her head. 'I don't think so, but put some blankets under him so at least he's not lying on the stone floor.'

'And move him further away from the fire,' said Fran. 'We don't want him going up in the middle of the night.'

Beaton dragged the paste-boy a safe distance from the flames, then bowed and left to fetch blankets.

'What do we do with him now, Aunty?'

Fran sucked her teeth. 'I suppose we could try lifting the shell up and see if he falls out, or we could chisel him out, or we could dangle him in the moat to soak him out. We'll think about it tomorrow – after we've had some shut-eye.'

'Good idea. Night-night.'

'Night-night, love.'

Fran set off towards the doors at the back of the hall.

'Oh, Aunty,' said Rosa, halting Fran's progress. 'Earlier this evening... if you were on your way to bed, what were you doing walking *away* from your bedroom?'

At the landlord's command, the last few stragglers from the Lamb and Werewolf's evening session jerkily tiptoed across the sticky floor, pulling their reluctant feet into the night.

Rigton emptied the drip trays and tankard dregs back into the barrels in the taproom and skilfully replenished the spirit casks using a ratio of alcohol to water that was his trade secret.

He washed and dried the tankards, standing them to attention in serried ranks on shelves behind the bar.

He cleaned and polished the tables and upended the parlour chairs and stools onto them before washing the floor, scraping and scouring to remove all trace of the earlier pasting.

He shot home the locks and bolts on the street door as loudly, pointedly and hintingly as he could.

And still the only customer left in the parlour did not move. He'd sat in the same spot all night, not even getting up for a drink but hailing vociferously for refills of his tankard.

'Will my lord be going up to his room tonight?' asked Rigton. 'Or should my wife bring a blanket for him?'

Rudolf let out an irritated sigh, as if he'd been puzzling over something all evening and had found an answer that would fit, but wasn't really satisfactory.

'No, I'll go. Give me your knife.'

Rigton's face retained a mask of utter indifference as he took the paring knife from his belt, handed it to Rudolf, and watched him plunge it into the moquette covering of the deep cushioned seat beside him. Rudolf sawed at the upholstery alongside his right leg, then his left, then lifted his knees and cut through the material across the front of the seat. He returned the knife to the landlord.

'You'll have to finish it,' he said, and leant forward.

Rigton bent over Rudolf's back. Had Rosa been in Rigton's position – holding Rudolf down while hefting an extremely sharp knife – the outcome might have been very different. However, the landlord's talent and inclination were directed towards business rather than butchery, and so behind Rudolf's back Rigton cut through the seat material, joining up the first two incisions that Rudolf had made. He straightened up and held out his arm.

Rudolf clasped Rigton's forearm as if it were the last bar of gold in the country, and Rigton hauled him to his feet. Rudolf gingerly straightened up and tottered off to his room, a large piece of red moquette securely pasted to the seat of his britches.

NOTES ON

Death

At one time, everyone knew that certain things just were. One of those things was Death, and everybody took it on trust that he was who he said he was. Then an image arose of Death wearing a monk's habit and carrying a scythe, an image drawn and perpetuated not by anybody with first-hand experience of him but by those wishing to make Death a recognisable figure of fear, which is barking up two wrong trees: people don't need to recognise Death – it's not as if they'll come back and tell their friends what he was wearing – and it's pointless to fear Death because it's not Death who hurts you. Disease, decay and injury are the ones to watch out for, because they'll make life a living hell before Death releases you.

Fear of Death is completely different from not wanting to meet Death, which should be fairly high on the list of anybody who's sound in wind, limb and faculties. Neither is fear of Death the same as fear of what happens after death. If you believe in post-mortal judgement, condemnation and reward, the time to influence that is during your life. By the time Death comes along, your actions have already decided whether or not your milk and honey will be rancid.

Despite the robe-and-scythe image gaining near-universal acceptance, Death doesn't use any form of agricultural implement for his harvest. He severs the lifelines of the body and soul – much as an umbilical cord is severed – using concentrated energy, which generates heat and burns brightly, hence erroneous accounts of people 'moving towards the light'. It's actually moving towards them.

Death shares a dwelling with Pat – Parturicia, Earth Mother, The Bringer of Life. It's an arrangement which makes as much sense as any, because they're rarely at home together. In fact, they're rarely at home at all unless time stands still – in which case nobody is born and nobody dies and Pat and Death can sit with their feet up, watching the repercussions; the usual outcome is that lots more babies are born late, and sick but wealthy individuals cling on long enough to ensure that the wayward youngest son gets a good going-over from his creditors before he inherits anything.

Death has many faces: an old friend, a complete stranger, a loved one or a sworn enemy. Perhaps the worst is when he appears as the object of our desires, because nobody ever dreams that something so beautiful could be so lethal.

However, much more common is when the object of someone's desires leads to the death of someone else.

~•~

In the upstairs room of a drinking establishment known as The Field Digger, a blanket of thin, grey smoke swirled under the rafters.

At one end of the long room was a sturdy bar counter and at the other, sixteen ropes cordoned off a large, square, blood-spattered area.

In one corner of the square stood a blue post, diagonally opposite was a red post and in each of these corners a low three-legged stool supported a bucket. Draped sadly over the rim of each bucket was a length of mucky rag, commonly used for wiping down those brave or stupid souls who stepped through the ropes and used their fists to knock seven bells out of each other while using their feet to keep as far away from their opponent as possible.

Around the walls of the room, tattered and peeling posters advertised the exploits of those whose job it was to get half and possibly fully killed for the benefit of other people who made money on the outcome of the fight. For the simplicity and arrogance of this concept, there was little wonder that everybody said boxing was a man's game.

The newest posters showed a heavyweight fighter with a spread eagle tattooed across his massive chest: Battling Bill Baldicott was back in town and taking on all comers.

On this occasion, however, the main event came not from that end of the room where short men who wore flat caps and tucked their jumpers into their britches hunched over the buckets and yelled encouragement to slaughter, but from the bar area. It would have been the talking point of the evening if only people had stayed long enough to talk about it. Around the almost empty room, beer still slopped in hastily downed tankards and the smoky air continued to swirl and curl, especially around the single doorway, through which died the echoes of a mass panic evacuation.

Four people remained in the room; only two of those were breathing. They hid behind the bar until the noises ceased, then hauled themselves to their feet and leant over the counter.

'Looks like tha needs a new prize-fighter,' said the barman, surveying the heavyweight tattooed corpse.

87

The boxing manager moaned. 'Oh, marvellous.'

'Mind,' said the barman, 'it's t'other bloke I feel sorry for.'

'Other bloke? What other bloke?'

'Him that were standing behind your man when he got his nosebleed. Him that your man's using as a mattress.'

The boxing manager dashed to the late Battling Bill, whose nosebleed had been caused by an axe, still embedded in his face. At a slight angle, crushed under the fallen warrior, lay another man who had previously been so thin only his large boots stopped him blowing over in the wind; now he was so thin he could have lived in an envelope, had he been living.

The boxing manager groaned.

'Oh, no. Not the bloody tailor an' all!'

'A tailor?' said the barman. 'You brought a tailor with you?'

'Who d'you think makes the shorts and vests and dressing gowns? Who d'you think stitches up the cuts?'

'Hadn't really thought. I've not been a barman very long.'

'Ever considered being a travelling prize-fighter?'

'No,' said the barman firmly.

'Pity. I've just had an' – the manager kicked savagely at Bill's boots – '*unexpected vacancy* come up on my team. Of my team. The whole of my bloody team.'

He turned to the barman.

'Oh, go on,' he said. 'Be a fighter. It's a good life – plenty of travel, you get paid to get fit, and at roughly an hour a day actual graft, it's a short working week.'

'An' a short working life,' said the barman, nodding towards the corpses.

'Are you any good with a needle, then?'

'No.'

The boxing manager snarled.

'Bloody typical! You spend half your life training these hulks to championship level and how do they repay you? By getting themselves killed. I mean – look at him. Six foot six of prime beef and he has to go upsetting a dwarf! Why couldn't he pick on someone his own size, for pity's sake?'

'Prob'ly couldn't find anybody,' said the barman. 'Besides, he didn't get himself killed. Somebody had him killed.'

The manager blanched.

'*Had* him killed?'

'An axe in his head, sharp end first? Thrown by a dwarf? That's got "contract killing" written all over it, that has.'

The boxing manager gulped.

'In that case, where's the nearest burial ground?'

The following morning, Rosa and Fran looked at the still-sleeping paste-boy.

'You do it,' said Fran. 'You've been married.'

'Yes, but not to him,' Rosa countered. 'You do it – you're the one who's helped out at thousands of births.'

'Births, aye. Conceptions, no. They're two entirely different... sets of...'

'Equipment?'

'Circumstances.'

The double doors opened.

'Ah, Beaton,' smiled a relieved Rosa. 'The paste-boy's not as bad as we first thought. Apart from his face and hands, most of the pasting's on his clothes so we need to get him out of those and into some clean ones and you're the best man – let's face it, the only man – for this particular job.'

'Certainly, milady. I have a suit from my younger days which should fit the boy.'

'Excellent. And use Rudolf's clothes if necessary.'

'Damp flannels laid on his face should soon soak off the paste,' added Fran.

Beaton bowed, then bent down and clasped the boy's wrists, straightened up and towed him along the corridor, passing Igress on the way.

'Who's that, Mr Beaton?'

'Someone Lord Rudolf actually caught, miss.'

'Yedder,' said Guildman, looking at the newly patched area on the upholstered bench in the Lamb and Werewolf, 'do you recall the colour of Rudolf's britches last night?'

Yedder, to whom the term 'understated elegance' had never been applied and whose sartorial taste was sweet, sour, bitter and salt all at the same time, said, 'Same as ever, Gil. He's only got the one pair – a rather boring lovat green colour. Why?'

Guildman's answer was forestalled by Rigton coming in from the taproom.

'My lords,' he said, 'Lord Rudolf sends this.'

He handed a note to Guildman.

As Guildman read it, a mischievous glint came into his eyes.

'Because of some mishap last evening, we must purchase new britches for Rudolf. Measurements are enclosed.'

He grinned. 'One for you, I think, Yedder.'

Rosa tapped a calendar on the laboratory wall.

'Big day today,' she said.

'Today we send that horrible little creep to meet his maker?' asked Fran, glee evident on her face.

'Aunty! I thought that you were trained to hold all life sacrosanct.'

'Existence, not life.'

'There's a difference?'

Fran looked at Rosa in disbelief.

'Call yourself a scientist? Existence is what's given to you; life's what you do with it.'

'Ah.'

'And however much or little you're given, you've got to make the most of it.'

'Which you intend to do?'

'Which I intend to do. Possibly by sending that horrible little creep to meet his maker.'

The look on her aunt's face made laughter the most obvious and desirable reaction for Rosa.

'Well, maybe tomorrow if you're a good girl, Aunty. Today we test my latest invention: never-stick pan paint.'

A massive metal grid was suspended over the laboratory workbench. Resting on it and hanging from it was all manner of equipment, some designed for laboratory work, some not. Rosa lifted down a saucepan and tapped a pencil against the inside.

'It's been hardening for a month,' she said, 'so it should be ready by now.'

Fran eyed the pan distrustfully.

'If that's food, don't expect me to test it for you.'

'It's not food. It's to stop food sticking on the bottom of the pan when you're cooking.'

Fran took the pan and examined it.

'Food won't stick if you season your pans properly.'

Rosa waved a finger in the air.

'Seasoning pans could be a thing of the past if my never-stick pan paint works.'

Fran turned the pan over.

'Are you sure it won't affect—'

She stopped as a glutinous, dark grey glob slapped onto the workbench.

Rosa snatched the pan. The inside was as clean as if she'd just washed it.

'I don't understand why it's done that,' she said. 'It should've stuck to the pan.'

'Why?' asked Fran. 'You said it was never-stick.'

'Yes, but only on one side. It's sticky on the other side.'

Fran picked up a knife and sliced through the grey mass. She had fast enough eyesight to see that where she cut was black but immediately turned grey on exposure to the air.

'It may well be sticky on the other side,' she said, 'but the other side's the inside.' She held her palms upwards in a gesture that said that any fool with half an eye could see the problem.

Rosa opened her mouth before she realised that she didn't have any words to form in it.

Igress knocked and opened the door slightly. 'Can I...?'

Rosa threw the pan onto the bench.

'Please! Come in. I might get some sense out of you.'

Fran waved Igress in.

'Take no notice, love. Her pan's just come unstuck, that's all. Come and have a seat – we need to talk.'

Igress paled as she sat. 'That's usually a sign of bad news.'

'It is, but you have to know sometime,' said Rosa. 'The thing is, the situation with Rudolf's getting worse. He'll do anything to get his hands on the castle and my fortune, and I do mean anything. You saw what he did to the paste-boy.'

'The poor soul,' said Igress.

'Quite,' Rosa continued. 'And that's somebody he doesn't even know. Imagine what he'd do to someone he hates – like you or me or Aunty Fran, although he probably won't do much about her because she's a witch.'

'He's stupid enough to try,' said Fran.

'And his stupidity makes him dangerous,' Rosa said. 'And he's greedy, which makes him ruthless. I believe he'd quite happily have us killed to get what he wants.'

'Killed?' squeaked Igress. 'As in killed to death for the rest of your life, killed?'

Rosa nodded. 'Afraid so. I'm his main target, but I should imagine you're a close second, unfortunately.'

Igress folded her arms.

'That does it. I'm not moving out of this castle ever again.'

'You can't stay hidden away forever, flower,' said Fran. 'Life's not worth living like that.'

'With all due respect, Mistress Stein, try telling that to someone who's dead.'

'Let's not get too carried away,' said Rosa. 'Maybe if he had the castle and the money, he'd be satisfied at that and he wouldn't come after us if we got away.'

'Will you give them to him?' said Igress. 'The castle and the money?'

'Not if I can help it, and not without a fight. But we need to be aware that we're in danger.'

'No,' said Igress, 'we already know we're in danger – what we *need* is a bodyguard.'

'A bodyguard?' said Rosa.

'A bodyguard...' said Fran, speaking as if she were watching an idea grow and bloom in front of her. 'What would we need for a bodyguard? Well, obviously the first thing'd be...'

Into the parlour at the Lamb and Werewolf strode an irate aristocrat hugging a large black velvet cape around him.

'Yedder!'

'Yes, old b— oof!'

Yedder had made the mistake of turning to face the person speaking, and so Rudolf's blow caught him on the side of the head rather than the back.

'You are unsporting sometimes, Rude.'

'Unsporting? I'll give you un-bloody-sporting, you—'

He raised his arm to berate Yedder again, but Guildman's dagger blocked him.

'Now, now, Rudolf. Let's calm down, shall we?'

Guildman did not sheathe his dagger until Rudolf had slumped onto the bench.

Rudolf raised an angry finger towards him.

'I blame you for this. I sent that note to you, not to Yedder. To you.'

'Note? Ah, your new britches, I take it.'

'Yes. You do take it. You take it something chronic, and one of these days—'

'What's wrong with your new britches, old boy?' asked Yedder. 'Do they not fit?'

Rudolf's words were clipped tighter than an ornamental box hedge.

'Yes, they fit very well, thank you, Yedder...'

Yedder tilted his head to one side, but it didn't make him any the wiser.

'Sorry, old thing – don't understand the problem then.'

'Black and white stripes?' seethed Rudolf.

Yedder's face lit up.

'Oh! Right... Ripping, aren't they? They're the very latest style, you know.'

'Just the thing for the modern lord-about-town,' smiled Guildman.

Rudolf bared his teeth.

'So why aren't you wearing them?'

'Because as you have pointed out on numerous occasions, I know absolutely nothing about lording.'

Rudolf's nostrils flared and he said nothing as angrily as he could.

'Well, I think they're absolutely spiffing,' chirped Yedder. 'I've ordered a pair for myself.'

Rudolf slowly turned his full glare on Yedder.

'Oh good. Then we can both run away to the circus and join the white-faced clowns because we'll both have the costumes, won't we?'

'Although Yedder will have to buy a red nose,' said Guildman. 'Unlike yourself. But at least he'll be able to. Unlike yourself.'

Yedder snorted.

Rudolf twitched. 'Meaning?'

'Meaning,' said Guildman, 'that that even if you needed a red nose – which you don't – you couldn't buy one.'

'What?'

'No dosh, tosh,' explained Yedder. 'The whole town knows Roz's cut you off without a penny, so nobody'll give you credit any more.'

A hand shot out from under Rudolf's cape and grabbed Yedder's collar. 'In that case, Yedder, you get the beers in.'

As Yedder headed for the bar, Rudolf kicked at his empty chair. 'No credit?!' he spat. 'No credit?! I've spent thousands in this town. For years. Lavish, me. Like a proper lord.'

Guildman said nothing.

Rudolf scowled. 'Oh, that's your answer to everything, isn't it? Smile and say nothing. I bet you laughed in sweet silence when Yedder bought these sodding pantomime britches.'

'That's the point, Rudolf,' said Guildman. 'Yedder bought your britches. Without credit, and without a second thought.'

'No bloody thought at all.'

'Without Yedder, the only thing you can get in this town is murdered. And then there'd be no money to bury you.'

'I notice you never put your hand in your pocket.'

'I prefer my hands intact, not bitten by those I feed.'

'He'll get his money back. Two and three times over. Just as soon as—'

'Just as soon as you get the castle and the fortune, yes, yes.'

'It's only a matter of time.'

'And money. And where will you get that?'

'Yedder!' beamed Rudolf to the approaching cheerful one who carried three tankards, each adorned with a slice of star fruit. 'You haven't told me what my cow of a wife said when you took the paste-boy to the castle.'

'Erm...' Yedder screwed his face up with the effort of recall. 'Roz said... stop taking your anger out on innocent people like the paste-boy and that wench, and... if you've got any further messages for her you should drag your... what was it, Gil?'

'Sorry little carcass.'

'That's it. Drag your sorry little carcass up to Castle Stein and she'll... tear you limb from limb. Something like that.'

'An adequate précis, Yedder,' said Guildman, dropping his star fruit into Yedder's ale.

'Sorry little carcass?!' cried Rudolf. 'I'll give her sorry little carcass when I get up there with an army!'

'Is this the army you can't afford to recruit, pay, equip, accommodate, feed or train?' said Guildman.

'Yedder'll loan me the money, won't you, Yedder?'

'Ah. Truth to tell, old boy, Lady Yedder's made noises in that direction lately. Used the word "profligate" once or twice.'

'What Lady Yedder doesn't know won't hurt her,' said Rudolf. 'Unlike you. You know what'll hurt you.'

A balding, overall-clad, dust-covered individual with a pencil behind his ear cradled an enormous chipped mug covered in dirty fingerprints in the kitchen of Castle Stein, and spoke to the back of Mrs B, who was busy at the sink.

'You've got have the right kind of rope for hauling, Mrs B,' said Mason, tilting his head to one side to fully appreciate the way the light fell onto Mrs B's ankles, which were the only bits of her below the neck – apart from her hands – that were allowed plenty of fresh air on a daily basis.

A newly peeled potato plopped into a large saucepan.

'And there's me thinking a rope is a rope is a rope,' Mrs B replied, dipping into the potato sack again. The temporary shortening of her skirt as she bent raised Mason's eyebrows.

'Oh, no. It's got to be the right rope, and I'm having the devil of a job to get it.'

Mason was fascinated by the way Mrs B's quick arm movements made her body shudder.

Another plop, another dip into the sack.

'And if you don't get one, Mr Mason, you'll never get the job finished and I shall be forever making tea for you.'

He closed one eye and ran his hand over the shape of her full body, even though she was well out of reach.

'You're a... generous woman, Mrs B, that you are.'

His hand was still outstretched when the kitchen door opened so he pretended to examine his fingernails.

Beaton, trailing behind Rosa as she strode into the room, glared a warning at the builder.

Rosa returned the never-stick-less saucepan to the pan rack.

'Mason,' she said, 'I suggest you leave before I start charging you rent for that chair. Besides, you won't want to hear the rest of this conversation – I know how delicate builders are.'

Mason gave her his best 'don't mess with me' smile and raised the chipped mug.

'I'll finish my tea first, your ladyship.'

Rosa shrugged. 'Suit yourself. Now, Beaton, are you clear on what you have to get?'

'Yes, milady. A thermometer, a large clock, long leather straps, telescopic metal tubing, a catering-size tub of grease...'

Mason's chair scraped on the floor as he stood up.

'I'll leave the tea.'

'Well, I've never seen that before,' said Mrs B, who, despite holding a half-peeled potato and a knife, put her hands on her hips and watched the builder depart.

'...a weather forecast from FitzRoy's Office,' continued Beaton, 'some waxed button thread and a dead body.'

'Preferably strong.'

'And can you get me two blocks of kitchen soap?' said Mrs B brightly, returning to her potatoes.

'I'll need a bag, Mrs B,' said her husband. 'It's a lot to carry.'

'Ask the paste-boy,' said Rosa. 'He might help you.'

'I'll see if his face has softened up yet, milady. Otherwise it may be difficult to gauge his reaction.'

'But—'

'It's quite simple, Yedder,' reasoned Rudolf. 'I've got a hot tip for the third race this afternoon. It's a good runner – could go all night. We go down, put the bet on, collect the winnings and come away again.'

'But the old girl's getting a bit suspicious. What if she asks if you've been spending my money again?'

'Tell her I haven't.'

Yedder looked horrified.

'What? Lie? Oh, no. Couldn't do that, old boy.'

'And why not?'

Guildman stretched out his long legs and put his hands behind his head. 'Never tell a lady a lie, Rudolf.'

'Look,' said Rudolf, tapping his forefinger on the table, 'you two'd better start behaving like proper lords and that includes lying, all right?'

Guildman winked at Yedder.

'All right, we'll lie, won't we, Yedder?'

An open-mouthed smile sprang to Yedder's face.

'Yes! Splendid idea! Of course we'll lie, Rude. No problem. Lie, lie, lie, lie, lie.'

'You're lying, aren't you?' said Rudolf, flatly.

''Fraid so, old thing,' Yedder laughed. 'See? Told you I couldn't do it.'

Guildman chuckled.

Rudolf sighed heavily.

'In that case, Yedder, *you* put the bet on, and *you* collect the winnings. Then *you* can tell her the truth.'

'Which would be?' asked Yedder.

'Which would be,' said Rudolf, adopting a look of self-satisfaction, 'that I hadn't touched your money.'

'It's unlikely that Yedder's winnings will be enough to fund an army for an assault on the castle,' said Guildman.

'I know,' smirked Rudolf. 'But it'll be enough to pay for a dwarf.'

Gambling

In Maund, the unsuspecting, unlucky or just plain stupid can be parted from their money in a variety of interesting locations and humiliating ways.

Most of the townspeople risk financial ruin simply by going to the market, where shoppers completing a transaction are strongly advised to count their fingers as well as their change.

In the local pubs, a smiling mine host will relieve you of both your money and the ability to stand up and communicate coherently.

Eating-houses will charge exorbitant prices for minuscule portions of food, usually when both you and the food are celebrating birthdays.

And, if you know where to go, a variety of beings will provide unusual, often intimate, occasionally eye-watering services for an equally eye-watering price.

However, it's generally agreed that not even vampires can suck as much blood as the owners of the gaming houses.

And for those overburdened with wealth who believe it's not healthy to sit in darkened, smoke-filled rooms betting on the spin of a wheel, the turn of a friendly card or the digestive system of a fellow creature, there are two main outdoor centres of money-squandering.

The first, patronised chiefly by people for whom the idea of having no money is as difficult to grasp as a greased snake, is the Equestrian Racing Circuit, affectionately known as the Horse Course. The second, attended by those who not only know the concept of penury but the theory, practice, machinations and repercussions of it, is the Maund and District Workers' Co-operative Sports, Social, Welfare and Recreational Club (Canine Branch) (Affiliated) – appropriately known as the Dog Flog.

Indulgent owners and skilled trainers spend vast amounts of time and money on pedigree animals, building strength, regulating diet, curing ailments, cosseting, comforting and training them to the very peak of physical fitness so that punters can bet on the animal's speed, staying power or ability to jump over bizarre obstacles. Such wagers are usually made after very careful consideration of a variety of factors, chiefly the sound of the animal's name, the colours it carries and whether or not it empties its bowels in the parade ring.

There's one major difference between the Horse Course and the Dog Flog: thoroughbred horses are clever enough to race against each other, whereas dogs need a hare to chase or else there's a lot of unnecessary sex, violence and sniffing. And, of course, the Dog Flog hurdles are lower and there's very little use of the whip by jockeys.

The punters are a world apart too, although the large-hatted lords and ladies who wine and dine elegantly in the Course grandstand line the pockets of the same bookmakers as the flat-capped and scarved men and women who eat out of paper bags in a field watching their beer money ride on a canine that couldn't get around the track as fast as their own grannies.

~•~

'Aren't you coming in, Rude?' asked Yedder as he and Guildman stepped down from the carriage at the end of Shuffler Gate Road opposite the Horse Course grandstand.

'How many more times, Yedder? I'm staying put in this coach to ease your precious conscience,' growled Rudolf. 'Now don't forget – you've got the name of the horse, you've got the money, and you know where the bookies are. Even you shouldn't go wrong on this one.'

'Worry not, old thing. Leave it to me.'

'And don't be long! The quicker I get my winnings, the quicker I get my castle.'

Rudolf slammed the window up and flopped onto one of the bench seats.

Yedder and Guildman strolled across to the betting area.

'This nag of Rude's going to take any honours, Gil?' said Yedder, scanning the bookie's blackboard.

'The longer the odds, the shorter the chance, I believe,' replied Guildman, noting that the odds on Rudolf's choice were longer than the distance the horse had to run.

The bookie windmilled his arms for a few seconds then added another nought onto the figure.

'I fear it may have fallen in the parade ring,' said Guildman.

'Tell you what,' said Yedder cheerfully, 'I'll put as little as possible on Rude's nag – then he can't say I didn't do it – and I'll put the rest on a choice of my own. How's that?'

'An admirable strategy, Yedder, and bound to increase the chances of success considerably.'

As Yedder placed his wagers, Guildman surveyed the crowd. As usual, the racegoers fell into two distinct camps: the minority, who had at least a cursory interest in what was happening on the track, and the vast majority, who paid large amounts of entrance money for the privilege of ignoring the racing completely as they busied themselves gossiping to friends, talking about enemies, eating, drinking, flirting, matchmaking and business dealing.

A familiar face winked then signalled for him to keep quiet.

He tilted his head very slightly, smiling lazily as the figure crept forwards and thrust a pair of plump arms around Yedder's thin frame.

Yedder started.

A smooth, attractive, familiar voice filled his ear.

'Gotcha, you handsome brute!'

'Gorgeousness!' cried Yedder, telling no lie.

The lady he turned to face had flawless skin and long, curling lashes framing dark brown eyes that a man could stare into all evening. Two soft crimson cushions of lips parted to reveal white, even teeth. The curls of her dark, silky hair bounced as she moved, and her figure filled every rounded letter of the word 'curvaceous'.

She and Yedder laughed, hugged and kissed.

He stood back and held her at arms' length, and his eyes shone as he looked her up and down.

'Gosh! You look divine – absolutely divine.' He kissed her hands. 'Isn't she a cracker, Gil?'

Guildman clicked his heels and bowed.

'My lady is beautiful and, sadly, spoken for.'

Lady Yedder giggled as she put her hand on Guildman's arm and kissed him lightly on the cheek.

'You are so smooth, Gil.'

'And so enchanted, my lady.'

She laughed again, and her beauty lit up the surrounding area, drawing admiring glances from passers-by.

'What are you doing here, my sweetness?' asked Yedder. 'I thought you were taking your aunts to the dressmakers or the milliners or something.'

She threw her hands up in mock horror.

'Oh, don't! Aunty Anna wanted a new dress, Aunty Maria wanted a new hat and Aunty Elise wanted new shoes, but that would have taken forever, going in and out of every shop. So, I've promised to take them individually on different days.'

'But how did you end up here?'

'Uncle Billy wanted wildlife, Uncle Bill wanted fresh air, and Uncle Will wanted to go out for lunch. Or was Uncle Bill who... Anyway, no matter. I decided that all three Williams would be happy if we came racing so I asked cook to pack up some goodies for us, and here we are! We're all having a completely spiffing time!'

'All, my angel?'

'Eleven aunts, seven uncles, Lady Guildman, me, four cases of wine and two enormous hampers. It's an absolute riot!'

Her laughter radiated true happiness to all who heard her.

She linked arms with both her husband and Guildman.

'Now then, my darlings, will you come and join us? We've got a huge picnic with plenty of drinkies, and we're having so much fun.'

'Well...' Yedder began.

'Please? Do say you'll stay.'

Yedder tried to resist, but took one look at her and melted.

'Hang it all – we will! Just for the next race, though.'

'Oh, darling, do you have to dash off somewhere?'

Guildman smiled. 'How could we leave when one so beautiful asks us to stay? Our... business... can take care of itself for a while. For you, my lady, we have all the time in the world.'

Lost somewhere in one of Beaton's old suits was a tall, gangly youth with freshly chapped hands and face. He stood before Rosa's desk catching the full radiance of her smile.

'Hello, Aidan,' she said. 'Have I got your name right?'

'Yes, miss... madam... milady.'

'Do you know where you are, Aidan?'

'Mr Beaton says this is Castle Stein, milady.'

Rosa nodded. 'Do you remember how you got here?'

Aidan shuffled his feet and cleared his throat.

'Not exactly. The last thing I remember is being in the pub, and then waking up here with cold flannels on my face being told that everything'd be all right.'

'And is everything all right?'

'Apart from my hands and face, milady. A bit sore.'

Rosa winced at the understatement; he had a face like a glazed strawberry tart.

'Aidan, do you enjoy being a paste-boy?'

Bewilderment filled his brain and spilled over onto his face.

'Er... I don't know, milady. It's just something I do. I don't think about enjoying it.'

'Right,' said Rosa, but the door opening halted further words for the moment.

Igress peeked round the door.

'I've brought a pot of ointment, ma'am.'

Rosa waved her in. 'Thank you, Igress. I'm sure Aidan would be glad of some cream for his sore skin.'

Igress walked over and stood by Aidan. He turned to look at her, she smiled, and the room seemed to fill with the sound of him gulping; he blushed as well, but nobody could see that. Igress put the tub of ointment on the desk, dipped her finger in it, lifted Aidan's hand and gently circled the cream into his palm. Somewhere in the depths of one of Beaton's old suits, a pair of gangly legs went weak at the knees and a heart was lost forever to the beautiful scientific assistant.

'I've been thinking for quite some time,' said Rosa, 'that we need a new footman in the castle to take some of the work off Beaton. Would that be a job you'd like to do, Aidan? Aidan!'

He tore his eyes away from Igress.

'What? Oh, sorry, milady!'

'Would you like—'

'I'd love to, milady.'

'But you don't—'

'I don't care.'

'Splendid.' Rosa's face was smiling, but her soul was rolling around on the floor laughing its socks off.

'That's settled, then. You'll be our new footman. Beaton will instruct you.'

'Oh, thank you, milady.'

He held his other palm out to Igress. She plonked the tub of cream on it and grinned mischievously.

During his working life, Innsted the coachman had heard many sounds coming from his carriage as he sat on the driving board. The tuneless bawling of unsavoury songs after respectable gentlemen's dinner parties. The desperate wails of young ladies as their fathers tore them away from unacceptable suitors. The agonies of men too slow to win the duel. The heart-piercing screams of a mother as her babe was snatched by its father.

But nothing had ever eaten into his soul with such relentless ferocity as Rudolf's snoring. Each hideous rasp was followed by a tantalising silence seeming to signify the coming of peace, and each silence was brutally curtailed by a dry, open-mouthed wheezy sigh that was the prelude to another hideous rasp.

When Rudolf had first dropped off, all had been silent, but as his sleep had deepened into near hibernation, Innsted had tried a crescendo of tactics to stop the reverberations. Coughing, tapping on the carriage roof and bouncing on the driving board had no effect. Shouting at the horses only confused them, as did jogging the reins to make them walk forward then pulling them up sharply again.

For the past hour, Innsted had seriously contemplated the professional repercussions of smothering a passenger. But when the chimes of the grandstand clock struck six, his gloom lifted like the lid on a pirate chest full of gold and jewels. Relief flooded through him and he leapt from the driving board a man renewed. He ripped open the carriage door and shook Rudolf roughly by the shoulder. 'Sir! Sir! Wake up!'

The snoring stopped, replaced by a goldfish impression as Rudolf realised that his mouth was dry. He licked his lips and rolled over on the seat.

'Hnh.'

'Sir, the hire time on this carriage has expired.'

'Hnh.'

'Sir, you must either re-hire or vacate this carriage immediately.'

'Wa?'

'Either pay up or get up.'

'Sod off.'

For someone who had spent many evenings delivering burly drunken sportsmen to various destinations, a semi-conscious aristocrat was hardly a challenge. Innsted grasped Rudolf's collar, and before Rudolf had time to get both eyelids open he'd been bounced off the seat, onto the carriage floor, out of the door, across the grass and into a ditch. He struggled to his feet in time to see Innsted turning the coach around prior to heading back into town. Rudolf scrambled out of the ditch, ran across the grass and made a lunge for the driving board. The sole of Innsted's boot met Rudolf's chest with some force and ensured that Rudolf did not achieve his desired goal, but crashed back onto the grass as the carriage hurtled away.

Rudolf punched the ground. 'Bastard! Agh, ya— ow!'

He shook his hand sharply before examining it. Blood welled up in a gash between his knuckles and he looked down to see what he needed to take his revenge out on. A gold piece lay on the grass; the pain subsided considerably.

Rudolf hammered on Millie's door which was, as usual, locked.

'Lemme in, Mills!'

'Go away! You know I don't work after six.'

'Aw... come on, Mills, it's me, Rudi.'

'Bugger off! Now!'

'I've got money...'

The door opened and a manicured hand shot out of a dressing-gown sleeve, grabbed Rudolf's tunic and jerked him into the house shortly before the door slammed shut again.

Rudolf lifted his arms and smiled, broadly and drunkenly.

'Millie, Millie, Millie,' he sang. 'I knew you couldn't resist me.'

Without her shoes she was a good foot shorter than Rudolf, so he bent over to engulf her. His progress was stopped by a stinging slap to the face.

'On your knees, you sorry wretch!' she commanded, and he obeyed, offering no resistance save putting his arms across his face as she beat him about the head and shoulders.

'How dare you!' she raged. 'How dare you come here at this time, making an exhibition of yourself on my doorstep! I've a bloody good mind to heave you out into the back lane.'

'Aw, Mills, don't,' Rudolf whined. 'I'm sick of being thrown out of places. Don't be rotten to your Rudi. Haven't I always been good to you?'

Millie laid into him again, fury powering her arms.

'Good to me?! I'll give you good to me, you tow-rag! We were engaged – remember? *Engaged!* – and you married *her!* But you still came to see me, didn't you? Still wanted me, and you were happy to pay through the nose for me, but not leave her and marry me. And now she's stopped your money I've had to go cap-in-hand to her – to your *wife* – to get paid! So no, you haven't always been good to me, you little shit!'

She stopped suddenly, panting. The physical effort of taking her anger out on Rudolf had loosened the cord on her dressing-gown. She had not yet changed out of her traditional costume, and as her corsets valiantly tried to constrain a bosom which swelled and threatened to overspill with every angry breath, Rudolf felt a shiver ripple the insides of his thighs.

'I've got money now, Mills,' he gasped. 'I have.'

She lifted a fishnet-stocking-clad leg and planted a small foot defiantly in the middle of his already bruised chest.

'You're a liar as well as a cheat and a drunkard, you disgusting runt.'

Silver and copper coins clattered across the floor as he turfed out his pockets. He timidly put one hand on her calf.

With a well-practised and surprisingly powerful flick of her ankle she kicked him onto his back. As he sprawled, she walked up his body and stood on his chest.

'Make me some tea.'

'Tea,' squeaked Rudolf.

'Then prepare my bath, which I will take in front of the fire while you're locked in your cage in the corner.'

'Cage.'

'And once you've emptied the bath and cleaned up, you will massage my feet.'

'Feet.'

'And then, only if you've been a very good boy, you can wash my underwear.'

'Underwear,' he quivered.

She stepped off his chest and stood with one foot on each side of his head. From Rudolf's viewpoint she'd have looked much taller if only his eyes had got that far.

After a few seconds she put one foot on his cheek, pushed his head to one side and said, 'What are you waiting for, you worm?'

Rudolf's eyelids fluttered.

'Oh, Mills, you're the best.'

She imprinted a fishnet pattern into his cheek.

'And you're so pathetic.'

~•~

NOTES ON

The Dead

For a lot of people, the presence of a dead body – whether their own or someone else's – signifies the end of their problems. For others, it's only the start.

All cultures have developed their own way of making people dead, both accidentally and on purpose. Some have been spectacularly successful by using positive effort and systematic methods, others through neglect, and some by carelessness, stupidity and ignorance. The size of the success may often be disputed, but the end result is the same: the dead. And whether on a large scale or small, something must be done with them. It's a problem that increases with every succeeding generation and shows no signs of going away. It can't just be brushed under the carpet, because sooner or later someone will fall over it and the cat keeps scratching at it.

Through the ages different civilisations have dealt with the problem in various ways. Some ancients encased their wealthiest dead in the centre of huge pyramids along with animals, food, fabulous treasure and occasionally servants, which shows that they didn't subscribe to the concept of 'you can't take it with you'. The pyramids were sealed by means of complicated sliding stonework, designed to keep out grave-robbers; however, if you don't want people running off with your fabulous wealth, don't build a huge stone marker indicating its exact location.

113

Certain people still believe that the best thing for the dead is burning. Whilst this removes the nagging doubt that someone may have just been in a very deep sleep, it's hardly environmentally friendly. At best, it merely reduces the size of the problem, as the ashes still need to be disposed of; at worst, cremation actually exacerbates the problem. The extravagant nature of the funeral pyre and the penchant for throwing relatives onto it, regardless of their state of health and their degree of guilt in causing the death, means that the pile of ashes is frequently much bigger than the original single dead body.

Some tribes leave their dead out in the wilderness, to be recycled by wild animals and birds. Cheap, with little heavy labour involved, not only is the food chain sustained but there's always enough bones around for a nourishing soup or a reasonable xylophone.

For those lacking a wilderness, the nearest available option is burial. The biodegradable body is recycled by those elements of the natural world that live below ground, again sustaining the food chain. By burying the dead, a valuable educational resource is being deposited for future generations of archaeologists; grave-digging, floristry, woodworking and stonemasonry keep people employed. A burial site gives us an indication of how far back in history we stretch as a people, and how short a distance we may reach into the future as individuals. A marked family grave serves as a touchstone to our memories and a friend to confide in, who gives neither advice nor reproof, but a chance to talk things out.

And the best place to bury someone is a burial ground, for several reasons.

Firstly, on a purely practical level, the digging is a lot easier in a burial ground, because somebody's already done the hard work and cleared out all the rocks and stones.

Secondly, people assume that they know why a person digs in a burial ground. If you start riving up a patch of waste ground, someone's bound to walk by and ask you what you're doing. In a burial ground, no-one will question what you're up to with that spade. If you've got to bury someone 'unofficially', where better to bury them than in a place where everybody expects to see people being buried? If you're still unsure, do it at night, because the only people brave enough to go near a burial ground at night are drunks, who won't remember what they've seen anyway and if they do, they'll think they dreamt it.

Thirdly, if you bury something in a farmer's field, the chances are it'll be dug up again at some point. However much your loved ones meant to you, you don't want them surfacing again just when you'd thought you'd got over it. And if it's an unofficial burial, you definitely don't want a major piece of incriminating evidence being ploughed up and used against you. So, stick with the burial ground. The only way there'll be any resurrection from there is courtesy of grave-robbers or unofficial undertakers, and if they find something untoward, they're hardly likely to go running to the rozzer shop with the mud still on their hands.

Lastly, if you dig somewhere that's not been dug before, you never know what you might find; in a burial ground, you most certainly do.

~•~

Aidan was not at Dafferd Hill burial ground through choice.

'I'm really not sure about this, Mr Beaton.'

Beaton folded back the tarpaulin on the handcart and picked up a spade and a long thin cane. He held the spade out to Aidan.

'Whatever would Miss Igress say? A big strong lad like you, afraid of a few holes in the ground?'

Aidan took the spade.

'I'm not afraid of the holes,' he said confidently. 'Only what's in 'em.'

A corner of the tarpaulin rose from the handcart without any help, accompanied by an ethereal wailing. 'Woooh...'

Both Aidan and spade dropped to the floor.

'You'd forgotten all about me, hadn't you?' teased a gleeful feline emerging from under the tarpaulin.

Aidan's lip curled.

'Come along,' said Beaton, helping Aidan up and handing him the spade again before setting off through the lych-gate.

Sooty jumped from the cart.

'Don't worry about the bodies, Aidan. *I'm* the scariest thing in here.' Lifting his front legs, he floated upwards and his body faded until all Aidan could see was a skeleton dancing in the air.

Aidan whimpered and ran to Beaton, who had stopped under the branches of a yew.

Sooty laughed, reassumed his normal cat form and breathed deeply. 'Ooh, don't you love the smell of moonlight? Clean and crisp and' – he licked his lips – 'just that tiny taste of silver. Can't beat it.'

He leapt onto the low wall surrounding the burial ground.

'Shop!' he called. 'Anybody in?'

'What sort of summoning's that?' rasped a dark voice out of an even darker corner.

Beaton sensed Aidan's body getting ready for flight, and so held onto his arm.

'Just testing,' said Sooty, then cleared his throat and straightened his back. 'Spirit of Co-operation desires to speak with the Burial Keeper,' he declaimed.

'Spirit of Co-operation, eh?' growled the other voice. 'Not seen him about these parts for donkey's years. Not since that fight over the lady cat from The Shambles. Not since I thrashed him and got the girl.'

'Boggis, you old scrote!' laughed Sooty. 'Show yourself, you worthless bag of bones!'

As Boggis emerged from the shadows, Aidan realised why he hadn't been able to see where the voice had come from. Boggis was not so much a black cat, more a hole in the night. Sooty jumped off the wall, and the two old friends greeted each other enthusiastically. Aidan relaxed, and Beaton let go of him.

'So,' said Boggis, 'what does the White One desire of the Burial Keeper?'

'Hah! I haven't been called the White One for years!' said Sooty. 'And fancy you being the Burial Keeper. Didn't anybody else turn up for the job?'

'Ahem,' coughed Beaton.

'Oh, sorry,' said Sooty. 'Burial Keeper, I desire to know who's new and who's strong.'

'Oh you do, do you?' said Boggis in an attitude that in a

human usually came from under a peaked cap.

'Yes I do.'

'Ooh, don't know if I can tell you. Privileged information, that is.' Boggis sucked in the night air through his teeth and left a hefty silence that could only be filled by one word.

'Please,' Aidan begged.

'Glad to see somebody round here's got some manners,' said Boggis, ducking before Sooty's paw could connect with him. 'New and strong, you say?'

'Yes sir, please sir, three bags full sir,' jibed Sooty, and it became his turn to duck.

'You're in luck,' said Boggis. 'I've got somebody over here who fits the bill.'

He led them over to a patch of recently dug soil.

'In here,' he said. 'Not too far down, I shouldn't think. Bit of a rush job.'

Beaton prodded the long cane into the soil. It passed through the earth easily until it struck something buried.

'Thank you, Burial Keeper,' Beaton said, then he turned to Aidan. 'Start digging, Aidan.'

'Me?' said Aidan. 'Why me?'

'Because you've got the spade.'

Boggis drew Sooty to one side.

'I should warn you,' he whispered, 'there's a tiny complication with this one.'

Most of Rudolf was blissfully happy, chiefly because most of Rudolf was exceedingly drunk. One tiny corner of his soul still nurtured vengeance against Rosa, but had decided to suspend operations for the night and return to recolonise Rudolf in the morning when it'd get a great deal more sense out of him.

For once, he felt one up on the Fates who ordinarily conspired to thwart his every endeavour. He'd found enough money for a ritual humiliation by the best dominatrix in Maund and still have the price of a bottle of cheap brandy, so once his body was satisfied he could continue indulging his thirst.

Which he did, as he staggered back to the Lamb and Werewolf, not caring that Rigton would have long since locked up, nor that it was pitch dark and he had to walk through areas where even the muggers daren't go out on their own. However, he did notice that the milestones seemed to be getting increasingly close together, and the slope he walked up was soft underfoot yet extremely steep. And when he fell down the other side, he knew that the drop was longer than the climb had been. But because he was exceedingly drunk he didn't hurt himself when he fell into the newly vacated grave, nor did he bother about the smell which permeated the soil of its walls and base. After a couple of futile attempts to climb out, he decided that a hole in the ground six foot by six foot by three was as good a place as any to curl up and go to sleep.

Boggis peered over the edge of the grave.

'Now then,' he said. 'There's something you don't see every day – a corpse that snores.' He shuddered at a sound that would not only frighten the daylights out of the living, but was in very real danger of waking the dead.

NOTES ON

Colour

The only colours that really interest the people of Maund are the colours of money. Copper, silver and gold are powerful colours indeed.

The colour of people's skin is of interest only to a physician or healer, and then only if it's not the colour it's supposed to be. To judge someone's character by the colour of their skin is as ludicrous as judging the value of a treasure hoard by the colour of the field it's buried in.

The skin people inhabit is not a matter of choice; they're born with it, they live with it and they'll die with it. And that'll be the end of it.

Unless something very unexpected happens.

~✦~

Although it was approaching midnight, Beaton, Aidan and Sooty were enjoying a well-earned drink in the kitchen at Castle Stein while in the cold store, three women were viewing things with a much stronger stomach than Aidan had.

'I know there's a family tradition of eccentricity,' said Fran, 'but isn't two bodies a bit ambitious?'

'I didn't ask for two,' replied Rosa. 'They were in the same winding sheet. What I don't understand is why they're naked.'

Fran opened her mouth, but Igress beat her to the words.

'No point burying good clothes if you can use them again.'

That wasn't the theory Fran had been going to put forward,

but to save further discussion she kept quiet.

'And it's the law, ma'am,' Igress added.

'What?' said Rosa. 'If you steal a body it's got to be naked?'

Igress nodded. 'If you're caught in possession of a completely naked dead body, there's nothing on it that belongs to anybody and so the most you can be done for is indecency.'

'Which in this town's like being done for breathing,' said Fran.

'Exactly, Mistress Stein – a minor offence. But if they catch you with a naked dead body which is wearing even one bit of clothing or jewellery, that clothing or jewellery obviously belongs to somebody and you can be done for theft.'

'Which carries a much higher penalty?' said Rosa.

'Trust me, ma'am. Mr Beaton could've gone to the gallows if either of these corpses'd had so much as a sock on.'

'Anyway,' said Fran, 'it's a good job there are two because this one's head's been stove in.'

'That thin feller doesn't look strong enough to do that,' said Igress.

Rosa peered closely at the boxer's caved-in face.

'No... he's too tall. Unless he was on his knees. No – this has been done by somebody much shorter. Look at the line of it. See how deep it is at one end compared to the other. My money says it was a dwarf throwing-axe.'

'Well, whatever it was,' said Fran, 'we can't use him.'

'And this one's way too weedy for a bodyguard,' said Igress.

'Too weedy to breathe in and out,' confirmed Rosa, running her hands over the tailor's slim body. 'Feel that. Ribs like broken biscuits. He's had the life crushed out of him. His spine feels intact, so he wasn't picked up and squeezed... no, something – or somebody – heavy fell on him. Probably the other chap.'

'You can tell all that from looking at them?' said Igress.

'She's not a scientist for nothing, you know,' said Fran.

'In every death there is the image of the parting,' said Rosa, lifting the end of the sheet covering the men's feet. 'The trick is knowing where to find it.' She grimaced and replaced the sheet. 'It's academic anyway. We can't use either of these.'

'And after all the trouble Mr Beaton's been to,' said Igress. 'It's a pity you can't just swap the heads over, isn't it?'

'It is,' said Rosa glumly. 'Still, that's how it goes... wait a minute – what did you say?'

'I said it's a pity you can't just—'

'Swap the heads over! Oh, Aunty, do you think we could?'

'You're the scientist – you tell me,' said Fran. 'Mind you, it's not like they're going to complain if it doesn't work.'

'Shame they won't match, though,' said Igress.

'How d'you mean they won't match? They're both people, aren't they?'

'Yes, but the big beefy bloke's the colour of birch wood and the little thin feller's more of a conker. Put 'em together and you'll end up with somebody who's like a longcase clock with a birch base and waist and a mahogany bonnet.'

There was a pause as Fran and Rosa looked at each other for interpretation. Rosa shook her head. Fran shrugged and unbuttoned her cuff. 'Roll your sleeve up, Rosa.'

'What's up?' said Igress. 'Have I said something wrong?'

'No,' said Fran, 'you said something interesting.' She put

her bare arm next to Rosa's. 'What colour are we, then?'

'Erm... Mistress Stein, I'd say you were cherry, and Lady Stein's almost as a pale as holly wood.'

'She doesn't get out much,' said Fran.

'And what about you?' asked Rosa. 'What colour are you?'

'Me? I'm more of a golden oak, really.'

'You seem to know an awful lot about wood.'

'My mum died when I was little,' said Igress, 'and my dad couldn't look after me during the day because he's a blacksmith and it'd be too dangerous to have a nipper in the smithy. But my uncle Hep's a cabinet maker, and he took me into his woodworking shop during the day and back to Dad at night. He taught me all about wood and veneers and sums and angles and stuff like "measure twice, cut once" and all that. Used to make wooden toys for me all in different natural colours.'

'Aww, how lovely,' said Rosa.

'Anyway,' said Fran, 'back to the job in hand. This bloke's hardly pure – what was it? birch wood? – is he? Look at him.'

The boxer's chest bore a spread-eagle tattoo in blue, black, grey, scarlet and orange. Patches of his skin were purple, green, yellow and brown from bruising; old scars were a dusky pink; the rest was a mottled beige which paled even further in the areas where his shorts and boots would normally be.

'And after all,' said Rosa, 'it is a human head we're putting on him. It's not as if we were giving him a troll's head, is it?'

Igress nodded. 'Fair point.'

'And at least these are the same basic material,' said Fran. 'Look at Pirate Polly from the chandlery. She's got half a leg made of a bit of tree most days, and a metal one if she thinks there's going to be trouble. No, we've got one good body and one good head and as long as they fit and they work together, I couldn't care less if the dial doesn't match the pendulum.'

In death, Alderman Alexander Constantine Barrington della Vittorioso McGillicuddy achieved what had eluded him in life: a stone monument with his name on it. His wish was for two blindfolded cherubim, one holding a wreath and the other an extinguished torch, standing by a broken column supporting a weeping virgin who crushes a rose beneath her bare foot while carrying a classical urn and an open book with a torn-out page bearing his name, the date of his death and a wilting lily.

The family, however, whether in an outbreak of parsimony, good taste or simple embarrassment, deprived the stonemasons of a steady income for several years by commissioning a plain oblong altar with a flat top. This fulfilled all the requirements of cemetery architecture: sufficiently high not to be stumbled over in the dark, no ornamentation that people would break off and steal to use as garden statuary, and it bore its occupant's name in a single line, albeit round a few corners.

And it was ideal for a cat to stretch out on in the morning sunshine, which Boggis did, as the lack of sound from below ground reminded him why he'd become the Burial Keeper – for the peace and quiet that the dead bring, that the living all too frequently do not. He yawned and rubbed his ears.

'Either I've gone deaf or he's woken up.'

He dropped lightly from Alderman McGillicuddy's resting-place, padded to the open grave and peered down at the dishevelled aristocrat clutching an empty brandy bottle.

'Awake, are we?' Boggis asked in as friendly a manner as possible bearing in mind that all night Rudolf had made more noise than a carpentry school.

Rudolf opened a bleary eye and looked up.

'Not sure,' he said sourly. 'Talking cat, are we?'

'Yup.'

'Then apparently I'm awake. But I've no idea what you're doing on my headboard.'

Boggis's tail swished. 'I'm not on your headboard, mate. You're in one of my graves.'

Rudolf jumped to his feet with all the renewed vigour of a man who's just discovered that as a bad start to the day, a hangover comes a very long way behind being buried alive. He leapt about in the hole, ferociously brushing himself down.

Boggis laughed.

'You're supposed to dance *on* people's graves, not in 'em.'

'Get 'em off me! Get 'em off me!'

'What?'

'The worms! The worms! Get 'em off me!'

'There ain't no worms on you! Blimey! What *were* you drinking last night?'

Rudolf stopped dancing. 'Last night? I've been here all night? Didn't anybody come looking for me?'

'They wouldn't've needed to look,' Boggis sniffed. 'They could've just listened.'

Most of the castle household rose late, and the two newest members didn't rise at all but lay in the cold store oblivious of the further injury that was to be inflicted upon them.

In the kitchen, the hardened and cracked hands interlocked around an enormous chipped mug belonged to a man mesmerised by the sight of Mrs B knitting, although those of a suspicious nature – including Mr Beaton – might say that this was because the main arena of action was immediately in front of her ample bosom.

'You've got skilful fingers, Mrs B,' said Mason dreamily.

'It's easy once you get into the swing of it,' she said. 'The worst problem's getting the tension right.'

He drooled as her hands darted back and forth in a rhythm he was sure he could put to better use. 'Tension?'

'Tension's how much you pull the wool. Some people pull their wool hard, and others pull theirs hardly at all.'

Mason gulped. 'And does the tension matter?'

Mrs B laughed a pink, moist, inviting, open-mouthed laugh.

'Of course it matters, Mr Mason! Imagine you're knitting a jumper. If your tension's too slack, your jumper'll be huge and you'll be stranded inside it like a sausage in a barrel. If your tension's too tight, you won't be able to get your jumper over your head. All depending on the size of your head, that is.'

Mason bit his lip. He knew all about the size of his head and he knew all about tension. What he wanted was relief. And he wanted it from Mrs B. He cleared his throat.

'So, how much do you pull the wool, Mrs B?'

At the end of a row, she turned the knitting round.

'Well, personally, I like to play with it until it feels right.'

Mason's eyes glazed over momentarily as he enjoyed a short private fantasy.

Mrs B ran the empty needle back and forth through her fingers and then clamped it under her arm ready for knitting.

'Why did you do that?' he asked, mimicking her movement.

'Oh, that? That helps me get the feel of things.'

She started another row, and Mason continued to stare, lost in his own thoughts – mainly about Mrs B pulling wool for him. Under the table he gripped the side seams of his trousers.

At the end of the next row, she said, 'Are you all right, Mr Mason? You've gone very red.'

'What? Oh, I was just wondering... I don't suppose you'd do something for me, would you, Mrs B?'

'And whatever would that be, Mr Mason?'

The kitchen door swung open.

'Ah, Mason,' said Rosa. 'The very man.' She took a seat opposite him. 'What new delay prevents you finishing my tower? Found a rare species of parrot nesting in your scaffolding and it can't be disturbed? The Maund Builders' Co-operative have instituted a twenty-minute working week? Problems with the foundations of the castle, is it?'

Mason sucked on his teeth for many reasons, and in what normally passed for an air of finality, he said, 'Can't get matching stone, your ladyship.'

Puzzlement contorted Rosa's face, as if she thought she hadn't heard him correctly. 'Can't... *can't get* matching stone?'

He threw out his arms in a gesture of complete helplessness. 'Just can't get it.'

'Mason, need I remind you that my family *quarries* stone?'

He pointed a finger gravely. 'Ah, that's a mistake a lot of people makes, your ladyship. The stuff they's quarrying now's not been exposed to the vagaries of wind and weather for hundreds of years. It's not got the patina of old age that... age-old stone's got. You sticks the new stuff on your West Wing and it'll shine like a beacon for fifty years or more. Won't blend sympathetically into the local landscape for at least a lifetime.'

'Mason, if you don't get a move on, you'll be blending sympathetically into the local landscape under a turf covering.'

'Now, now...'

'Use the original stone. It's very handy – it's scattered within a half-mile radius of the West Wing Tower. Including in the moat. I'd be happy to lower you down on a rope myself.'

He smiled smugly. 'I can't swim, your ladyship.'

She smiled back. 'I don't care, Mason.'

He looked over-affronted, as only builders can, but it had no effect. 'It still wouldn't be enough, your ladyship. Some of it's bound to have shattered in the explosion.'

Rosa's smile broadened. She'd spent too many years blasting holes in Rudolf's excuses to be outwitted by a builder.

'Then you'll *have* to use new stone, won't you?'

Mason's mouth twitched. He'd never given in gracefully, and he wasn't about to start now. 'It won't age properly.'

'I know what'll age it, Mr Mason,' Mrs B piped up.

Mason let out a heartfelt sigh. How bitter to have the object of his affections siding with the enemy.

Mrs B put her knitting on the table, walked to a milk churn that stood in the corner of the kitchen and lifted the lid. She dipped her hand into the churn. When she brought it back out a thick, creamy goo clung to the end of her finger. 'Yoghurt.' She licked her finger clean, and Mason immediately forgave

129

her for stabbing him in the stonework. 'I read it in last month's *Castles and Courtyards*,' she said. 'Rub it on your new garden statues, and quick as you like, all sorts of mosses and lichens have moved in and you'd never know it hadn't been there for hundreds of years. It should do the same for new stonework.'

Rosa beamed.

'Mrs B, you're a gem. Let's give it a go, shall we, Mason?'

Mason blew out his cheeks. 'Ooh, I wouldn't recommend it, your ladyship. Anything might happen.'

'And that could only be an improvement. You will do it and you will start work just as soon as you've found me a saw.'

Mason was taken aback by this sudden departure from the stonework. 'A saw?'

'Yes, a saw. I'm sorry, I simply assumed that being a builder you'd know what a saw is.'

Mason looked at the ceiling, breathed in deeply and said, 'And what sort of thing is your ladyship going to saw?'

'I've got two dead bodies in the cold store and I need something to cut the heads off them.'

Mason laughed. 'Oh, ho ho – good one, your ladyship. You had me going, there. Dead bodies. Oh, ho. Oh dear.'

While Mason was wiping his eyes, Rosa looked at Mrs B, who shrugged, unable to offer an explanation as to why Mason thought truth was not only stranger than fiction but apparently a lot funnier as well.

Rosa tried again. 'All right, Mason. I need a saw that can cut through something the thickness of your neck. And unlike the West Wing Tower, I need it now.'

In her bedroom, Fran made final adjustments to a tea-tray on a side-table, then opened a drawer and took out the carved wooden box that she had brought from her cottage months ago. In it was a white silk pouch holding a finely engraved silver bangle; she slipped the bangle onto her left wrist, clasped it with her right hand and held her arms above her head as far as they would go.

'*I call on the Power of the Bracelet of Life:*
A Favour I need of some Time on a lease.
This Favour I ask to a task undertake
In order my niece can live life safe in peace.'

She replaced the bangle in the silk pouch, enclosed it in the box, put the box back in the drawer and picked up the teapot.

There was a knock on the door a second before it opened and a cheery voice lilted, 'Hello-o, anybody ho-ome?'

'Come in, Pat,' said Fran.

Parturicia, The Bringer of Life, bustled into the room as only a statuesque, eminently sensible, blue-uniformed midwife can. She plonked herself on a chair by the tea-table and put her stiff black leather bag on the floor.

'Is one of those teas for me?' she said. 'I'm *so* ready for a drink. Hello, Fran – haven't seen you for a while.'

'Semi-retired,' said Fran, handing her a full teacup.

As Pat reached across to the tray of biscuits, the silver buttons on her black elasticated belt vanished under the shadow of her generous bosom. 'Oooh, shortbreads. Very classy. I tell you, some places you're lucky if you get a rich tea thrown at you these days.' She took a slurp of her tea. 'Now. What can I do for you? Not for yourself, is it?'

Fran gave her a withering stare, such as only those who have known each other for a long time can give.

'Give over – I'll be talking to your other half soon. It's for my niece... indirectly. She's having trouble with her husband.'

'Oh, tell me more...'

When you've given life to as many creations as Pat there tend to be very few fresh scenarios, but this one was new to her. At the end of the tale she let out a long breath.

'And how much Time do you want?' she said, lifting her teacup to her lips again.

Knowing that her reply was extraordinary, Fran said it in as small a voice as possible through clenched teeth.

'I need a couple of years of Twicetime.'

Pat spluttered, sending tea over the side of the cup.

'A couple of years?! I thought you were only building one bodyguard, not two. Twicetime's only supposed to be for twin lives, you know.'

'I know, but I've got to keep two lives going in one entity, haven't I? One life for his head and one for his body. Standard Time won't work because he'd have to stay as two separate entities and the body wouldn't be able to see where it was going and the head wouldn't be able to go where it was seeing.'

'But two years...' said Pat, mopping up tea splashes with her hankie. 'The biggest bag of Twicetime I do is six months and they're only for exceptional circumstances.'

'Please,' said Fran. 'Rudolf's greedy and stupid enough to attack at any time. He's already tried it. He might hold off if he thinks *I'm* in the castle in case I kill him with magic, which I can't do, but he won't know that. But the minute I'm not here, one way or another he will attack. So, I need somebody here now in case he attacks and I need somebody here after I've gone who's got enough time to make sure Rosa's safe.'

'And when do you meet Death?'

'In about nine months.'

Pat drummed her fingers on the table as she pondered.

'You can have one year of Twicetime. That'll give you your bodyguard while you still live and for three months after you've gone. If the pair of you can't get this sorted out in a year then your niece is on her own.'

Rigton's was a well-trained nose at the height of its powers. Under the right conditions it could detect at least forty different cheeses and twenty-seven types of beer. In blind ale-sniffing competitions it could analyse individual malts, barleys, hops and yeasts, water content and alcohol rating, and therefore profitability. He could tell not only that a beer was off, but by how far it was off and how long he could carry on selling it before somebody noticed. However, during a normal day behind the bar, so many smells of business, pleasure and differing standards of personal hygiene circulated through the Lamb and Werewolf that as a matter of course his olfactory senses shut down until actually needed.

So when he lifted the bowl to his nostrils and sniffed, he was disappointed not to smell anything. His wife had said that the things in the bowl were fruit, but he was yet to be convinced that they weren't cobs of animal dung. Each one was shaped like a large plum without the indentations, and the bottle-green skin was given a brown haze by hundreds of tiny hairs. He picked one up, wincing slightly, not entirely comfortable with the feel of it in his palm. He gently squeezed it, half-expecting it to squelch through his fingers like mud, but it was surprisingly solid and withstood his grasp.

The street door opened and in walked two aristocrats: one tall, elegant and unhurried; one shorter, cheerful and lively.

Rigton put the fruit back in the bowl, his suspicions not entirely allayed, and reached for two tankards.

'Good morning, my lords. The usual, is it?'

Yedder rubbed his hands together.

'Why not? Oh, look! Oriental goosegogs!'

He picked up three fruit and flawlessly juggled them with the effortless ease that only comes from bags of natural talent and years of practice, unwittingly providing evidence that the clowns weren't the only ones from the circus who had been involved in extending the Yedder family line.

'One of my nieces loves 'em,' he said. 'Slices the top off and eats the middle out with a spoon, like a boiled egg.'

'Does she have soldiers as well?' asked Guildman.

'If the rumours are true, Gil!'

Yedder laughed ostentatiously and put the fruit back.

Rigton cut one in half. It was firm beneath his knife and sliced easily, and for a moment he was taken aback by the brilliance of the moist green flesh. Had he been anything other than a landlord he might have marvelled at the depth of colour and the perfect symmetry of the fibres and seeds, and reflected on what mighty hand or greater intelligence could have framed such a creation. But he was a businessman, and the mention of boiled eggs prompted him to speculate on the possible popularity of pickled kiwi fruit. He cut two slices and hung one over the rim of Yedder's tankard. Before he had the time to adorn Guildman's drink, a firm grip around his wrist stayed his hand. He looked up and saw Guildman, smiling but shaking his head. Rigton nodded, and dropped the extra slice into Yedder's ale. Guildman released his grip.

Yedder picked up his drink. 'Is Rude about, Rigsy?'

'I've not seen Lord Rudolf since he went out with your lordships yesterday.'

'Really?' exclaimed Yedder. 'Hear that, Gil? Rude's gone missing. Maybe Roz's taken him back.'

'A likely possibility?' smiled Guildman.

Yedder thought for a second then grinned.

'Not unless she's completely lost her mind. So then, it looks like the rest of the day's our own.'

Rigton's nose tingled. 'I fear not, my lord,' he said, shortly before the street door swung open and an unkempt and malodorous Rudolf strode in.

'A tad hasty there, Yedder,' said Guildman, as Rigton reached for another tankard and narrowed his nostrils.

'What the hell happened to you two yesterday?' demanded Rudolf. 'All you had to do was put the bet on and collect the winnings when my horse romped home.'

'We did,' said Guildman, walking away from him.

'It didn't,' added Yedder.

'Eh?' said Rudolf.

'Your nag, old boy. We did exactly as you asked: put the money on, waited for it to romp home.'

'We're still waiting,' said Guildman, propping open the

135

street door with a chair as the other patrons in the Lamb and Werewolf's parlour opened as many windows as they could.

'What?!'

'True,' said Yedder. 'Shot off up the straight, missed the turn, jumped the rail and ran off towards Roibrough.'

'For all we know, it's still running,' said Guildman. 'Apparently it could go all night.'

Rudolf bared his teeth at Guildman but made no move.

'So, no fortune for me,' he growled.

''Fraid not, old boy,' said Yedder. 'I hit a lucky streak, though – made a packet. Didn't put a foot wrong, did I, Gil?'

'Until now, Yedder,' chuckled Guildman as a smiling villain's arm went around a gullible victim's shoulder.

'Well, we can't leave that money burning a hole in your pocket, my friend,' said Rudolf, demonstrating both the mental agility and the ruthlessness that could have made him a vast fortune in commerce in no time if it hadn't involved actually working for an hour a day. 'We must make it work for us.'

Yedder wafted a hand in front of his face. 'Must we?'

'Oh, yes. If I'm going to pay a dwarf to top Rosa—'

'Then you won't get a penny out of me, old boy.'

Rudolf sighed. 'All right. If I'm going to pay for a select band of men to take the castle—'

'And evict Roz, not hurt her...'

'And throw the baggage out, yes...'

Yedder stepped away from him. 'You promise?'

Rudolf crossed his fingers behind his back.

'Yes, yes, yes, I promise!'

He leant towards Yedder conspiratorially, as if he were

136

about to impart the secret of eternal life.

'But if I'm going to evict her I need money, so sup up and let's get off to the Dog Flog.'

Yedder screwed his nose up. 'Not a good idea, really.'

Rudolf slumped. 'What now?'

'Um, no offence,' said Yedder unhappily, 'but the way you smell, the dogs are more likely to chase *you* than the hare.'

Fran laid two filled paper cones, each gathered and tied at the top with a noose of string, on the mantelpiece in her bedroom.

She grinned. Always ask for more than you'll settle for.

Alongside the bags she placed the Timekeeper, a flame-shaped black crystal which would gradually change colour as the Twicetime was spent. She stood back and pulled at her bottom lip. 'Hmmmm. On second thoughts...'

She left the Timekeeper as it was, but put the paper cones in separate pockets within her gown. 'Better safe than sorry.'

In ways undreamt of, a man's news can be a woman's heartbreak, and a client of Millie's brought gossip of the events at the Field Digger.

She curled up on her bed and wept convulsively for the love who would never return. He had been torn from her life, all trace of him obliterated and, denied knowledge of his burial site, her misery was complete.

Three aristocrats stood at the side of the road. The first, paying the coachman, sported the honest, open grin of someone looking forward to a jolly good afternoon's entertainment. The second wore the lazy, enigmatic smile of someone whose heart's desire came closer with every misfortune of the third, who carried the petulant scowl of someone whose journey through life lately seemed to be on a midden cart.

'Why are we stopping here?' asked Rudolf. 'The entrance is round the other side. We must be half a bloody mile away.'

Guildman pushed him away. 'Downwind, please.'

'What's wrong now? Yedder, why have we stopped here?'

Yedder concentrated on the money-bag in the palm of his hand and avoided Rudolf's gaze.

'A bit of fresh air, old boy. A brisk walk in the breeze.'

'I don't particularly want a brisk walk in the breeze.'

'Want and need are not the same thing,' hinted Guildman.

'What?' snapped Rudolf.

Yedder avoided Rudolf's gaze still further by watching the coach and horses turn a wide semicircle.

'Gil's right, old thing. You are a bit... pungent.'

Rudolf dragged Yedder towards him by the collar.

'Yedder. This morning, did you or did you not tell me that I stank like a polecat?'

'Not in so many words,' squeaked Yedder.

'So did I or did I not wash and get tarted up to please you?'

Yedder's eyes started to water, and not from Rudolf's grip.

'Yes.'

'So what's your problem?'

'The problem is,' said Guildman, calmly pressing on Rudolf's wrists so that he had to release Yedder, 'you've been a tad heavy-handed with the aromatic oils.'

'My perfume? What's wrong with my perfume?'

He stood at the centre of an ever-increasing circle of wilting flora. Blossoms closed up as delicately scented bushes surrendered in the face of such stiff competition. The faint hum of distant activity and the hoofbeats of the coach horses were almost drowned out by the swish of leaves as greenery went into sudden collapse.

'It would be improved by some time in the fresh air,' said Guildman.

'About a fortnight,' said Yedder. 'Ow!' he added, as Rudolf slapped the back of his head.

Guildman drew his sword and rested the point in the middle of Rudolf's chest. 'Downwind.'

The faint hum grew more noticeable. Rudolf rolled his eyes as he took a step backwards. 'Make your minds up. First, I'm too smelly and now I'm too sme—'

He spun round. The hum had taken on a form: a cloud of bees, courted by all the winds that brought them an amber scent of odorous perfume. The swarm darkened the sky, each bee jostling good-naturedly while vying to be the first to the source of the scent.

If Rudolf's instinct for self-preservation was well honed, his execution of that instinct occasionally left something to be desired – complete success, usually. He lifted his cape to cover his head, thereby releasing even more of the aroma so enticing to the pollen-gatherers. By the time he'd snatched Yedder's money-bag, the apian force had arrived and were looking for somewhere to stretch their legs and set to work.

Rudolf ducked and ran under the humming cloud with such speed that the resultant air turbulence caused the bees to swirl and tumble out of control for a few seconds. The light hum that had characterised the happy swarm changed to a menacing drone as the bees hitched up their trousers, pushed up their sleeves and shot off in mass pursuit of the perfumed but pollenless aristocrat who in turn was chasing the coach and horses so recently vacated by himself and his friends.

The swiftest bees reached the edge of Rudolf's cape as he leapt onto the running-board and wrenched open the carriage door. 'Drive!' he yelled. 'Drive like the wind!'

The coachman sagged.

'Now what does that mean?' he said, turning to address his customer, but seeing instead a very nasty stinging heading his way. As Rudolf bellowed 'Getthehellouttahere!' the driver whirled around and cracked the whip violently. The horses reared and Rudolf fell inside the lurching carriage, trapping his cape as the door slammed shut. He opened the door just enough to drag his cape inside, along with a lone bee.

As the speeding coach separated him from his community, the bee accepted the mission on behalf of his swarm and single-handedly prepared to launch an offensive.

However, Rudolf's exertions had raised his temperature considerably, greatly magnifying the effects of the perfume, and in the confines of the carriage the air rapidly became polluted to toxic levels. Instead of dying a heroic death inflicting a serious wound on his mortal enemy, the striped avenger blacked out, clutching his throat and choking.

Rudolf rolled his cape into a pillow and stretched out on the bench.

Aidan shivered, and not simply from being in the cold store.

'Mr Beaton, I've got a bit of a problem.'

Beaton answered without raising his eyes from the work he was doing at one end of a large table.

'The best way to get rid of a problem is to solve it, Aidan.'

'But I've never had a problem like this before.'

'Then you will bring an entirely fresh eye to the situation, possibly leading to a solution never previously attempted.'

Aidan didn't want to bring any eye at all to the situation if he could help it, which was why he was wincing and had one eye closed. Aidan was having enough trouble bringing a hand to it, which was why he was holding it very warily by the ears and as far away from himself as his arms would reach.

'Mr Beaton, could we change ends, please?'

Beaton looked up.

'If this is your solution, what precisely is the problem?'

Aidan grimaced as he lifted a stove-in and recently sawn-off head.

'I don't know what to do with this, Mr Beaton, because it doesn't fit the rest of it.'

'Very well,' said Beaton, laying down the bandage he was using to secure the feet of the body which the head didn't fit. 'On this occasion only, I shall make allowance for your inexperience. We shall indeed – as you put it – change ends.'

Aidan was halfway to the other end of the table before he remembered he was still carrying the head.

'Maybe we could tuck it under his arm,' he suggested. 'You know, so that he can go haunting with it.'

Beaton took the head. 'Unfortunately, that would be both

141

impractical and aesthetically undesirable.'

'Mr Beaton?'

'The grave accommodates a body within a very narrow dimension of width. If that width is exceeded – for example by an elbow, set at a jaunty angle – then we may not be able to return the body to the grave.'

'Oh.'

'Also, although I cannot confirm this with an extract of any written regulation, I do believe that one haunts with one's *own* head underneath one's arm.'

The sensitive nose started to twitch. Rigton knocked on a tankard with his paring knife.

'Ladies and gentlemen,' he said. 'Please cover your drinks and take them into the taproom for a few moments. By the pricking of my nose, something wicked this way blows. Something milk-curdling and beer-souring.'

Knowing that he never bothered them with trivialities, his customers dutifully emptied the parlour. Rigton threw open the street door and all the windows, put a tankard of ale on the end of the counter closest to the door that led upstairs, opened that door then moved as far away from there as possible.

Rudolf, carrying his rolled-up cape, swept through the parlour in a smooth arc from the street to the stairs, picking up the ale without breaking stride. Streaming out behind him, fumes shimmered in the air.

'Bath!' he called from halfway up the stairs.

'Just the one?' murmured the landlord.

~+~

NOTES ON

Bathing

Bathing has never really caught on in Maund for a host of reasons.

On the whole, the people prefer to stay dry. They get quite wet enough during the winter – and every other season – and so, like work, they'd rather not do voluntarily what is forced on them during the rest of the year. Also, they associate being wet with being cold, shivering, catching a chill, developing pneumonia and being one cough away from eternal rest.

Plus, there's not enough space in the average Maund house to lay down a bath. Every room is always occupied, and trying to cram everyone else into the rest of the house while you have a room to yourself is as dangerous and futile as herding wasps.

Furthermore, very few people own a bath, and if by some freak combination of circumstances you did want to have a bath, you'd have to borrow one from a neighbour, who'd probably charge you for the privilege.

But above all, for most people in Maund, having a bath is far, far more trouble than it's worth.

Even assuming that you can find a private space, other people – especially those on a different shift trying to sleep – won't exactly be overjoyed at hearing a lidless tin coffin being dragged across a wooden floor, particularly when it scrapes on a nail-head standing proud of a floorboard, or catches the corner of a bedstead, or clangs into a cast-iron fire-grate. Then you have to gather all manner of pots, pans, buckets and bowls, draw the water, stoke the fire and heat the water. Even if you have the foresight, space and funds to have a hot-water boiler on the premises, the boiler and the bath are never in the same room so you have to make several forays through the household, carrying pots, pans, buckets and bowls of boiling water through crowds of already disgruntled and muttering fellow residents, up flights of stairs and across landings, while skilfully avoiding scalding anybody or anything that chooses to run across your path. You pray to all the gods who may be listening that your last earthly thought is not 'This pan-handle seems very light all of a sudden.'

When the bath is full of steaming water, then you must wait for it to cool sufficiently. This calls for fine judgement: you need to avoid turning any of your bodily parts into a boiled ham, but still be able to sit in the bath for longer than two minutes without the water going cold. Just when you've decided upon the ambient temperature and lowered yourself gingerly in, you can be sure that someone you haven't spoken to for years will hammer on the door demanding to see you.

Then there's getting dry. Sanding yourself down with a thin square of scratchy rag that's been used for everything from wiping the stove to flaying thieving dogs is hardly just reward for all the time and trouble you've gone to. Keeping a soft, fluffy bath sheet specifically for your personal use is impossible; once the family finds out where you've hidden it, it'll be used by all and sundry as a tent, a curtain, a makeshift stretcher, a floorcloth and a blanket – for both humans and any livestock that's the least bit valuable and looks like it might succumb to a sudden mystery illness, taking the family's investment with it. But whatever you wipe yourself with, there's the problem of getting that dry as well.

Once you are dry, you must decide whether or not to put on clean clothes – always assuming you have some, of course. It's an enormous waste of effort to have a bath and climb back into your everyday rags, but who wants to put clean clothes on when the first thing you have to do is get all hot, sweaty and probably wet again emptying out a bathful of mucky water and dragging the bath back to its rightful owner? The steam from your bath will have soaked into every piece of fabric in the room anyway, so whatever you put back on will be damp, as will any bedding, curtains and rag rugs in the immediate vicinity. Hang those out to dry and you'll have to post a sentry to stop them being stolen and ending up on a market stall.

One summer, Maund Town Council did open up a public bath-house, but it closed within a week when the man who scraped the scum off the top of the water died from overwork.

So, for most people in Maund, the idea of having a bath remains an idea, and one that is only brought out for high days and holidays, moments of delirium and pipe-dreams, depending on what substance is in your pipe. Simply the thought of all the effort involved is enough to put people off attempting it, an effect also found whenever anybody suggests eating a pomegranate with a pin.

However, some people have always had other people to do all the hard work, and so can't see what all the fuss is about.

~•~

The business partnership running the Lamb and Werewolf was efficient, born of the knowledge that both Rigton and his wife each had their own interests at heart and knew exactly how to make money to keep those hearts interested. The division of labour was fair and equitable: he ran the bars and the cellars, whilst she interpreted the term 'bed and breakfast' as literally as possible. To certain selected customers crossing his threshold Rigton would subtly recommend the charms of the landlady and the advantages to be gained from hiring a room; for her part, Mrs Rigton would reassure clients that residents of the establishment were free from petty restrictions such as closing time.

Mrs Rigton differed greatly from her husband. She was much younger, physically desirable, highly sexed and, unlike her nasally-enhanced spouse, blessed with no sense of smell whatsoever which, bearing in mind her particular definition of 'room service', was a great bonus.

With a series of echoing clangs and a swish of skirts, Mrs Rigton backed into Rudolf's room dragging a tin bath. Rudolf concentrated on the rhythmical swinging of her rear end as she manoeuvred the bath, and something stirred within him.

He lounged on the bed, watching her come and go as she brought him drink and bath water. With each trip, the exertion and the increasing steam dampened her. Wisps of hair clung to her face and neck, and as she bent over to empty the pails of hot water into the bath, beads of perspiration trickled down her cleavage, a journey that was watched intently by a recumbent aristocrat with an accelerating pulse.

As she turned to make another trip, Rudolf leapt from the

bed, kicked the door shut and lolled against it. She walked over to him, breathing heavily from her exercise. Rudolf reached down to her ankles, and as he straightened, he ran his hands up the outside of her legs, lifting her skirts.

She looked him in the eye and leant into his lust.

'Does my lord want this bath filling, or what?'

He licked his lips. 'What.'

As darkness fell, clouds looking for trouble gathered around the castle as if it were the only place in town to get a drink.

The inhabitants of the moat were unconcerned as the first light splashes of rain sent gentle ripples across the water. As the frequency of the drops increased, the more cautious fish mothers herded their small offspring back under rocks to gaze out in safety at the pattering sky. Soon only the teenage piscine daredevils were foolhardy enough to dodge the liquid pellets piercing the surface, and eventually even they had to seek refuge from the water bombs that ripped into their world.

High above them, rain-drenched gales howled, clawing at the castle, taunting its solidity. Heavy, gunmetal clouds roiled overhead, echo chambers for the hammer-blows of thunder given birth by lightning that forked on every side, relentlessly seeking a place to earth. Pinpricks of light leaking out through closed shutters were gobbled up by the vicious darkness.

In the laboratory, flickering oil lamps cast darting, uneasy shadows across the last-minute preparations. Resting in a counterbalanced cradle just under the shuttered window was a plank, fitted underneath with a grappling hook at one end; on top, fixed along the length of the plank, was a long telescopic metal pole. One end of a wire as thick as a hawser was soldered onto the pole; the wire coiled on the floor before stretching upwards, the other end being soldered onto the large metal grid over the workbench. From the grid hung eight more wires: two connected with the ankles of a body on the workbench, two with the wrists, two with the chest and two with the temples.

Leather straps were nailed to the workbench; Igress fastened them across the naked corpse.

'He was a fine figure of a man, ma'am,' she said.

Rosa adjusted the temple wires and patted the body on its new forehead. 'Yes, and now he's the fine figure of two men.'

The creak of the laboratory door announced Fran's arrival. Tagging along was Sooty, whose curiosity didn't have to work too hard to get the better of him.

'Are we nearly ready?' Fran asked, re-creaking the door before walking across to the workbench. 'Oh, cover him up, can't you? He might be embarrassed at being brought back to life completely starkers in front of strange women.'

Igress grinned as she tightened the strap across his chest.

'Yes, Mistress Stein.'

'We got the new head on, Aunty,' Rosa beamed.

'I can see that,' said Fran. Large, uneven, childish stitches encircled the neck of the corpse. 'It's a good job you're a scientist – you'd never make it as a seamstress.'

'Nor you a diplomat,' said Rosa, stepping out of Fran's reach.

'Cheek,' said Fran, taking a swing all the same.

'All ready,' said Igress, dragging up the winding sheet to cover the body.

Sooty leapt up onto a nearby bench and settled down with a grandstand view of the proceedings.

'Right,' said Fran. 'All we're waiting for now is the weather.'

As if to underline her words, a thundercrack threatened to rend the very earth in two.

Rosa stood by the shuttered window, raised her arms and cried to the heavens.

'Waiting for a mighty bolt of unearthly power to galvanise the spirit and send life coursing through the veins of my creation once again!'

'If you say so,' said Fran, 'but I'd rather it wasn't so fierce.' She whispered conspiratorially to Igress. 'Cast a spell in the middle of this lot and you never know what might happen.'

Rosa dropped her arms and put her hands on her hips as she turned around. 'Aunty, just get on with it.'

Fran took a deep breath. 'Well, on your own head be it. Which is more than we can say for this poor soul on the table.'

From her pocket she took a large paper cone, gathered up and tied at the top with a noose of string which she paid out until the point of the paper cone skimmed the floor. Then she lifted the cone up, and plucked a silver pin from her lapel.

Suddenly an enraged thunderclap rattled the window shutters. Startled, Fran dropped the pin.

Rosa covered her face with her hands.

Fran stooped and retrieved the pin.

'See a pin and pick it up...' said Sooty.

'And all the day you'll have good luck,' said Igress and Rosa.

'No,' said Fran. 'You'll have a pin. Stands to reason. How can you get good luck by picking a pin up? I mean...'

'Aunty!'

'All right, all right. Get to your places.'

Rosa and Igress moved to each side of the counterbalanced cradle under the shutters as Fran pierced the point of the cone several times before dangling it by her side. Sands of Twicetime trickled out of the pinholes as she circled the workbench, leaving a golden, silver, black-flecked continuous sand line on the floor.

This Circle of Life I give to you now:
Once outside this Circle, the days will be yours
To do as you're bidden in any way how.
I ask for your help in pursuit of my cause.'

Once all the Twicetime had run out, Fran crumpled up the cone and string and threw it inside the sand circle. After a few moments' pause, she lifted her head.

'Now!' she shouted.

Rosa and Igress threw back the shutters, hurled the plank across the window-sill and flattened themselves against the wall. The grappling hook bit into the stonework and jerked the plank to a halt; momentum sent the telescopic metal pole stabbing into the heart of the night.

This was just the chance the lightning had been looking for. It struck the pole with a ferocity that sent tiny gobbets of molten metal plummeting towards the moat. The plank sundered along its scorched length as power surged through the pole, rampaging down the thick wire, arcing and spitting as it coruscated across the metal grid, blasting the eight wires away in a shower of iridescent sparks, melting the sizzling filaments on its way to the body. A drop of molten wire landed on the length of string inside the sand circle, starting a flame of such blinding white intensity it obliterated the lightning. When the paper cone caught fire it flash-burned, filling the laboratory with an orgy of colour.

The table juddered and the women heard the leather restraints snap before a deafening roar filled the room, followed by a heavy thud.

In Fran's bedroom, the Timekeeper on the mantelpiece suddenly glowed white then faded to a lustrous green.

'Uuuuuhhhhhhh,' moaned the newly created bodyguard, slumped on the floor.

'Stand back,' said Fran. She bent over and murmured to him; he rose horizontally and floated gracefully under his sheet back to the bench.

'Ooohhh... my head,' he groaned, putting one arm across his still-closed eyes.

'He's right on that one,' said Fran. 'It's his head.' She tapped his cheek. 'Come on... wake up, love. What's your name?'

'Gussie,' came the reply.

'And how do you feel, Gussie?' asked Rosa.

Gussie licked his lips. 'Like I've got a monster hangover. Any chance of a drink of water? I know landlords don't usually like you asking for water...'

'You're not in a pub, Gussie.'

Gussie lifted his arm and opened his eyes slowly. The first thing he saw was the grid suspended above him. He closed his eyes again.

'Am I in prison?'

'No,' said Rosa, 'You're—'

'Am I flat on my back?'

'Er... in a manner of speaking.'

'I've got some water,' said Igress, holding out a glass.

Rosa and Fran helped Gussie to sit up, and Igress passed him the water. His fingers closed around it but forgot to stop and the glass splintered in his fist.

'Ooowww!' he said. 'Sorry, don't know my own strength.'

He lifted his hand to survey the damage and immediately fainted, leaving Fran and Rosa to catch him before his head hit the bench. They gently laid him back down.

'Igress,' said Fran, 'get a pitcher of water and a stone mug. Rosa, you're the tallest – lift his feet up.'

Rudolf's cup of happiness was decidedly more full than it had been that morning, but how could a day go downhill when it starts in the bottom of a grave? In the bathtub, he was as warm, content and relaxed as any aristocrat who'd been thrown out of his castle could be. His belly was full of beer, his body was full of the afterglow of Mrs Rigton, he had a bagful of money – albeit Yedder's – and he wasn't outside in the violent thunderstorm. What more could a man ask, apart from more? And more he might get, when Mrs Rigton came back up to empty the bath. He slipped his hands under the water and started housekeeping; everything must be clean and tidy for the landlady's return. His mind began to wander, and water sloshed over the side of the bath.

Water was already darkening the laboratory floor before Gussie's face caught up with the feeling of being drenched then slapped.

'Come on, Gussie,' said Fran. 'Can't hang about all day.'

Gussie shook his head. The three women winced, but the stitches held and there were no unwelcome noises of a skull rolling off a table and hitting a flagstone floor. He lifted one hand slowly and stroked his wet face.

'Oh... that's rough... what have I been doing?'

He opened his eyes to look at his hand but instead he groggily saw a wrinkled face looking down at him. He dropped his hand, which thudded back onto the bench.

'Who are you?' he asked.

'I'm your... er...'

Fran struggled for a suitable word.

'Nurse?' suggested Igress.

'Yes, nurse. I'm your nurse.'

'Don't you remember?' said Rosa, putting his feet back on the bench and walking round to look at him. 'You cut your hand and then fainted.'

Gussie slowly turned his head to look at her. 'Who are you?'

'She's the doctor,' said Fran quickly.

'And I'm training to be a doctor,' added Igress, dabbing at his cut palm with a clean lab cloth.

'Lady doctors,' said Gussie. 'Now I know I'm dreaming.'

'You're not dreaming,' said Fran, 'just a bit slow wakening up, that's all.'

'Believe me, nurse, if I was awake and felt as awful as this, I'd be dead.'

153

Rosa mopped Gussie's face. 'So how awful do you feel?'

'I think I've got flu. I'm freezing, my arms are as heavy as lead, I feel like I've put on eight stone overnight, my head feels like it doesn't belong to me and my stomach thinks my throat's been cut. I'm starving.'

He started to sneeze.

Rosa clamped his head in her hands.

'Oh, dear, yes, it does sound a lot like the flu, doesn't it?'

Sooty leapt onto the bench and walked along Gussie's chest.

'Hello!' he said.

In between sneezes Gussie started to struggle.

'Uuurgh! Get it off! Atch – I'm al-le-le-lergic to cat-choo!'

He sat bolt upright, dislodging Sooty, who twisted and turned and dropped lightly to the floor.

The sneezing Gussie heaved his legs over the side of the bench and stood up, swaying as he shouted, 'Get it out of here!'

'Oh, charming! Thank you very much,' Sooty said pointedly and stomped out of the laboratory.

Gussie bent over as he sneezed violently. Only when he straightened up did he realise that things were wobbling far more than they used to, and there were breezes where breezes shouldn't be in mixed company of more than two people outside of an art class. He looked down at his naked body and did the only thing advisable under the circumstances.

Rosa and Igress managed to push him onto the bench as he fainted again.

NOTES ON

Second Chances

Sometimes in life you get a second chance – the opportunity to wipe the slate clean, start again, make amends, put right what's gone wrong. The only rules regarding second chances are: they always come after the first chance, and you never get a second chance to make a good first impression.

Because second chances are notoriously unpunctual, some people decide to make their own rather than wait for something to turn up. However, attempts to create a second chance rarely work first time round, and before you know it the ingredients start to run out. So, people pop out for more time, place, ambience or circumstance, only to get back and find a note on the kitchen table that says, 'Sorry, I missed you. Better luck next time. Best wishes, Second Chance.'

Some people are so desperate for a second chance that their lives become entirely focused on it. They hang around the house all day, waiting for opportunity to come knocking. After some time, they begin to suspect that opportunity has missed its turning, so they start roaming the neighbourhood in search of that lost opportunity, peering into other people's windows in case their second chance is being entertained by someone else. And while they're walking the streets trying to track down something they don't even know is there, opportunity could be kicking their door in and throwing stones through their windows, but they're not at home to see it.

Some people miss the first opportunity because their brain power isn't strong enough to cast light as far as the end of their nose, so they wouldn't even see a second opportunity coming, let alone have the gumption to stop it and use it.

But happily, some individuals are only too prepared to grab any passing opportunity with both hands, or whatever the equivalent is in their species. And sometimes, an individual takes up the opportunity on behalf of a group.

~•~

Rudolf soaked in the bath, clothes scattered across his room, their abandonment reflecting the urgency of their casting-off. His frockcoat, waistcoat and shirt were slumped behind the door, one boot was on the hearth, one by the window, and his britches dangled from a chair. On the floor lay his black velvet cape, which had unrolled when it had been kicked off the bed during Rudolf and Mrs Rigton's sheet-rumpling session.

Those whose horizons were not clouded by steam might have seen a thumbnail-sized area of the velvet move, change from black to black and yellow, put out shiny, unsteady little legs and totter over the folds of the cape into the fresh air. Those whose eyes were not closed in hot water relaxation might have been fascinated by the sight of a small striped creature putting intense concentration into a series of slow stretches then grooming itself as if for a great occasion. Those whose thoughts were not dwelling on the return of Mrs Rigton might have pondered on the reason that the creature then sat absolutely still. Those with any imagination at all might have said that it was watching somebody.

156

'Now let me get this straight,' said Gussie, who still lay on the table. He took a much bigger breath than he'd ever been able to with his own body without going dizzy. 'You're saying I was killed, I was buried, you dug me up, cut my head off, sewed it onto another body and brought me – us – back to life?'

'In a nutshell,' said Rosa.

'I don't believe you. I'm dreaming.'

'All right, then,' said Fran, bandaging his hand. 'Wake up,'

'What?'

She put her mouth close to his ear. 'Wake up!'

He screwed his eyes shut, but it didn't blot out the sound.

'See?' said Fran triumphantly.

'I'm in a very deep sleep,' he pouted.

Igress nipped the skin on the underside of his arm and twisted it until her fingers slipped.

'Ow!' he protested.

'Only trying to wake you up,' she said brightly. 'It always works for me when I'm having nightmares.'

'I bet you don't have nightmares where somebody cuts your head off and sews it onto another body.'

'Neither do you,' said Rosa. 'This is real.'

'It can't be!'

Rosa threw her hands up in despair and turned away.

'Listen,' said Fran. 'You think you're dreaming and at some point you're going to wake up and everything'll be fine. Yes?'

'Yes,' said Gussie.

'So what's the problem?'

'Aunty?' said Rosa.

'No matter what this dream brings,' said Fran deliberately,

glaring at Rosa before smiling at Gussie, 'you'll wake up.'

'And...' added Rosa, '...when you wake up... everything'll be back to normal, so to speak.' She gesticulated to Igress as wildly as she could using only her eyes.

'Oh... yes,' said Igress. 'And so... because it's all a dream... whatever happens, you'll be all right. You're invincible!'

'Invincible,' said Fran flatly. 'Hmm... well.'

'I suppose I am,' said Gussie. 'Hadn't really thought about it that way.'

Fran patted his hand. 'Why should you, love? You haven't been in this dream very long, have you?'

'Would you like some water?' asked Rosa, holding out the stone beaker. 'You look... thirsty.'

Gussie looked at the beaker, then at Rosa, then at the beaker again. He'd been tricked like this before – usually into a back alley and out of his money. 'Is it just water? It's not a drug or poison or a sleeping draught or anything?'

Fran tutted. 'Oh, get it down you. We didn't bring you back from the dead just to poison you. And why would we give you a sleeping draught? You're fast asleep already, aren't you?'

'Am I?'

'You're dreaming, aren't you?' said Rosa.

'And in your dream, you're invincible, so it wouldn't matter if it were drugged, would it?' said Igress sweetly.

Gussie wrestled with the logic of this for a few moments, but found himself flat on the canvas with the referee standing over him counting him out. He sat up, took the stone beaker and drained it. He was unaware that as he did so, three women had stopped breathing as they concentrated very hard on the stitches around his throat, and they only breathed again when it became apparent that the water was heading downwards towards his stomach and not outwards towards his shoulders, chest and back.

'Hold on a minute...' he said, looking at his hand.

Fran's eyes widened and huge hints stretched her smile as far as it would go as she turned to her niece.

'Rosa, why don't you and Igress go... and find something for Gussie to wear? It can get awfully chilly round the castle.'

'What? Oh, right... yes. Come on, Igress, let's find something for...'

'...Gussie to wear,' finished Igress, heading for the door.

Gussie had put the beaker down and was looking at his arms and his body. 'Oh, well, now I know I'm dreaming.'

'Don't worry,' said Fran as Rosa and Igress left the room. 'Everybody has that dream where they're going somewhere completely naked. It's quite common.'

'Well, that's very interesting, but it's not what I meant,' Gussie replied. 'I know I'm dreaming 'cos this isn't my body.'

Fran hesitated. 'Ah. You noticed.'

'This is a bit of a giveaway,' he said, pointing to the spread eagle tattooed on his new chest. 'Wait until I tell him.'

'Who?'

'Battling Bill Baldicott, the Peripatetic Prize-Fighter.'

Fran looked nonplussed.

'This is his body,' explained Gussie. 'I've never dreamt I had someone else's body before... Hey! This proves my theory about dreaming. You know – that it's the body's way of sorting out everything that's happened during the day. All the stuff you're too busy doing to actually take notice of? It all surfaces when you're asleep.'

Fran's own theory was that dreaming let your mind have a good old run round on its own, free from the chore of managing the body, which could then heal itself of life's injuries without worrying too much about what the mind was getting up to. But Gussie seemed to be relaxing, so she encouraged him.

'Surfaces?' she asked.

'Oh, yes. How else do you explain it? I've often wondered what it'd feel like to be Battling Bill, and now I am him.'

'Not entirely.'

'You say I've still got my own head? Are you sure?'

Fran looked at him, and saw long, curling eyelashes, high cheekbones, a straight, unbroken nose, an angular chin and a graceful, slender neck leading onto a body so muscular it looked as if it had been overstuffed with balled-up socks.

'Oh, no. It's your head all right.' She walked over to a row of cupboards and started opening the doors. 'There's one round here somewhere... ah, here we are.' Screwed onto the back of one of the doors was a full-length mirror. She beckoned to Gussie. 'Come and have a look, if you want.'

He stood up and clumsily manoeuvred the winding-sheet around his waist. 'Sorry,' he said. 'These fingers are much fatter than I'm used to.'

'And you have cut your hand,' she said gently.

'Yes.' He tied the winding sheet in a complicated fashion. 'There we go.' He noticed Fran's face. 'What's wrong with it?'

'Nothing,' she smiled. 'Just admiring how... elegant it looks.'

'Thank you. It's my own design, you know. Right. Let's have a look-see.'

'Be careful,' she warned as he approached the mirror. 'You're not used to seeing yourself as you are.'

He saw his reflection. 'Oh, for crying out loud!' he exploded. 'This is a nightmare!'

'I did warn you,' said Fran.

He lifted his head. 'Who put those stitches in?!'

'My niece...'

He turned his head from side to side.

'How old is she? Four?!'

'Twenty-seven...'

'So why didn't somebody take the blindfold off her?!'

Fran's brow furrowed. 'The stitches may be a bit rough...'

Gussie pawed at his neck. 'Rough?! You're not wrong there. What did she use for a needle – a bloody crossbow bolt?!'

Fran slammed the cupboard door shut and folded her arms.

'Oh, and you're an expert on needlework, are you?'

He folded his arms back at her.

'I should be – I've been a tailor for over twenty years!'

Fran put her hands on her hips and glared up at him.

'Well, I'm sorry, but we couldn't very well ask you to sew your own head onto a different body, could we?!'

'I'd have made a better bloody job of it than this!'

Unaware of his new strength, Gussie wrenched the cupboard open again. The hinges sundered and the unfettered door swung towards Fran.

The scream chilled the foundations of the castle.

It was rising now, round and white and wet, like the moon over the sea in a rainstorm. As large, unmissable and perfect a target as any bee could ever hope for.

Rudolf was too busy towelling his hair to hear the buzz, but everybody in the Lamb and Werewolf heard him scream.

First into the laboratory was Rosa. 'What in the— Aunty!'

'Mistress!' called Sooty, and they ran over to the prone figure on the floor.

'Stop screaming, Gussie!' shouted Igress, but Gussie continued to hop from foot to foot, pointing at Fran and bawling, 'Help her! Somebody help her!'

'The gentleman is hysterical, miss,' said Beaton. 'Aidan and I will immobilise him if you'd be so good as to slap his face.'

'If he's hurt Mistress Stein, I'll flamin' murder him!'

'I didn't! It was an accident!' Gussie wailed, waving his fists by his face in complete helplessness but enormous strength.

'Aidan, take the gentleman's arm,' ordered Beaton.

Aidan looked around to see if there was anybody else in the room who could possibly be called Aidan.

'Please,' Igress begged.

That was all the encouragement Aidan's weak knees required; he shot forward and hung on to Gussie's arm for all he was worth.

Igress took a swing at Gussie and connected with thin air just in front of his chest.

'Hang on!' she said, climbing onto the bench while Beaton and Aidan manoeuvred the jigging Gussie closer to her.

'Imagine... it's... Lord Rudolf... miss,' shouted Beaton, in between the wailing and the jolts from Gussie's arm.

Igress pushed her sleeve up, swung her arm and let fly.

A slap which any tidal wave crashing onto a beach would have been proud of silenced the screams and stopped Gussie jigging, but left Igress bent double on the bench with her hand tucked under her arm.

In the lull, Beaton shoved a stool into the back of Gussie's knees. Gussie sat down abruptly, dragging Aidan to the floor in the process. Gussie bent to help him up but Aidan scrambled away, and Beaton put a firm hand on Gussie's shoulder. Gussie looked up at him. Beaton shook his head.

Gussie started to cry.

Igress glowered and pointed a stern finger.

'One more wail out of you, that's all,' she threatened.

Gussie took hold of the bottom of Beaton's jacket and buried his face in it, his body shaking with sobs.

'It – it was – an accident,' he snuffled between sneezes.

Beaton put his arm around Gussie and gave him a handkerchief. 'Come along now, sir, let's get you to the kitchen. Mrs B will make you a nice cup of tea.'

'But... but what about...'

'Now don't you worry; Miss Frances is in good hands. Aidan, help Igress off the bench and go and see if milady needs you. Come along, Mr Gussie.'

When you don't know what's happening, the easiest and most instinctive thing to do is to obey someone who does seem to know. As this applies universally to all sides in a crisis, Beaton was soon leading Gussie out of the laboratory and Aidan, having had his arms around Igress for a short while as he lifted her from the bench, was awaiting further orders with greatly renewed enthusiasm.

Had any poor unsuspecting souls been glancing idly round The Horse Fair, their attention might have been drawn to a certain window at the Lamb and Werewolf, and in years to come they'd probably have told their children and grandchildren the story of the birth of a bizarre new religious cult, whose main ritual took the form of dancing round naked apart from a head towel, clutching your backside with one hand and stomping on the floor with one foot.

However, no-one did see into the room where Rudolf, fired by rage and illuminated by sporadic flashes of lightning, stamped and ground a bee to dust and a valiant death.

'Milady never was much good at needlework,' said Mrs B, helping Gussie into one of her old dressing-gowns and fussing over him as no-one had done for many a year.

'I wish she had been,' said Gussie pulling the collar up to hide his neck. 'Then I might not have been in this mess.'

Mrs B tied the dressing-gown cord and popped a clean hankie in the pocket.

'Well, whatever the mess is,' she said, 'you can't face it on an empty stomach.' She held him at arms' length and took a good look at him. 'That's better. Now let's get you fed. You must be starving after all the excitement.' She sat him at the kitchen table and pushed a plate of sandwiches towards him. 'Go on – a big lad like you needs to keep his strength up.'

Gussie picked up a sandwich; the bread compressed under

his grip and sloppy filling shot across the table.

'No, Mrs B, I think I need to keep my strength down.'

'Soup and bread, then.'

She scooped a ladleful of steaming soup from her ever-bubbling stockpot into an earthenware bowl and placed it in front of him. 'Spoons are in that drawer behind you.'

'Thanks, Mrs B. You're very kind.'

As Mrs B opened a bread crock and retrieved half a loaf, Gussie turned around and pulled at the drawer, which raced off its runners and hung horizontally in mid-air for a second before breaking off its handle and sending knives, forks and spoons clattering to the floor in a deafening cascade.

Gussie's face started to crumple.

Mrs B put the bread on a tea-towel on the table and patted him on the hand. 'Don't you fret yourself, Gussie. It's forever doing that,' she lied as she bent to scoop the cutlery back into the drawer. She passed him a spoon. 'Here you are. Give it a quick wipe on the tea-towel – it'll be all right.'

The snap of a silver stem told Mrs B that Gussie had done as she'd said, and it wasn't all right. She lifted the cutlery drawer onto the table then put her arm around Gussie's shoulder as silent tears began to drip from his cheek into his soup.

'Perhaps you'd best drink it out of the bowl, eh?'

He nodded sadly and Mrs B wiped his tears with her apron. 'Come on now,' she said. 'The soup'll do you good.'

He gingerly picked up the earthenware bowl half-expecting it to crumble to dust in his grip, but it stayed the course and before long it was emptied and bread-polished, and a few crumbs were the only tangible reminder that half a large loaf had graced the table not so long ago. Gussie was just putting himself outside of his third mug of tea when Mrs B stood up and took two more china cups and saucers from a cupboard.

'They're on their way,' she said.

'Who?'

'Milady and Mr Beaton.'

'How do you—'

The door opened and Rosa and Beaton swept in. Rosa plonked herself on one of the kitchen chairs, looked at Gussie and shook her head.

'What am I going to do with you?' she said.

Gussie's hand went to his mouth.

'Oh, I am so sorry,' he whispered. 'So very, very sorry.'

Whenever thumping came from upstairs at the Lamb and Werewolf, Rigton looked for his wife. If she was nowhere to be seen, he assumed that she was fully in control of whatever situation the thumping was about, possibly actively involved in it or at least making money from it. If she was downstairs, however – perhaps helping a young gent to spill his beer in a variety of interesting ways – Rigton would draw her attention to the thumping and hand the situation over to her.

Attention drawn, Mrs Rigton entered Rudolf's room to empty the bath, and saw Rudolf naked, moaning and face down on the bed, one of his favourite positions. Having spent enough time with him to recognise one of his opening gambits, she pushed her sleeves up as a prelude to giving the proffered bottom a damned good spanking.

'You could be a lot sorrier once she gets her strength back,' said Rosa.

Gussie's eyebrows shot up.

'What? She's not... you mean I haven't...'

'No, she's not and no, you haven't.'

Gussie let out such a sigh of relief that all the crumbs were blown from the kitchen table.

'Oh, gods be praised,' he said, delving into the dressing-gown pocket and pulling out the handkerchief. 'That is such good news.' He dabbed at his moistening eyes.

'How is Miss Frances, milady?' asked Mrs B.

'She's sleeping now. We'll see how she is in the morning.'

'It was an accident, truly,' pleaded Gussie. 'It just came away in my hand. I never meant to hit her. I've never hit anybody.'

'Then it's a good job you missed Aunty Fran.'

'But – if I didn't hit her...'

'She's an old lady, and not very well at that. But don't tell her I told you so. She doesn't want anybody to know.' Rosa sighed. 'She fainted. She's been overdoing it. You pulling the cupboard door off startled her. That's what she says, anyway.'

Rosa rubbed her hand across her face. 'I'm sorry. It's very late – or is it very early? – and I'm very tired. Beaton, show Gussie to his room, will you?'

'My room?' said Gussie.

Rosa looked at him in puzzlement. 'Yes. Your room. You know, where you will have your bed and your... things. Oh, what's the matter now, for goodness' sake?'

Gussie was sobbing again. 'I've never had a room of my own before,' he choked. 'I've always had to share with

167

somebody. Usually several somebodies. I just – oh – you've all been so kind...'

His face crumpled again and he buried it into the handkerchief.

Rosa picked up the earthenware mug, dropped a tablet into his tea and swirled it.

'Here, drink this. It's some of Aunty's herbal remedy to help you sleep.'

Deep in the recesses of his brain a bell rang faintly.

'But I'm already asleep. This is a dream.'

'All right, it's some of Aunty's herbal remedy to help you wake up,' Rosa snapped. 'Just drink the damned thing.'

As Gussie drained the mug, Rosa swept her hands to one side as a signal to Beaton, who said, 'Come along, Mr Gussie. I'll show you to your room.'

'Could I stay with Mistress Stein tonight, please?'

Rosa's expression darkened.

'Certainly not! That's my maiden aunt you're talking about!'

'I meant on the floor. At the side of the bed. So that if she needs anything... please.'

'Sorry, Gussie. Sooty's in there with her, and I'm not sure the sound of you sneezing all night'd do her any good.'

'What about outside the door? Please.'

Rosa looked into his red-rimmed eyes and saw someone as frightened and bewildered as a lost child. 'Oh, all right,' she said softly. 'But if you're up first in the morning, come straight here to the kitchen and don't go wandering about.'

'I'll have a nice big breakfast waiting for you,' called Mrs B as Gussie and Beaton left the kitchen. She handed Rosa a cup of tea. 'Milady, you know when you sewed his head on...'

'Oh, not you as well, Mrs B. Aunty's already given me an ear-bashing about the size of the stitches.'

'Oh, no, milady, it's not that. It's just that he's put out so much water I wondered if you'd connected his bladder directly to his eyeballs.'

Despite both his good intentions and the excitements of the day, Gussie enjoyed a sound and an untroubled sleep thanks to Fran's herbal remedy, but a few seconds after he woke up, he was an emotional battenburg. There was disappointment and anger at being in the same dream again, coupled with curiosity and gladness that he'd be able to find out how it ended. Sandwiched between all these feelings was a worry that he couldn't remember anything about his life outside of this dream, and wrapped around the lot was a looming fear that this wasn't a dream at all.

In this sea of bewilderment, he decided to cling onto the life-raft of what little knowledge he had, which was the route to the kitchen. As he turned back the covers that Beaton had provided, he heard the tearing of material, reminding him that he was now a lot stronger than a tailor needs to be. He stood up, carefully pulled the dressing-gown around him and set off, uttering staccato oohs and aahs as he tiptoe-hopped from foot to foot along the cold stone floor.

Mrs B was putting a steaming plate of breakfast on the table when Gussie pushed the kitchen door off its hinges, just managing to catch it before it brained Mrs B and obliterated his breakfast.

'Sorry, Mrs B, sorry, sorry. Accident. Sorry,' he said, his eyes pleading for help.

'Don't fret. Rest it against the wall and get your breakfast. Aidan'll fix that.'

He sat down in front of an earthenware plate piled high with various hot meats, eggs and traditional accompaniments.

'I'm sorry, Mrs B, I can't eat this.'

'Yes you can,' she replied. 'We've found you a cast iron knife and fork.'

'No, I mean – I have a bit of a delicate stomach.'

'Oh, I don't think you have any more.' She filled an earthenware mug with tea. 'Eat up, there's a good lad.'

He counted the items on the plate.

'Could you spare a bit of greaseproof paper please, Mrs B?'

'Greaseproof? Whatever for?'

'Well... when I leave here I don't know when I might eat again, so I thought I might take some of this with me...'

His words trailed off as tears welled in his eyes.

'Why, wherever are you going?' said Mrs B.

'I... I don't know.'

'I'm sure milady wants you to stay.'

Gussie brightened slightly. 'Really?'

'Whyever else would we have got your room ready?'

'I thought that was just for the one night.'

Mrs B patted his hand. 'I'm sure they wouldn't've brought you back from the dead just for the one night. Now eat up before it's dinnertime and you've two platefuls to get through.'

'I get dinner as well?!'

Mrs B, who thought that people should have as many

square meals a day as they could possibly manage, laughed out loud. 'Of course! But not until you've had your elevenses. And you can't have elevenses until you've had your breakfast!'

Gussie smiled as he realised that in this kitchen he might possibly get through more food in twenty-four hours than he had done in the previous twenty-four years. The only decision now was whether to binge and diet or binge and bugger it. The plateful in front of him did look like the sort of thing he'd always denied himself for fear of putting on weight.

Reason threw Fear out of the window by saying that his weight was now out of his control, seeing as somebody else had made him several stones heavier. Greed then told the broken Fear that if this existence was a dream, it didn't matter what he ate, because when he woke up it wouldn't have made a ha'porth of difference anyway. His taste buds simply drooled and ordered his hands to start work.

On the window-sill in Fran's bedroom sat a mound of fur as white as an angel's wing, holding in his front paws Cecil, the small, honey-coloured teddy bear with the fading red ribbon and the raggy ear.

Sooty gazed through the leaded glass: the outside world was sodden after the ferocity of the previous night's storm. In time, the earth would steam as the morning sun burned off the wet, but for now all was heavy, laden with a grim stillness that blanketed Sooty's soul and drenched his bones with foreboding. He lowered his head, resting his chin between Cecil's ears, and when he looked out of the window again, he saw the world through another layer of moisture.

'Cracker of a storm last night,' said Fran from the bed.

'I notice you managed to sleep right through it,' said Sooty.

Fran hitched herself up to lean on the pile of pillows against the headboard. 'Well, I've never really seen the point in having a sleepless night.'

Sooty picked Cecil up by the ear and jumped off the window-sill. He padded round to the ottoman at the foot of the bed and used it as a step to get up and over the footboard. He dropped Cecil onto the bedcovers.

'How are you this morning?' he asked.

'I'm fine. Why?'

'Last night? Being attacked?'

Fran sighed irritatedly. 'He didn't attack me, I fainted. If he'd attacked me, I'd have been dead by now, wouldn't I? Or at least badly minced. Can you see a mark on me? No, you can't. Not so much as a scratch.' She pointed an admonishing finger at Sooty. 'He did not attack me. I fainted, all right?'

During the silence that followed, the two of them stared out an unspoken compromise: neither side gave way, but they would not speak of the matter again.

Fran smoothed the bedcovers.

'Nip and ask Mrs B if I can have breakfast in bed this morning, would you?' she said.

'You never have breakfast in bed.'

'I think I'm old enough to start, don't you?'

Sooty frowned. 'You're not very well, are you?'

'No, I'm not *very* well, but I'm well enough. Satisfied?'

'No, not really. How well's "well enough"?'

'I'm... not as strong as I was.'

'So you're weakening.'

'All right! Yes, I'm weakening. And I'll be dead of starvation and interrogation before me time if you don't get a move on.'

'Oh, pardon my concern!'

The bedroom door flew open. Sooty jumped off the bed and ran out of the room; the slamming door echoed all over the castle.

Fran sniffed and reached across the bedcovers for Cecil. His ear was raggier than usual, and the top of his head was very definitely damp.

Rosa and Igress were at the kitchen table when Sooty padded in just as Mrs B put down breakfast for him.

'Morning, Sootbags,' said Rosa, finishing off the last mouthful of her breakfast. 'How's Aunty Fran?'

'Alive and kicking,' he said bitterly. 'Oh, and she'd like breakfast in bed, this morning, if you please, Mrs B.'

'I thought she might,' said Mrs B, placing a single rose into a bud vase on a tray laden with breakfast.

Rosa pushed away her own plate and stood up. 'I'll take it.'

'Watch yourself, Rosa,' warned Sooty. 'She's liable to bite your head off.'

'You and Mistress Stein had a row, Sooty?' asked Igress.

'Let's just say we failed to see eye to eye about something.'

Rosa winked at him. 'Oh, now, there's a novelty – Aunty Fran failing to see eye to eye with somebody.' She picked up the tray and left the kitchen.

'Want to talk about it?' Igress asked Sooty.

'Not really. But thanks for the offer.'

Suddenly his ears pricked up. He turned abruptly away and concentrated on his breakfast, all his fur standing on end as if he'd had an unexpected starching.

An eager Gussie bounced into the kitchen, followed by Aidan and Beaton. 'Look, Mrs B! Don't I look posh?'

'You do indeed, Gussie. Mr Beaton, is that one of your father's old suits?'

'It is, Mrs B. It's his special occasion uniform – the one that he wore when buttling at civic receptions in the Mansion House.' Beaton's chest swelled with pride, but still came nowhere near his late father's upper-body measurement.

Gussie twirled, beaming broadly. He wore shiny black shoes, black socks, black trousers, a matching tailcoat with silk lapels, a white waistcoat over a formal, high wing-collar shirt and a white bow tie. His head still didn't look as if it belonged on his body, but at least the wing-collar covered up the stitches in his neck.

'It's rather grand just to wear around the castle,' said Igress.

'It's only until we can get him some workaday clothes, miss,' said Beaton. 'Mr Gussie can keep the suit for formal dinners and dances.'

The word 'dances' only heightened Gussie's joy. He started to sing, then pulled Igress from her chair and waltzed her around the room, even though her feet didn't touch the floor as he held her in his arms.

Aidan's unhappy face was set, his bottom lip sticking out. When Gussie dipped the giggling Igress towards the floor Aidan shouted, 'Watch out for Master Sooty!'

To Aidan's satisfaction, Gussie screamed, dropped Igress

and ran behind Beaton. Aidan helped Igress to her feet as Gussie began sneezing violently.

'Ask him how the old – choo! – lady is. Tell him, Mr Beaton – choo! – tell him I didn't mean to – choo! – hurt her! And I'm sorry I called him an it, Mr – choo! – Beaton! Tell him!'

'I'm sure that Master Sooty understands, Mr Gussie. Master Sooty, how is Miss Frances this morning?'

'She's alive, Mr Beaton,' said Sooty, 'but it's no thanks to that monster.'

'I'm not a – choo! – monster,' Gussie wailed. 'I'm a nice person...'

He broke into large sobs and more sneezes.

'Oh, not again,' said Igress, walking over to him. 'Come on, Gussie, let's go for a walk.' She tried to take his arm, but he flinched away from her. 'It's all right,' she said. 'I'm not going to hit you again, I promise. I only want to show you round the rest of the castle.'

'I'll come with you,' said Aidan.

'Unfortunately, Aidan,' said Beaton, 'you and I have a lot to do. This way.' Aidan didn't even get chance to gaze wistfully after Igress as she led Gussie away.

In the now quiet kitchen, Mrs B sat in her rocking chair and looked at Sooty. 'He's not really a monster, you know,' she said softly. 'And he wouldn't hurt your mistress.'

Sooty grunted, but did not resist as Mrs B lifted him onto her lap.

She began to rock gently and stroke him. 'He wouldn't deliberately hurt anybody – it's not in his nature.'

'So why did he pull the door off and frighten her?'

'Because his nature's in his head, not in his body. It's the same reason the kitchen door's off its hinges. He doesn't know his own strength; he still thinks like a little lamb instead of a prize bull. You're a shape-shifter – you're used to this sort of thing. He's not. Imagine what you'd be like if you got stuck half-way through a transformation, your head being one thing and your body another. It'd take some getting used to.'

'Suppose so.'

'He's lost... and scared,' said Mrs B. 'His old life's vanished overnight – along with his old body – and he's faced with a bunch of complete strangers. He hasn't got a thing he can call his own, and he's forever breaking other people's things because he can't help it. Wouldn't you be unhappy?'

'Maybe.'

'I mean, whatever must it feel like to wake up one day and find that the life you knew has gone forever?'

She said no more, but continued to rock gently in her chair, and after a while she felt that the place where his head lay on her lap was wet with his tears.

'I understand that certain people haven't been seeing eye to eye this morning,' said Rosa, laying the tray across the bedclothes.

'I don't know what's up with him,' said Fran. 'Damned fool's got me dead and buried already.' She flapped out her napkin and tucked it into the neck of her nightgown.

Rosa sat on the bed.

'We aren't all as matter-of-fact about this as you are, you know. We haven't all had your Union training.'

Fran sawed at a sausage. 'He has.'

176

'Maybe he was away when they did Stoicism In The Face Of Personal Tragedy.'

Fran dipped the sawn-off end of the sausage into her egg yolk. 'He'll get over it. I'm not his first Mistress and I certainly won't be his last.'

'True... but I think sometimes—'

Fran threw her cutlery onto the plate.

'Sometimes what? Sometimes we just have to accept what happens and get on with it – ever thought about that? Mm? Well, we do. Now if you don't mind, you're putting me off me breakfast.' She picked up the knife and fork, thrust the eggy sausage into her mouth and chewed defiantly.

'Sootbags was right about one thing,' said Rosa levelly.

'Oh, aye?' said Fran, hacking at the brown and crozzled rind of a rasher of bacon.

The slightest smile twitched the corners of Rosa's lips.

'He said if I came in here I'd get my head bitten off.'

The tough rind suddenly gave way and the knife cracked onto the plate as bacon shrapnel shot across the bedroom.

'The cheeky sod!' exploded Fran. 'Wait till he shows his face. I'll give him what for... What? What are you laughing at?'

Rosa's slight smile had broadened into a huge grin.

'You.' She cupped her hands and called out. 'Are you all right down there in the deep end?'

Fran waved her knife at her niece. '*I do not go off the—*'

She got no further as Rosa flopped back on the bed and laughed helplessly.

Fran returned to work on her breakfast.

'All right, all right, you've made your point. Anyway, how's

177

Gussie today? Have you told him why he's here?'

Rosa sat up, chuckling and wiping her eyes.

'Haven't said a word. Haven't seen him.'

'What if he doesn't want to be your personal bodyguard?'

'I'll just have to convince him.'

'And if you can't?'

'Then you'll have to.' Rosa waggled her fingers out in front of her. 'Do whatever it is you *trained* people do.'

'Typical civilian. If you can't get what you want by normal means you want to resort to magic.'

'What's the point in having the power if you don't use it?'

'That's the whole point of having the power – so you don't have to use it.'

Rosa screwed her face up in childish concentration.

'No, can't see that one at all.'

Fran tutted. 'Look. If I used the power to get whatever I wanted whenever I wanted, there'd be no point in anybody else living, would there?'

'Wouldn't there?'

'Of course not. Take this breakfast, for instance. I could make this, and all my meals, and do all the housekeeping, just with a wave of my hand if I wanted to, but then I don't need Mrs B or Beaton.'

'But they could still work for me.'

'Not if I chuck you out on the street.'

'Then we'd all work for someone else.'

Fran gave a short laugh. 'You?!'

'All right,' said Rosa. 'They'd work for someone else and I'd throw myself on your mercy.'

'Live in your own castle under somebody else's tyranny? Isn't that why you threw Rudolf out?'

'True. But the others could still work for somebody else.'

Fran rolled her eyes in mock despair. 'And you're supposed to be the brainy one of the family. Think about it. The most powerful mortal employer in this town is powerless against me if I put me mind to it. Whatever he makes and sells, I can make and give away. Whatever he pays for, I can make for nothing. So, whoever he employs, I can put out of work.'

'Then what stops you taking over the town?'

'If we could all get what we wanted when we wanted it, what'd be the point in getting up in a morning? Folk have to have summat to do. Take away their livelihoods, and you take away their lives. We all need to work at *something*, otherwise how are you going to test your mettle, fulfil your potential, develop as a person? If we never work at anything, we're just grown-up kids, bickering and fighting until somebody bigger than us puts a stop to it all.'

'I can't imagine you trained ones as grown-up kids.'

Fran's long years of experience gave vent to a snort.

'We're the worst. Believe me, you don't want a cartload of Systers of the Black Cauldron hanging about, every one of 'em self-sufficient, and every one of 'em bored witless because they've nowt to do. Boredom leads either to creation or destruction, and if somebody's got the power and turns it to destruction you can kiss everything goodbye.' She took a swig of tea. 'Besides, you can't just go round magicking this that and the other – you'll get run down. Why do you think I fainted? There's only so much energy in a body, and you can't afford to get run down.' She tapped her finger on the breakfast tray to emphasise the point. 'You've always got to be ready in case somebody needs you to be ready. D'you understand me?'

'Oh, I understand,' said Rosa, 'but I do have one question.'

'Yes, well,' said Fran, 'scientists always do. "What's this for? What's that do? What happens if I mix this with that? Let's take it apart to find out how it works in case it ever goes wrong and we have to take it apart." And then when you put it back together you've usually got a handful of bits left over.'

'Thus proving that it doesn't necessarily need all its components to fulfil its designated function.'

'Why can't you accept that some things just work and some things just are?'

'Because I have to find out *why* they just work and *why* they just are. It's my job.' Rosa smirked. 'And as a wise old woman once said: everybody's got to have something to do.'

Rigton whisked the coins from the bright daylight of the counter to the dark recesses of the pocket under his apron and reached for the tankards.

Yedder rubbed his hands together and laughed.

'A bee sting, Gil, a damned bee sting! In the arse!'

'Fruit, my lord? Mango today,' said Rigton over the swish and glug of beer into tankard and the giggle and gurgle of merriment out of Yedder.

'For Yedder,' smiled Guildman. 'And one for yourself.'

'Thank you, my lord.'

Yedder bounced his hands on the bar. 'And your good lady goes and damned well slaps it! Oh, I wish I'd seen his face!'

'Apparently, his face was not visible, my lord.'

A fresh wave of amusement drenched Yedder.

'I bet he howled!'

'He did, my lord. And I'd venture to say that—'

A thump from upstairs caught Rigton's attention.

'I believe Lord Rudolf is rising.'

Yedder gave one last chortle then coughed.

'Oh! Righty ho! Thanks, Rigsy. Here we go, Gil.'

With greater ease than many would have thought possible, Yedder subdued his laughter and his features, and when Rudolf entered the parlour, the picture he saw was that of a landlord wiping clean the area of the counter from where two aristocrats carried three tankards of ale towards a rickety table.

'Yedder! Bring that beer back!'

'It's all right, Rude, we've got a table.'

Rudolf strolled over to the bar.

'I don't want to sit at a table, I want to stand at the bar. Now bring that beer back.'

'But we always sit at a table.'

'Not today!'

Yedder looked at Guildman.

'Sorry, Gil. He wants to stand up.'

'Perhaps he has some master plan which is better explained in the perpendicular.'

They moved back towards the bar.

Rudolf grabbed one of the tankards.

'Why the hell do you have to make such a song and dance about everything? It's perfectly simple. We're going to stand here, drink our beer and then go to the Dog Flog.'

'Again?' said Yedder.

'As yesterday's attempt was such a dismal failure we're going to try again.' He looked hard at Yedder. 'Any questions?'

A short pause and a distant look in Yedder's eye signalled concentrated activity in the question-forming section of his brain. He picked up a slice of mango, chewed it thoughtfully, then – with a face as innocent as a baby – turned to Rudolf.

'Are you sure you don't want to sit down?'

Rudolf grasped Yedder's lapel. 'Positive. We'll stand here, finish our beers and then go and make me enough money to get that festering fishwife out of the castle. All right?'

Yedder raised his hands in surrender.

'Fine by me, old thing. Standing up it is.'

Rudolf released Yedder and returned to drinking his beer.

Yedder grinned and picked up another slice of mango.

'Landlord,' said Guildman, 'please arrange a coach.'

'My lord,' said Rigton, resting one hand on the counter and bowing slightly.

'No coach,' said Rudolf.

Guildman's tankard stopped halfway between counter and mouth. Rigton froze in his bowing position like a gardener with a bad back. Yedder missed the mango and bit his finger.

'Ow! Otch! Ooh! What? No coach?'

'You heard,' said Rudolf.

Rigton's head was the only part of him moving as it swivelled from side to side watching the three men.

'No coach?' said Guildman.

'That's right.'

'No coach?' tried Rigton.

Rudolf banged his tankard on the bar.

'Hell fire! Has there been an outbreak of spontaneous deafness in here? Watch my lips. No coach! We are walking to the Dog Flog.'

Yedder's eyes almost fell out.

'Walking? You never walk anywhere unless you have to, old thing.'

Rudolf glared at him. 'Maybe I fancy some fresh air.'

'I'm not surprised after that perfume you had on yesterday,' said Yedder, shortly before Rudolf slapped him on the back of the head. 'Ow! Steady on, old boy. Just a joke.'

'Well har bloody har. We're walking.'

'You?' said Guildman. 'Push through crowds of the lower orders? And probably creditors? Hardly lording behaviour.'

'Oh, no,' chimed Yedder. 'Far too unpleasant, Gil. A real pain in the arse.'

Gussie's incredulity echoed around the library in Castle Stein.

'Me?! A bodyguard? Do I *look* like a bodyguard?'

'Certainly,' said Rosa. 'Apart from the suit.'

'It'd be like getting beaten up by a waiter,' added Igress.

'Beaten up?' said Gussie with a look of horror. 'Nobody said anything about beating people up.'

'Not people,' said Fran, 'person. Rosa's ex-husband.'

Gussie folded his arms.

'I never get involved in divorces – far too messy. And talking of messy, I could never face Mr Beaton again if I got blood on Beaton senior's special occasion uniform.'

'You won't,' said Fran. 'You'll have some working clothes.'

'Working clothes? You call beating people up "working"?'

'Isn't that what Battling Bill used to do?' said Rosa.

'Wer... well, yes, but—'

'And haven't you got Battling Bill's body?'

'Er... apparently, but—'

'So isn't this sort of thing that your body's been trained for?'

'Aaa...I suppose so, but—'

'But what?'

'But he used to fight other fighters,' protested Gussie, 'not poor saps chucked out of the house by their wives.'

'Poor sap?!' choked Igress. 'The raving lunatic who had a go at me? Some poor sap?'

'Had a go at you?'

'He belted Igress,' Fran explained. 'Chased her through town, threatening to murder her.'

Gussie blanched. 'That's not helping. You should have stuck with the divorce scenario – at least that was only messy, not usually fatal.' He turned to Igress. 'Did you manage to fight back at all?'

'Oh, yes,' beamed Igress. 'I gave him a good right-hander.'

'Now that does it. I've had one of your right-handers and it nearly emptied my gums. If he could stand that *and* chase you through town, he's a lot tougher than I'll ever be.'

'But we really need your help,' said Rosa, vulnerability sweeping across her face. 'We three helpless females—'

Gussie pointed to Igress.

'All right,' conceded Rosa, 'two helpless females and one who's got a good right hand – we're at your mercy. Protect us from Rudolf.'

Gussie looked at Fran.

'You're a witch, aren't you? Can't you do something?'

'Alas,' she replied, coughing her way into a convincing lack of breath, 'I am trained to hold all existence sacrosanct, and what few powers I have are waning. I fear my time is short.'

No consumptive heroine ever faded more dramatically, and Igress rushed to her side.

'Is he really that bad?' said Gussie.

'He attacked me, and he beat up Aidan,' said Igress.

'Again, not helping.'

'He wants to murder me and take the castle,' said Rosa.

'The castle?' said Gussie. 'Does that include my room?'

'Oh, yes. If he gets hold of this place, we'll all be out on our ear. Including you.'

'And it'll be winter soon,' added Fran, shivering for dramatic emphasis. 'How easily the cold seeps into the bones. Winter's no time to be roaming the icy streets, with nothing to call your own.'

'Pressing your nose up to the windows of the eating-houses,' whimpered Igress, 'remembering the good old days when Mrs B would feed you any time of day or night, and fuss over you, and make your bed...'

'*Your* bed,' said Rosa, 'in *your* room, with *your* chair, and *your* table, and *your* wardrobe, holding *your* clothes...'

Gussie gulped. 'Can I think about it?'

Rosa patted his hand. 'Dear, dear Gussie – of course you can. In the kitchen? Over a cup of tea? With biscuits?'

'Chocolate ones probably,' added Igress.

'You need a day out,' said Mrs B, half-persuading, half-commanding. 'Take yourself off for a long walk somewhere. It's a beautiful day.'

'I can't,' said Sooty, lying on one side on her lap.

'Whyever not?'

'I can't leave her.' He pushed himself to his feet and faced Mrs B. 'What if... something happened... while I was out?'

'It won't. Besides, if anything was going to happen, wouldn't you be the first to sense it, wherever you were? And wouldn't she call you back?'

Sooty frowned, but Mrs B ignored it and continued.

'You're not carrying this burden all on your own, you know. Isn't that why she came here? To be with family? You can't make it go away, and you can't do it for her, because you can't *be* her. So you've got to be you. And this isn't you, is it?'

He sighed. 'Not really.'

'And will it do her any good to see you moping about?'

He wrinkled his nose. 'Suppose not.'

'That's better.' Mrs B stroked his ears. 'Off you go. Get yourself out for the day. Look at things from a bit of a distance. Closer isn't necessarily clearer.'

'True.' He stiffened. 'Oh-oh. Enemy approaching.'

Three women sat around a sturdy workbench in the laboratory of Castle Stein. One was tall, elegant and determined; one was smaller, neat and worried; one was short, stout and sensible with a deep-seated streak of mischief.

'He'll do it,' said Fran.

'You seem very sure, Mistress Stein,' said Igress.

Rosa chuckled. 'Aunty Fran's spent her whole life being sure – or at least convincing other people she's sure.'

'I am sure. His body doesn't need an excuse to fight – it's trained for it. It's probably itching to have a go at something.'

'You don't think dying might have affected his ability?' asked Igress. 'Being dead hardly qualifies as the peak of physical prowess, does it?'

'We'll get him back in training,' countered Fran. 'Skipping.'

'Skipping?' said Rosa. 'It's not the all-Maund playground championships, you know.'

'It'll help him be light on his feet. Fancy footwork's a great asset to a boxer.'

'I want him to punch Rudolf's lights out, not join him in a social foxtrot.'

'Aye, but you'll want him to get out of the way quick once Rudolf starts flailing about.'

'I don't want Lord Rudolf to have the chance to start flailing about,' said Igress. 'I want Gussie to land him one he won't get up from.' She flexed her arms. 'Shouldn't he be lifting weights or something? Build up his muscles again?'

'Ideally, yes,' said Fran. 'But what's heavy enough for him?'

'I'll sort that out,' said Rosa.

'Good. Then there's only two things to worry about.'

'Oh really?' said Igress. 'Only two? What are they then, death and death? My, my, things are looking up.' She stopped short and looked at the other two. 'Sorry. It's just that I've never been threatened with death so many times in one week.'

'Remind me to make you up a stress-reliever,' said Fran.

'With all due respect, Mistress Stein, I'm not suffering from stress, I'm suffering from impending death.'

'We're all suffering from that.'

'Girls, girls,' Rosa overruled. 'Can we get on, please? Aunty, what have we got to worry about?'

Fran took a deep breath. 'Firstly, Gussie's only got a limited lifespan so he'll have to sort Rudolf out fairly sharpish.'

'Poor soul,' said Igress. 'He'll only just have got used to the idea of living again and he'll have to die again.'

'That's the way it is, flower. I know it sounds callous, but he was brought back for a purpose, so we've got to make the best use of him while he's here.'

'Otherwise we'll have brought him back for nothing – which'd be even worse,' added Rosa. 'What else, Aunty?'

'Let's hope Rudolf doesn't knock his block off.'

In the kitchen Gussie cradled his stoneware beaker, stared at the empty plate and bit the inside of his mouth. His inner torment manifested itself as facial contortions, and he sighed a much deeper sigh than he'd ever done in his life but which could become a regular occurrence of his death. He stuck out his bottom lip and laid it over his top one, giving the impression that his face was deflating.

'Hm,' he mused.

'Miles away, aren't you?' asked Mrs B, taking his beaker.

'Hmm. What? Oh, sorry, Mrs B. What did you say?'

'You're miles away,' she replied, filling up his beaker with more tea. 'And if you're miles away, wherever are you?'

He blew out his cheeks, rasping as he expelled the air.

'That's just it,' he said dolefully. 'I don't know.'

She gave him his tea; he cupped his hands round it as if it were the only friend he had.

'Well, you're here, for a start,' said Mrs B. 'Because if you're not, whoever am I giving this tea to?'

'Apparently it goes through my mouth but into someone else's stomach, which is something I try not to think about.'

'Then whatever do you think about?'

He looked into his tea.

'I think I'm dreaming,' he said, 'but everybody in my dream thinks I'm not.'

'People are like that in dreams. Everything makes sense to them that's in it.'

'But that's what's so worrying – it's starting to make a kind of sense to me.'

'So whatever's the problem?'

'That is.'

'Hold on,' said Mrs B. 'We need more biscuits for this.'

She reached into a cupboard and pulled out a large round tin embossed in varying shades of purple. On the lid was a picture of a lord and lady looking in a decorated shop-window during a blizzard, and around the side in white letters was written *Walpurgisnight Greetings*. She removed the lid and placed the tin in the centre of the table. An assortment of home-made chocolate biscuits begged to be eaten; Gussie obliged.

'Right,' said Mrs B. 'If you're dreaming, what's your life like when you wake up?'

'I can't remember,' Gussie replied, trying desperately not to spray crumbs everywhere. 'I know I'm called Gussie and I'm a tailor and that's all I know. The rest of it's gone – like... like...'

'Like a dream when you wake up?'

He thought for a moment.

'Er... yes, I suppose so. It's as if dreams and reality have swapped over.'

'Whatever's wrong with that?'

Gussie spluttered. 'I'm sorry? Did you say—'

'As long as you've one set of reality and one set of dreams, does it matter which is which?' said Mrs B. 'When you're in real life it's real and when you're dreaming it's just as real as if it *was* real, so I don't see that it matters much.'

He searched her face for signs of humour and found only the self-assuredness of a woman who was a damned good housekeeper and didn't let little things like whether she really existed or not get in the way.

He pulled at his chin. 'It matters when you've been asked to kick seven bells out of someone you've never met.'

Mrs B smiled. 'You can't lose.'

'I might get hurt.'

She laughed. 'A big strapping lad like you? You're twice the size of Lord Rudolf.'

'Then there's twice as much of me to get hurt.'

Mrs B tutted. 'Haven't you been listening? If this is a dream, Lord Rudolf doesn't really exist, so he can't hurt you.'

'Er... I suppose so,' said Gussie slowly, aware that he'd lost control over the conversation as well as his life. 'But it still seems a bit mean, beating up a man who's not only not real but who's never done me any harm.'

'Only because he hasn't met you yet. Very few people get away from him unscathed. Anyway, you're going to have to kill him because beating him up'll only make him angry.'

'Kill him?! I can't *kill* somebody!'

'Of course you can,' said Mrs B brightly. 'He'll be trying to kill you – and milady, Miss Frances, Igress and Aidan – so why shouldn't you kill him? And if this is a dream, he's not real anyway so it won't matter if you do kill him.'

'And it won't matter if I don't.'

'It'll matter to the people that he kills. And if this isn't a dream, that'll include you. More biscuits?'

To call it a bar was an act of generosity, but the barrels and crates served their purpose as efficiently as Rigton's polished woodwork, albeit at a greater risk of drinking splinters.

'Three beers, barkeep,' said Yedder to the large, unshaven man who stood behind the plank of wood that formed the counter by dint of being both reasonably flat and supported by three upturned barrels.

'Make it two flask, one cask, please,' said Guildman.

The barman dipped into a battered wooden crate, picked up two flasks of ale, pulled the corks out with his teeth, spat them into a barrel and placed the flasks on the counter.

'Your bar seems to be on some sort of fire circle,' commented Guildman.

'Aye, well,' said the barman, stooping and picking up a wooden tankard from a jumbled heap on the floor, emptying its dregs back onto the pile as he straightened up. 'There were a bit of an incident yesdy afternoon.' He knocked the tankard against one of the barrels to dislodge the insect life.

'Incident?' asked Yedder.

'Aye.' The barman dipped the tankard in a half-full drip-tray and wiped it on a cloth that looked as if it was older than most of the barrels and had been rolled around the floor more times. 'There were a terrible pong 'anging over everywheer.'

'Pong?' Yedder repeated, laying a coin on the counter.

'Sweet. Perfume oils, or suchlike. Don't know wheer it come from but it med your eyes water.' The barman filled the tankard from a battered and bird-lime-encrusted barrel. 'In t'end we had to gi' up racing coz it were confusing t'dogs. They kept running round in circles.'

Guildman wiped the tops of the two flasks with a white silk handkerchief. 'There seems to be no trace of the smell now.'

The barman put the tankard on the counter and pocketed the coin. 'Only one way to clear a pong like that: fire.'

'You had a bonfire?'

'We did after some silly bugger dropped his flaming torch on t'bar.'

'Hence the charred area underfoot.'

'Correct,' said the barman, and moved off to serve someone else.

Yedder and Guildman clunked their flasks together then turned to survey the crowd as they drank.

'Thought I recognised those britches,' said a voice from ground level. 'You two are slumming it a bit, aren't you?'

Yedder laughed and crouched down to stroke Sooty.

'Pot and kettle, old chum.'

'If one wishes to gamble on the outcome of events,' added Guildman, 'one has to go where the events are, Spirit.'

Sooty's eyes narrowed. 'Is one gambling, Guildman?'

'Indeed, no, Spirit, one is not. But one other is, on behalf of a third.'

'Who?'

Yedder withdrew his hand from Sooty and moved out of reach. 'Yours truly. On behalf of Rudolf.'

Sooty's hackles rose. 'Yedder!'

'Now, now, old thing. Don't go jumping to conclusions.'

'Why not?'

'Look, Rude's only gambling – he's just using my money, that's all.'

'Why can't he use his own?'

'He hasn't got any.'

Sooty's hackles calmed slightly.

'Yedder,' said Guildman, 'hold my drink, please.'

As Yedder stood up, Guildman bent down and rubbed a gloved hand in the remains of the fire circle.

'Forgive me, Spirit, but we must disguise you.' He stroked the cat, darkening his fur with charcoal. 'Rudolf is heading this way, and he must not recognise you.'

'Let me change,' said Sooty.

'Not in such a public place. And say nothing.'

'Absolutely,' said Yedder. 'Talking cat? Dead giveaway.'

'Understood,' said Sooty.

Guildman took hold of Sooty's head and blackened his face. 'And remember, Spirit, no matter what you might hear, or however bad it sounds, remember that there are those who love Rosalind as much as you do, and will not see her come to harm. Do you trust me?'

Gussie sat in Mrs B's stove-side chair, legs stretched out, staring into the orange glow from the cooking range fire.

'Don't sit too close, Gussie; we don't want you getting scorched, do we?' said Mrs B gently. Without blinking or taking his eyes from the fire, Gussie bent his legs so that his feet were under the chair. 'Good lad,' said Mrs B.

Gussie said nothing, his eyes fixed on the burning coals which collapsed in on themselves with the same suddenness that his life had, except the coals did not rise again. Flickering embers were drowning in the flames that consumed them as surely as he himself was drowning in a sea of troubles that would consume him – if he let them. He gazed deeper and deeper into the fire; down and down his mind plunged, into the white-hot heart of confusion.

Rudolf's concentration on liquid refreshment was such that he almost tripped over one of his companions.

'What the hell are you doing, Guildman?'

'Merely trying to explain to this poor benighted feline that the Dog Flog is not necessarily the best place for a cat to be.'

'Decent of you to take the trouble, I'm sure,' scorned Rudolf, snatching one of the flasks out of Yedder's hands.

Yedder snatched it back. 'Ah-ah.' He indicated the battered wooden tankard on the counter. Rudolf glared. Yedder smiled. 'Thought we'd get you a full pint, old thing,'

'I should think so, too. Guildman, shift that mangy bag of bones and let me get to my beer.'

'Meow,' said Sooty.

'What?' said Rudolf.

'Never said a word, old thing.'

'Not you, Yedder – that cat. It said "Meow".'

'That's what cats say.'

'No, I mean it *said* "Meow", you fool.' Rudolf scrutinised Sooty, who tried to look as gormless as he could. 'Is it one of those witch's cats from The Union? They can talk, can't they?'

Guildman stood up, took his flask back from Yedder and handed Rudolf the tankard. 'They can, but I don't think "meow" is at the top of their list of conversation starters.'

'I say, Gil,' grinned Yedder, 'if it is one of those cats ask it what's going to win today's racing. Rude needs all the help he can get in that direction.'

Rudolf spluttered his beer.

'Are you saying that a *cat* can pick a winner better than me?'

Guildman bent down to Sooty again.

Yedder coughed. 'No... no... it's more like I'm saying that you've been a bit... er... unlucky... with some of your choices... over the last few months.'

'Choices? Choices?! Did I have any choice when that cow threw me out? Did I? Did I, Yedder?'

'W— er... um...'

'No! I had no bloody choice at all! And let me tell you – once I've got my hands on that castle and that fortune, my choice will be to hold her upside down in the moat for a couple of hours and then use her for archery practice and see how she likes it! That'll be *my* choice.'

Yedder could see Sooty struggling in Guildman's grasp.

'I say, steady on, old thing.'

'Steady on? Steady on? Yedder, I'm going to march an army

across the drawbridge and into the Great Hall. I'm going to give that harridan the seeing-to of the century and then feed her to a pack of hounds. I'm going to hollow out her head to use as a spittoon. I'm going to cut off her hands, nail them to the wall and use them as cloak-hooks and I don't want to hear a weedy little voice saying "Steady on, old thing"! All right?!'

'All right, old boy, calm yourself,' said Yedder into the space vacated by the crowd round the bar who had moved a safe distance away during Rudolf's rant.

'You'll need a lot of money for an army,' said Guildman.

'Not necessarily a full army,' said Rudolf, 'just a small select band of killers, that's all.'

Sooty ran off. Guildman stood up.

'Which is why,' Rudolf continued, grabbing Yedder's elbow and propelling him towards the bookmakers, 'Yedder is going to put some money on *my choice* of whippet.'

'Your choice. Good,' said Yedder. 'Which one?'

'Number six.'

'Not a good idea,' said Guildman, strolling alongside.

'And pray tell me why not, Guildman? Bearing in mind that you know as much about betting as you do about lording.'

Guildman looked pointedly at Rudolf's black and white striped britches. 'I know that you should never bet on anything wearing the same outfit as you.'

Mrs B poured steaming fresh tea into an enormous chipped mug covered in dirty fingerprints. She dropped in a splash of milk and eight sugars and set it on the table just as Mason walked into the kitchen.

'Mrs B, you certainly knows how to please a man. Oh, sorry – I didn't realise you'd got company.'

'Oh, don't mind Gussie. He's only having a good old think.'

Mason sat at the kitchen table, cupped his hands round the tea-mug and studied Gussie, whose only sign of animation was a pouty bottom lip that moved in and out very slowly.

'Why's he wearing an evening suit?'

'Well if he wasn't, Mr Mason, he'd have nothing on at all and I'm not having nakedness in my kitchen.'

It was Mason's turn to stick his bottom lip out.

'Not even a little bit?'

'Not even at all.'

Mason took a sip of scalding tea, but it didn't warm him as much as the thought of nakedness in Mrs B's kitchen. After a while he said, 'Hasn't he got a little head for such a big body?'

'Yes,' shot Gussie, causing Mason to spill tea on areas that were already overheated, 'but his ears still work.'

Mason's eyes crossed in pain.

'Oh, my dear!' cried Mrs B, but the fresh snows of Mason's fervent expectation became a slush of bitter disappointment as she rushed past him to put her arm round Gussie's shoulders.

'Are you back with us, love?' she said.

Gussie covered her hand with his. 'Yes, Mrs B. I'm back.'

'Are things any clearer?'

'No and yes.'

Mason temporarily uncrossed his eyes and rolled them heavenwards, but nobody noticed.

Gussie sighed. 'No because I still don't understand it, but yes because that doesn't matter any more. If this is real life, I'll spend so much time trying to understand it I'll have no time to live it, so I ought to stop trying to understand it and start living it. And if it's a dream, there's no point in trying to understand it because it's only a dream. Either way, I might as well just get on with it and see what happens.'

She ruffled his hair. 'Good lad,' she said fondly.

'Who's a good lad?' asked Rosa as she came into the kitchen followed by Igress and Fran.

'Gussie,' said Mrs B proudly.

'We knew that already,' said Igress, walking over and assuming the shoulder-hugging responsibility as Mrs B vacated the post to pour more tea. Gussie smiled.

Fran winked at him. 'Didn't think you meant Mason, Mrs B,' she said. 'He doesn't qualify as either good or lad.'

Gussie chuckled. Mason looked daggers at him.

'Which is why,' added Rosa, 'I've found a good lad to be your labourer.'

'And why do I need a labourer, your ladyship?'

'Because you and labour appear to be strangers.'

Mason snorted.

Gussie laughed. 'It'll be all right, Mr Mason. You'll get on well with Aidan.'

'Who said anything about Aidan?' asked Rosa.

'But you said... oh, now wait a minute... you don't mean...'

'I do.'

'Me?!' squealed Gussie.

Mason's eyebrows raised as he pointed at Gussie. 'Him?'

Gussie frowned. 'And what's wrong with me?'

'Can you do heavy work? I'm not employing you unless you

can do heavy work. Building's all heavy work.'

'You're not employing him,' said Rosa, 'I am. Gussie has enormous strength but needs to tone up his muscles so we thought he could do a bit of weightlifting for you.'

'What?' said Gussie.

'Weightlifting?' said Mason.

'Fetching and carrying stone for you,' explained Igress.

'Now hang on...' said Gussie.

'You need to build up your strength,' said Rosa, 'and Mason needs to finish the West Wing Tower. It's perfect.'

Mason disagreed. 'He's still not working with me.'

'Why not?'

'He's not wearing overalls.'

'Look again,' said Fran, and all eyes turned towards Gussie, now clad in a sludgy-brown all-in-one.

'Oh!' he wailed. 'Where's Mr Beaton senior's suit gone?'

'In your wardrobe, flower,' Fran reassured him. 'Don't fret.'

'Still no good,' said Mason.

'Because?' asked Rosa, her manner suggesting that somewhere a fuse was burning.

'Them's dancing shoes. He needs proper boots with reinforced toes. And gloves. Health and safety, y'know. Wear and tear on your hands. Sharp edges, rough ropes, wood splinters, grazes, cuts, friction burns.'

'That'll be the day when you move fast enough to cause any friction,' said Rosa.

'Boots and gloves,' said Fran.

Gussie looked at his feet with horror, then at his hands, now encased in stout, tan leather gloves with wide fingers and wrist-hugging orange knitted welts. His mouth dropped open.

'Awww, you are joking, aren't you? My godfathers, I've seen sausages with better tailoring than these!'

'Satisfied, Mason?' asked Rosa.

'I'm not, your ladyship.'

'He's got overalls, boots and gloves,' said Igress, 'what more do you want? Blood?'

'That's what I'm worried about, miss.'

'Sorry?'

'I'm worried that blood could come spurting out of his head if he had an accident. Stonework doesn't have to move too far or too fast to cause injury, specially to the head.'

'He'll be perfectly safe with you then,' said Rosa. 'The stonework hasn't moved at all since you got here.'

'He needs a helmet, your ladyship. I mean, what'd happen if he got his head stove in by some falling stonework?'

Rosa rested her knuckles on the table and leant across to the builder.

'In that case, Mason,' she hissed, 'we'd just sew him another one on.'

The gods who normally damned Rudolf must have taken the afternoon off and forgotten to leave clear instructions, for whoever was in charge of luck poured their beneficence upon him unceasingly, and his winning streak was only stopped by the end of the racing. A succession of outsiders and one extreme long-shot had resulted in a bulging moneybag.

'Here, Yedder,' he sneered, handing over two gold pieces, 'your original stake money. Your precious conscience is clear.'

'Top hole, Rude,' said Yedder. 'Well done.'

'Congratulations,' said Guildman. 'A tidy sum.'

'More than tidy. Enough to get that harpy out of the castle.'

'Indeed. We'd better start making plans.'

'Tomorrow. I have... things to do tonight,' Rudolf leered.

Yedder winked knowingly.

'Going to see a man about a dog, eh?'

'Yes. And tomorrow, I'll see a dwarf about a bitch.'

In the laboratory, the large sheets of paper on which Rosa and Fran were detailing the next stages of Gussie's training rustled as the door opened to admit Sooty.

'Rosa,' he said, 'you'd best sit down. I've got something—'

'Look at the colour of you!' interrupted Fran. 'Where the hell have you been?'

'For a walk,' Sooty replied, his tone rising to match the incipient hysteria.

'Where? Up a chimney? Look at the state of you!'

'I went to the Dog Flog.'

'The Dog Flog?!'

'Aunty...' said Rosa.

Fran's voice was so squeaky she was in danger of being heard only by passing bats.

'You went to the Dog Flog?! Have you forgotten you're a cat? Dogs chase cats, you stupid animal!'

'And have you forgotten that I'm no ordinary cat, you stupid woman?!'

Fran's mouth dropped open.

Rosa tried again. 'Sootbags...'

'And even if the dogs had've chased me – which they didn't – at least it would've meant that *somebody* wants me!'

He ran out of the laboratory. It could have been a gust of wind that slammed the door behind him, but it wasn't.

The bell-pull had seen this drunk many times, and it put up as much resistance as it could when Rudolf tugged it almost out of the wall. However, it was only a bell-pull and it had a function to fulfil, distasteful or not. It jangled its folk-tune bells and shrank back into its socket. The door opened and stopped short on its safety chain. Rudolf stuck his foot in the gap.

'Go away. I'm busy,' hissed Millie, tightening the silk belt of her dressing-gown.

'Not too busy for me, Mills.'

She stamped on his foot. 'I'm too busy for paupers.'

'Ow! I'm not a pauper, look – I've got money!'

Rudolf held out a gold coin. Millie reached out but Rudolf whipped it away from her grasp. 'Ah-ah. Got to let me in first.'

'Please yourself.'

Rudolf smiled as she shut the door in his face. Both he and the door held their positions for a full two minutes before one of them cracked.

He knocked on the door.

Millie opened it on the safety chain and held out her palm. Rudolf placed the coin in it, and Millie withdrew her hand and closed the door again. When she reopened it, there was no sign of the coin.

'Get in here!' she snarled.

Rudolf tried to put his arms round her as he entered the

house, but his only welcome was a smack across the face.

Millie shoved him into a side room which was decorated very plainly, the only relief from the unrelenting magnolia colour being the interesting variety of instruments of torture hanging on the walls plus the occasional bloodstain.

She pushed him onto a hard wooden chair; he landed on his bee-sting and yelped. She slapped him. 'Hands and feet,' she ordered, taking two leather straps from the wall.

Rudolf meekly allowed her to buckle him up at the wrists and ankles and lash him to the chair with a rope.

'Oh, Mills,' he sighed.

She slapped him again. 'Quiet! I'm with another client.'

'Another client? Oh, Mills, let me watch. Can I watch?'

'No, you can't watch,' she said with unconcealed disgust as she walked towards the door, 'but you can listen.'

He heard her climb the stairs, and shortly afterwards he was tugging ineffectually at his bindings as sounds which stirred up his envy and lust tortured him in his helplessness.

'Cow!' he yelled, and the syllable floated upstairs to where a scrawny individual clad in grubby vest and shorts jumped up and down on a bed, uttering cries of sexual ecstasy that indicated a long history of fruit abuse.

Millie controlled the scrawny man's actions with a whip and a well-developed wrist, occasionally flicking him if it seemed that enthusiasm was waning. This she did from the comfort of an armchair several feet away from the scrawny man, as she delicately picked at an assortment of fine quality chocolates and devoured the latest available work of romantic fiction.

The clunk of a heavy latch rang out, causing those nocturnals who snuffled and scratched in dark corners to pause and test the air with twitching noses and trembling antennae. Creaking hinges heralded the exit into the night of a butler and a gangly youth, whose dancing golden torch flames overran the moonlight that silverwashed the back courtyard at Castle Stein.

'Fetch the handcart, Aidan,' said Beaton.

Aidan's footsteps echoed across the yard – not as crisply as Beaton would have liked – but on the return journey, they were masked by the rumbling of the handcart.

A tarpaulin swished and the loose end of a thick rope bobbled behind it as Beaton cleared the flat bed of the cart. He and Aidan went back into the castle only to re-emerge carrying a bundle resembling a gift-wrapped headless statue holding a cannonball. They loaded it onto the cart along with a long thin cane and a spade then lashed the tarpaulin over it. Beaton checked the knots as Aidan wedged the flaming torches into iron hoops on the side of the cart.

'Right. Close the door,' said Beaton.

Aidan almost fell over a streak of fur that shot out of the castle and leapt onto the cart.

'Thought you were going without me there, Mr Beaton,' panted Sooty.

'Certainly not, Master Sooty.'

Aidan heaved on the door. The hinges grated and creaked again. 'Mr Beaton, shall I put some oil on the door hinges?'

'For what purpose?' asked Beaton.

'To stop that creaking. So it doesn't disturb people.'

'Ah,' said Sooty, 'but the whole point of having a creaking

door is so you know when people are coming in and out. You don't want the likes of Rudolf sneaking in the back way and you not being able to hear them, do you?'

'Er... I suppose not,' conceded Aidan.

'Lesson learnt,' said Beaton. 'Come along. Let's go.'

Sooty turned to face the front of the cart, drew back one ghostly white paw and thrust it forward. 'Wagons roll!'

The torches cast nervous shadows as the three comrades in clandestineness trundled the cart across the courtyard, their progress watched by a solitary figure who by rights should have been in a sleep much deeper than the foundations of the castle.

Gussie was tired to the very bones he'd been given, and ordinarily would not have been able to rise from his bed for a king's ransom. But something tugged at his soul and denied him rest, pushing him on through the maze of corridors and stairs until he leant against the cold stone framework of a window overlooking the courtyard, responding to whatever call of the spirit compelled him to witness the night's events.

Instinct guided his hand to the glass, urging him to make his farewell for the peace of his soul. His heart cried out for intervention, but his mind told him it would be worse than useless. As the deepest shadows of the night took the cart from sight, he was left with only faint remembrances of what had been, and no hope of return. He knew that the memory of this misery would be his alone to carry for ever; desolation overwhelmed him, and he wept the most anguished of all his life's tears until his tortured body gave him release and he slumped to the floor.

The threats that streamed up the stairs disturbed the scrawny man not at all; on the contrary, at the thought of arousing another man's ire, he capered about on the bed with renewed vigour, shouting unfulfilled demands which would have both gladdened and unsettled the heart of any wholesale fruiterer.

However, Rudolf's bellowing of what he'd do once Millie untied him broke her concentration on her reading. She clapped the book shut, rose from the chair, removed her dressing gown and hung it up in the wardrobe. When the scrawny man caught sight of her traditional costume, he immediately stopped cavorting and calling for fruit.

'Keep going,' said Millie, taking an extremely long red silk scarf from the back of the door. 'This is extra.'

She looped one end of the scarf under her breasts and threaded the other end around her body – over each shoulder, around her waist and between her thighs, not quite fully covering the parts other scarves don't even reach. She threw the loose end back over her shoulder.

'I'll pay,' wheezed the scrawny man.

'You can't afford it,' she replied.

Downstairs, Rudolf continued to express his envy and lust as loudly as he could until Millie entered the room and walloped the back of his head.

'Shut it!' she commanded.

'Make me.'

'Oh, I will.'

She stood in front of him, close enough for him to see every detail of her body but just out of reach, even though he was strapped up. She waited for a few moments, making sure his eyes drank in all her possibilities, and when she knew he was concentrating she tugged the scarf sharply, releasing both her breasts from her corset.

Rudolf's eyes came out almost as far as her chest and he choked on air he didn't even know he'd been breathing.

Millie pulled the scarf and the red silk snaked round her body, mesmerising Rudolf, who quickly concentrated on that tiny triangle of space at the top of her thighs through which the majority of the scarf had to pass. He squealed as she brandished the scarf above her head and swayed towards him.

'Oh, Mills,' he beamed. 'You're the—'

Further communication was suspended as Millie forced the scarf across his mouth, wound it round his head a few more times for good luck, and tied it tightly.

'Nnnnn?' said Rudolf.

Millie undid the rope that lashed Rudolf to the chair. She looped it over the strap binding his wrists and under the one binding his ankles; when she pulled it tight his hands hit his feet and his chest hit his knees. She secured the rope with a complicated knot.

'Nnnnnn!'

Ignoring his moaning, Millie walked behind Rudolf's chair and tilted it forwards, pitching him on to the floor.

'Nnnnnnnnnnnnn!' he muffled-yelled as she walked out and closed the door.

Back upstairs, the scrawny man sat on the bed. He looked up in hope as Millie re-entered the bedroom.

'You haven't the price,' she said, opening the wardrobe and putting her dressing gown back on. She sat in the armchair and picked up her book, looked at the scrawny man and flicked him viciously with the whip. 'Get on with it!'

At Dafferd Hill burial ground, Sooty leapt from the cart.

'Coo-ee!' he sang. There was no reply. 'Boggis, you half-hearted excuse for a Burial Keeper, where are you?'

In the darkness, something far darker tutted.

'Tch! This used to be such a quiet place to live. The neighbourhood's gone to wrack and ruin since certain people started showing their face.'

'At least my face is worth seeing,' Sooty retorted, shortly before a black paw cuffed him round the ear. He swiped out into the blackness, but disturbed only night air.

'I'm surprised to see it so soon,' said Boggis. 'You've not come for another, have you?'

Sooty laughed. 'On the contrary – we've brought one back.'

'Brought one back? I'm not sure that's allowed. We don't operate on a sale or return basis, you know.'

'No, but you did give us two for one last time whether we wanted it or not.'

Boggis sniffed. 'Fair enough.'

They walked along the wall until they drew level with a patch of ground that had been turned so many times it was in danger of being classed as a whirlpool.

'You're sure you're not going to want this one back again?' said Boggis. 'It's just that the worms are getting dizzy.'

Both of them giggled, and were still chuckling when Aidan and Beaton carried their burden across the grass.

Moonlight illuminated the misshapen shroud, and Sooty

could not tear his eyes away as it was lowered into the grave.

'Blimey!' said Boggis. 'What kind of poor soul is that?'

Sooty's heart twinged with unease. 'He's... they're... it's...
'I'll see you around, Boggis,' he said quietly.

'In daylight hours, next time, eh?' quipped Boggis, but his
old friend had already walked away.

In a sleep hastened on by several small sherries, Fran dreamt
of the days when her hair was black, her limbs were supple and
she could get both arms around the waist of a certain young
man with no shirt on.

The Spirit of Co-operation was, to quote from *The Book of
Procedures Volume III – The Procedure of Graduation*, 'a Spiritual
Essence housed, for the Purposes of Convenience, within the
Body of a Cat'. And he was as broadminded, friendly, open
and honest as the next spiritual essence. Indeed, his mind was
a good deal broader than some other familiars, chiefly because
he'd been assigned to many a witch during all his lifetimes, and
consequently there was very little left that could perturb him.

Except, of course, himself.

As he'd watched Beaton and Aidan lower the bundle into
the grave, Sooty had sensed a wrong, and he could no more
ignore it than he could a thorn in his paw. But if someone had
asked him where the trouble was, he'd have pointed to his
chest, where he experienced the almost physical feeling of
something niggling at his heart.

And so padding through the castle, ostensibly in search of
echoes of old friends long departed or hints of new mischief,

was a familiar with a bad case of irrational emotional indigestion.

So deep in thought was he that, although he didn't know where he was going, he knew when he'd got there, because he walked head-first into it. 'Oh, sorry,' he said automatically, before raising his head to find out what he'd bumped into. Even as his hackles rose when he saw it was the prone Gussie, a small voice inside him told him he was overreacting.

'It's all right,' he sighed, 'you can open your eyes. I'm not going to bite you.'

Gussie did not respond.

'Please yourself,' said Sooty. 'If that's your attitude, I'm off. I'm not mucking about here playing dead dogs with you.'

He walked away, but with each step he took, his indigestion grew until he thought his heart would burst. He stopped, wheeled around and retraced his steps. 'Look, I think we might have got off on the wrong foot, so I— well, the least you could do is open your eyes when I'm talking to you!'

Gussie did not flicker.

Sooty reached out and pushed his paw into Gussie's cheek. The skin rucked up under the pressure, and slid back into place when he took his paw away, but there was no other reaction. Sooty ran.

'Rosa!'

His night's work finished, a couple of Beaton Specials took Aidan to a dreamland where he threw open the doors of a packed Lamb and Werewolf, the crowd parting in deference as he strode to the bar. An overflowing tankard was slammed on the counter by a barmaid with a well-aired, gravity-defying bosom; as beer slopped over the side of the tankard, she scooped up the escaping foam with her finger, which she lifted to her mouth and sucked provocatively. It was Igress.

Rosa crouched and felt Gussie's cheek.

'Gussie! Gussie! Can you hear me?'

Deep in the heartlands of sleep Gussie shouted a reply, but he was so far away that by the time his cry reached the real world, it had diminished to a barely audible 'Mm'.

Rosa lifted one of his hands. It carried the cold of stone slabs but not the chill of death. 'I think he's just very, very, very fast asleep. But he'll catch his death if... I mean he'll freeze, lying on the floor. I'll go get some bedding; you snuggle up to him and give him a bit more body heat.'

'What?!'

'Do as you're told. He's cold, you're warm, so lie on top of him and warm him up a bit.'

'But you're bigger than me and you're warm — why can't you do it?'

'For all sorts of reasons.'

'Such as?'

'Such as... can you carry eiderdowns, blankets and pillows?'

'No...'

'Then shut up and lie down.'

'But what if he starts sneezing?'

'Listen, he's so far gone that he wouldn't sneeze if I stuffed you up his nose, which I might well do if you don't lie down.'

Half a bottle of wine ensured that Igress slept soundly if not quietly, reliving the moment when she threw beer over Rudolf. Except instead of running away, she kicked him half to death on the floor of the Lamb and Werewolf, then stretched out on the bar and let Guildman pour champagne all over her body.

Tottering up the corridor was a headless mass of bedding held together by two arms whose interlocked fingers would have twanged apart upon the insertion of one more feather.

'Stop!' called Sooty, before Rosa fell over the prostrate Gussie. The bedding landed on the floor with a muffled thud.

'How's he doing?' asked Rosa.

'Much the same, really.'

Rosa folded two eiderdowns together and laid them along Gussie's right-hand side.

'You can get down now. We're going to turn him over.'

'Us? We can't lift him. Shall I fetch Mr Beaton?'

'No. I'm not disturbing Mr and Mrs B at night – they work hard enough during the day as it is. Come on, we can do this.'

Rosa knelt by Gussie, put his left arm by his side and his right hand under the left-hand side of his face.

'It's all a question of weights' – she straightened his left leg and bent the right one until the knee pointed to the ceiling – 'and pivots.'

She gripped his knee and shoulder and heaved; Gussie's back slowly came up off the floor and Rosa tilted him over until he was balanced against her thighs.

'Now,' she said, 'push those quilts into his back.'

Sooty did as he was told and Rosa lowered Gussie onto the

eiderdowns. She stepped over him and tilted him over on his other side, Sooty helped her to pull out the folds of the quilts and she laid Gussie back on his new mattress.

'Right,' she said. 'I'll go get some more bedding.'

Soon Gussie's body had vanished in a mound of blankets, and his head, topped with a nightcap, rested on a couple of pillows. Sooty, under orders, lay next to him.

Rosa picked something up off the floor.

'A hot-water bottle?' said Sooty. 'At your age?'

Rosa pushed the bottle under the covers towards Gussie.

'Why not?' she said. 'I like to be kept warm at night.'

Sooty chuckled. 'I know someone who wants that job and you wouldn't have to fill him up with hot water every night.'

'I'm not going through witch training up at The Union to adopt you just because you've fallen out with Aunty Fran.'

'I wasn't talking about me.'

Rosa brushed the blankets straight with her hand in short bursts. 'That makes a change.'

'Me-ow,' said Sooty, rucking up the top blanket with his front paws. 'Anyway, wouldn't you rather have a hot Guildman than a hot bottle?'

She slapped at his paws and smoothed the blanket again.

'Stop trying to take your mind off your troubles by putting mine on mine.'

'Guildman doesn't look like he'd bring you any trouble.'

Rosa sat on the bedding, pulling a spare blanket around her.

'There's trouble and there's trouble. And you never know who's going to bring you trouble until they do.'

Had anyone been watching Guildman as he slept, they'd have seen him smile his long, slow smile, and would have been in no doubt as to what he was dreaming about, and would have marvelled that he was able to dream what he wanted.

'He's not a monster, you know,' said Rosa.

'Guildman? I never said he was,' replied Sooty.

Rosa prodded him through several layers of blanket.

'You know who I'm talking about.'

Sooty wrinkled his nose. 'Yes, well... I don't want to talk about it.' He turned his head sniffily to one side.

'You need to talk about it. And if I have to go get half a dozen Beaton Specials to get you to talk about it I will. But I'd rather not because I don't want any earache from Aunty in the morning about leading you astray.'

Sooty lifted his head. 'Oh, go on... let's have one at least.'

'Start talking and I'll think about it.'

He let his head flop back on the pillow. 'Typical.'

'I'm waiting,' said Rosa, 'and so is your drink.'

Sooty sighed. 'The first time I met him, I was all nice and friendly, and before you know where you are he's shouting and bawling and sneezing like there's no tomorrow.'

'He can't help being allergic to you.'

'I can't help being been allergic to. Do I get my drink now?'

Rosa folded her arms. 'You've got to do better than that.'

Sooty scowled. 'The next thing was, my mistress was flat out on the floor and he was – he was – standing over her.'

'He didn't hit her, she fainted.'

'It's a bit of coincidence that she fainted right at that

particular moment, don't you think?'

'Aunty Fran said she fainted, and I believe her. You've only to talk to him to see he wouldn't hurt her; he wouldn't hurt anything. He's scared of most things, including you.'

'Oh, yes – a huge great bloke like him's scared of a cat.'

'It's only his body that's huge. His brain still thinks he's little and weedy and liable to be picked on, particularly by people he's upset, like you.'

'I'm not people.'

'But you are upset.'

'I think I've every right to be.'

'As long as you're upset with the right people for the right reasons.'

'And you don't think your monster's given me a good enough reason?'

Rosa prodded him again. 'Stop calling him "monster". His name's Gussie. And no, I don't think he's given you a good enough reason, and neither do you or else you wouldn't have legged it half-way round the castle to tell me he was out cold.'

Mr Beaton and Mrs B passed the night in the brewhouse making Beaton Special. They had no need of sleep, being in a state of animated suspension after an accident at The Union some generations ago. They were at their daughter's graduation ceremony when a wayward spell cast by a third-year student blew the doors off the Globe Hall and sent a light ball careering through the gathering. Afterwards, those it touched found themselves never ailing and never ageing, becoming by default the keepers of the history of Maund because they were the only ones old enough to remember what the place was like before it was ruined by Town Council improvement schemes.

Sooty pawed at the blanket as he searched for the right words.

'At the cemetery tonight... it seemed so sad and... dismal. Oh, I don't know, not much to show for a life, really... such a... pathetic bundle. Nobody to mourn him, nobody to miss him. Boggis said that first time round he – they – were just chucked in the hole. Said it wasn't so much a burial as a get rid of.'

'Oh.'

'And I felt... oh, all right, I felt sorry for him. Nobody should be that... anonymous... unloved, I suppose.'

'Particularly when some of us are so well-loved?'

He said nothing, but swallowed hard.

Rosa gently stroked one of his ears. 'Come on. It doesn't take a genius to know what's really troubling you.'

Sooty began to lick her hand frantically, but broke out into sobs. She lifted him from the bedding and held him to her.

'It – it was when they started – started lowering the body into the grave,' he choked. 'And I saw... I saw that's what'll happen. I saw that's what'll happen to her, and... and I knew... I *know*... it won't be too long in coming.'

'Oh, Sootbags. She's not going unmourned and unloved.'

'No, but she is going. I'm losing her, Rosa. I'm losing her and there's nothing I can do about it.'

She held him tightly and kissed the top of his head.

'Let's go,' she whispered, her voice breaking. 'It's time for you and me to drown our sorrows.'

Across town, in a sumptuous four-poster bed festooned with rich velvet drapes exquisitely embroidered in fine gold thread, Lady Yedder lay with her head on soft silk-covered pillows and dreamt of parties and picnics. At her back, exactly matching the contours of her body, slept her husband. They were as close as two spoons in a cutlery drawer, and Yedder draped his arm protectively over his wife and dreamt only of her.

There's a time in most households when beers and tears flow in equal measure, and so it was for a while that night in Castle Stein. The talk was deep, rambling and progressively less coherent, suppositions grew wilder and proposed courses of action ever more unworkable.

And during the long night, somewhere between the wee small hours and 'bloody hell, is that the time?', the pain of the impending parting was anaesthetised sufficiently for Sooty and Rosa to wander unsteadily through the castle to their respective destinations.

Rosa flopped into her bed, reached for one of the remaining pillows and cuddled it. A childish grin spread across her face as a vision of Guildman swam before her eyes and she and descended into happy oblivion.

Sooty's route took him to a mound of bedding. He patted at a pillow, testing every place where he would place his paws as he tottered towards the earhole of the sleeping figure. He swayed unsteadily as he spoke.

'Now listen. Me and you haven't been seeing eye to eye, and I think maybe we should.'

As he lifted one paw to emphasise his point, he lost his

balance. His legs buckled under him and he slid down the pillow, ending up in between layers of bedding.

'Oh, buggrit,' he slurred. 'Talk about it tomorrow.'

Rudolf spent the night on the floor at Millie's. Unfortunately for him, this arrangement seemed to completely slip Millie's mind until the following morning.

Sooty was awakened by a violent shaking.

'And what d'you think you're doing?' hissed a voice.

Sooty opened his mouth to speak, and once he'd managed to prise his tongue from his palate, yawned as widely as he could in the hope that fresh air might make his tongue taste better.

'Yeugh... oh, who's been sleeping in my mouth?'

'Are you drunk?'

'I'm sure bits of me still are.' He opened his eyes. 'Oh, it's you. Wassup?'

'What the hell are you playing at?' said Fran, hauling him out of the blankets. 'Go back to your own bed!'

'Wha— wha— what's going on?' he flailed as she plonked him on the cold floor.

'If he wakes up next to you he's going to start sneezing again. Now go on – off you go.'

Sooty rolled his eyes. 'Oh fine. Thanks for your concern. Don't let me come between you and wonder boy.'

'His condition probably isn't self-inflicted.'

'Meaning?'

'Meaning he hasn't spent half the night on the booze!'

'He doesn't need to, does he?' Sooty bit back. 'He's got you fussing over him all the time.' He started to walk away.

'You come back here and explain yourself!'

'No! You've told me to go and I'm going. Goodnight – good morning – whatever flaming time it is. Who cares?'

Fran glared after him, turned sharply and set off for the kitchen. Halfway down the stairs, she met Aidan coming up.

'Morning, Mistress Stein. Mrs B said you might need this.'

Aidan was staggering under the weight of a tray containing two full breakfasts under silver domes plus teapot, milk jug, assorted cutlery, one china mug and one stoneware mug.

'Oh, excellent!' said Fran. She led Aidan up the stairs and through the corridors to where Gussie lay, still sleeping.

'Why isn't he in his room?' asked Aidan.

'He's had some sort of collapse.'

'Oh, no,' said Aidan with genuine dismay. 'Does that mean we've got to go back to the cemetery and get another one?'

Fran's mouth opened, but no words came out for a few seconds as she realised where Aidan's main worry lay.

'Er... no, Aidan, you won't have to go back.'

He brightened considerably. 'Oh, good.'

'Pop the tray on that window-sill. We'll bring it down when we've finished. Run along now and thank Mrs B.'

'Right you are, Mistress.' He skipped off.

Fran sat on the window-sill next to the tray, drinking a mug of tea as she contemplated the prone figure under the mound of bedding. At length she turned her attention to her breakfast, and as she lifted the silver dome from her plate, Gussie stirred and sighed.

'Is that true what he said?' he asked quietly. 'The bit about getting me from the cemetery?'

Fran replaced the dome.

'What's it matter? You're here now.'

'Everybody should know where they come from, otherwise how do you know how far you've gone?'

This time it was Fran who sighed. 'Yes. It's true.'

'I was dead, now I'm alive again.'

'Yes.'

'And this really is my life now. I live here, amongst you lot. After all, I do seem to keep waking up here.'

'I know it's difficult to grasp...'

'No. A slimy eel is difficult to grasp. Some people's choice of spouse is difficult to grasp. This is something else entirely.'

Fran scratched her head. 'Couldn't you just... stop trying to reason it out and... and look on it as a chance to... to be somebody else, live someone else's life, and do all the things that you couldn't do in your own life?'

Gussie put his head on one side and thought for a moment.

'Are there big meals involved?'

Fran lifted the domes from the breakfast tray.

In Fran's bedroom, the cold stone flags were too harsh for Sooty; he needed somewhere soft for his aching body and breaking heart to drown in. There was only one place to go, and for him there was only one way to get there.

He stared at the ottoman at the foot of the bed for some time, each passing moment reminding him that if he'd only had the courage to risk the jump, he'd have been in bed by now, fast asleep and getting better with every snore. But knowing in your heart of hearts what the right course of action is and actually wanting to do it are two very different things. Sooty's heart of hearts told him to leap onto the ottoman – 'It'll all be over in a second and you'll feel much better' – whilst his experience said, 'Jump up there and your brain'll thud against your skull like a wet sponge.'

Heart of Hearts said, 'Go on. It's lovely and soft up there. You'll be in dreamland in no time.'

Experience said, 'Always assuming you don't misjudge it and slam into the footboard.'

'You've done it loads of times and not hit the footboard.'

'You've never done it with a hangover like this before.'

Experience was settling in for a long toe-to-toe stand-off, but Heart of Hearts was getting fed up and kicked Sooty up the backside. He leapt onto the ottoman. He didn't hit the footboard but his brain did thud against his skull like a wet sponge, so Experience danced away claiming victory as Sooty closed his eyes and moaned.

He clambered over the footboard and shambled up the bed, leaving indentations in the recently straightened coverlet and wishing he'd got a spare paw to hold to his head. Laid against the pillows was Cecil, the small, honey-coloured teddy bear with the fading red ribbon and the raggy ear.

Sooty sank into the bed, dragged Cecil into a tight hug and chewed on the raggy ear. His body and his heart already hurt too much to cry himself to sleep, so he closed his eyes, blocking out the world until his dreams became his reality.

Gussie put the much lighter breakfast tray by the kitchen sink.

'Did you have enough to eat, my dear?' asked Mrs B.

'I should think he did,' Fran chipped in. 'He had half of mine as well as his own.'

Mrs B laughed and put a plate of biscuits on the kitchen table. 'Aw, he's a growing lad, aren't you, Gussie?'

'If he grows any more we'll have to have the doors widened.'

'Oh, w— excuse him,' said Gussie, taking his place at the table, 'but it's not his fault he's put on an awful lot of weight very recently, is it?'

He reached out and took a biscuit.

Fran slapped his hand. 'It'll be his fault if he gets that fat he can't move about, won't it?'

Gussie stuck his tongue out at her then bit the biscuit, grinning mischievously.

Mrs B ruffled his hair and went to wash up.

'Which is why,' Fran said, moving the biscuits out of his way, 'we're adding extra training to his fitness regime.'

'What?' said Gussie, spraying crumbs onto the table.

'You heard,' said Fran. 'You're here to be a bodyguard, and for that you've got to be fit. You need to get back into shape.'

'This wasn't my shape to start with.'

'Well it is now. And you're going to look after it, and that means training.'

He looked at her petulantly and chewed what was left of his biscuit in a marked manner before reaching over and taking two more biscuits.

'I can't go training. I haven't got any training gear.'

'Not a problem,' said Fran, taking a biscuit for herself. 'You're already going to be lifting weights, shifting stone for Mason; we'll get you a length of rope for your skipping routine, and I'm sure Beaton could rig you up a punchbag.'

'Not equipment,' said Gussie, 'clothes.'

Fran rolled not just her eyes but her whole head. 'Clothes? Again? You're obsessed with having the right clothes!'

'I'm not obsessed! I'm *supposed* to be interested in clothes. I'm a tailor!'

'Not any more.'

'My hands might not be but my head is.'

'Then I'll get you a hat!' She chomped her biscuit angrily.

'Listen, fishface,' he said, wagging a fat finger at her. 'Has it occurred to you that one of the reasons I might be interested in clothes is the fact that I don't have any of my own?'

For the first time, Fran looked at Gussie the outward image of Gussie the person she'd been talking to. 'Ah.'

He pulled at his clothes. 'This is one of Mrs B's old nighties, and this is one of her old dressing-gowns. The gods only know whose nightcap this is and the socks came with that awful labourer's outfit. Apart from that, I have Mr Beaton senior's best dress uniform and I am not going to ruin that by running about in it.'

'All right,' Fran conceded, 'you've made your point. We'll get you some more clothes.'

'Thank you. But I'm still not going training.'

'What? Why not?'

Gussie snatched the rest of Fran's biscuit and ate it.

'Can't go training on a full stomach.'

'And how would you know?'

'Call it my sporting intuition,' he smiled.

'I didn't think tailors had any sporting intuition.'

'Ah,' he said. 'You're forgetting – I'm seventy-five percent boxer.'

Fran's lip curled.

'Aye, and twenty-five percent terrier, apparently.'

'Not at all, Rigsy?' asked Yedder as the landlord of the Lamb and Werewolf filled two tankards.

'Not at all, my lord.'

'Damn me, Gil. Rude never came back last night.'

'Really, Yedder?' said Guildman. 'And he was carrying such a lot of money. Where *could* he have gone?'

'I say, Rigsy – not wishing to be rude, old thing, but you don't think your good lady might be losing her touch a tad?'

Such a slur on the landlady's talents from a lesser man would have earned the utterer a swift half round the head, but Rigton was, on this occasion, the very model of restraint.

'My lord?'

'I mean, damned fine woman and all that, but...'

'But not enough to satisfy Rudolf, it seems,' Guildman finished.

Rigton put the two tankards on the bar.

'Rest assured, my lords, Mrs Rigton is working flat out.'

'We would expect nothing less,' said Guildman, as Yedder flipped a coin to the landlord, 'but possibly something more.'

Rigton caught the coin with an easy grace and a glad heart as the street door opened and across the floor slurred the feet of the most bad-tempered aristocrat ever to be bent double in the cause of pleasure and unable to straighten up afterwards.

'Bath! Hot!' Rudolf called.

'Yes, my lord.'

Knees bent, elbows stuck out as he clamped his hands to his bowed back, Rudolf swayed from side to side as he shuffled across the parlour.

'I say, Gil – a talking turkey!'

'One that's been trussed up all night, Yedder.'

'Sod off,' snarled Rudolf, without breaking his shuffle.

'From that cheerful greeting, may I take it that you will not be joining us today?' asked Guildman.

'Yes, you can take it, and you can shove it, Guildman.'

Guildman's face broke into a grin that Rudolf didn't see on account of his head being level with Guildman's waist.

'Yedder and I will have to amuse ourselves, then.'

'You usually do,' snapped Rudolf, hobbling over to the door that led to the stairs. There were several blind thumps until he located the door handle. He held the door open for a few seconds. 'And I want a massage, Rigton.'

'My lord.'

'And beer!'

The door closed behind Rudolf, and halting thuds indicated that he was crawling upstairs on all fours.

'Now, where were we?' said Guildman.

'I believe we were discussing Mrs Rigton's contribution to the welfare and happiness of her fellow man, Gil.'

Rigton polished the bar around their tankards. 'My lords were asking if Mrs Rigton could provide... something more.'

'Something more like that we've just seen,' said Yedder, perfectly aping Rudolf's shambling gait.

Guildman slowly pushed a gold coin across the counter.

'Tell your good lady to buy herself something. Something...'

'Something more?' suggested Rigton.

'Or less,' smiled Guildman.

Gussie opened the wardrobe door and caught his breath. Fran had been as good as her word.

Shirts, ranging from short-sleeved silk to long-sleeved brushed cotton, accompanied trousers – short, long, casual, formal and working. Lightweight jackets draped against heavyweight jumpers. There were overcoats and underwear, shoes, socks, pumps and slippers. It was a large wardrobe and as full as Gussie's heart, which overflowed when he saw a small wooden sewing box beside his footwear. His face crumpled.

'What's up now?' said Fran. 'What have I forgotten?'

'Nothing,' whimpered Gussie. Tears started to trickle down his face as he touched the clothes. 'It is all real, isn't it?'

'Yes, it's real. What kind of a witch do you think I am?'

Gussie sniffled. 'I was thinking of that story – you know, about the girl who wants to go to the ball and she hasn't got anything to wear and the fairy godmother comes along—'

'Fairy godmother?' Fran bristled. 'I am way past fairy frigging godmother, I'll have you know! This lot's not going to disappear at midnight, matey.'

Gussie gathered up some of the shirt sleeves and buried his face in them.

'Oh, thank you, thank you. They're wonderful.'

'Yes, well,' said Fran, somewhat placated. 'You'd better get changed if we're going out.'

Gussie cheered up visibly. 'Going out? Where?'

'For a walk. You can walk on a full stomach, can't you?'

Gussie beamed.

'Oh, yes, yes – I just need to decide what to wear.'

'I've already taken the liberty,' Fran said, pointing towards the bed.

Gussie picked up a pair of floppy dark trousers, elasticated at the waist and ankles. Underneath lay a dark sweater, elasticated at the welt and cuffs, complete with a hood through which ran a white drawstring. Beneath that was a pair of white socks and black pumps with thick rubber soles.

Reluctance spread across his face. 'Do I have to?'

'What's wrong with them?' asked Fran.

'Nothing in themselves,' said Gussie. 'I just hope nobody sees me wearing them, that's all.'

Repeated clanks and thuds announced that a tin bath was being dragged up the staircase at the Lamb and Werewolf. At the top of the stairs a door whined open, followed by the muffled scrape of the bath being pushed across a bedroom floor.

The only two customers in the parlour waited to hear Mrs Rigton's footsteps come clonking back down the uncarpeted treads. However, the succession of shuffles and rhythmical thuds and creaks indicated that she was occupied with the non-food aspect of bed-and-breakfast, and it would be a while before Rudolf's bath was anywhere near ready.

Yedder drained his tankard and rubbed his hands together.

'So, Gil, the day's our own. How shall we spend it?'

'Well, Yedder,' said Guildman, stroking his beard, 'if I were an aristocrat who'd been thrown out of what I considered to be *my* castle, and I were trying to get my castle back, I'd expect my friends to help me in any way they could.'

Yedder's eyes lit up.

'By, perhaps, doing a reccy on that particular castle?'

'A fine idea. But first – a small detour.'

'Detour, old love?'

'Rudolf now has the money to attack Rosalind. We must ensure that he doesn't use it.'

The panel behind the grille in the oak door slid back.

'Welcome to Top Chop,' said the dwarf behind the door.

Yedder didn't understand what Guildman said but the effect was obvious. Seventeen locks were released and the door was opened before Guildman had finished speaking.

He and Yedder ducked through into the courtyard. The dwarf on the platform built onto the back of the door bowed and pointed.

'Gil?'

'Yes, Yedder?'

'My Dwarfish... a tad rusty.'

Guildman smiled. 'I told them I brought greetings to the clan, respect to the overlord and gold to the executioners.'

'Oh.'

'And I enquired how much they charge to murder a member of the aristocracy.'

Mrs B was putting some recently baked goodies into a large wicker basket that sat on a pile of folded-up empty flour sacks on a counter in the kitchen at Castle Stein.

'Aidan,' she said, 'run and fetch me a machete from the tool-shed would you, please?'

Mrs B could have been perched on Aidan's shoulder and he wouldn't have heard her. He was in another world, gazing adoringly at Igress who was eating her elevenses. Mrs B picked up a rock cake and threw it with unerring accuracy. It bounced off Aidan's skull and dropped to the floor.

He spun round, rubbing the back of his head.

Igress smirked.

'Ah, you *are* there, Aidan,' said Mrs B. 'Fetch me a machete from the tool-shed, would you?'

'A machete?'

'Long sharp knife? For cutting down branches and suchlike?'

'Right you are, Mrs B.' Aidan got to his feet and she threw another cake, but this time to him rather than at him. He grinned as he caught it and ambled off to the tool-shed.

'He's got it bad for you,' said Mrs B.

'He's only a lad,' Igress replied.

'You're not much more than a lass yourself. And lads have a tendency to turn into men when you least expect it.'

Igress nodded. 'But I don't think we can expect it out of Aidan for a while, do you?'

They laughed together, and Mrs B picked up the rock cake from the floor. When she threw it into the fire it flared as the flames caught the sugar.

Igress rose from her chair. 'If anybody wants me, I'll be—'

'In the laboratory.'

'Mrs B, do you know everything?'

'Oh, no, dear. I have to filter some things out or else my head'd get ever so full, wouldn't it?'

'I suppose it would.' Igress turned to go but the way through the kitchen door was temporarily blocked. 'Ooh, Gussie, aren't you the proper athlete!'

'Really? I've never gone in for leisurewear myself.' He pulled at the seams of his baggy training suit. 'I'm much more your bespoke fully fitted kind of man. Mind you, that was in the days when I knew what size I was.'

'Not sure about the gloves, though.'

Gussie waggled his hands and pulled a sour face.

'No. Granny Grumpy here says I've got to wear them – although we're only going for a walk.'

Behind him, Fran dug him in the ribs.

'Oi! Less of the grumpy – and pick up that basket.'

'Aidan's getting a machete for you,' said Mrs B, draping a couple of brightly checked teacloths over the contents of the wicker basket.

'A machete?' said Gussie. 'What the hell do we want with a machete?'

NOTES ON

Secret Passageways

Castles are built for various reasons: as an ostentatious display of wealth; to reinforce the dominance of the builder over the built-upon; as a safe haven against wind, weather, over-enthusiastic friends and bitter enemies; as protection and security – for kith, kin and neighbouring community – against the one family member who is clearly deranged and must be kept well away from the matches behind the strongest non-flammable door with the most locks on it.

But, whatever the reason, castles are built to a template. The layout varies from site to site, but the components are always present. Any self-respecting castle must have steep smooth walls, crenellations, turrets, arrow slits, a courtyard big enough to hold post-battle re-enactments and at least one round tower with a high window and a pointy roof.

And all castles must be twice as big on the inside as they are on the outside. This is to accommodate not only those long, draughty corridors and innumerable identical rooms (a feature which explains why an aristocrat's favourite entertainment – apart from the usual countryside pursuits involving death and peasants – is farce) but also dungeons, priest-holes, hide-outs, blind staircases, false panelling, doors that don't open, hidden libraries and, of course, secret passageways.

If you want to use a secret passageway, there are a few things you need to consider, apart from the necessity to take a light, a weapon and possibly some sandwiches.

Firstly, you must know your way around. Twisting the candlestick to rotate the bookcase and hurling yourself into the darkness is fine if you know where you're going, but stumbling around a maze of identical tunnels – with the attendant scrabblings of wildlife and wailings of spirits of those who last came down here without a map – is not for the faint-hearted.

Secondly, have a good reason for using the secret passageway. This is usually to escape from your enemy – although frankly, if your enemy has managed to penetrate your defences to the point where you're even considering using secret passageways to flee, you've shown an appalling lack of judgement and don't deserve to keep the castle anyway.

Good reasons do not include: hiding birthday presents, especially perishables; putting the children in there for a bit of peace and quiet; playing party games when drunk. Many a Walpurgisnight celebration has been ruined by an interminable game of hide and seek.

Thirdly, the only way to keep secret passageways secret is to ensure nobody sees you go into or come out of them, which may mean being cooped up behind the false panelling in the drawing-room for hours on end until the last of your guests decides to go to bed. Wherever possible, have spy-holes drilled through the wall, and cover them on the other side by a large portrait with removable eyes that can be operated on your side.

Fourthly, you need someone to keep all the mechanisms in good working order. The lack of natural daylight in secret passageways means that the ideal employee for this job would be a vampire, but do bear in mind that they will suck the life-blood out of anybody who gets lost, and they may have difficulty flying round the tunnels carrying an oil can.

~•~

'I've never been horse-riding,' said Gussie as he and Fran approached the thatched stable-block.

'Don't worry,' said Fran, leading Gussie into one of the unoccupied stalls, 'you're not going to start now. There's been no horses here for donkey's years. Right – pick up that torch.'

Gussie lifted a bundle of rushes and twigs from an iron ring on the back wall of the stall. Fran traced a pattern on the cobblestone floor with the end of the machete then stamped her foot twice; the back wall swung away from them, revealing another floor disappearing into a dark void out of which slunk the faint musty smell of damp.

Busy staring into the darkness, Gussie jumped when Fran took the torch, and he gawped open-mouthed at her as she tucked the machete under her arm and ran her palm across the business end of the torch, which glowed then flamed.

She handed it back to him then took hold of the machete again. 'What's up? Never seen anybody light a fire before?'

'Not with just their bare hand, no.'

'You'll see better things than that before the day's out.'

Fran pushed Gussie through the opening, the torchlight revealing a set of steps leading down to a tunnel. She followed him through and closed the wall. 'There. All done.' She set off down the steps.

Gussie didn't move. At the bottom of the steps Fran turned back to him. 'Come on!' she called, and went into the darkness.

Something in Gussie told him he didn't want to be down

here on his own. Both the basket and the torch creaked as he held them, reminding him of claws on stone, and the flames cast swift shadows, not unlike the darting of small animals. He ran down the steps after her. 'Where are we going?'

'Outside.'

They strode on, past unmarked junctions and blind alleys. Once or twice Fran led him up a spur tunnel.

'I'm glad you know your way around,' said Gussie. 'All these tunnels look alike to me. Couldn't we have gone out of the front door and walked round?'

Fran snorted. 'You've obviously no idea how big this place is. Besides, we don't want anybody to see us, do we?'

Gussie stopped. Being in a dark alley where nobody could see you, with somebody who was carrying a large knife and didn't want to be seen anyway, only added up to one thing in his book. 'You're not going to kill me again, are you?'

His question stopped Fran in her tracks. She turned, walked back to him and glowered. 'Oh, yes. Now I remember. That's why I brought you down here.' Anger made her voice rise in tempo, pitch and volume, and she stabbed at the basket with the machete. 'Is this what gave it away? Me taking' – stab – 'confectionery with me when I go out murdering?!'

Gussie dropped the basket and the torch, put his hands to his mouth and whimpered.

Fran sighed, picked up the torch and the basket, scowling as she handed them back to him.

'Just what kind of world do you come from?'

'Truth to tell, I can't remember,' said Gussie. 'But I do know that in this world people with large knives make me break out in bloody cuts and very bad stitching.'

'Oh, get a hold of yourself, you great pudd'n. I'm not going to hurt you. I wouldn't have brought you back from the dead if I was going to hurt you, would I?'

'How do I know? You forget – I'm the new boy around here. I wasn't expecting to be brought back from the dead with someone else's body but you made it happen. I didn't think anybody could change my clothes just by looking at me but you can. How do I know what else you've got planned?'

Fran tutted. 'Hell's bells. I've known winters that didn't go on as long as you do. I – won't – hurt – you. Now come on!'

He followed her until she stopped at an empty cast iron ring on the wall. He put the picnic basket on the floor as Fran traced along several lines of the mortar between the vast stones of the wall with the point of the machete.

A section of the brickwork swung open. The light in the tunnel faded as she took the torch from him, went through the opening and strode down a short passage into a room. She lit a candle on each side wall, brought one back and gave it to Gussie, then ran her hand over the flaming end of the torch.

He snatched it from her. 'What the hell are you doing?!'

'Only taking back that which I gave.'

The flames vanished. Gussie examined the torch closely, but no mark of smoke nor hint of warmth remained to indicate that it had ever burnt or even smouldered.

'Don't stand there looking at it,' Fran said, 'tidy it away.'

Too bemused to refuse, Gussie put the torch back in the iron ring. Fran took the candle from him, gave him the basket, pushed him into the room, followed him in and shut the door.

On the back wall of the room was a large wooden ship's wheel from which hung a long closed loop of rope.

Fran replaced the candle in its holder and pulled the loop of rope from the wheel. 'Turn that wheel until you can't turn it no more but don't let go of it,' she ordered.

'Which way does it go?'

'Round – which way do you expect a wheel to go?'

There was a pause. 'Of course,' said Gussie. 'Silly me.'

He did as he was told, his hands finding the task a lot easier than his mind had led him to believe, despite a variety of grinding and straining noises issuing from behind the walls. He screwed his face up.

'What's up?' asked Fran. 'Does it want oiling?'

'No...' he replied, 'it's just that I've got this rising feeling of... well, rising, to be honest.'

'You're winding us up.'

'I'm not – I wouldn't dare.'

'No, you fool, you're winding us up to another level. It's my own invention – I call it a lift.'

'Not a wind-up, then.' He grinned at her as he turned the wheel, and Fran saw a flash of the mischievous Gussie who must have existed before she'd known him; a Gussie who'd temporarily forgotten what he'd become in favour of being comfortable with who he was.

'What's that?' he asked, pointing at a trapdoor in the ceiling.

'It's a way out in case the lift gets stuck.'

'Is it going to get stuck?'

'No, of course it's not going to get stuck,' said Fran, her indignation evident. '*I* built this – it's not going to get stuck.'

'Then why put in—'

Gussie broke off as the wheel jammed. 'It's stuck now.'

'No it's not. You've just reached the top. Right – now don't let go of that wheel.'

Gussie leant on one side of the wheel, bracing it against a series of hidden ropes, pulleys and counterweights.

Fran passed part of the rope loop behind the ship's wheel, pushed it between two spokes, then threaded it back through itself, pulling it tight. She stepped through an opening in the side wall of the lift and dropped the other end of the loop round an iron hook on the floor outside.

'Now release the wheel. Gently, mind.'

'Yes, your majesty.'

'Call me Fran. "Your majesty" sounds a bit too formal.'

'Right you are, gal.'

Fran put her hands on her hips.

'Honestly! It's all or nowt with you, isn't it?'

Gussie grinned again and winked at her. He gingerly lessened the pressure on the wheel; the lift lowered slightly and the rope became progressively taut as it took the weight. When he could see the wheel was secured, he let go altogether.

'Wouldn't it have been easier to put stairs in?'

'Stairs is for up and down. This lift's only for up. Putting in an up and down when you only want an up's a waste of effort. Come on, bring the basket – and don't fall over that hook.'

Gussie's brow furrowed as he reran her logic in his mind, then relaxed as he came to the conclusion 'oh, just do as you're told'. He picked up the basket and walked out of the lift, stepping lightly over both rope and hook.

Fran took the basket and put it on the floor, then manoeuvred Gussie by the elbows. 'Turn round and sit down.'

He did so, uttering a small cry as he stretched his legs out in front of him and they came to rest at a downward angle, generating a resounding clang. In the little light afforded by the candles in the lift, he could see the glint of polished metal.

He tapped his heel on it. 'Is this a slide?'

'In a manner of speaking.'

She wrapped the machete in a teacloth and laid it in the basket which she gave to Gussie. 'Put your ankles together and hold this on your lap. And whatever you do, don't let go of it.'

He folded his arms over the basket.

She patted him on the shoulder. 'Good lad. Now don't worry, I'll be right behind you.' She gathered up her skirts and sat close behind him with her legs astride his body. 'I'm just going to put my arm round you.'

He steeled himself so he wouldn't flinch. This was a situation completely outside his normal sphere of experience; the last time he'd been in anything approaching this position with a woman was when he'd been born the first time.

'Turn around and watch the lift,' said Fran. 'I love this bit.'

They half-turned in unison. She pressed a tiny lever at the side of the hook in the floor. The hook flipped backwards, releasing the rope, which shot into the fast-descending lift. The resultant rush of air blew the candles out, plunging Gussie and Fran into darkness, and the roar of the descent filled all available space. Gussie twitched. Fran put her other arm around him. 'Hutch up then,' she shouted. 'Let's go.'

With a whimper from Gussie and a whoop from Fran they

started a rapid descent of their own in the darkness, the air cold against their faces and loud in their ears. After a few seconds, the levels of light increased gradually, unlike Gussie and Fran's travelling speed which decreased considerably as the polished metal floor of the slide abruptly changed into a distinctly more carpety surface, stopping them spilling out into dim daylight.

Fran leant back on her hands and laughed.

'Ee, I haven't done that for ages.'

'You and me both, gal.'

Their way ahead was barred by a network of overhanging branches and vigorous bramble growth. Gussie looked at Fran, who stared back. 'Don't stand there like tripe at fourpence,' she said, 'start chopping, else we'll never get out.'

Gussie put the basket down and unwrapped the machete. He hefted it and tentatively prodded at the interwoven bramble tendrils, which rustled and sprang back into place.

'No, no, no,' Fran chided. 'You'll never build up muscle strength like that. Give it some swing,' she demonstrated, flattening her hand to resemble a blade.

Gussie mimicked her action. The blade was extremely sharp and sliced through the growth with little resistance.

'Wa-hey!' he said, and soon was clearing a decent path through the woods. After a while he stopped hacking and looked at Fran. 'There's something I'd like to talk about.'

Fran sighed bad-temperedly then scowled at him.

'Look – how many more times do I have to go through this? You were dead. You are alive. Now live with it!'

Gussie looked startled for a moment. 'Oh, that's easy for you to say, isn't it?' he retaliated. 'You don't know what inner turmoil I might be suffering as a result of being resurrected, do you?' He jabbed a finger at her. 'No. After all, you've never been dead, have you?'

'Don't be stupid! If I'd been dead I wouldn't be standing here talking to you now, would I?'

'Exactly!' Gussie crowed. '*I'm* not supposed to be standing here talking to *you* now, am I?'

Fran sucked her teeth, but said nothing.

'Even though that's not what I wanted to talk about,' he said quietly.

'Oh.' She softened. 'Perhaps we'd better start again, then.'

He did. 'There's something I'd like to talk about.'

'What's that?' smiled Fran.

'You.'

The smile disappeared. 'What about me?'

Gussie took a deep breath. 'Well, although you've never been dead... you are dying, aren't you?'

Fran coughed. 'I'm not very well, I'll give you that.'

'It's more than that, isn't it? You're dying.'

'All right, I'm dying. What's it to you? Or to anybody for that matter? It's my life, it's my death, it's my business.'

'Oh, don't be soft. You've not been a lone soul, have you? You haven't gone through *your* life without affecting other people's. What about Rosa? And the cat? And me? You gave me a new life! You're practically my mother.'

Fran's eyes narrowed. 'Don't you dare start calling me—'

'Don't worry, I won't. But...'

'But what?'

Gussie pulled a face, trying to stave off the worst possible reply to his question. 'But... do I have to die when you do?'

'What? Oh, no.' Fran put her hand on his arm. 'No, love, you don't have to die when I do.'

'Are you sure?'

She was about to lambast him for doubting her word, but the eyes she looked into belonged to a man who was genuinely afraid to live until he knew he wasn't going to die.

'Yes,' she said softly, 'I'm sure.'

Gussie blew out his cheeks.

'Hoo! Hah! Hmm. I can't pretend I'm not relieved at that. You know: tried it once, think I got away with it.'

'The whole point about you being here is so that you can take care of Rosa after I've gone.'

'I thought that's what husbands were for.'

'Haven't you been listening? She tried it once, didn't get away with it.'

'So how's work going upstairs?' asked Mrs B, putting a mug of steaming tea on the kitchen table.

'Upstairs?' the deeply concentrating Mason replied automatically. Life in the building trade had taught him to pick one word out of a customer's question and focus on that, asking the customer to explain exactly what was meant by it. The degree of stupidity he was prepared to assume usually corresponded with the magnitude of the excuse he was trying to come up with. In this case, however, it was merely a delaying tactic to allow him to further enjoy the sight of Mrs B's ample form bustling about the kitchen.

'The tower, Mr Mason? The one that you're rebuilding?'

Mason came out of his reverie. 'Oh, that.'

Mrs B laughed. 'In a world of your own there, weren't you? Whatever were you thinking about? The things you need to finish the job?'

Mason wrapped his fingers around the tea mug and raised it towards his mouth. 'There are one or two things I'd like to get my hands on, that's for sure.'

'Anything *I* can help you with, Mr Mason?'

Mason started and scalding tea slopped across his knuckles. He put the cup down and stuck his fingers in his mouth.

'Oh, don't do that,' said Mrs B, coming around the table to him. 'You're keeping the heat in.'

She seized his arm and led him towards the sink, where she plunged his reddened fingers into a bowlful of icy water, putting her arm around his shoulders and gripping his wrist tightly to keep his hand submerged.

'Haaaaa...' he gasped as equal measures of pain and a peculiar kind of pleasure raced round his body, watering his eyes, tightening his trousers and buckling his knees.

'Stay there, Mr Mason,' said Mrs B, 'and I'll get you a seat.'

She fetched a chair, and when she put her arm round him again and guided him into it, his pleasure overtook his pain.

'Now you sit here and keep that hand underwater until I tell you otherwise,' she said.

'Right you are,' he squeaked.

She picked up a cloth and was dabbing at the spilt tea on the table when Sooty ambled into the kitchen.

'Not so loud, Mrs B, please. I've got a head like a bucket.'

'That must be why you're so pale,' said Mason, and started

grinning. 'Pale. Get it? Pail. Bucket. Oh, never mind.'

Sooty curled his lip in reply.

Mrs B smiled. 'So that's why there's a big hole in the stock of Mr Beaton's Special this morning.'

'Well,' drawled Sooty, 'it could have been me, or it could have been Rosa. But let's just say... it was both of us.' He slumped in front of the fire.

'Never you mind, my love. I've got something for you.'

Mrs B chuckled as she poured out a saucerful of highly perfumed liquid. She put it on the floor in front of Sooty.

His nose twitched tentatively. 'Phew – it's a bit strong.'

'Strength didn't worry you last night when you were drinking Mr Beaton's Special.'

'Fair point. What is this, anyway?'

'This is Mrs Beaton's Special.'

Sooty shut his eyes and tasted it. His eyes opened. 'Mmmm. Nice.' He lapped it up. 'Any more?'

Mrs B laughed and refilled his saucer.

'There – that'll put new life in you.'

Sooty drank as Mrs B finished wiping the table. She threw the cloth into the sink and it slapped into the water, which splashed ice-cold up Mason's arm. The builder shuddered.

'Oh, I'm sorry, Mr Mason,' said Mrs B. 'I wasn't thinking.'

'Not a problem, Mrs B. It was a bit cool, that's all.'

Sooty looked up. 'For a moment there I thought Mr Mason felt an estimate coming on.'

'See, Sooty?' said Mrs B. 'It's working already.'

'More than Mr Mason is.'

Fran led Gussie into a clearing crossed by a rutted track, where a weather-beaten cart stood outside a hovel built partly into the side of a mound.

'It's amazing what some people class as a cottage these days,' he said.

Fran tutted. 'Oh, and I suppose you imagined something half-timbered, white-rendered, thatched, roses round the door, poppies, delphiniums and lupins standing tall in a sea of baby's breath, a wisp of smoke from the chimney curling lazily into an endless blue sky, and across it all a big red bow stretching from corner to corner of your mind's eye?'

'There's no need to be facetious about it.'

'You people – you're all alike.'

'What's all the "you people" business?' said Gussie. 'Who the hell are you talking about? The living or the dead? Or the undead? Boxers? Tailors? Machete-wielding ramblers? Who?'

'You city folk with your rosy picture of life in the country. It's all sunshine and lazy days with you lot, isn't it?'

'What?'

'You've no idea of the sheer grind of scraping a living from a patch of land. Having to forage for your food—'

'Excuse me,' Gussie overrode her, lifting the picnic basket in front of her face. 'I hardly call this foraging.'

'That's a rare treat,' sniffed Fran.

'Anyway, who rattled your cage? I was only saying I thought the house could do with a lick of paint, that's all.'

'Paint? What does it matter how the house is painted as long as it gives him protection? What does he care whether or not the sky's blue as long as it doesn't rain on him? What does he need with scarlet poppies and yellow roses?'

'Oh, now—'

'What good's colour to him? He needs food and shelter like the rest of us and he needs touch and taste and smell and sound. He doesn't need—'

'You didn't tell me,' Gussie interrupted.

'What?'

'You didn't tell me he was blind.'

Fran looked surprised. 'Oh.'

There was a pause born of irritation at an unfamiliar task about to be undertaken. 'I'm sorry,' she said loudly, waving her arms theatrically. 'I forgot to tell you. He's blind.'

'He's blind, he's not deaf,' called a voice from behind the cottage. 'And he's just heard summat he's never heard afore.'

'Oh aye? What's that?' Fran called back.

'My sister apologising for something.'

Gussie laughed. Fran thumped him.

'Charming,' she said. 'A girl gets no respect in this wood.'

'If you've brought a girl, I'll respect her,' said the voice.

'Cheeky sod. Bring yourself round here.'

'Some things even you can't control,' came the reply. 'Go inside; there's a pan of soup on the stove. I won't be a minute.'

Gussie had to stoop to get through the doorway into the cottage, and was rewarded with aromas suggesting that the soup was far more pleasant than he'd thought possible, given the potential basic ingredients he'd smelt outside.

The only light came from the firebox of the small cooking range. Fran reached into the fire, picked out a glowing coal and gently blew on it until its comforting redness had changed to a brilliant white light. It slowly rose from her hand until it bumped the ceiling and there it stayed, illuminating the room.

'Wow!' said Gussie, setting the basket and the machete on the kitchen table.

'Oh, there's no need for that,' Fran primped, 'it's only a—'

'Look at all those!'

The white-hot coal had thrown light on shelf after shelf of clay heads. Gussie reached up to take one.

'Don't!' warned Fran. He looked at her in surprise. 'Sorry,' she said, 'but you don't know your own strength yet. And they are rather precious to him.'

'Ah,' said Gussie, folding his arms.

He leant forward and peered at the intricately and precisely modelled faces. It would have been all too easy for a fertile imagination to see muscles twitching beneath the undecorated clay skin. Gussie saw cracked lips and furrowed brows, heavy jowls and scrawny wattles. He saw laughter lines etched around chillingly dead eyes. Whole life histories offered themselves to him, written with painful clarity in the scars from old wounds and disfiguring illnesses. He shivered.

'They're good, aren't they?' said Fran, stirring a stockpot on the stove.

'Good? They're remarkable.'

'Not bad, considering he can't see what he's doing.'

'*He* makes these?'

'His *name* is Durney,' she said with a hint of reproach.

'You didn't tell me that either.'

'Oh. Well. Yes, he makes them.' Fran lifted a small, battered tin from a shelf, opened it, took a pinch of dried herbs from it and sprinkled them into the stockpot. She snapped the tin shut, momentarily trapping a fold of her skin. She took a sharp breath and pulled her hand away from the tin. 'Ooh!'

She instinctively put her hand to her mouth and sucked at the sore area, splaying her fingers across her face. After a few seconds she took her hand from her mouth and shook it, then examined the tiny blood-blister that was forming.

'Daft beggar,' she muttered.

Gussie turned. 'You all right?'

'Yes of course I'm all right – why shouldn't I be all right?'

'I'm sorry, I thought you'd hurt yourself.'

'Well I haven't.' She replaced the tin on the shelf and stirred the stockpot again. 'And sit down.'

He sat, and gazed at her back for a while before turning around to study the clay heads again. 'They're amazing.'

'Aye. Think what they'd be like if he could paint 'em.'

Gussie thought for a moment. 'Can't you help him?'

'Me? I can't paint.'

'No... can't you... give him his sight back? I'd have thought it was a piece of cake after bringing somebody back from the dead, giving somebody their sight back.'

She banged the spoon on the rim of the stockpot. 'I can't give back what he's never had. Mother Nature made him like that.' She straightened up and looked at the wall. 'And who am I to go against Mother Nature?'

'An interfering old busybody, that's who,' said a man standing in the doorway.

Gussie laughed and started to rise.

Fran pushed him back down. 'Keep still, you.'

Durney was wiping his hands on a thin towel as he walked into the room, and his hands were the first thing to make contact with Gussie, hitting him in the middle of the back.

'Sit down, lad, sit down – don't make the place untidy.'

'I am sitting down.'

Durney raised his eyebrows and put the towel on the table.

'Damn me! You must have been well fed when you were a kid.' He ran his hands across Gussie's back until he could grip him by the shoulders. 'What's your name, lad?'

'Gussie.'

'And where do you come from?'

'Now that's a bit of a long story...'

'Is that your real voice?'

'What do you mean, my real voice? Yes, it's my real voice. What's wrong with it?'

Durney stepped sideways and patted Gussie on the chest and the back. 'Well, with a ribcage this size you ought to be a least a basso profundo, if not molto profundo.'

Gussie looked pointedly at Fran. 'Let's just say I haven't had the musical training.'

'You're not here to sing,' said Fran.

'Fair enough,' said Durney, stepping back behind the chair again. He ran his hands along Gussie's collarbone, then up his neck until he cradled his cheeks. He opened his mouth and took a breath, abruptly closed his mouth and put his hands back on Gussie's shoulders. His mouth opened once more, as if he couldn't quite believe the evidence of his own fingers. Several times he clapped his hands round Gussie's face, then his shoulders, then his face again.

'Oh do stop it, Durney!' said Fran. 'You're going to knock his bloody head off if you're not careful!'

'Feels like somebody's beaten me to it.'

'Thanks very much,' muttered Gussie.

Durney patted him on the arm.

'No offence, lad, but you do seem like you're out of...'

'A horror story?'

'...proportion. A very unusual head-to-body ratio. Not exactly classical styling.'

'That's supposed to make him feel better, is it?' asked Fran.

'Of course it's supposed to make him feel better,' said Durney. 'Every Tom, Dick and Harry's got a normal head and shoulders. I've waited years for somebody like him to turn up.'

Gussie brightened considerably.

'Mind you,' continued Durney, 'I'd have summat done about them stitches.'

Fran took a clay bowl from the shelf, nudged Gussie and pointed to the picnic basket.

'Get me your bowl out, flower, and take no notice of him.'

Dejectedly, Gussie removed his gloves, lifted the picnic basket onto the floor and retrieved his bowl and spoon.

Fran ladled out soup from the stockpot into the two bowls.

'I thought we'd brought lunch with us,' said Gussie. 'I didn't know we were imposing upon Mr Durney.'

'You're very imposing, lad, but not on me. And it's just Durney.'

Fran yawned and shook her head before she gave them their soup. 'There's gallons in the pot, so get stuck in.'

'All right... if Mr – if Durney doesn't mind...'

Durney picked up a spoon. 'You heard the woman.'

Gussie got stuck in. 'Where's yours, gal?' he asked between slurps as Fran put two large round bread cakes on the table.

'I'm not hungry. I had half a good breakfast this morning.'

'Only half?' said Durney, breaking one of the bread cakes.

'Yes. Some hungry-nosed devil had the other half.'

'You said you'd finished!' Gussie retorted.

'So I had. Now stop talking and concentrate on eating your soup.' She yawned loudly. 'Oh-wo-wo-wo-wo-wo-wah!'

'Sounds to me like somebody's tired,' said Durney.

'Well,' said Gussie, 'it's bound to take it out of you, being right all the time.'

Fran took a swing at him, but once he'd dodged the blow he had to catch her as she fell.

'Oh, come on,' he said. 'It was only a joke.'

She made no reply except to weigh heavily in his arms and slump against him.

Beaton closed the heavy front door behind the two aristocrats who strode into the Great Hall.

'I'm afraid milady is indisposed, my lords,' he said.

'Still in bed,' grinned Aidan, miming the drinking of a pint. 'Indisposed, Aidan.'

Aidan's grin vanished. 'Indisposed, Mr Beaton. Sorry.'

'Been getting sozzled, has she?' chuckled Yedder. 'Hardly surprising with the problems she's got. Fran about?'

'Miss Frances has gone out for a walk.'

'Hmm. Not scoring very highly here. What about Sooty?'

Aidan leapt in. 'He's indisposed as well.'

Beaton held out his arm. 'Would your lordships care to wait in the library? I'm sure milady will be available shortly.'

'Prefer the kitchen, if that's all right, Beaton. Not in the mood for reading.'

'Are my lords in the mood for a little light refreshment?'

Yedder beamed. 'Always. Lead on, old love, lead on.'

The jangle of Gussie's spoon hitting the floor alerted Durney.

'What's that noise? What's happening?'

Gussie struggled to support Fran on his knee. 'Aah... I don't know – wake up, gal, come on, wake up... I think she's fainted.'

'Fainted? Slap her face.'

'I haven't got a spare hand!'

'Fran? Fran!'

'Besides, I think that's hysteria.'

'Put her head between her knees... or put her feet in the air.'

The white-hot coal bobbing against the ceiling was starting to glow orange as Gussie manhandled Fran until she sat on his knee with her head drooping towards the floor.

Durney felt his way along the table until he touched Fran; his hands found her face and he tapped her cheek.

'Fran!' said Durney. 'Wake up, Fran. Come on, stop mucking about.'

'It's no use,' whimpered Gussie. 'I'll have to go for help.'

'We'll both go.'

'We can't leave her here!'

'Carry her out and put her onto the cart,' said Durney, stepping forward and picking up an unlit torch from a pile by the cooking range. 'I'll just get this lit.'

He stuck one end of the torch into the firebox.

In the fading light from the now red coal, Gussie hoisted Fran back into his arms and stood up easily; for someone with so much power, she was surprisingly light. He bent low to get through the door then ran along the path and lifted her into position over the side of the cart, too concerned for her welfare to notice something fall from her pocket. He rubbed one of her hands as he hopped from foot to foot.

'Oh, come on,' he groaned at the recumbent figure, 'don't do this to me. Don't leave me. Wake up... don't go... where are you?... Come back... don't leave me... I'm not ready yet... I don't know what for, but I'm not ready...'

He turned round to bellow for Durney and cannoned into the blazing torch Durney was holding out, knocking it to the floor in a shower of sparks.

'Whoa!' cried Gussie. 'What's that for?'

'So you can see where you're going.'

A brilliant ball of light exploded from the ground: a brief, blinding, roaring, incandescent rainbow sphere.

'What was that?' asked Durney as the roar died away.

'The torch...' said Gussie, blinking at the space where the ball of flames had been. 'Must have landed on something.' He warily picked up the glowing torch and placed it into an iron ring on the front of the cart. 'Right! Where's the horse?'

'Horse? I an't got a horse,' said Durney, clambering aboard. 'You'll have to pull it.'

'What?!' squealed Gussie.

'Well, I can't pull the cart and Fran and you, can I?'

'But I don't know the way!'

'Just go in the direction the cart's pointing, and when you come to a fork in the road, take a right-hander. Don't worry, the cart knows the way.' Durney braced himself and Fran against the backboard of the cart. 'On you go.'

Gussie's mouth gathered fresh air and his eyes darted from side to side as he weighed up the options. In this particular kingdom, it would appear he qualified as king.

A king who didn't know why the torch had flared. A king who didn't see a coal drop from the ceiling onto the kitchen table. A once white-hot coal that was now cold, black and dead.

He ducked between the shafts of the cart, threaded his arms through the leather traces and firmly grasped each shaft.

In his previous life, Gussie had run away from many things: mice, spiders, debt collectors, angry boyfriends, poverty and a persistent landlady with a ferocious dog which was so ugly that all its creators must have had their eyes closed when they threw its ingredients together. But he couldn't remember ever having to run towards something.

Until now.

Mrs B put a tray of drinks on the kitchen table as Yedder and Guildman walked in. 'My lords. What a pleasant surprise.'

'The pleasure is all ours, Mrs B,' said Guildman.

'No it's not,' said a voice from the floor. 'She's still in bed.'

'Good day, Spirit,' smiled Guildman, taking off his gloves. 'We were led to believe you were... indisposed.'

'You old rogue, you,' teased Yedder, picking Sooty up and shaking him. 'Been leading someone astray, have you?'

Sooty retracted his claws before lashing out at Yedder's

chin. 'Put me down! I'm in no fit state to be thrown about.'

Yedder laughed, held him at arms' length and wobbled him very gently before putting him on the table. Sooty lashed out again. Yedder caught his paw.

'Awww. Iddums got a wittw headache, den?'

'The sooner the peasantry rise up against the cruel and heartless aristocracy the better,' Sooty said sourly.

'Mrs B, would you have a saucer of the milk of human kindness for our friend here?' asked Guildman.

Yedder tapped Sooty's nose. 'He'd probably curdle it before he had chance to drink it, wouldn't you, chum?'

'Yedder, when I'm feeling better, I'm going to sharpen my claws, come round to your place and rip all your silk shirts into tiny little pieces. But right now—'

'Right now you can have another refill,' said Mrs B, giving him another saucer of her perfumed pick-me-up. She placed Beaton Specials in front of the lords and kept a cup of tea for herself; Mason looked at her in hope, but was disappointed.

Durney cradled Fran's head as the cart jolted through the woods. Between the shafts, Gussie's body kept up the pace as disparate thoughts crowded his head. 'I hope I'm going the right way' battled with 'Just keep going' and 'Hold on, gal, hold on'. Gradually overpowering all of those, however, was a creeping feeling of well-being backed up by a sense of purpose. There was a job to be done, he was the best man for it and his body had responded, taking his mind by surprise. Running was physically taxing, yet somehow easy and familiar. The even pounding of his feet on the earth was reassuring, and for the first time since his rebirth he was a man entirely suited to his task and not a maladroit lump at odds with a gracious world.

Durney had been right. The cart did seem to know the way, rolling steadily in well-worn ruts in the earth. The tree canopy of the woods thickened and all daylight faded. When the springy forest floor gave way to solid stone, the earth ruts became chiselled channels and the rumble of wheels and Gussie's footfalls reverberated through a tunnel.

Sooty's ears pricked up. 'Durney's on his way. And it sounds like he's got a full load on.'

'How do you do that?' asked Yedder. 'I can't hear anything.'

'It's a gift,' said Sooty, 'although when I can hear you, it's a curse.' He smirked and put his paws in his ears. 'Now if you don't mind, I've got some more sleeping to do.'

Mrs B moved to the corner of the kitchen and beckoned.

'Lord Guildman – a word, please?'

Mason's eyes followed the aristocrat intently.

Mrs B handed Guildman an empty flour sack and motioned silently towards Sooty and Yedder. Mason's eyes darted back and forth as Guildman opened the sack and walked towards the kitchen table, where Yedder scooped up the unsuspecting cat and threw him into the sack.

In the tunnel Gussie's voice jogged along with him, and echoed as he gasped, 'Where are we?'

'It's a short cut to the castle,' answered Durney from the back of the cart. 'Stop when you go through the bead—'

A clack and a swish, a stream of expletives and a sudden

jerk of the cart told Durney that Gussie had gone through the bead curtain which now clattered against the side of the cart.

'That *is* a short cut,' panted Gussie.

Durney had already jumped down and was feeling his way along the curtain. 'Shorter than I've ever done it. Ah, here we are.' He tugged at an iron ring set into the wall. 'Lift her up.'

'What the— oh very funny, Yedder,' sputtered Sooty as Mrs B tied the top of the sack with string.

'Forgive me, Spirit,' said Guildman, 'but it's better this way.'

'It's not better for me, mate.'

'The good of the many versus the good of the one.'

'Guildman, you let me out of here.'

'All in good time, Master Sooty,' said Mrs B.

'Not you as well, Mrs B? So, I had a few drinks, got a bit tipsy; is that any way to— hold on, that's not why I'm in here, is it?' The floppy bundle in the sack suddenly stiffened. 'Something's wrong, isn't it? Something's wrong and you don't want me on the loose. It's her, isn't it? There's something wrong with her!' The sack began to thrash wildly. 'Let me out! Let me out of here now! If you don't let me out right this minute I'm going to kill the lot of you!' Underlining this threat, claws pushed through the fabric of the sack.

Guildman and Mrs B double-bagged the thrashing Sooty in another flour sack as stone grated on stone, the wall started to pivot and heavy thumps in quick succession indicated someone's approach. Mrs B pulled Guildman aside seconds before a panting and sweating Gussie burst into the kitchen, carrying the unconscious Fran.

Sooty stiffened again. Suddenly he knew why he was in the sack, as surely as if he could see her.

'Miiiiiiiissssssstreeeeeeeeeeessssssss!' he howled, shooting pain into the heart of all in the kitchen.

'Take her to her room, love,' said Mrs B, grabbing her first-aid basket and hurrying after Gussie.

Sooty pounded inside the sack.

'Miiiiiiiissssssstreeeeeeeeeeessssssss!'

Yedder held out his hand. 'I'll take Sooty, Gil.'

'No,' said Durney, by the open wall. 'Give him to me.'

Guildman handed over the distraught sack and ran.

'What's this?' asked Durney, expecting fur and receiving thrashing, howling hessian.

'We had to restrain him, Durney,' explained Yedder.

'Spirit of Co-operation, I bid thee cease!' shouted Durney.

All movement and noise from the sack stopped abruptly.

'Oh, well done,' said Yedder, guiding Durney to a chair.

'Fran taught me the knack years ago. Couldn't see the point at the time. Didn't think I'd ever have to use it.'

'You never know what's going to come in handy until it does,' said Mason.

'Or who,' said Durney, sitting and putting the sack on his knee. 'Spirit of Co-operation, I bid thee speak – quietly, mind.'

Only Durney's tight grip on the sack prevented the agitated Sooty from falling to the floor.

'Durney, what's happened? There's something wrong but they won't let me out! Is she all right? Durney, tell me!'

'She'll be all right, Sooty, calm yourself,' replied Durney. 'She fainted, that's all.'

'Fainted? Again? Why has she suddenly started fainting all over the place?'

'Trust me,' said Durney firmly. 'She's fine. She's just in a very deep sleep.'

'Are you sure?'

'Of course I'm sure. I was the one cradling her all the way back here. I didn't need eyes to tell me she was snoring.'

Judging by the constant agitation within the sack, Sooty was not reassured.

'So if she's only sleeping, what's all the fuss? Why did your cart sound like it was going at double speed and why am I in a sack if she's only sleeping?'

'The big feller was pulling the cart. That's why it—'

Sooty stopped moving. 'The big feller?'

'Yes, whatsisname, Gussie. Owwwwwwwww!'

Durney suddenly lifted the sack from his knee and held it in the air. Sharp claws stuck through the hessian.

'And that's why you're in a bloody sack!'

'Two, actually,' said Yedder, taking the writhing, swearing bundle and putting it on the table.

Durney rubbed his thighs.

'Shame it wasn't half a dozen.'

Guildman ran through the castle, hoping that Rosalind still slept in the same bedroom. His feet had run these corridors many times when he was a child; in his mind, many more times since then. The route was as familiar to him as his own castle. He stopped and hammered on the door.

'Mmmmm,' murmured a sleepy Rosa. 'Just leave it on the

floor, Beaton, I'll get it later.'

He knocked again. 'Rosalind, it's your aunt.'

'Come on in, Aunty.'

He sighed for as many reasons as the heart has emotions.

'Rosalind, it's Gil. Your—'

The latch clicked and the door swung wide.

Rosa had not yet reached that age when she needed an hour's notice to smooth out those sleep wrinkles which make most of the population look as if they've been folded up damp for the night. Consequently the seductive, tousled, still-warm-from-the-bed vision framed in the doorway tested Guildman's willpower to the limit. Years of training conquered centuries of instinct as he tore his gaze away from the close-fitting silks. He bowed his head. 'Your aunt needs you. She has met with an accident. She is—'

'Where?! Where is she?!'

'In her room. You must—'

The rustle of silk told him that she had already gone. He leant on the door frame, tipped his head back and bit his bottom lip. His head lolled to one side, his gaze coming to rest on the rumpled sheets and dented pillow on Rosa's bed.

Guildman quickly looked away, staring at the ceiling for a few seconds before pushing himself from the door frame and walking into the bedroom. He sat on the edge of the bed, the last vestiges of her body heat warming his palm as he touched the bedsheet. Her scent enticed him to rest his head where hers had been, and he breathed in as much of her as he could. A single strand of her hair lay on the pillow; he picked it up and placed it inside his shirt, next to his skin.

He ran his hand lightly over the hills and valleys of the deep-buttoned headboard, its claret leather cracking and peeling with age. Suddenly he hooked his fingers behind one of the large buttons and ripped it from its anchors. As his fist closed tightly round the prized object, the broken metal gouged his skin; a drop of blood fell from the wound and soaked into the pillow.

With his other hand, he tore a silver-crested button from his sleeve and laid it on the bloodstain.

Sooty was threatening Yedder and Durney with all kinds of murder and destruction.

'Spirit, I bid thee silence!' commanded Durney. 'Your mistress is sleeping. You'll go to her when Mrs B says so.'

The noise stopped; the writhing didn't.

'So who is the big chap, Durney?' asked Yedder.

'Gussie? One of Fran's friends.'

Claws scrabbled on the table.

Yedder looked at the sack.

'I'm not sure that was the right answer, old love.'

The sack shimmered and the claws disappeared, as did the bulk of the cat which was replaced by a much smaller, faster-moving shape.

'Oh-oh,' said Yedder, to the accompaniment of tiny chomping noises.

'What's he doing?' asked Durney.

'I think he's changed into a mouse. He's eating his way out.'

'Maybe you'd better get another sack ready.'

Fran's bedroom door flying open startled Gussie. He knocked Cecil from the window-sill, caught him and then cowered with him in a corner as Rosa raced towards the bed.

'Aunty!'

Mrs B was smoothing the blankets.

'Don't you worry yourself, milady, she's all right.'

Rosa sat on the bed and clasped one of Fran's hands which was, thankfully, warm. 'Aunty Fran... can you hear me?'

'She'll hear nobody for a few hours, milady. She's fast on.'

'Oh, Mrs B, are you sure? What happened?'

'I got her back as quick as I could,' wailed Gussie.

Rosa wheeled round.

'Got her back? From where? Where did you take her?'

Gussie flapped his hands in defence.

'I didn't take her anywhere! She took me!'

'They'd been to see Durney, milady,' said Mrs B. 'Miss Frances had me make up a basket for them.'

Gussie nodded vehemently. 'Durney.'

'So what happened? Had she been overdoing it?'

'I don't know... she – she was giving us soup. Durney had some soup on the go and... and – and she put something in it and I thought she'd hurt herself because she said "ooh" but she said she was all right and then she started yawning and then she... collapsed. And then me and Durney brought her back.'

'What did she say "ooh" for?'

Gussie squeezed Cecil in agitation.

'I don't know, I don't know... she said she was all right...'

Rosa turned at a knock on the open door.

'My lady?' said Guildman.

Rosa flashed him a sad smile. 'Gil... would you escort Gussie— ah, where are my manners? Lord Guildman, Gussie. Gussie, Lord Guildman.'

Guildman bowed; Gussie looked more terrified.

Rosa took Cecil from his hands. 'Gil, would you escort Gussie back to the kitchen? I'll be there in a moment.'

'Of course.'

'Go on, Gussie. Guildman won't hurt you.'

'Yedder, this is Gussie,' said Guildman.

'Pleased to meet you,' said Yedder. 'Sorry I can't shake hands – bit busy.' He was constantly rotating the sack to stop Sooty from getting a toothhold.

'Pleased to meet you, my lord. Where's the cat?'

'He's in—' Mason began, but his pearl of wisdom never got out of its shell because Mrs B walked into the kitchen, shortly followed by Rosa.

'Oh, Mr Mason,' said Mrs B, 'whatever are you playing at? Still sitting there with your hand in the sink.'

'But you told me to...'

'And I'm telling you now,' said Rosa. 'Get off that chair and go and build.'

Mrs B dried his hand on a towel. 'There you go.'

'Hear that Mason?' said Rosa. 'There. You. Go.'

Mason stood up and grudgingly left the kitchen, muttering.

Rosa put her hand on Durney's arm and kissed his cheek. 'Hello, Uncle D.'

He patted her hand. 'Hello, love. How is the old trout?'

'Sleeping. Mrs B says she'll be sawing the bed legs off for a couple of hours and she'll be all right after that.'

'Hear that?' Durney said. 'What did I tell you? She's asleep.'

'Who are you talking to, Uncle D?'

'Sooty,' answered Yedder, nodding towards the sack.

'What's he doing in a sack? Come to think of it, what are you two doing here? Sootbags, what's happened?'

'Spirit, I bid thee speak,' said Durney. 'But watch your language – there are ladies present.'

The sack emitted distraught high-pitched squeaks.

'I can't understand you!' Rosa shouted over him.

The sack shimmered and once again contained a cat.

'Rosa!' he bawled. 'They won't let me out, Rosa! She's hurt and they won't let me out. They won't let me see her and she's hurt and it's all the fault of that great ugly git and everything bad's happened since he got here and he's using up her time and I hate him I hate him I hate him and they won't let me see her and they won't let me out let me out let me out!'

'Give me the cat,' said Gussie, holding out a hand.

Violent spitting and hissing came from the sack.

'I don't think that's such a good—' started Yedder.

'Give me the cat.'

'Gussie—' said Rosa.

'*Give me the cat!*'

Guildman's hand went to his sword.

Gussie closed his eyes against the welling tears.

'Do not draw your weapon, my lord. I've never harmed a creature in my life and I'm not about to start now. Just... give me... the cat.'

It was Mrs B who stepped forward and lifted the sack and

its bristling contents. 'There you are, love,' she said. 'You do what you have to do.'

Gussie clutched the sack to his body all the way to Fran's bedroom. The more the writhing Sooty beat at his chest and scored his skin with claw-marks, the tighter Gussie held him.

'Let me out! Let me out of here! Where are you taking me? Let me out of here! I want my mistress!'

'Hold your horses, cat.'

The thumps against Gussie's chest intensified as Sooty's voice began to crack. 'I am not "cat"! I am The Most Ancient And Venerable Spirit of Co-operation! My working name is Sooty! I am not "cat"! I have a name!'

'And so do I!' Gussie spat. 'And I seem to recall we've not been formally introduced!'

He held the sack level with his head. Sooty stiffened as Gussie spoke close to the hessian.

'My name, for what it's worth, is Gussie. Not "monster", not "great ugly git" nor any of the thousand other vile things you've seen fit to call me since this whole nightmare began. My name is Gussie, and it is the only thing I have of my own in this world. I have no home of my own, no friends and no family. I do not own the clothes I stand up in, and I don't even own most of the body I stand up in, but *I have my name.*'

The hessian sagged, and Gussie heard the sound of stifled sobs. He clutched Sooty to his chest again with one hand, and with the other he opened the door into Fran's bedroom.

'Mistress!' called Sooty, trying to claw his way out of the sack again.

Gussie walked over and put the sack on the bed. 'Now keep

still while I get this undone.' He fumbled at the intricate knots. 'I can't undo this with these bloody fat podgy sausages... I used to have such lovely slender fingers.'

'Oh, come on,' pleaded Sooty, keeping his agitation in check as long as he could. 'Get me out. Please, Gussie.'

'Right. I'm going to turn the sack upside down, and I want you to make yourself into as small a ball as you can at the knot end, all right?'

'All right.'

Gussie gathered the material at each side of the seam in his hands. 'Here we go.' He pulled, and the seam gave way along its length in a cloud of hessian strands and flour dust.

'Oh,' he said, looking at another intact sack.

'They double-bagged me.'

Gussie gripped the second seam.

'Oh well, same again.'

Another rip. Sooty spilled out onto the bed and immediately clambered over the sleeping Fran. 'Mistress, oh mistress,' he sobbed, pressing himself against her body. Gussie lifted Fran's arm and rested it on Sooty. Without waking, Fran hugged Sooty to her.

Gussie picked up the flour sacks as he left the room.

Rosa put her hand on Durney's arm. 'Won't you stay a while, Uncle D? Stay for dinner.'

He patted her hand. 'No thanks, love. As long as I know the old nagbag's all right, I'm fine. Besides, I had a particularly delicious soup on the go when she keeled over. No offence, Mrs B, but I don't want it boiling dry.'

Mrs B was arranging a tea-tray, but the smile in her voice overrode the chink of crockery.

'If you change your mind, Durney, you come back. There'll be more than enough to go round.'

'Mrs B, you're a marvel. If ever you decide to leave that no-good husband of yours, you know where I live.'

Mrs B chuckled. 'I do, Durney, I do.'

Rosa kissed Durney. 'Take care, Uncle D. See you later.'

Yedder stood up. 'Mind if I accompany you, Durney?'

'What for? I'm not going to get lost.'

'Oh, I fancy the walk, old sport. Besides, I haven't seen your place for ages. And it's years since you modelled me.'

Durney tutted. 'Come here, then. Let's have a feel at you.'

Yedder put his face into Durney's hands. Durney ran his fingertips lightly over the smiling aristocrat's face and gently slapped his cheek. 'I don't know if you're worth doing again, Yedder. You still haven't grown a chin.'

'Well!' said Yedder in mock indignation. 'I'm outraged!'

'You're outrageous, you mean,' replied Durney. 'Come on then – you can push the cart back to the cottage.'

'Yes, sir, Durney, sir!' laughed Yedder, and he allowed Durney to lead him out of the kitchen.

'That's Yedder taken care of for the afternoon,' said Rosa, 'which just leaves you, my lord.'

'Indeed,' said Guildman. His face assumed a look of innocent puzzlement. 'What *shall* I do?'

Rosa held out her hand. He kissed it tenderly and allowed himself to be pulled to a chair next to her.

'You shall tell me, my Lord Guildman, exactly how you and

Yedder came to be sitting in my kitchen.'

'Can two old friends not visit a third without a reason?'

'Of course. And yet there is suspicion lurking in the back of my mind.' She leant towards him. 'Speak, noble lord.'

He leant towards her. 'If I speak, what shall be my reward?'

She smiled broadly but remained silent.

'What's this?' he said. 'No reward? No inducement? Speak, dearest lady, speak.'

She moved even closer. 'My lips are sealed.'

He moved closer still.

'Then I shall have to find a way to open them.'

Her eyes dared him to do it. 'Come now, my lord. Is—'

'Tea up!' said Mrs B over-brightly, lifting the tray laden with a large teapot, a milk jug, two cups and a mound of biscuits.

Rosa and Guildman leant back but held each other's gaze.

'Mrs B?' said Igress, walking into the kitchen. 'Any tea on the g— Oh! Lord Guildman.'

Guildman stood up and bowed. 'Mistress.'

Igress's sigh carried an unspoken 'If only.' She started to run her fingers through her hair. 'What a pleasant—'

'Come along, dear,' bustled Mrs B, the tea-tray blocking Igress's way. 'You're just in time for tea. I thought we'd have it in the laboratory today.'

'Sorry?'

Mrs B pushed the tray into Igress's hands.

'Tea. In the laboratory. Today. Now.'

'Oh,' said Igress, finding herself with no excuse to go anywhere except wherever Mrs B was going.

Gussie lay on his bed, his body drained, his mind anguished.

What if Sooty had been right? What if it was all his fault? What if the old lady had only taken poorly since he got there? Suppose she *had* given him life in exchange for hers? He'd no idea what force sustained him; anything seemed to be possible inside these stone walls. Could he, who'd had no control over his own death, now be responsible for the death of another? She'd said that he didn't have to die when she did; could it really be that he was draining the life out of her?

If that were true, he'd have to end it right away. Living his life in someone else's body was bad enough, but using up somebody else's life was a thing too terrible to accept and too big to be left to supposition. He had to know. He had to ask the one person who could tell him the truth.

Instinct bade him release the monumental pain welling inside him. Anger and frustration built into a mighty howl of despair, then his exhausted body found the strength to curl up and he cried himself to sleep.

Rosa and Guildman ran from the drawing room but stopped when they saw Mrs B standing at the entrance to the corridor where Gussie's room was. She put her finger to her lips, held her hand up, turned and listened down the corridor. After a few seconds she turned back again.

'He needs to be alone, milady.'

In an oversized armchair in the drawing room, Rosa leant back on Guildman and his arms wrapped protectively round her.

'Can't we buy Rudolf off, Gil?'

'His pride wants more than money; it wants revenge. My love, you have finally succeeded where his parents and tutors failed: you have given Rudolf a purpose in life.'

'My death,' she said disconsolately.

'An event that – one way or another – he will not live to enjoy, for with your death comes his own. And mine.'

Rosa sighed, and pulled his arms round her more tightly.

'Oh, let's just run off together, Gil.'

'And live as fugitives? Didn't you throw Rudolf out because you couldn't stand living a lie?'

'I threw him out because I couldn't stand *him*.'

'Nevertheless, what profit in swapping one lie for another?'

'Happiness?'

'Tainted by cowardice? And Rudolf running riot through your ancestral home, besmirching your family name? Forever looking over your shoulder in case he's come after you, as you know he will?'

'Hmmm,' said Rosa. 'What will you tell him about where you've been today?'

'The truth. I came to see how good my lady's defences are.'

She stood up and faced him.

'And what about your defences, Gil?'

'Mine?'

She pulled him to his feet. 'Yes, yours.' She kissed him. 'How is your stronghold? Is it...' – kiss – '...in grave danger of being overwhelmed...' – kiss – '...and quite easily taken?'

Guildman smiled his long, slow smile.

'My lady is welcome to try.'

And so the afternoon passed at Castle Stein.

Fran, Sooty and Gussie retreated into sleep; Mrs B prepared dinner; Beaton taught Aidan the art of table-setting; Igress experimented with formulas in the laboratory; Mason avoided building; Rosa tested Guildman's stronghold to the limit.

The dwarf behind the desk at Top Chop read from the paperwork Rudolf thrust at him.

'Name: Lord Rudolf Dibkiss; victim: Lady Rosalind Dibkiss of Castle Stein; to be terminated: as soon as possible. Method of payment?'

Rudolf hefted his bag of gold.

'Sign here,' said the dwarf.

'What?' said Rudolf. 'I've never had to fill forms in before.'

'New procedures. Sign.'

Rudolf signed, and the dwarf whipped the paperwork away.

'Wait here,' he said, leaving the room.

The paperwork returned, affixed to the clipboard of a dwarf whose name-badge proclaimed him to be Top Chop's Head of Customer Relations. He spoke rapidly.

'Ah, Lord Dibkiss. Now before we assess your case, I must explain about a new joint initiative we're trialling with the Town Council.'

'Must you?' said Rudolf wearily.

'Yes. It seems we're much more likely to integrate into the local community if we rationalise our termination services, so to prove our commitment to harmony within the community, we've decided to downsize our operation somewhat.'

'Downsize?'

'We're targeting our range and expertise to a more specific customer base whilst still retaining our high level of commitment to the community as a whole. It's been decided that the aristocracy have the means necessary to facilitate a termination for themselves and therefore should do so, freeing up valuable resources to be redeployed in areas of most need, i.e. the less fortunate members of society, shall we say. The aristocracy can still come to us for aid, and each case will be assessed on its merits – the level of assistance being pro-rata'd on a sliding scale concomitant with the level of income of each applicant, of course. So, under the terms of the new joint initiative we regretfully have to decline your application and refuse your commission.'

'You won't kill my wife?'

'No.'

Rudolf closed his eyes but said nothing. Even he knew better than to argue the toss in the home of the hired killers. He snatched up his bag of gold and stormed out.

When he had gone, the dwarf heaved a sigh of relief, threw the clipboard onto the desk and ripped off his name-badge.

'Wolfson!' he called.

The first dwarf stuck his head round the door. 'Yes, sir?'

'Prepare a final invoice. Usual stuff: job complete, but payment as agreed at twice the usual rate, and send it to Lord Guildman.'

Fran stretched out in bed, then relaxed, and then wasn't relaxed. She sucked her teeth and gave a hum of unease.

'You're back!' Sooty cried, and started nuzzling her.

'I've only been asleep.'

'And now you're awake! How are you feeling?'

Her brow furrowed. 'There's something wrong.'

Sooty jerked his head up to look at her.

'What's wrong? Does it hurt? Where does it hurt? Tell me where it hurts.'

She squinted at him. 'What? No, not me, you fool – I'm fine.' She looked around. 'But there's something wrong, somewhere.'

'Wrong? What? Where? Here? Why?'

'Well, if you'd shut up a minute and let me concentrate, I might be able to find it.'

Sooty slumped. 'You're back all right.'

'Shh!'

Fran scanned the room, trying to locate the source of her disquiet which grew stronger the closer she got to the fireplace. When she saw the Timekeeper, she stopped looking. She got out of bed and checked the pockets of her gown. 'Oh-oh.'

She walked over to the mantelpiece, held the Timekeeper in both hands and closed her eyes; a vision formed in her mind of a paper cone on the forest floor and a dropped torch flaring unexpectedly. Her head drooped.

'Oh, bugger.'

'Come in,' said Gussie flatly, in reply to the knock.

'Only me,' said Fran, sticking her head round the door. 'There's somebody here who'd like to see you,' she added in that sing-song way adults use when trying to mollify children.

'That'll be a first.'

Fran gave up all pretence at tiptoeing round his emotions and sat on the bed.

'Oh, come on. Don't be like that.'

Sooty leapt onto her lap.

Gussie bit back what he was going to say and instead settled for, 'How are you feeling?'

'Me? Fine. Why shouldn't I be?'

'Oh, stop it!' Gussie flashed. 'Stop treating me like some kind of half-wit!'

Fran looked chastened. 'Yes. Well. Anyway, I do feel fine, thank you. Quite recharged.'

'No wonder I felt so exhausted, then.'

'What on earth do you mean?'

Gussie looked away. 'Nothing.'

Fran folded her arms.

'Now you're treating me like a half-wit.'

He looked at his hands. 'Am I using up your life?'

'What?'

'Your life. Your energy. Am I using it up?'

'Using up my— No... whatever gave you that idea?'

He looked her in the eye. 'Are you sure?'

'Of course I'm bloody sure! You're using up your own life, not mine.'

'You're getting weaker as I'm getting stronger. You didn't start having fainting fits until I got here, did you?'

'Ah, I see. You've been listening to this silly little sod.'

She prodded Sooty, who said nothing.

Gussie threw his hands up in despair. 'There you go again. Treating him like a half-wit as well. Treating him like he's got

273

no feelings, like it doesn't matter to him what happens to you.'

'All right!' shouted Fran. She looked at Gussie and spoke slowly and deliberately. 'I have just been telling my very good friend here exactly what happened today.'

'Which was?'

'You haven't noticed, have you? Nobody's noticed.' She rolled her eyes. 'I don't know – you take all that time and trouble and nobody even notices.'

'I didn't notice,' murmured Sooty.

'You'd be too busy going off the deep end, I expect.'

Gussie sat up in bed. 'Notice what?'

Fran rubbed her hand along Sooty's back then rubbed the same hand all over Gussie's face.

'Puh!' he spat. 'What are you playing at?'

'Give me strength,' she muttered. 'Fancy a sneeze? No? I wonder why? Could you be cured? Hmmm, let me think...'

Gussie brightened. 'Cured? I'm not allergic any more?'

He reached out, stroked Sooty with both hands and then smelt his fingers. 'I'm not allergic any more! Nothing! Not a prickle! Not a tingle! It's gone! Oh, you don't know – all my life – sneezing – oh, thank you, thank you. You're a marvel!'

'At last we agree on something.'

'Tee-hee! I'm not allergic any more! Hee hee hee...'

'Well, now you've got over the shock,' Fran said, 'you can come and join the rest of us.' She leaned forward to look at his chest. 'What's happened to your jumper? Why is it— are they claw-marks?'

Gussie pulled the bedcovers up.

'Ah,' said Sooty, 'that was—'

'That was in the woods,' Gussie butted in, staring Sooty out. 'On the way back. I – er – took a wrong turning. Ran into some sharp bushes. Got stuck. Panicked. Sorry.'

'Hmmm,' she said, and sat back. 'You'd best get changed. We'll be in the kitchen.'

Walking away from Gussie's bedroom, Fran said, 'Interesting how he managed to take a wrong turning in the woods when that cart runs in ruts.'

'Baffling,' said Sooty.

Fran sniffed.

'Getting a cold?' asked the cat.

A volcano of anger burned and churned in Rudolf. How *dare* the dwarves refuse his money? And after all he'd been through to get it in the first place. Dwarves would *kill* for the right amount of gold. Literally.

It never occurred to him that they'd also *not* kill for an even righter amount of gold.

He stormed through town a seething mass of venom and blinding rage, heedless of other people's welfare as he pushed them aside, ignorant of the gang of children who exchanged silent signals about the stripy-trousered aristocrat, and oblivious of the child whose accurately timed leg tripped him. As Rudolf went sprawling so did the gold from his moneybag; he was trampled underfoot in the resultant melee, and ten seconds later was alone in the cleanest, emptiest street in Maund. Everyone had disappeared, as had his money.

When Gussie walked into the kitchen Mrs B was delving into a large pan, testing its contents with a fork; Yedder and Sooty were playing slap-hands, with Fran keeping score; Beaton was trying to teach Aidan napkin-folding – Aidan whose attention kept wandering to Igress, who kept darting glances at Guildman, who smiled his long, slow smile, having spent the afternoon with Rosa, who positively glowed after having thoroughly tested Guildman's stronghold.

'Come and sit by me, flower,' said Fran.

As he sat, Gussie swept Sooty into his arms and buried his face in the cat's fur.

'Oi! Cut that out!' shouted a startled Sooty.

Gussie laughed and put him back on the table.

'Sorry! Couldn't resist.'

Sooty stuck out his jaw, twitched his head and, mustering as much dignity as he could, walked over to Rosa.

'I'm not allergic any more,' Gussie beamed, by way of explanation. A murmur of surprise ran around the table.

'Well, seeing as you've brought that up...' said Fran. As all eyes turned to her, she took a deep breath and rattled through the rest of what she had to say. 'This morning I took Gussie to Durney's so I could cure his allergy to Sooty but I managed to make meself collapse but now I'm better so we can get on with the business in hand, Rosa?'

'Hang on,' said Gussie, 'hang on. Why would you make yourself collapse?'

'I didn't do it deliberately!' she snapped. 'I nicked me hand on the tin that Durney keeps one of the herbs in.'

'You lost so much blood that you keeled over?'

'I didn't lose any blood.'

'Then I've missed a vital point of the story because—'

'*I'm* allergic to the herb that cured *you*! I nicked me hand, stuck it in me mouth without thinking, sucked in the herb and bang! Over I went. Satisfied?'

Gussie looked thoughtful. 'Erm... no, not really.'

'Look,' said Fran, clearly intending to finish the issue, 'if I'd been really poorly – proper badly – then Sooty wouldn't have been lounging about in the kitchen, he'd have been racing to be with me. All right?'

'Why?'

'Mother Nature! If anything serious happens to me, he' – she pointed at Sooty, who pointed at himself – 'will find me, wherever I am. That's the way it works. Now can we get on?'

Gussie tilted his head to one side.

'Why did we have to go to Durney's?'

'Because he's the only one round here who grows the stuff!'

'Oh.' Gussie paused. 'Why doesn't he live in the castle?'

'What?!'

'If Durney's your brother, why is he out in the forest? Why doesn't he live in the castle?'

Fran's face said that this was the most ridiculous question yet. 'Because he doesn't want to. Happy now?'

Gussie pouted for a few seconds.

Yedder leant across to him.

'I'd say yes, old sport, or she'll explode.'

Fran smacked Yedder on the arm.

Gussie giggled. 'Happy.'

'At last,' said Rosa. 'Perhaps now we can eat. If nobody has any objection – and you'd better not have – I'd like all of us to dine together tonight, and that includes you two, my lords.'

During dinner, the talk was of the weather, fashion, science, art, sport and in the event of a victorious attack by Rudolf exactly how many of them were likely to perish.

After dinner, Sooty stretched out by the kitchen fire while Beaton, Mrs B and Aidan cleared up. Rosa led the rest of the party into the library.

'I'm sorry, I don't play cards,' said Gussie, as they moved towards a large round table covered in green baize.

Yedder clapped him on the back. 'Have to, old thing, if you want to be accepted into polite society.'

Gussie chortled. 'Oh, yes, I'm going to be a must at the posh parties, aren't I?' He pulled open his collar and pointed to his stitching. 'It's supposed to be the ladies who have the most interesting necklines.'

'Don't fret, old love – my tailor says ruffs could be making a comeback.'

Gussie looked horrified. 'If that's what he's thinking he needs his scissors taking off him.'

Fran sat at the table and picked up a pack of cards.

'If Yedder's tailor told him holeless balaclavas were in fashion, he'd walk round with a sock pulled over his head.'

Yedder leant over the back of Fran's chair and tickled her. She squirmed in her seat and slapped at him, and he laughed as he took a seat beside her.

Gussie sat on her other side. 'I'll just watch.'

Fran tried to push him away. 'Oh, no. I'm not having you

sitting next to me going, "if you've got three of them does that beat his two of those and one of that?" Go to bed.'

Gussie stayed put. 'Go chase your granny round the graveyard! If you remember, I didn't say I *couldn't* play cards – I said I *don't* play cards.'

The other players smiled in varying degrees at Gussie having the temerity to bite back at Fran.

'What are you lot grinning at?' she demanded.

'Nothing, nothing,' chuckled Rosa from the safety of the other side of the table, onto which she lifted a flat wooden box the size of one of Mrs B's biscuit tins.

'And the reason you don't play, Gussie?' asked Guildman.

Gussie tutted. 'Oh for crying out loud! Your life's not your own round here, is it?'

'Come on, Gussie,' said Igress, putting her hand on his arm. 'Why don't you play cards?'

'All right,' he said, and he gave a tight little shake of his head. 'I can't afford it.'

'Dashed good reason,' said Yedder.

Guildman nodded. 'Very wise.'

'One of the best reasons there is,' said Igress.

'You're not very good, you mean,' said Fran, closely examining the cards before starting to shuffle them.

'Aunty!' chided Rosa. 'Gussie, how much money have you spent since you've been here?'

He looked down and fussily smoothed the nap on the baize but said nothing.

Fran divided the pack into two and expertly interleaved the cards, merging them in a pattering riffle.

279

'Gussie?' Rosa said again, lifting the lid of the wooden box.

He put his hands together and banged them on the table in front of him.

'Nothing,' he said tartly, looking up but refusing to meet any of their gazes. 'Not a bean. Not a sou. Not a red cent. Not a cent of any colour whatsoever. Nothing. All right?'

'So why do you need money?'

'What?'

'You heard,' said Fran. 'Why do you need money?'

She slapped the pack on the table and smoothed the cards out into a long straight line. She lifted the bottom-most card which flipped all the rest over in a continuous wave.

'Things,' he said.

'What sort of things?' asked Igress.

'You're fed and watered, clothed and housed, warm and dry,' Fran said, gathering the cards in a smooth sweep. 'What else do you want money for?'

She split the pack, fanned half of it in each hand, merged the two fans in one swift movement and squared the cards up by banging their edges on the table. She finally placed them face down in front of her and clasped her hands together.

Guildman reached across and took the pack. He slid the top five cards onto the table and turned over the sixth, which would have been Fran's card. He held it up towards her; it was an ace.

Yedder looked mock-shocked. 'You bad girl,' he said.

Fran pursed her lips and primped the back of her hair, then winked at Guildman and grinned. He smiled, remade the pack, shuffled it and handed it back to her.

'What do you need money for, Gussie?' said Rosa.

Gussie shrank slightly in his chair and wrinkled his nose.

'Card games?' he said, with a hint of hope.

She shook her head. 'No.'

From the box on the table she took a small, thin, wooden trough containing carved roundels with differently coloured centres. She pushed it across to him.

'We play with these.'

He picked up one of the roundels and looked at it closely as Rosa pushed a wooden trough towards each player.

'You play for bits of wood?' said Gussie.

'Chips,' said Rosa.

His face lit up. 'Yes, please.'

'They're *called* chips.'

His face fell again. 'Oh.'

'Each one has a certain value, and you use them like money, except they all get handed back at the end of the game.'

'What's the point in that?'

'It's fun, Gussie,' said Igress. 'Don't people play for fun where you come from?'

'Fun?' he said. 'They're too busy playing for survival.'

By the end of the evening the gambling chips in front of Gussie far outnumbered those of the other five players put together.

'You wouldn't be getting tired at all, would you, Gussie?' asked Rosa haltingly.

'Funny you should mention that,' he replied, with an enthusiasm which made five hearts sink, 'I was just thinking I'll win one more game and then I'll get some shut-eye.'

'You win one more game and I'll shut your eyes for you,' said Fran.

'Ooh,' said Rosa. 'It sounds like Gussie's not the only one who needs sleep.'

Igress stifled a yawn. 'I'm surprised any of us are still awake after a day like today.'

'Very true, sweet thing,' said Yedder.

'In that case,' said Gussie, laying down another winning hand, 'may I wish you all a very good night.'

A consensus groan fell into the middle of the table along with the losing hands of cards. Gussie picked up the remaining chips and added them to his hoard. His mouth formed a tiny, irritating smile and he tapped his steepled fingers together.

'Mmmm. Now let me see. What does this add up to?'

'You not being asked to play cards again,' said Fran.

Gussie's grin broadened.

'Ooooh, Miss Grumpybum. Nobody likes a sore loser.'

'You've got ten seconds to get out of here before you become a very, very sore winner.'

'And on that happy note,' Rosa broke in, 'I think it's probably time to call it a night.'

Yedder stood up. 'Miss Igress, would you take my arm please? Fran, would you take the other one? Gussie, be a love and get the door, will you? I can't get both of these gorgeous creatures through the one side.'

Gussie rose and bowed exaggeratedly.

'Why, certainly, my lord,' he said, and after Yedder had seen his charges safely into the hall, Gussie closed the doors on Rosa and Guildman.

Guildman enveloped Rosa's hands in his and held them close to his chest. 'Thank you for the best day of my life.'

A thin veil of sadness clouded the hope in her eyes. 'Oh, Gil,' she whispered, 'couldn't we have so many more?'

He wasn't expecting to be dragged into her bedroom.

'Madam, I must protest! I'm not that sort of lord.'

'No, Yedder,' said Fran, closing the door, 'and you're not as stupid as you make out, either.'

He giggled. 'Curses! You've seen through my disguise.'

She pushed him onto the ottoman at the foot of the bed.

'Shut up, you fool, before I change my opinion.'

Yedder folded his arms, mock-pouted and said nothing.

Fran faced him. 'Why have you and Guildman stuck by Rudolf all these years?'

Yedder looked at her as if she'd asked him why he breathed.

'Rude? Why shouldn't we? We were at school together, in the army together...'

'But he's a snake!'

'He wasn't always, and even snakes have their beauty. When things are going his way, he's a good laugh. And he's mostly harmless. Oh, he's full of sound and fury, yes, but that blinds him to reality and makes him the architect of his own misfortune half the time. And for the other half—'

'I was wrong,' said Fran. 'You are as stupid as you make out. He's threatened to kill Rosa!'

'Yes, but he won't,' said Yedder.

Bafflement spread across Fran's face. 'Why not?'

'Rude's been threatening Roz ever since their wedding

reception. And yes, he's a bit more intense about it now but all his threats come to nothing – Gil makes sure of that.'

'What?'

'Oh, come on, don't tell me you don't know. If someone threatens the person you love, where's the best place to be?'

'At their side, defending them.'

'No – at their enemy's side, making sure he doesn't get anywhere near them.'

'So why doesn't Guildman kill Rudolf?'

Yedder looked aghast. 'Kill him?! Why?'

Fran grimaced. 'Because I don't think Rudolf's harmless any more. By stopping his money, Rosa's turned his idle threat into a raging ambition. And besides – if Rudolf's dead, it's Rosa and Guildman happy ever after!'

'Oh, I see...'

He sat for a moment, nodding, as if working through the scenario, and his demeanour changed entirely as he sloughed off the clownish aristocrat; he spoke quietly and deliberately, his words heavy with authority and experience.

'Killing is a savage and sordid business, Fran, and Gil is neither savage nor sordid. Killing Rudolf to get Rosalind would be unthinkable to such an honourable man.'

Fran softened her approach. 'He doesn't have to do it himself, does he? Just make sure that it's done.'

'Blood is blood, whether it's on the hands of the killers or on the money that pays them.'

In Fran's mind, two jigsaw pieces suddenly fitted together.

'Money! You said all Rudolf needs to launch an assault on the castle is money, didn't you?'

'How ironic,' said Yedder. 'When Roz gave him money, he didn't use it against her; now she doesn't, all he wants it for is to pay an army to go after her. And that won't come cheap.'

'So why doesn't Guildman give him the money to attack? Then Rudolf can get killed in the fighting.'

'What man pays to endanger the woman he loves? What man pays another for purposes of instigating violence? Certainly not Guildman.'

Fran sighed. 'No, no, I know. Guildman is an honourable man.' She pulled at her chin. 'Isn't there anything *you* can do?'

'Me being a less honourable man?'

Fran closed her eyes momentarily and sagged.

'Oh, Yedder, I am sorry – I didn't mean that at all.' She ran a hand across her face then walked towards him. 'Forgive me, love – you know I never meant it that way. I'm just— I want to see an end to this thing, that's all.'

Yedder stood up, put his arm round her shoulders and kissed the top of her head.

'We all do, Fran. We all do.'

Gussie changed into his pyjamas, once again gleefully running his hand in wonderment along the contents of his wardrobe and marvelling at how well his life seemed to be going since his death.

He turned towards the bed; on his pillow rested a squiggle of fading red ribbon that had severe and ancient creases from being long tied around a teddy bear's neck. As he picked it up it curled, trying to regain its usual shape. Gussie smiled, bit his lip and swallowed hard.

He opened the wardrobe and delved into the sewing box for a pin; he crossed the ends of the ribbon over to form a simple loop and pinned it to the lapel on Mr Beaton senior's best dress uniform.

Fran charmed the creaking hinges into silence as she opened the back door of Castle Stein and carried her broomstick into the courtyard at the height of the moon. Only Beaton and Mrs B would have been awake anyway, but stealth would save Fran time, explanation and unnecessary fuss.

She rose, flew over the castle roof and hovered silently for a moment, surveying the ever-expanding agglomeration of wood, masonry, glass, slate and canvas which housed Maund's great unwashed – literally, for the most part. Scattered mansions that had once stood out as solitary magnificences in vast landscapes were now in danger of relegation to mere gatehouses in an invisible curtain wall that was gradually being overwhelmed by the sprawl it sought to contain.

Fran coughed, fixed her sights on a distant point, and flew.

'Come in, Mistress Stein.'

'How did you know it was me?' she said to the back of the armchair.

The occupant of the chair chuckled.

'I receive no visitors here. No-one calls without invitation, and I invite no-one. There are no matters in my life pressing enough to warrant the invasion of my privacy – except one.'

'I might have been that one.'

Guildman stood, turned to her and bowed.

'Mistress Stein, you have my highest regard and respect, but my heart will know when Rosalind comes to me.'

'Humph.'

'Also, my lady would not be as stealthy as yourself.'

'True, true.'

'Nor would she come through the open window on a broomstick.'

'Ah.'

She dismounted and leant the broomstick against a wall.

'Please take a seat,' Guildman smiled. 'Tea?'

He tugged on a tapestry bell-pull richly embroidered with gold thread, bordered by thick burgundy cord and weighed down by a fat tassel. Just the sort of thing to adorn a rich lord's bedroom. In this case, almost the only thing.

Despite the solidity that castle walls bring, the room's austerity told Fran that this accommodation was temporary rather than settled, and could – and would – be vacated for a better life at a moment's notice, if that moment was the right one. It was the room of someone whose life was suspended, awaiting fulfilment; the room of a young man whose reason for moving to a bigger room had been cruelly ripped from him and given to someone else.

Where the semicircle of fire-glow petered out, the room became spartan; cold, harsh and dark except for a thin line of light which invaded under another door at the back of the room but died before making any appreciable impact.

'Not exactly the lap of luxury, is it?' she said.

'It suffices.'

The door opened a little, but the servant did not enter.

'Tea for Mistress Stein,' said Guildman, 'and a bottle of the Volunteers '39, please.'

The door closed again.

'A good year for Volunteers,' said Fran. 'I see you're not entirely without comfort.'

'The wine is for taste, not comfort. I want no comfort other than my lady.'

Fran looked around the room.

'Rosa deserves better than this, Guildman.'

'As Lady Guildman she would have the best of everything.'

Fran sniffed. 'Isn't that title already taken?'

Rudolf's lifelong dedication to vigorous sports of every description – involving variously sized animals and women, though not usually at the same time – had ensured that his body was accustomed to all kinds of physical abuse, and had subsequently developed an extraordinary capacity to bounce back. He lay on his bed in the Lamb and Werewolf, the ministrations of Mrs Rigton having straightened out his body. However, his mind was still twisted, and by their refusal to kill Rosa the dwarves had tightened the screw.

The situation had gone on too long. Each darted glance, elbow nudge and fresh piece of speculation about himself and his continued presence at the Lamb and Werewolf stabbed him to the very remnants of his soul. Every tiny misfortune, every slight, every unhappy mischance where he emerged worse off poisoned his life and robbed him of contentment. And today had been the last of a very large number of straws.

'Mistress Stein – or should I say Lady Frances Stein? – I feel there is mischief in your question. As you well know, my mother would relinquish her title as the current Lady Guildman and become the Dowager Lady Guildman.'

Fran pulled a face.

'Never could get the hang of how the titles worked. And I might've been Lady Frances once, but I also became someone else many years ago, as *you* well know, Lord Guildman.'

He smiled and bowed briefly, acknowledging her point.

'Besides,' Fran continued, 'if I know your mother, she won't take kindly to being called the Dowager Lady Guildman.'

'Nevertheless, that's what she'll be.'

Fran took a deep breath.

'So, as Lady Guildman, Rosa shall have everything her heart desires.'

'Everything she doesn't yet know she desires.'

'And I suppose you'll go to the ends of the earth to fetch these wonderful things for her.'

'No, I shall send others to fetch them. I shall never leave my lady's side.'

Fran frowned.

'All this "my lady" stuff, Gil... she's a living, breathing, intelligent woman. She has needs, wants, desires...'

'As do we all.'

'She doesn't need adoring, worshipping, handling with kid gloves – she needs stimulation, challenge, passion... love.'

'She will have all that. I do love her.'

'I know. I can hear your heart breaking from here.'

Lady Yedder stirred in her sleep and stretched out her hand to her husband. He clasped it in his and kissed her gently on the forehead. 'Hush, my love. Go back to sleep.'

She mumbled and slipped back into a dream, a luxury that for once escaped Yedder as he clung to his wife's hand and stared at the ceiling.

'Why don't you buy Rudolf off?' said Fran, pouring tea.

'He could have this castle and all it contains but she would still not be safe. Only revenge will satisfy his wounded pride.'

'Kill him, then.'

'Kill a man to take his wife? Become not only a thief but a murderer as well? Mistress Stein, you ask too much of me.'

'I thought nothing was too much to ask for Rosa's sake.'

'What life for me if I lose the lady's respect?'

'What life for you if you lose the lady altogether?'

Although the headboard had lost a button, a silver chain around Rosa's neck had gained one – one with the Guildman crest on it. She slept soundly, blissfully unaware that she was the subject of protracted discussions. Sooty also slept blissfully unaware: firstly that Fran was out, and secondly that she'd made him unaware to avoid an inquest when she returned.

'Can't you provide the money for him to get himself killed?'

'Mistress Stein, that is merely an extension of your second suggestion, which is not open to me as an honourable man.'

Fran put her teacup down sharply on its saucer.

'Honourable man! That's all I hear about you – bloody

honourable man.' She clattered the cup and saucer onto a side table. 'Do you want to be the most honourable and most miserable man in Maund all your life? Or do you want to be the most honourable and most miserable corpse in the cemetery as well? Because that's what you're going to be if you don't get up off your honourable backside and do something!'

Guildman held up his wine glass and examined it.

'I cannot – and will not – provoke a confrontation.'

'Because you are an honourable man.'

'No. Because I cannot guarantee that he will be killed.'

Fran leant towards him. 'I can.'

He held her gaze. 'Is it not one of the precepts of The Union that those who hold the power will do no harm?'

She cocked her head on one side and winced. 'Technically.'

He said nothing, but his silence asked all his questions.

Fran looked down at her hands.

'I wouldn't kill him myself, just ensure that it happens.'

He still said nothing.

'What on earth do you think Gussie's for?!' she said.

Guildman rolled his glass in his hands. 'I did wonder.'

Fran clenched her fists and forced her words through gritted teeth. 'Oh, Mother Nature, give me strength! There's no helping some people!'

She took a breath and studied him as she calmed down. His was a face that was open, honest, a little mischievous and infinitely sad.

'What kind of man are you, Gil?' she asked softly. 'I thought you yearned for her.'

'Yearning is for beginners, Mistress Stein.'

'So go get her.'

He drained his glass. 'Sadly, impossible, I think.'

'It'll change from impossible to inevitable. And I don't think that, Gil, I *know*. And you ought to know by now.'

'But until it does change, it is my duty as a gentleman to maintain the status quo – in my lady's favour, of course.'

'And it's my duty as Rosa's aunt to see that she's happy. I don't mind Rudolf wasting his life, but it saddens me to see you wasting yours and I'm damned if Rosa's going to waste hers. And for her, a life without you is a wasted life. So, it looks like I've got to save both your hides.'

Rudolf seethed as he bit his nails and spat them out. The roof over his head was not the one he wanted. He was fed and watered, but at the castle he hadn't had to pay for that.

Mind you, he wasn't paying for it now. Yedder was. He'd have to pay him back at some point, he supposed; then again, Yedder wasn't the sharpest tool in the box and it was unlikely he was keeping a tally anyway, the generous, soon-parted-from-his-money fool.

Not like the other pompous prig who kept everybody and everything on a tight rein and made sure fair was fair.

At the Lamb and Werewolf Rudolf did have the use of hot and cold running landlady, something that he'd never had at Castle Stein. Rosa had always run icy, and the only times she'd run anywhere near hot was with temper, not temptation.

Well, see how long her temper kept her warm at the bottom of the moat.

Alone again, Guildman stared into the fire. Fran had given him much to think about. Not that he hadn't thought about it before, over the years.

Every year.

Every day.

His honour was the one rigid framework upon which he had built his life, but was it also a cage that kept him within narrow, unhappy confines? Did the code that made his life worthy also bleed that life of all pleasure and render it, ironically, worthless?

In the depths of his soul a flame started to burn, casting light onto a pain that he could no longer keep buried. Illumination of his hurt forced him to acknowledge its presence, but didn't ease it; visibility simply made it impossible to ignore a heartache that would, he knew, grow to agony.

And now Fran had imparted urgency. With her involvement came the growing feeling that things would, as she had said, change from impossible to inevitable, and there wouldn't be a damned thing he could do about it. His future was no longer his to determine. The tide of his life was turning, and he must ride it at the flood or be swept away.

A tiny wellspring of hope bubbled inside him. He refreshed his wine glass and carried it towards the back of the room where the thin line of light offered an invitation; he opened the door and stepped forward, crossing the threshold of a future.

Light and warmth from a blazing fireplace flooded over him. In this room, opulence was standard. The finest carpets entirely covered the floor, themselves bestrewn with thick rugs. Luxurious swags and drapes cosseted the windows and door frames; vibrant tapestries and needlepoints obliterated the starkness of the walls, and were half-hidden by the best furniture money could buy: sofas, dressing tables, chests of drawers and wardrobes.

All, though, were dwarfed by the magnificence of the room's centrepiece – a majestic mahogany four-poster bed drowning in silks and velvets.

Every available surface was piled high with gifts of all shapes and sizes. And everything, from the tiniest ring box to the largest clothes chest, was neatly and artfully wrapped in hand-blocked paper, secured by gold and silver ribbons. From each ribbon-plaited fastening hung a hand-written tag bearing the name 'Rosalind Guildman'.

He raised his glass in salute and drained the wine. Suddenly he turned and hurled the glass back across his spartan room. It smashed into the fireplace, and he smiled his long, slow smile.

She must die. And if the dwarves wouldn't do it, he must. He must have an army. He must get some money.

Moneylenders? They weren't called sharks for nothing. No respecters of rank or class either, those thieves; it didn't matter to them whether the limb they snapped was clad in coarse woollen or fine silk.

Did anybody owe him money? That'd be the day. Very few people were prepared to ask him for an opinion, let alone cash.

Sell something? He'd gladly sell everything he possessed, but even in Maund there was a very limited market for second-hand hair and teeth.

Theft? Anybody who left *that* amount of money lying about

where he could steal it would have long since been done over by everybody from the council to the clergy.

That left one course of action.

'Mugged?' Yedder repeated, as Rigton placed two beers – one unadorned and one stuffed with fruit, little paper umbrellas, a tiny carved and painted parrot and several ferns – on the bar counter in the parlour at the Lamb and Werewolf and polished his own fingerprints off the ceramic and brass hand pumps.

'Lucky to get away with his life, he says, my lord.'

The street door swung open and a small man walked in. His face was partially obscured by the large hood on his cloak and he brandished a handful of oblong cards.

'Good morning!' he announced. 'It's a good morning for a gamble! Who will buy my lottery tickets? One in five wins! Get your lottery tickets here!'

'Push off,' said Rigton, gesturing. 'This is a respectable establishment. No gambling here.'

'I'm shocked – do you hear me – shocked, to find out that gambling has not been taking place on these premises,' said the man, glancing around the parlour as he walked towards the bar.

'Get out or I'll throw you out.'

'Come now, kindly barkeep! Pennies for a possible fortune? What harm is there in that? You wouldn't deny a friendly lottery seller a living, would you?'

'I'm warning you...'

The man looked wildly around the room.

'Surely there must be some penniless soul here today in need of a fortune.'

'I shan't tell you again.'

'He shall have everything his heart desires. Everything he doesn't yet know he desires.'

'Right!' said Rigton, throwing his bar towel across his shoulder. 'Enough!'

'Hold hard, kindly barkeep,' Guildman grinned. 'I feel that the friendly lottery seller would appreciate a cup of tea. Is that not right, friendly lottery seller?'

'What?' said the man.

'You're wasting your time, Mistress Stein.'

'Fran!' squealed Yedder.

The man's face flickered to that of its true owner as Fran hit Yedder. 'Shut up, you fool, you'll give the game away.'

'I thought that's what you were here to do,' said Guildman.

Her lottery seller's face returned as the door to the stairs opened.

Mrs Rigton came in, buttoning her blouse. 'Better get a beer ready,' she said, before spying the parlour's occupants, whereupon at least three recently fastened buttons burst open again as she sashayed towards Guildman, her smile as wide as her expanse of chest. 'My lords,' she said silkily, 'pray forgive my state. I am not long risen.'

'I bet something was,' murmured Fran. Yedder snorted into his beer. Rigton started to fill another tankard.

Guildman held up a silver coin. 'Madam?'

'Yes,' breathed Mrs Rigton, her chest swelling as he whispered in her ear. 'Oh, a silver piece will buy you much more than that, my lord.'

'That is all I require,' he said.

Her chest deflated as she grabbed the coin with one hand and Fran's hand with the other.

'You've got to get out of here,' she said. 'Come on! Through the back.'

Fran was too startled to argue as Mrs Rigton dragged her out of the parlour.

Yedder and Guildman moved to the rickety table. Rigton put the full tankard on the counter at the same time as the door to the stairs opened again.

Rudolf strode in, swept up the tankard and joined his companions, slapping a folded parchment in front of Yedder.

'Read that!' he said.

Yedder unfolded the paper. The angular writing was occasionally punctuated by large black blobs where Rudolf had obviously changed his mind about various terms and conditions. Yedder's eyes popped. 'I say, Gil, listen to this. *I, Rudolf Dibkiss, do hereby contract with the undersigned*... blah blah... *advances the sum of*... is that a two or a seven?'

'Seven,' said Rudolf.

'*The sum of*... huge number... *to be a loan from the undersigned party*... blah blah... *for the period of*... oh, seems to be a gap there.'

Rudolf waved his hand. 'We can fill in the details later.'

'*The amount to be paid back being the original capital plus*... how much? Is that a six or a zero?'

'Zero.'

'Thought so.'

Guildman took the paper from Yedder.

'I thought you were going to see the dwarves yesterday, Rudolf. Have your plans changed again?'

'Yes,' snapped Rudolf.

'You had rather a hefty bag of dosh too,' added Yedder.

'And I don't now. If you must know, I was viciously robbed of my hard-earned cash.'

'As Yedder will be if he agrees to this document,' said Guildman. 'You're asking him for a virtually interest-free loan of a huge amount over an unspecified time period.'

'I'll pay him back,' sneered Rudolf.

'When, old thing?'

Guildman peered at the manuscript.

'According to the small print, the loan will be repaid sometime after Rudolf has retaken Castle Stein. And according to the tiny print, that can be anything up to ten years after.'

'Sorry, Rude, no can do,' said Yedder.

'Oh, what? Why not? It's a business deal, that's all. You have my word you'll get your money back.'

Guildman laughed. 'Your word changes to suit your situation. That's no guarantee.'

'And that's where you're wrong, know-it-all. I'll have to pay him back – it's a legally binding document.'

'And you have as much respect for the law as Yedder does for the long and venerable tradition of brewing.'

Yedder raised his crowded glass. 'Anyway, old sport, I haven't got that kind of money.'

Rudolf's retort was lost in the creaking hinge of the street door, which opened to admit what looked like a small man in a large hooded cloak.

'Oh,' said Rigton stiffly. 'It's you, friendly lottery seller. What is your business here today?'

The lottery seller looked at Rigton for a long moment, then waved the lottery tickets in the air and pointed to them.

'Oh, yes, of course,' the landlord sputtered. 'You have come to sell your winning lottery tickets, have you not?'

'Indeed, kindly barkeep. Who will buy my lottery tickets? One in five wins! Get your lottery tickets!' The friendly lottery seller walked towards the three aristocrats. 'A little outlay for a large income! Surely there must be some penniless soul here today who needs a fortune and what better way to gain it than by a lucky lottery ticket from a friendly lottery seller?'

'Are they winners?' chirped Yedder.

'One of them is, my lord. Guaranteed. Sure-fire winner. Can't fail.'

'Good-oh. Let's have one.'

'You don't even know what the prize is,' said Rudolf.

'Many, many small prizes, sir,' said the man, 'and one massive jackpot. Riches beyond imagining. Enough to buy this pub. Enough to buy a brewery. Enough to buy a mansion with servants and the carriage of your dreams. Why, enough to buy the castle that my lords look like they already own.'

Yedder chuckled. 'Well, you can never have too many castles, I say. I'll take a ticket.' He handed over a coin.

The friendly lottery seller weighed it in his hand.

'The fortune only comes to those in need. This coin tells me that my lord has inherited money, scavenged from the wealth of the common people.'

'I say, that's a bit strong, isn't it?' said Yedder, taking a ticket and opening its three cardboard windows.

'Has my lord won?'

'Wa-hey!' cried Yedder. 'It says *You're — a — winner!*'

Rudolf snatched the ticket 'Oh, what?!'

The lottery seller took it from him, delved in his pocket and withdrew a lollipop, which he gave to Yedder.

'Your winnings, my lord.'

'One of the many, many small prizes?' laughed Yedder.

'Quite right, sir. Sadly, there's no extra fortune for you, but justice is served; the money is one step closer to those who need it.' The friendly lottery seller gestured to Guildman. 'My lord — care to chance a coin?'

'Alas no. I will not obstruct your justice, and as another scavenger of the wealth of the common people, I would not wish a common person to work one hour more to provide me with coin to give those who prey on the gullible and greedy.'

'Touchy,' murmured the friendly lottery seller.

'Don't you mean touché, old thing?' said Yedder.

'I know what I mean. You will not play, my lord?'

'I will not play,' said Guildman. 'I would rather those in need of a fortune had more chance of taking one from you, however slim the odds.'

'Hell fire!' Rudolf spat. 'Guildman, it's only a game! I'll have a ticket, especially if Lord Prig here won't.'

'My lord must provide me with coin first,' said the lottery seller. 'Otherwise the fortune will not come to him.'

'Yedder, give the man a coin.'

'That would make it my lord scavenger's ticket, and therefore his fortune.'

Rudolf breathed heavily down his nose.

'Yedder, give me a coin to give to this lunatic.'

Yedder did so.

'Now that you have coin, my lord,' said the lottery seller, 'you shall have a ticket. A sure-fire winner, sir. I foretell that justice will be served and my lord will get his reward.'

Rudolf tore at the three false panels on the front of the card, and let out a shout.

'Have you won, Rude?' asked Yedder.

Guildman stared the friendly lottery seller in the eye.

Rudolf threw the card on the table.

'There's justice for you!'

Yedder picked it up.

'Gil, what does it mean when your winning line is *seven, seven, banana*?'

Guildman raised an eyebrow and continued to stare at the lottery seller, whose eyes were widening.

'It means that your coin has gone into the coffers of those who prey on the gullible and greedy,' he said, 'and the friendly lottery seller has gained our trust under false pretences.'

'Sorry, Rude – it looks like you've lost.'

'Despite stating that this was a sure-fire winner and the gamble could not fail,' stressed Guildman. 'What went wrong, friendly lottery seller?'

'I've not been well?' offered the friendly lottery seller.

'In that case, you'd better go home and have a lie down,' said Yedder.

'Before I lie you down permanently,' snarled Rudolf, clenching his fists and starting to get up.

Guildman put his arm out, blocking Rudolf and forcing him back into his seat.

'I think we should give the friendly lottery seller one more chance, don't you, Yedder?'

The friendly lottery seller nodded frantically.

'Oh, why not,' said Yedder, reaching for his money.

'No,' said Guildman firmly. 'I will pay.'

'You?' laughed Rudolf. 'Lord Prig? After all you've just said, you're going to—'

Guildman's gloved hand clamped over Rudolf's mouth, halting the rest of his jibe. Squeezing tightly, Guildman pulled Rudolf's head towards him and spoke very deliberately.

'Forget what I said. I will pay.'

He pushed Rudolf's head away.

Rudolf stretched his mouth and rubbed his face.

'By the gods, Guildman,' he blustered, 'I think you're finally picking up what lording's all about.'

Yedder's grin vanished as Guildman spoke to the friendly lottery seller.

'Or perhaps I have realised that in order to win anything in life, you have to take a gamble.'

He pushed a coin across the table.

The friendly lottery seller pocketed it, held up a ticket and with the slightest vocal tremble said, 'Is my lord certain that he wishes to play?'

'Certain.'

'Is my lord prepared for the consequences of his actions?'

'Well prepared.'

'Even at the cost to his soul?'

'Oh, for the love of—' wailed Rudolf. 'Will you give him the bloody thing and have done with it?'

'It's my lord's first gamble. I'm trying to make sure—'

Guildman's hand closed around the lottery seller's wrist.

'I'm sure,' he said quietly, and took the lottery ticket. He freed the lottery seller and opened the first panel on the card as Rudolf peered over his shoulder.

'I say,' piped Yedder, 'wouldn't it be a hoot if Gil won the jackpot!'

'Oh, yes, a real barrel of laughs,' said Rudolf.

Guildman opened the second panel.

'I mean,' added Yedder brightly, 'out of the three of us, who needs the money least? Gil!'

Rudolf groaned.

Guildman looked at the friendly lottery seller, whose eyes burned encouragement into his soul. The air between them collapsed under the weight of the unheard messages passing across the table in eye contact.

Rigton stopped polishing.

Yedder had nothing to say.

Guildman opened the third panel.

'Bastard!' spat Rudolf, and rested his forehead on the rickety table.

The friendly lottery seller handed Guildman a folded note.

'Be at this address at the stated time this evening.'

Guildman pocketed the paper without unfolding it.

'I'll be there.'

'Where? What time? I've got—' said Rudolf.

'You won't be there,' Guildman cut in. 'I shall be alone.'

'Alone, Gil?' said Yedder.

'Alone, Yedder. I'll join you later.'

'You're mad, picking up your winnings on your own,' said Rudolf. 'There's people in this town who'd kill you for a thousandth of what you'll be carrying.'

'Then I'll make sure you're otherwise occupied, Rudolf.'

When she returned to Castle Stein Fran went to bed. She was a little tired from her exertions and knew she would need all her strength for the coming times, but she also wanted to mull over – yet again – the possible consequences of her actions without interruption or suspicion from anyone. She had set something in motion, and wanted to make sure she'd done everything she could to help it get to the right destination.

At five o'clock, Rudolf's bedroom door opened and Mrs Rigton entered, the bottom corners of an envelope tucked into the low neckline of her dress. 'A boy brought this for you.'

'Bring it here, then,' said Rudolf, from the bed.

She sauntered across the room and bent over Rudolf, proffering him the note on the plate that was her bosom.

Rudolf ran both his hands from her neck down her chest to the note, which he then plucked from its perch. He broke open the seal and lifted the piece of paper with one hand while playing with the laces on Mrs Rigton's bodice with the other. His eyes scanned the note.

'I have to go out this evening,' he said, throwing the piece of paper onto the floor. 'But not yet,' he added, as the loosening bodice became the focus of his attention.

~•~

NOTES ON

Lawyers

In Maund, few members of society are more despised than lawyers, because right or wrong, win or lose, justice or injustice, they make money out of everybody – criminals and honest folk alike. Because of this, their trade association is called The Sinidexters, indicating that lawyers can take their fee from either side, or, more usually, both.

And lawyers have another ace up their sleeve: the more honest a client wants a lawyer to be the more it will cost, and the more dishonest a client wants a lawyer to be the more it will cost. A beautifully simple financial plan. To train as a lawyer in Maund and go broke shows not only a spectacular lack of financial acumen, but also a serious personality defect.

Most people think that the secret of success as a lawyer lies in knowing all there is to know about the law.

Not so. If you can find a lawyer like that, you'll be looking at someone who has far too much time and money on his hands. To reach such a detailed knowledge of legal matters is incredibly tedious, takes years off your life and involves costly rooms lined with oak-panelled bookcases holding endless yards of leather-bound, gilt-embossed hardcover volumes which constantly need updating with every new precedent set. And that only leads to more expense, keeping the volumes safe from the thieves who may one day depend upon the very same books for their freedom – not that there are particularly literate thieves in Maund, but a good legal textbook can keep a fire going for quite a while, once the leather's been stripped for footwear and the cover boards are replacing broken windows.

Some people think that the secret of success as a lawyer is to know enough to not get caught.

Again, not so. Legal dealings always involve more than one party, and you can't legislate for unexpected stupidity by others: there's no declared standard for foolishness, and many a foolproof plan has come a cropper because it's been based on the wrong kind of fool.

Neither can you legislate for chance. If your trusted courier is mugged by a low-life and your vitally important secret missive falls into the wrong hands, will it be your fault? No. Will your life – professionally and literally in some cases – be over as a result? More than likely.

The secret of success as a lawyer is to know enough so that if you do get caught, you can get yourself off and put away those who didn't know enough and who may want to come after you because you did. It's always best to stay ahead of the game, or at least make sure you've read and understood all the rules before play starts. That's why the best lawyers in Maund don't employ clerks or operate from offices insulated with thick legal tomes, but work from their heads and their wits, rarely using more than one sheet of paper and a pencil.

And it has to be said that knowing vast amounts about the law is one thing, but knowing a small amount about a judge can be far more effective.

The Sinidexters own several rooms across the town available for lawyers to rent by the hour, giving them access to office space for as long or as short as they need it without them having a fixed address that disgruntled clients could camp outside. The standard of room varies according to the level of impression that the lawyer wishes to leave upon his client, and gives the lawyers' association a foothold in several properties in what may, one day, be prime locations in Maund. If property prices ever rise and the developers move in, compensation may be the word on everyone's lips, and Maund's lawyers have bigger lips than anyone – all the better to suck the last penny out of everybody's purse.

~•~

Behind the desk in Mr Grimpweed's office-for-the-evening was Mr Grimpweed himself, a small, neat man whose rounded, cushiony features hid the most incisive legal mind that money could buy. Lounging against one wall was a tall, bearded aristocrat newly come into a vast fortune. Sitting next to each other opposite Mr Grimpweed were two further aristocrats: one whose cheerfulness, for once, seemed a little forced, and another who was only there because he'd been told it'd be to his advantage.

'Gentlemen,' Mr Grimpweed began, 'can I assume that we all know why we're here?'

'Sorry, old sport – haven't a clue,' said Yedder.

Rudolf's jaw dropped. 'What? You haven't told Yedder what's going on either? That's not like you, Guildman – you don't normally make a move without your little pal here.'

Guildman seized Rudolf's lapels and hauled him to his feet with a speed and ferocity which surprised everyone.

'You have no idea of the moves I make, Rudolf. Now if

you want to live in the castle, sit there and keep your mouth shut until someone asks you to open it.'

He pushed Rudolf back into the chair.

Rudolf straightened his tunic. 'All right, keep your hair on.'

'Gentlemen,' Mr Grimpweed began again, 'you are aware that Lord Guildman has this day won a considerable sum.'

'I should say so,' said Yedder.

'And Lord Guildman has engaged me to formalise the disposal of said fortune.'

Rudolf laughed. 'Lord Prig? Spend money? You must—'

He got no further as Guildman slammed his foot into the side of Rudolf's chair. Even Yedder jumped.

'I say, Gil, steady on.'

'What *is* the matter with you?' asked Rudolf.

'I don't know. Maybe I don't like being called Lord Prig. Especially by someone who wants what I've got.'

'Ahem,' said Mr Grimpweed. 'On Lord Guildman's instructions I have drawn up a contract in which he undertakes to provide the money to enable Lord Dibkiss to live in the property known as Castle Stein.'

'Hell's teeth,' whispered Yedder.

'What?' gasped Rudolf, starting to rise. 'Let me have a—'

Guildman pushed him back into the seat. 'It's very simple. I have the money; you want it. You'd slit my throat to get it; I don't want my throat slit. So I'll lend you the money.'

Rudolf looked up at him. 'This is some sort of trick.'

The lawyer bristled. 'Most assuredly not, my lord.'

'Read the contract, please, Mr Grimpweed,' said Guildman.

Mr Grimpweed consulted his paperwork. '*By this signed and*

duly witnessed legally binding contract, the undersigned Lord Guildman pledges to provide all monies necessary to enable the undersigned Lord Dibkiss to take residence of the property known as Castle Stein, this pledge being dependent upon the following conditions...'

'Conditions?' said Rudolf. 'I knew it. It's a trick.'

'Every contract's got conditions, Rude,' Yedder pointed out. 'And as far as I can tell, you're in no position to bargain.'

Guildman patted Rudolf's cheek. 'No position at all.'

'You bastard. You've thought of everything, haven't you?'

Guildman smiled. 'Not me, but Mr Grimpweed has. Pray read the conditions, Mr Grimpweed.'

'One: that Lord Guildman and the undersigned Lord Yedder jointly, severally and only will have possession, access and use of the monies provided for the assemblage of a private militia to facilitate the enterprise.'

'A private army?' said Yedder. 'To take Castle Stein?'

'What's all this severally and jointly business?' asked Rudolf.

'It means Yedder and I will keep control of the money and use it to train and pay the army,' said Guildman.

'So you're not lending me the money after all.'

Guildman grabbed Rudolf's hair and pulled his head back; his other hand went to Rudolf's throat.

'I am willing to use more money than you will ever have, to raise an army to get you what you most want in all the world, and all you can do is carp?!' He threw Rudolf's head forward and nodded towards the lawyer. 'Mr Grimpweed, thank you for your time. Yedder, I shall see you later. Rudolf, I shall never see you again. Our acquaintance is at an end.'

He turned to go.

Yedder shot out of his chair and blocked the way.

'Gil! Gil, wait. Wait a minute.'

'For what, Yedder? Rudolf has obviously achieved the pinnacle of his ambition. He'd rather live in one squalid room over an ale-house, sharing the landlord's wife and at the mercy of his creditors than secure in a castle with his own servants.'

'You know he wants the castle. He... he doesn't always realise when people are being generous. Do you, Rude?'

There was a long pause, broken by Yedder's rarely heard steel-lined voice. 'I said he doesn't always realise when people are being generous, do you, Rudolf?'

Rudolf answered quietly. 'No.'

Yedder rolled his eyes. 'No.' He sighed. 'Give him another try, eh, Gil? Just one more? For me?'

Rudolf swallowed. 'I'm er... sorry, Guildman. Yedder's right. Please – I beg of you, continue with your conditions.'

Guildman looked at Yedder for a moment, then nodded briefly. 'Continue, Mr Grimpweed.'

'*Two: That once in residence at the property known as Castle Stein, Lord Dibkiss will assign one half-share in the said property to Lord Guildman and commence repayment of monies loaned.*'

Rudolf almost choked. 'What?!'

'Half of Castle Stein?' said Yedder. 'I'd like to hear what Roz has to say about dividing up the estate.'

'If I've anything to do with it, that bitch'll be up to her parting in moat,' muttered Rudolf.

Guildman glared at him. 'Rosalind will vanish from your life, as you desire. Is that not good enough?'

'It's a start. But you say you want half the castle? Why?'

Guildman walked behind Rudolf's chair. 'Why do you want

me to spend the sort of money that no-one else would – not even to ransom your life – and have nothing to show for it? All I'm asking for is a return on my investment. This is a loan and you have no collateral. To pay me back, you'd have to sell the castle, and I'm the only person rich enough to buy it.'

'He's right, Rude,' said Yedder. 'And half a castle's better than nothing, which is what you've got at the moment. Just think of what you could have.'

'I could have Guildman breathing down my neck all the time, telling me what I can and can't do in my own castle.'

'Half a castle,' said Yedder.

'I give you my word,' said Guildman. 'Once you're installed, I won't come near the place; you may live as you wish. Or, if you prefer, I could keep the entire place for myself...'

Rudolf frowned. 'You're handing the castle over to me, and I have to give half of it back. Why aren't you keeping your half to start with and then assigning me the other half?'

'That would be the better deal for me,' replied Guildman, 'but I'm not listening to you whining for the rest of your life that I promised you the castle and only gave you half. I'm doing the gentlemanly thing and trusting you to do the same.'

'And if I don't give you a half-share?'

'What?!' said Yedder. 'After all that? He's going to get you your heart's desire and you're thinking of cheating him?'

'I'm only asking,' said Rudolf.

'Mr Grimpweed?' said Guildman.

The lawyer cleared his throat and quoted the remainder of the document. '*If, for whatever reason, Lord Dibkiss fails to provide Lord Guildman with a half-share in Castle Stein or fails to start repayment of monies, then standard terms and conditions apply: everything Lord Dibkiss has becomes forfeit to Lord Guildman until either the debt is cleared or Lord Guildman considers the debt to be cleared.'*

Rudolf grinned. He had nothing, and so had nothing to lose. Unlike that idiot Guildman. 'Where do I sign?'

Formalities completed, Mr Grimpweed handed over a wax-sealed copy of the contract to each of the aristocrats and put the final copy in his own inside pocket.

'That is all, gentlemen.'

Yedder took the hint. 'Oh, righty ho... er... thank you, Mr Grimpweed. Most... er... efficient.'

'At your service, sir.'

As Rudolf rose from his chair, Guildman threw a bag of money to him. 'Go and celebrate your good luck.'

Rudolf caught the money. 'Is this part of the loan?'

'Let's call it a foretaste of what's to come, shall we? Yedder, would you go with him and start the celebrations?'

'You not coming, Gil?'

'Later. I have one or two things to tie up first.'

Rudolf hefted the moneybag. 'I might tie one or two things up myself tonight,' he sniggered, striding out of the office. 'Come on, Yedder. Party time!'

'In a jif!' Yedder called after him, then he turned a concerned face towards Guildman. 'Is all well, old love?'

'Fine, Yedder, fine. Why do you ask?'

Yedder bit his lip. 'It's just that...' he said, '...I'm starting to think I don't know you any more.'

Guildman watched silently as Yedder walked away.

'Will that be all, my lord?' asked Mr Grimpweed. When he

got no response, he coughed politely. 'My lord?'

'What? Oh, er... I beg your pardon, Mr Grimpweed. My mind was elsewhere.' He handed the lawyer a moneybag. 'Thank you for your service and I bid you a safe goodnight.'

Mr Grimpweed bowed. 'Goodnight, my lord.'

Guildman strode along the corridor and stepped outside into the evening, a time of day when being in the centre of Maund meant one of three things: either the visit was absolutely necessary and could not hold until morning, there was entertainment writ large to be had with a group of friends, or there was profit in it, legal or not.

As Guildman had profit written all over him, the cut-purse surveying the street couldn't believe his luck when Guildman took a side-step into the suffocating darkness of an alleyway.

After a few paces Guildman stopped and turned.

The footsteps behind him also stopped.

'You're 'andsome man, milord,' growled the mugger. 'Fine clothes an' all. Be a shame if your frock-coat or your face was to get a little torn.'

'It would,' Guildman said calmly. 'Thanks for the warning.'

'That's all right – it'll only cost you all your money.'

'Hardly a warning then; more of an unsolicited service.'

'Call it what you will, milord, but pay up. Or be cut up.'

Guildman opened his arms. 'Cut up? With what? I see no weapon. Hold it up, let's have a look.'

The mugger held his arm out in front of him and moved it from side to side.

'Sorry,' said Guildman, 'still can't see it.'

The mugger raised his arm slightly. There was just enough

light from the street bleeding into his opponent's end of the alley for Guildman to catch a glimpse of metal blade.

'Oh, I see it now. Come on, then.'

'What?'

'Come on, cut me. It's the only way you'll get any money.'

Guildman, arms outstretched, jinked from side to side across the alley as the thief made a few introductory slashes at him. Too busy trying to find a home for his dagger in Guildman's body, the thief didn't see Guildman's fingers grip the handle of a broom that was propped up in the alley. With a practised movement, Guildman swung the broom and the business end of it sent the knife flying from the mugger's grasp to clatter against a wall; a few more blows from the sharp twigs had the mugger reeling on the floor before scrambling back down the alley.

Guildman threw some copper coins after him.

'You forgot your money!' he called, then stooped and picked up the blade. 'After all,' he added quietly, 'it's bad luck if somebody gives you a knife and you don't pay them for it.'

He examined the broom. It hadn't suffered much, and so he took it back into the shadows of the alley.

A few moments later, nobody noticed that rising out of the blackness and into the night was an elderly lady on her own personal transport.

'You did what?!'

Guildman's long legs had been stretched out in front of the fire as he waited in his room, as instructed, for Fran. But once she'd arrived, and detail followed revelation in her story, he'd ended up pacing around, arms half-folded, the fingers of one hand covering his mouth.

She handed him his copy of the contract.

'It's all in here,' she said. 'Have a read.'

As he perused the document, she sat sipping tea, the fire-glow catching the gold rim of the china cup.

'You have enslaved me,' he said at length. 'You have enslaved me to the service of Rudolf and the endangerment of Rosalind. I cannot go through with this.'

'Oh yes you can. And you will. Because you are an honourable man who has given his word.'

'It's not my word, Mistress Stein.'

'Prove it.'

'What?'

'Prove that you didn't sign four copies of this document.'

Guildman was taken aback. He'd never been asked to prove anything before; after all, he was an aristocrat. 'My servants will swear that I never left the castle after six this evening and therefore could not have been at this meeting of yours.'

'The testimony of two noblemen and a lawyer will far outweigh that of paid servants – even yours.'

Guildman considered her words.

'Besides,' added Fran, 'I'm sure I could find the street scum who tried to mug you in an alley. He'd swear it was you who beat him – and he'd have the scratches to back up his story.'

Guildman read the document again then folded it up.

'I cannot agree to this, Mistress Stein.'

'Fine,' she said, standing up and taking the contract out of his hands. 'Don't do it. And tomorrow the whole town,

315

including Rosa, will know you're a fraud because you signed a contract you'd no intention of honouring. Everybody'll know you can't be trusted. Your good name and your precious honour will already be a fading memory. And as you'll no longer be an honourable man, you might as well murder Rudolf in cold blood, because you'll have nothing to lose. Mind you, you're going to have to kill him anyway because as soon as he hears you're backing out he's going to come after you.'

They stared at each other long and hard.

Eventually Guildman took the contract back from Fran and read it through again. 'A private militia,' he said despondently.

'Controlled by you and Yedder. Don't you see? You can train them up to whatever standard of battle you like. They'll be directly under your command. You, not Rudolf, will decide the success – or failure – of this enterprise.'

'This enterprise, as you call it, has to succeed.'

'And it will. I'll be there to make sure it does.'

For the first time in years, Rigton wondered whether to go to bed without tidying up. He wondered whether to go to bed at all. In truth, part of his brain was convinced that he was in bed already and the pandemonic scenes of excess and jollification that swam before his eyes in the Lamb and Werewolf were merely a sleeper's vision of what a pub landlord's life could really be like. And then his businessman's heart slapped him round the face and said, 'Get a move on – there's people in here just dying to be overcharged.'

And so beers, wines and spirits flowed one way, money flowed the other and everyone in the heaving pub was happy.

The same could not be said of the individual sitting on a cast-iron bench outside the pub, slowly eating beer-soaked fruit from a pint glass.

Yedder glanced towards the sound of the footsteps.

His lifelong friend slumped onto the bench and sighed heavily. Yedder held out the glass to him. Guildman shook his head. For a while, the only sound was that of intense merry-making, ever threatening to spill onto the street.

'Someone's having a good time,' said Guildman at last.

'He is that,' replied Yedder.

'I thought you'd be in there keeping an eye on him.'

Yedder snorted. 'There's plenty of eyes on him already – or on his money, anyway. You did give him a fair amount.'

Guildman looked puzzled for a moment. 'Did I?'

He rubbed his hands over his face and folded his arms.

'Believe me,' he said, 'when I woke up this morning, I had no idea that I was going to do that. Or that contract.'

'Ah, yes, the contract,' said Yedder, something in his voice demanding an explanation.

'Yedder, I know I've been acting a little... out of character, shall we say, this evening. And I apologise for not asking you about the contract beforehand.'

'It was... unexpected.'

'I know, I know. But I also know you won't let me down.'

Yedder nodded. 'True.'

'And let's not forget – Rosalind's life is at stake here.'

'So's yours.'

Guildman shrugged. 'That makes no difference to me.'

'It makes a difference to Roz.'

'Then help me to work this thing to her advantage.'

'Of course.' Yedder paused for a moment. 'By the way, this thing about you and me in charge of the army. Excellent idea. Can't have Rude in control – or out of it, for that matter.'

Guildman smiled.

Yedder leant towards him.

'You know you said you were out of character?'

'Yes...'

'Are you back in character now?'

'I am.'

'What on earth possessed you to be so out of character?'

Guildman gave a short sigh. 'Mistress Stein possessed me.'

'Ah,' said Yedder, leaning away again. 'Say no more.'

He offered the glass to his friend.

Guildman took a piece of beer-sodden fruit, ate it and pulled a face.

'How can you eat this stuff, Yedder?'

'Practice, old love, practice.'

Guildman chuckled and stood up. 'Refill?'

'Do you know,' Yedder grinned, 'I don't mind if I do.'

Rudolf clapped a seated man on the back, raising a small cloud of dust. 'Landlord! Fill this man's glass! Everybody celebrates with me tonight!'

'Thank you, my lord,' said the man. 'What's the occasion?'

Rudolf bent closer to him and waved a finger in his face.

'The occasion is— ah! Yedder! Guildman! There you are.'

He straightened, holding on to the man for balance. As Yedder and Guildman drew level, the man looked up.

'Oh,' said Yedder. 'What ho, Mason.'

Mason nodded. 'My lords.'

'What?' sputtered Rudolf. 'You know this man?'

'He's a builder,' said Yedder. 'Working at Castle Stein.'

Rudolf's face lit up. 'Is he? Well, isn't that' – he dipped his head dramatically to emphasise the word – 'excellent!'

Rigton put a pint in front of Mason. Mason reached for it but Rudolf gripped his wrist. 'Listen to me, Basin.'

'Mason.'

'Whatever.' Rudolf swayed unsteadily as he bent towards Mason again. 'I want you to listen. Are you listening, Basin?'

Mason sighed. 'Yes, I'm listening.'

'Then listen. I want you to do a really, really, really good job on whatever you're doing at the castle, do you hear me, Basin?'

'Yes, yes, I hear you.'

'Good. Because do you know why?'

'Why what?'

Rudolf stood up and looked over Mason's head to Yedder and Guildman. He laughed drunkenly and pointed at Mason.

'Why what, he says?'

Rudolf seized Mason's lapels and bent even closer.

Trapped in a chair with nowhere to back away to, Mason had no choice but to bear the alcohol fumes washing over him from Rudolf.

'Why you've got to do a really, really, really good job on the castle, you moron.'

Mason screwed his face up and held his breath. 'No, why?'

'Because it's going to be *my* castle. And do you know why it's going to be my castle?'

319

'No,' squeaked Mason, running short on oxygen.

'Because Guildman says so, that's why. He's buying me an army and we're going to take that castle and chuck that vixen of a wife of mine in the moat and serve her bloody well right.' Rudolf pushed Mason away and pointed to his own chest. 'My castle. There you are, Basin, whaddaya think to that, eh?'

'Will I still get paid?'

Rudolf bent backwards as he laughed.

'Ha ha ha ha ha! Will you still get paid? You'll get paid, Basin. Guildman'll pay you. Guildman's paying for everything!'

The following morning, at the kitchen table, Mason caught hold of Mrs B's wrist. 'I'm telling you. Straight from the horse's mouth.' He quickly let go of Mrs B as her husband strode into the kitchen with Aidan trailing behind.

The builder's familiarity with the butler's wife did not go unnoticed by the butler in question. 'Horse's mouth, Mason?'

'Lord Rudolf hisself. Last night. He said, "Guildman's paying for everything". Them's his very words.'

Beaton looked at him through narrowed eyes.

'"Everything" being exactly what?'

'Well, there's my wages for a start.'

'Minus a sugar tax, naturally.'

Mrs B giggled.

Mason looked at first hurt then, as he told his tale, superior.

'Lord Rudolf said Lord Guildman was going to pay for an army to come and take over the castle.'

'Why would Lord Guildman want this castle?' asked Igress, walking into both the kitchen and the conversation.

Mason swung round. 'Not Lord Guildman, Lord Rudolf.'

'Make your mind up, Mason,' said Beaton. 'You just said it was Lord Guildman.'

Mason swung back. 'Lord Guildman—'

'But Lord Guildman has his own castle,' said Aidan.

'Which lord doesn't?' said Igress.

'Lord Rudolf,' said Aidan, and Igress laughed.

Mason groaned and threw his arms wide.

'Ye gods! If you'd all get here at the same time, I could tell you all at once and then nobody'd get the wrong end of the stick!'

Gussie entered. 'Tell us what? Morning, everybody.'

The variations on 'Morning, Gussie' that greeted him and the subsequent idle conversations that threatened to fill the kitchen pushed Mason's blood pressure up. Eventually the builder knocked his fist on the table.

'Hold on, hold on... do you want to hear this story or not?'

Gussie sat on a bench and the kitchen fell silent.

'Thank you,' said Mason. 'Right. Lord Rudolf told me last night that Lord Guildman is going to pay for a private army to seize the castle and hand it over to Lord Rudolf.'

'Don't believe you,' said Igress.

'That's what I said,' added Mrs B.

'Was he drunk?' asked Gussie.

'Well, yes...'

'There you are then,' said Igress. 'He was rambling. It can't be true.'

'Oh,' said Rosa from the doorway, 'I'm afraid it is.'

All the windows and doors of the Lamb and Werewolf were gaping. An unseasonal gale was carrying away the stale odours of spilt beer, pipe smoke and body odour that had resulted from the best night's trading ever to fill Rigton's coffers, which is why he was polishing everything in sight with renewed vigour. He'd not seen Mrs Rigton since last evening, which only increased his happiness because he knew she'd been bending over backwards most of the night to satisfy customers and top up the takings. His huge smile only left his face during sporadic whistlings of the barkeepers' anthem: *Drink To Me Only With Thine Eyes And Then Get Another Round In*.

'Ah, what a fine day, my lords!' he said to the two aristocrats who blew into the parlour along with the chill wind.

Yedder and Guildman looked at each other for a moment.

Yedder went back outside, looked up at the front of the pub and then rejoined Guildman. 'It's the right place, Gil.'

'Intriguing.'

The landlord beamed as he took a tankard from the shelf.

'Forgive my exuberance, my lords. And by way of apology, the drinks are on the house.'

'I say, Rigsy,' enquired Yedder, 'is everything all right?'

Rigton pulled on the beer pump as they walked towards the bar. 'Quite wonderful, my lord.'

'In that case,' said Guildman, 'we wish to discuss business with you.'

Rigton's smile was so broad it threatened to decapitate him.

'My lord's words are the most harmonious music to my ears. To put even more business my way—'

A gloved hand closed around the beer pump and pulled it

out of his grasp. Rigton looked at Guildman, whose eyes carried a stern warning.

'Your cheerfulness does you credit, Rigton,' said Guildman, 'but forgive me, I have a lot on my mind at the moment so could we please resume our normal arrangement?'

'My lord?'

'That's the sort of thing. Yedder and I have the bonhomie, and you are the taciturn landlord.'

'Ah. No gushing?'

'No gushing, no effusing, no enthusiasm.'

'May I smile, my lord?'

'Can you do it quietly?'

Rigton displayed a much-reduced smile.

'Very well, then,' said Guildman, releasing the beer pump.

Rigton grasped the beer pump and pursed his lips.

'But no whistling,' said Guildman.

The landlord sighed and continued pulling the beer.

'The thing is, Rigsy,' said Yedder, turning around and leaning back on the bar, 'we'd like to hire this room if poss.'

'Will my lords be requiring any food or musical entertainment for the party?'

'Party, old thing? Ah, I see. No, not a party, is it Gil?'

'Indeed no, Yedder. No party – and no picnic, either.'

Sandwiches, pies, buns and biscuits had been piled high, but the long meeting had gradually reduced the mountains of food to scattered crumbs. Normally this would have induced in the diners a feeling of well-being and harmony with the world, but their world had suddenly become distinctly discordant.

All normal daily duties had been suspended and the inhabitants of the castle had spent the day around the dining table drawing up battle plans, contingency measures, fail-safe procedures, fall-back positions and desperate acts. Weaknesses and vulnerabilities in the castle's structure had been detailed and improvements discussed. Preparations for a lengthy siege had been tabled. The restoration and refurbishment of vintage fighting equipment had been mooted.

Aidan had come into his own, turning vague words into visible illustrations as he easily and confidently sketched out everything from practical suggestion to wild idea.

By late afternoon Rosa had a 'to do' list, supplemented by Aidan's drawings and reams of lists of materials needed to get the doing done. She interlaced her fingers, rested her hands on top of the paperwork and looked around the table.

'We've got some rough times ahead,' she warned, 'but if it gets rid of Rudolf once and for all, we've got to do it.'`

The assembled heads nodded silently.

'When I say "we", I mean *I* have to do it, but the rest of you don't. And if any of you feel that you can't go along with it, then please say so. This will be your last chance to get out. After this, we're fully committed. No going back. So speak up now. From here on in, we're in it together. All for one and—'

She stopped abruptly as a hand was raised.

The tremors in Rudolf's arm took quite a while to reach his brain, and even longer for his comatose thinking cells to work out that someone was shaking him.

'Whuh?' he said into the pillow.

'Get up! Do you hear me? Get up!'

'Mills?'

'Yes, it's me. Now get up! It's gone noon. Your time's up.'

'But—'

'But nothing. Now come on – I've got work to do.'

He rolled onto his back. 'Gimme my coat.'

A pile of clothes landed unmercifully across his face. Blindly he rooted in his pockets, took out a moneybag and threw it on the bed. A short time later – once Millie had checked the purity of the gold – a small, discreet notice appeared in her front window. 'Closed until further notice.'

'Can I say something?'

All heads swivelled towards Gussie.

'Er, of, of, of course,' stammered Rosa.

'You won't like what I've got to say,' he warned.

'I'd better like it,' said Fran.

Suddenly everybody else found the table-top a fascinating example of the wood-carver's art. Rosa coughed. 'I... erm... applaud you... for having the courage to say it, Gussie.'

'Thank you,' he replied. 'Now shut up.'

'What?'

'Shut up. Stop going on about last chances and you-don't-have-to-do-its and get-out-now-while-you-cans and stuff. We wouldn't dream of letting you down, and frankly,' he added haughtily, 'some of us are a bit upset that you think we would.'

Murmurs of agreement filled the air. Igress leant over and kissed him on the cheek.

'Bravo,' she said, then she leant back a little too far, almost overbalanced and grabbed at the table. In doing so she sent Aidan's drawing pad flying, scattering loose illustrations. The murmurs turned to gasps at what was on the drawn pages.

In the way that people do when they just *know* that trouble is heading their way and there's nothing they can do except sit there and take it, Aidan concentrated on twiddling his pencil.

There were sketches and sketches of Igress. She was a goddess standing on a sea-shell. She was lounging on a bed, gazing into a mirror. She was floating in a reed-bordered river. She was a warrior queen, her right arm holding a trident and her left arm balancing a shield. She was a countess, smiling enigmatically against the backdrop of a city.

She was red in the face.

'This one's got no eyebrows,' said Fran.

'It's only a sketch,' said Gussie. 'He'd have put eyebrows on the finished painting, wouldn't you, Aidan?'

'Erm... I hadn't thought about doing a painting.'

'What? Oh, you must! You've got real talent! We must get you some paints.' Gussie nudged Fran. 'You can get him paints, can't you, gal? He's got to have paints.'

'Yes, yes, calm yourself. Rosa?'

Rosa duly wrote down 'paints' and then, as if a sudden thought had struck her, she underlined it twice.

'Aidan,' she said, 'these sketches... why did you do them?'

He reddened worse than Igress had done, and gulped.

'Because I can?'

~•~

NOTES ON

Soldiery

Who joins an army?

Those who follow in father's footsteps, which can mean they end up standing in exactly the same place as he did when he was killed.

Those who are told to, whether by state decree or exasperated family member.

Those who want a lifestyle where somebody pays them to eat healthily and take regular exercise.

Those who can follow orders blindly. These are valuable troops to have, providing you give them very specific orders. It's no good telling them to 'Fire at will' unless you also tell them which one's Will.

Those who want to prove to their parents that they can stand on their own two feet, but need someone else to do the cooking and make all their decisions for them; the ones for whom marriage or a housekeeper would have been a safer bet.

Those with visions of how the world should be run – which is usually without the bother of democracy. Top brass officer material, very often they're the ones whose names are written in the annals of history, usually in everybody else's blood.

Those who believe that a cause is worth fighting for and who will sacrifice themselves to the greater good. These are the most dangerous, because unless properly regulated they will waste themselves before their time. This usually entails them breaking cover despite all orders to the contrary, and not only dying a needless death but also endangering the rest of their company by unthinkingly revealing their whereabouts.

Those who believe their very nationality makes them superior to others and are willing to kill people to prove it, thereby disproving it. Superiority by nationality is self-defeating, because once you've either annihilated or assimilated all others, there's no-one left to be superior to, and the whole basis for your argument dies with the last victim of it.

Those who are so full of youth and vitality that they think they're immortal, which in a way, we all are as long as we're alive. Sadly, they're usually the first to go. It's not only careless talk that costs lives; foolhardiness must take some blame.

Those whose lives have, or shortly will, become so wretched that death no longer holds any fears for them. These are the ones the enemy is most afraid of, for desperation knows no restraint.

Those with an innate propensity for violence. A certain section of society would like to see natural talent properly channelled: why should vicious thugs be on the streets roughing people up indiscriminately when an army can train them to be efficient killers? And if you do have the hankering to murder someone, why not do it within a hierarchy that not only sanctions it, but employs you to do it? Admittedly you don't get to choose your victim, but surely that's a small price to pay. And from the point of view of those governing, the violent criminals are off the streets and out of people's houses and pockets, the crime rate plummets and the nation's borders are ruthlessly safeguarded by those who have no compunction in repelling any marauding hordes. Of course, another section of society would say that giving naturally violent individuals easy access to weaponry is simply asking for trouble.

~✦~

Drawn by the prospect of guaranteed regular wages paid by an aristocrat you could trust, all kinds of men formed a queue round the block hoping to join Guildman's private army. They represented the entire scale of manhood from 'perfect illustration' through 'fine figure' and on to 'right specimen'. There were old soldiers, people pretending to be old soldiers, and people who'd been bored rigid by an old soldier telling them how he'd won a war single-handedly.

The majority of the queue was taken up by tradesmen, carrying their tools still fresh from their work; some, like the butcher, not only fresh but still dripping.

The rest were unemployed, unemployable, misfits, oddballs, desperate men and a few badly disguised women. The latter were the exception in Maund's female population: the vast majority of women were of the opinion that as wars were started by men, it should be the men who go out and get killed in them.

Rigton was only too happy to rent his parlour as a recruiting office, as those accepted for training were given a drink paid for by Yedder and Guildman, and those rejected were only too willing to drown their sorrows at the nearest bar.

Rudolf was initially unhappy that Guildman wouldn't let him take part in the recruiting, but soon found solace in a bag of money and a few days in the arms – and more – of Millie.

The day after Rosa's council of war, rooms in Castle Stein that had lain unused for years suddenly found themselves subjected to a thorough search for anything that might possibly be used as a weapon in its own right or looked like it could be fashioned into something dangerous.

Gussie trailed behind Beaton all over the castle carrying an increasingly heavy crate which he finally hefted onto a workbench in the laboratory close to where Igress and Rosa were decanting yellowish-brown fluid into dishes.

'Careful, Gussie,' Rosa warned, as her scientific crockery rattled and fluid splashed onto the workbench.

'Sorry,' he said. 'What are you doing? Distilling for Sooty?'

Igress chuckled.

Rosa put down a dish. 'No. I'm trying to – well, it doesn't really matter anyway. I've tried it forty times and it doesn't seem to work.' She peered into the crate. 'What's that lot?'

'I'm afraid it's all the potential weapons we could find, milady,' said Beaton, 'aside from Lord Rudolf's sporting equipment.'

Broken blades, blunt knives, old forks and distorted pieces of ancient armour lay jumbled together in the crate.

Rosa dipped into it and pulled out an old door hinge; she tried wiggling it, but it was rusted solid. She stood it on end on the workbench.

'Hmmm. Not exactly a terrifying arsenal, is it?'

'There's a spiky ball thing,' said Gussie. 'Mind, it's more ball than spike.' He rummaged about and lifted his hand. 'Ta-da!' A chain slithered from the crate and knocked the door hinge into one of Rosa's dishes. 'Oops!' said Gussie. 'Sorry.'

Rosa sighed. 'Oh, never mind. It doesn't matter.'

Igress took the object from his hand. 'It's a flail ball.'

'A what?' said Gussie.

'The ball from a ball-and-chain flail. You know – spiky ball on a chain fixed to a handle? It's one of them.'

She pointed to the chain that had fallen from the crate.

'That's probably its chain there.'

She turned the ball over. 'See that? The loop attaching it to the chain's broken. Wouldn't take long to knock up new spikes and a new loop for it.'

'Ooh, hark at you, Master Ironfounder,' teased Gussie.

Igress bridled. 'Excuse me, but that's Mistress Ironwringer.'

'Igress Ironwringer? That's your name?'

She frowned. 'No, Igress is my name; a Mistress Ironwringer is what I am.'

Gussie looked at her hard.

'I wring iron,' she explained. 'I work it. Try to think of it as a blacksmith and a half. My dad trained me.'

'But you were working as a barmaid in the Lamb and Werewolf when we met you,' said Rosa.

'That was Dad's idea. Nobody was coming forward wanting an ironwringer for a wife, and I'd never have my own smithy 'cos he's leaving his to my brother. Uncle Hep offered to train me as a joiner, but Dad said that was just as bad and I ought to do something a bit more girly if I wanted to be wed.'

'And do you want to be wed?'

'Not if your ex-husband's anything to go by, begging your ladyship's pardon.'

Rosa smiled. 'So you ended up barmaiding.'

'Mmm. I tried seamstressing, but it's not for me. If you go wrong with cloth, you can't melt it down and start again.'

Gussie flapped his hands.

'Wait, wait, wait. You really could make some spikes for this?'

'If I had a furnace or a smithy. And some tools.'

Rosa lifted the hinge from the dish. No longer rusted, it swung freely, scattering drops of her formula on the workbench. She looked at it as though a vague recollection was becoming clearer.

'A smithy, you say? Gussie, go find Aunty Fran.'

~✦~

NOTES ON

Heritage

Traditionally, aristocrats live in enormous castles on large estates with stabling for dozens of horses. Teams of servants do their bidding, look after their every whim, make their decisions and almost live their lives for them except in a few key areas, notably bodily functions and the taking of pleasure, and often these two become one.

However, too much pleasure may exert a deleterious effect on the mental stability of an individual, though sadly usually not enough of an effect to prevent them passing personality defects on to future generations, which is why most ordinary folk have to spend the majority of their lives working for others: any family fortune which may have been enjoyed by their ancestors was enjoyed out of all existence by a succession of gambling, drunken, gluttonous, womanising, manising, animalising, gullible lunatic spendthrifts.

And even if the fortune does come down to you intact or – by some miracle – increased, if there haven't been horses stabled at your place within your lifetime then you could be forgiven for not remembering you had a smithy and foundry on the premises until somebody mentions it in passing.

The ironworks at Castle Stein was built in the most sensible place – opposite the stable block so the horses didn't have a major trek when they needed shoeing, next to a well in case any fires got out of hand, and far enough away from the house for the noise not to disturb the residents.

And, as with everything else to do with Castle Stein, it was not built with economy in mind.

~•~

'Look out!' called Gussie, as he pulled at the ivy and found that rather than yield its anchors, it brought with it great lumps of cracked and split wood.

Fran, Sooty and Igress stood well back, shielding their eyes from dust and dislodged wildlife.

In less than a minute Gussie created a large pile of greenery and timber fragments by easily demolishing one of a pair of rotten wooden doors. He bent over and ruffled his hair, sending ivy leaves, insects and splinters flying in the sunlight that fought its way through the dust into the revealed chamber. He straightened up and looked around. 'Blimey O'Reilly!'

The others walked towards him and peered into the smithy.

'Hit me,' said Igress.

'What on earth for?' said Fran.

'I've got to know I'm not dreaming. Hit me. Hit me now.'

Fran and Gussie exchanged worried glances.

'Don't look at me,' he said. 'I'm too strong for that kind of work. Besides, I've got another door to get down. Stand back.'

The crashing and rustling didn't quite mask the scream from Igress when Fran pinched her under the arm.

'Ow! You might've warned me,' said Sooty, scowling and rubbing his ears.

The four of them walked into the smithy. With both doors demolished, the true size of the cavernous circular interior became apparent.

'It seemed big when I was a kid,' said Fran, 'but I thought it was big because I was little. But it is... actually... big, isn't it?'

'Slight understatement,' said Sooty.

Not only was the scale of the place revealed, there was also an insight into the mind of whoever had last used it. Apart from the long-dead ash in the huge forge and the forgivable cobwebby dust of over fifty years, it was immaculate. A place for everything, and nothing out of place. The walls were lined with hooks, clips and sockets, each especially made to take its own tool with its own stamped metal label underneath it.

Igress gently touched the tools she could reach, murmuring their names like an incantation. 'Fullers... ball-peins... claw hammers... pincers... snub-nose pliers... snipe-nose pliers...'

Each tool was available in at least five different sizes, as were the anvils lined up surrounding the central forge. Grinding wheels, whetstones and a foot-operated tilt-hammer with interchangeable heads stood to attention, ready for action.

'What's this for?' asked Sooty, pointing to a circular track in the floor following the arc of the walls.

A metallic scrape formed part of the answer as Fran attempted to push what would have been, in another room, library steps. Although seated in the track, the wheels had seized up and obstinately refused to move.

Igress grinned. 'Soon have those whizzing about.'

'What's this rope do?' said Gussie, unwinding it from a large cleat on the wall.

'No idea,' said Fran. 'Does it let fresh air in?'

Gussie dropped the rope and a deep metallic clang came from nearby. Igress's head jerked towards the sound, then back to Gussie. Her eyes traced the path of the rope from where he'd dropped it, up through a series of pulleys and capstans.

'That's no vent,' she began, 'that sounds like...'

Gussie pointed to another pair of doors. 'What's in there?'

'If memory serves me,' said Fran, 'that's the foundry.'

'What?!' said Igress. She ran to the doors and pushed them sideways. They rolled squeakily away between two stone walls.

Igress gasped. The massive space had been divided into two workshops by a full height stone wall which extended half way across the area. In one workshop stood a furnace and piles of foundry sand; in the other were various workbenches fitted with vices, clamps, lathes and treadles, only waiting for expert hands to make them useful again. The same order and discipline were as obvious in here as in the forge: lining the walls were several different sizes of every conceivable woodworking and foundry tool, each with its own labelled place. The only thing askew was a crucible cradle attached to the other end of the rope Gussie had dropped.

'Oh, I remember this!' said Fran. 'I used to love playing with this.' She pulled a lever on the wall.

'Whoa!' said Sooty, jumping out of the way as floor tiles flipped up under him, revealing a channel leading to depressions in the floor into which moulds could be slotted for casting everything from caltrops to cannonballs.

Tears welled in Igress's eyes. 'It's beautiful,' she whispered.

'Just promise me one thing,' said Fran.

'Anything at all.'

'Promise me you'll come back to the house for meals.'

On the third day of recruiting, Yedder and Guildman were at their usual rickety table when a large, muscly man barged into the pub and heaved people aside as he headed for the bar.

'I'm here to see the Lord Rudolf!' he shouted.

'Wait your turn,' said Rigton.

Using the shoulders of those beside him, the man hoisted himself on to the counter. Yedder and Guildman rose as his hobnailed boots scored through many years of dedicated polishing. 'Perhaps you didn't hear me,' he bellowed. 'I'm—'

'My bar!' shrieked Rigton. 'Get your boots off my bar! Go on, get off and get out!'

Pints were hastily lifted out of the way as the man stomped along the counter, leaving splintered dimples in the wood.

Rigton screamed.

'Go on then, Doris,' taunted the man, 'make me.'

The screaming stopped and the swearing began as Rigton brandished a cudgel. 'I'll bloody make you get off, you—'

The point of a sword dug into his heaving chest.

'Now, now, Rigsy,' said the cheerful aristocrat at the other end of the sword. 'Hold hard, old love.'

Rigton's eyes almost fell out as he pointed frantically to his pockmarked counter. The muscly man started to laugh, only to roar with pain as the point of another sword jabbed him in the backside. He spun round on the bar, gouging circles into its recently meticulous surface. Rigton whimpered.

A finger shot out from one of the man's fists.

'Who did that? Come on! I'll have you, you spineless—'

He was silenced by Guildman's sword point lightly pressing on his vitals.

'In these parts,' said Guildman, 'it's customary to offer a greeting when one enters a hostelry.' He pressed his point further. 'That's if you don't want to get hurt in these parts.'

'Hello?' said the man. Yedder slammed his arm across the back of the man's knees; as the man buckled, Guildman grasped his tunic and heaved him to the floor, where he lay still, two sword points pressing firmly against his neck.

'Hello,' said Guildman calmly.

There was a thud behind the counter as Rigton's cudgel fell to the floor. 'My bar,' he sobbed, tenderly stroking the woodwork. 'My beautiful, beautiful bar.'

Guildman looked at the prone man. 'Perhaps now you'd like to tell us why you're here.'

'Word is Lord Rudolf's wanting blokes to join his army. Men who aren't afraid of a good scrap. Word is the pay's good.'

'And did the word say who's paying?'

'No... only to turn up here.'

'Well, if you hadn't upset our friend here, I would have been paying,' said Guildman.

'Oh.'

'Oh indeed. I am raising this army on Lord Rudolf's behalf. My name is Lord Guildman. And your name is?'

'Temeraire, sir.'

'Temeraire,' said Guildman. 'Yedder, I think our army is now complete.'

Yedder grinned. 'I should say so.'

He and Guildman sheathed their swords and helped Temeraire to his feet. Yedder started to brush him down. 'A pint for the famous fighting man here, if you please, Rigsy.'

Rigton's anguish overcame his deference.

'After what he's done to my bloody bar?! Are you mad?!'

The balm of Yedder's money soothed the landlord's troubled soul. 'Would the gentleman like fruit with his beer?'

Rosa's fortieth-formula solution came into its own. Igress poured it into the channels that ran round the foundry floor, easing the sliding doors and the library steps. Buckets of it soaked movement back into pulleys, rusted wheels and jammed pivots, with Igress wire-brushing the worst cases. The rust and dust of thirty years was dissolved and polished away, and with it went any hint of Igress the serving-wench.

'I'm very sorry about your bar,' said Temeraire meekly, 'truly I am. If there's anything I can do...'

'Oh, don't you worry about that at all,' said Rigton jovially, putting three tankards on the rickety table. 'Any friend of my lords is a friend of mine.'

He patted Temeraire on the back and walked away.

Temeraire nervously twisted one of the bottom corners of his jacket. 'And I do humbly beg your lordships' pardon for my unseemly behaviour just now.'

'No hard feelings, old chap,' said Yedder, raising his drink.

'Your lordships are very kind,' said Temeraire, lifting his tankard. 'Very kind indeed.' He drained the full pint in one and wiped his mouth. 'Ahhhh.'

'Steady on, old thing. No need to guzzle.'

Temeraire blushed. 'No, sir. Sorry, sir. It's my nerves, you see. I'm... nervous.' He tapped the tankard on the table then lifted it up again, apparently unsure of what to do with it. 'I never drink when I'm on duty sir, never. Can't afford to. Slows your reaction times. Only have a jar when I'm off duty. And when I'm... nervous.' The tankard dropped onto the floor. 'Sorry.' He picked it up.

Yedder took it out of his hands.

'You didn't seem nervous two minutes ago.'

'Ah no, sir. That's because I was proving myself so I'd be taken on and I could earn good money for the family.'

'Does that mean we can expect more of you turning up?'

'Oh no, sir. There's only me available at the moment. Most of my brothers and sisters are in the far north, and the other brother is guard to Lord Margana of Scrubble. We don't let Father fight during autumn and winter, otherwise he suffers badly, feeling the cold too much in his scars. That just leaves me. Apart from the youngsters, that is, but they're a touch headstrong as yet. Uncontrollable. Fly off the handle a bit too easy, if you know what I mean, sir.'

Guildman smiled. 'Heaven forbid someone should turn up unannounced, picking fights with anybody for no reason at all.'

'Indeed, sir. Mrs Temeraire's trying to instil a bit of discipline into them.'

Yedder leant forward. 'What exactly is it about you lot that makes you such good coves in a scrap?'

Temeraire swelled with pride.

'It's in the blood, sir. A perfect mixture of low cunning, high speed, short fuse and long reach.'

'What about loyalty?' asked Guildman.

Temeraire looked affronted.

'Just because we're mercenaries it doesn't mean we've no loyalty, sir. Whoever comes up with the right money the soonest gets our allegiance, and once that bargain's been struck, heaven and earth will not move it.'

'But will more money?'

'Indeed no, sir. You'll not find a loyaller man than a Temeraire, sir. We never swap sides until the battle's over.'

Gussie put a bucket on the foundry floor.

'A prezzie for you from Mrs B.'

Igress put down the pliers she was cleaning. 'Oh?'

'She said your need for grease was greater than hers. Besides, there's always plenty more where that came from.'

Igress looked into the bucket, which held a soft white paste flecked with brown. 'Nice.'

'Don't get your hopes up,' said Gussie. 'Sooty's had the meaty jelly out of the bottom.'

That evening, Rudolf's incredulity echoed around the Lamb and Werewolf. 'You've only recruited thirty men?'

'Thirty's more than enough, old bean,' reassured Yedder.

'Don't you want me to get my castle back?'

Guildman raised an elegant eyebrow. 'How many men does it take to defeat two servants, one youth, one former serving-wench, a little old lady and her helpless niece?'

'I don't know,' said Yedder merrily. 'How many men does it take to— ow!' He rubbed his head. 'No need for that, Rude.'

'Glad to see my life gives you some amusement, Yedder.'

'Endless,' said Guildman.

'What?'

'Your life. Endless... amusement.'

Rudolf glared. 'Sometimes I wonder about you, Guildman.'

'Do you, Rudolf? Do you ever wonder who's paying for it all? No. Because you know that I am. Do you ever wonder how you'll get the castle back without my help? No. Because you know you won't. I'm paying the piper here, so I'm calling the tune. And you will dance to it or you will leave the party.'

Into the kitchen Gussie carried two patchworks of hide which looked as if they had been concertinaed for thirty years and the rats had assumed they were layer cake.

'Mrs B, have you got any—'

'Will this do?' she replied, laying a large piece of leather on the kitchen table next to a sewing basket and a pair of shears.

'Er – oh! Have you been sewing?'

'No, these are for you, love,' she smiled. 'You're making new bellows for Miss Igress, aren't you?'

'Erm, yes, but... how did you... oh, never mind. Thank you, Mrs B, that's very kind.'

Gussie laid the old leather over the new. Taking a triangle of tailor's chalk from the sewing basket, he expertly drew round the old leather leaving him an outline to follow on the new. He picked up the shears and gave a squeal of delight as they sliced effortlessly through the hide. His eyes darted backwards and forwards and he hummed a tune as he expertly cut the leather into shape.

'You're very good,' said Mrs H.

'I should be – I've been doing it long enough.' He laid the

shears down. 'I like cutting out. It's the point of no return. Once you've made that first cut, you're committed. You go from "this could be" to "this will be". Same with carpentry. You have to sacrifice whatever your materials *could* have been in order to make them what they *will* be. And it's the closest a feller'll get to having a baby really, creating something out of something else. But without so much pain and screaming.'

Mrs B hugged him.

'What's that for?' he asked.

'For doing what you've done. And for being you.'

'All I did was cut a bit of leather out. I didn't really put much thought into it.'

Mrs B looked up at him proudly.

'Exactly,' she said. 'You didn't think about it. You didn't think about who you are, or who you used to be. You just did it, because you know you *can* do it. And you know what you can do because you know who you are.'

Gussie smiled. 'I suppose you're right. Now I've settled down I don't think about things half as much as I used to. Unlike you. You think of everything. I bet you've even—'

She handed him a needle with waxed thread running through its eye.

'I assumed you'd be doing the stitching,' she said.

He sat at the kitchen table. 'Too right I am. Let's face it, everybody's as busy as bees trying to make this place safe, and if I can do my bit, I will. And there's no point in asking her ladyship to do any needlework.' He pointed in the direction of his neck. 'I think we've got enough evidence, don't you?'

Mrs B chuckled.

Gussie matched up two pieces of leather. 'It won't be perfect but it'll be better than most, even if it is these bunches of bananas doing the sewing.' He studied his hands. 'I used to have really long, thin fingers – very quick.' He pushed the needle through the leather. 'Fingers you could fit in a thimble. Not any more.' He sighed, and started to sew. 'So these'll just have to get used to my way of working. Maybe Igress can make me a thimble when she gets the foundry going.'

'Maybe,' said Mrs B, delving into a drawer and pulling out a set of ornate silver round-bowled measuring spoons held together by a ring through their handles. 'In the meantime, will one of these do?'

'Oh, Mrs B, I couldn't – they're too beautiful.'

'Beauty is a luxury that can only be afforded when all necessities are fulfilled.'

'What?'

'Needs first, looks second.' She lifted his hand and tried the ladles on him. 'Ah, there we are. How's that feel?'

'Er – fine, fine.'

'Good. Now break it off the handle.'

'Oh, I can't.'

'Well *I* can't.' She gave him one of her sternest looks. 'Now are you going to break it off, or shall I tell everybody you're not doing your bit for the war effort?'

To get his army into peak fighting shape, Guildman called upon his former regiment and secured the services of both the physical training instructor and the drill sergeant, and they bludgeoned the men into fitness. On an increasingly cold training ground the troops ran with heavy packs, jumped across ditches and swam in the lake. They crawled under netting, struggled hand over gloved hand up ropes and along beams, slithered through mud-mired barrels and ran on tiptoes through old cart wheels. But, for all the exhaustion, bruises, chills and soakings the men couldn't believe their luck. They were being systematically bullied, taunted, humiliated and kicked into shifting themselves. Except for the good food and the high wages, it was just like being at home.

Gussie's mornings took on a routine of breakfast, long walk, long run and back in time for lunch. Fran walked with him, and hovered beside him on her broomstick when he ran. They talked of important events and trivia, swapped stories of their lives and people that they'd known, they shared jokes and had arguments. Often Sooty went with them, sometimes changing into a horse or a dog to trot alongside.

In the afternoons Gussie exercised and built his muscles while helping the household. He dug out new vegetable plots and turned the compost heap for Mrs B. He helped Igress in the foundry when she needed a hand with the casting cradle. He lifted heavy furniture and equipment so that Beaton could effect repairs and he accompanied Durney on his wood-chopping expeditions.

And he danced with Rosa. One afternoon a week, he seemed freed from the weight of the body that had been thrust upon him. His brain taught his feet new moves, and he waltzed Rosa round the ballroom with a knowledge that had never been useful in his previous life and an effortless grace that had never been present in this. He sang as they danced, and Rosa giggled at his pleasure. Even Fran was surprised at how light and sure-footed he was, and she stopped telling him that he was only dancing to improve the speed of his footwork.

Over the weeks, Fran directed Gussie's path, monitored his progress, checked his health, nurtured him and came to cherish him. She changed his route every day, not only to save him from boredom but also to have a final look round the estate without weighing anybody down by the reason.

Gussie marvelled at the things his body could do, once prompted by Fran. He'd never before experienced sport as a participant, unless you counted running from trouble. If he was honest, he'd always considered Battling Bill Baldicott to be a punch-drunk lumbering brute, but now he realised just how well-trained Bill's body had been, even if his brain hadn't.

As Gussie's training progressed, the body responded to the clear head now guiding it. For years, it had suffered rigorous mindless exercise, followed by a quick bout with some sap and probably a quicker bout with a willing woman, a victory celebration and a drunken sleep in the back of a wagon rattling its way to another town. Now, it hardly got bashed at all; it was properly fed, had a comfortable place to sleep, a useful purpose in life and didn't waste any energy on base reactions to women.

Gussie blossomed.

It's an ill wind that blows nobody any good, and the malign breeze of impending hostilities unexpectedly propelled Aidan into seventh heaven. His artistic skills had never been so much in demand, Rosa bought him all the materials he asked for and certainly no-one had ever kept him so warm and well-fed for emptying paint pots and wearing out brushes.

He breathed life into Durney's clay heads which were used as decoys. He turned the castle into a palace of optical illusions with false doorways and dummy windows. Non-existent troops cast threatening shadows into corridors. Passageways were hidden by painted canvas walls melting into the stonework as Aidan coloured and shaded the very fabric of Castle Stein.

He couldn't have been happier. Excused normal household duties, he painted, sketched and chalked all day long, his talent flowered, his confidence grew and everybody praised him unstintingly, including the woman for whom he had reserved a square of canvas and frame in his bedroom and his heart.

After eight weeks of intensive basic training for Guildman's army, there followed silent signalling tuition, and for a week the training ground whispered with the flick and snap of flapping pennants. Each man was given a red flag and a blue flag, and had to memorise arm positions in relation to message content – everything from 'Enemy sighted two hundred yards due north' to 'Help! Help! My flag's on fire!'

However, as the autumn mists and long nights rolled in, it became obvious that a back-up communication system would be needed, and so another week's training was added as every man was issued with a shuttered lantern.

Perspiration ran in rivulets down her smooth skin, soaking her thin shirt until it crinkled and clung to her body. Her fingers closed around the tools, knowing instinctively where to grip, the pressure required and the angle of the blow. The tools responded to her expertise, and from time to time a cry of satisfaction burst out of her. Many a man would have paid good money just to watch her, and better money for half an hour in her hands. Igress was the hottest, sweatiest, most muscular and hard-breathing woman dressed in a leather apron in Maund, and the smithy was out of bounds to Aidan.

But not to Mrs B, who brought regular supplies of food, much-needed drink and obsolete metal kitchen equipment. As a thank-you, Igress made an exquisitely wrought set of thimbles crafted to withstand the rigours of Gussie's handling and a pair of flail-ball spikes drilled out as novelty salt and pepper pots.

'Don't let Mrs B know you've left a sandwich,' said Rosa, picking up the plate from the workbench in the smithy.

Igress looked up from fiddling with a modified mangle and patted her stomach.

'If Mrs B doesn't stop feeding me, I'll need a bigger smithy.'

Rosa chuckled, then pointed to a pile of paper-thin sheets of metal at the foot of the mangle. 'What's this?'

Igress picked a sheet up. 'I was wondering if I could make any weapons from rolled metal. You know, throwing weapons, with sharpened edges – but I overdid it with the rolling out.'

Rosa wafted the metal sheet in the air; it made a shimmering sound. 'It's like gold foil.'

'Mmmm,' said Igress despondently. 'Except it's not gold.'

'More like silver. You could call it silver foil.'

'Except it's not silver.'

Rosa scrunched the foil into a ball. It kept its new shape. 'Greenhouses aren't green, are they?' she said. 'And they're not houses, either. You can call a thing whatever you like as long as everybody knows that that's what it's called.' She smoothed out the foil; it retained an image of all its crinkles. She handed it back to Igress. 'Will it melt if it goes in the oven?'

Igress flattened it further.

'Not in Mrs B's oven. Needs really high temperatures to get it to melt again.'

'Will it crack if it gets cold? Like in the cold store?'

'Erm. . . no, I don't think so. You've just got to watch out for it tearing, that's all. It's pretty thin.' She slipped the foil under the left-over sandwich. 'Napkin, do you think?'

Rosa pouted. 'Maybe. Is it absorbent?'

'Ah – no. And a bit sharp on the corners.'

Rosa folded the foil over the sandwich a few times and held it up in the flat of her hand.

'Hey!' she smiled. 'It makes lovely wrapping paper.'

In the tenth week, the army was split for specialist training.

Yedder's ten men were the athletes. Agile and light of foot, they spent a fortnight at Castle Yedder practising rowing, ropework, grappling-hook-throwing and wall-scaling.

Guildman's ten were the weapons-masters, and they spent the fortnight in the private fencing hall on the Guildman estate.

Rudolf inherited the remaining ten, who generally fell into the category of not too bright but tough with plenty of stamina.

If Rudolf had owned anywhere to take his men for training he wouldn't have needed the men in the first place; but he didn't have anywhere, and he did need them, so he commandeered a corner of the Town Field as his own.

His men completed their fitness regime by playing rugby on frozen ground as Rudolf sat bawling instructions and basking in the warmth of a flaming brazier. The structure of the teams was changed from match to match, ensuring that whilst every man was a team player, he was also independent and versatile, able to adapt to playing in any position. Being such a contact sport, the rugby also toughened the men up and they were able to shrug off lacerations, dislocated shoulders, black eyes and broken teeth, earning them the reputation of being not only the hardest men in Guildman's army, but by far the ugliest.

'You're right,' said Guildman, as Rigton passed three tankards across the gleaming new bar in the Lamb and Werewolf.

'What?' exclaimed Rudolf.

'You're right. The training's complete. The men are ready.'

'Wa-hoo!' said Rudolf, clapping him on the back. 'I knew you'd come to your senses.' He snatched a tankard. 'Drink up! Let's go get that castle.'

'Not today.'

Rigton flinched as the tankard slammed down again.

'I knew it!' spat Rudolf. 'I bloody knew it! What is it this time?'

He held up his hand. 'No, don't tell me; the men need another week's training for oh, I don't know – horsemanship? Or is it mediaeval architecture? So they can fully appreciate the castle that we're never going to storm at this rate!'

'We will launch our offensive,' said Guildman quietly, 'the day after tomorrow.'

'Why not tomorrow?'

Yedder looked surprised that Rudolf would even ask.

'The chaps'll need tomorrow to get over their hangovers, old sport.'

'Hangovers?'

'Yes. Rigsy's going to shut up shop tonight so we can have a private end-of-training party for the men. They'll be in no fit state for anything tomorrow.'

Yedder noticed that Rigton instinctively put a hand on his counter.

'Fear not, Rigsy; Temeraire's promised to only dance on the floor.'

'Tonight the men will have the party of their lives,' said Guildman, pushing a large moneybag towards Rigton and the other beers towards Rudolf. 'So why don't you make a start? Yedder and I have work to do.'

Faces fell in the castle kitchen.

'The day after tomorrow?' repeated Rosa.

'I'm afraid so,' said Guildman.

Yedder put his hand on her arm.

'It had to be sometime, Roz.'

'And we're ready for it,' said Fran. 'Aren't we, Gussie?'

'As ready as we'll ever be, I suppose,' he replied.

He couldn't remember whether he'd told Fran that he'd never killed anybody before.

Only one thing stopped Rigton locking the drunken revellers in the parlour of the Lamb and Werewolf and leaving them to it: the damage they'd have inflicted, and after their training their capacity for inflicting damage properly was greatly increased. Sensing danger to his profit margin, he stayed at his post, serving, refilling and wiping – and glowering at anyone who so much as looked as though they might leap onto his bar.

Mrs Rigton was also increasing their income. Knowing that even she wouldn't be able to share her favours around everybody, she had allowed a couple of friends in to earn, as she put it, 'a bit on the side'. Their earnings were somewhat diminished by the charge she made for rent of the rooms, but the arrangement was such that everybody was satisfied – some people two or three times.

Outside, two aristocrats paused, their breath making clouds in the cold night air. Normally, the comforting orange glow from a tavern would have lured them into the warm, but the Lamb and Werewolf's welcoming light was tempered by the occasional sight of a body, accompanied by a rousing cheer, rising towards the ceiling before dropping down again.

Yedder drew his greatcoat a little tighter round him.

'If it's all the same to you, Gil, I think I'll be toddling off home now.'

'Can't face going in?'

Yedder wrinkled his nose. 'No, not really.'

Guildman smiled sadly. 'Me neither, Yedder. Me neither.'

As they left the celebrations behind, tiny snowflakes began to fall.

NOTES ON

Winter

Spring, summer and autumn in Maund hardly vary. One might be a bit windier, one a bit sunnier and one a bit damper, but generally, for three-quarters of the year the townspeople have to be prepared for any and all weathers during the course of a day, from freezing snow to blinding sun. This calls for a layered approach to clothing, but each new layer does tend to increasingly restrict body movement.

Winter in Maund differs from every other season for an obvious reason: it's cold all the time and only marginally less cold when the sun is up. This naturally requires even more layers of clothing, which is why, for the most part, the citizens of Maund appear bulkier and stiffer than normal people.

As in most places, a Maund winter starts with a light flurry of white flakes drifting benignly towards earth. Small children excitedly call their mothers and dance in the streets, sticking their tongues out to catch each tiny miracle of frozen geometry. Within the hour a bleak, howling gale is blowing tiny icy daggers into each inch of exposed skin and all idle thought and conversation is drowned out by the constant crunch of fresh snow underfoot. Every ounce of concentration is required just to remain upright, and if you fall over, your fellow man is so bound fast in ever-tighter layers of clothing there's no way he could bend over to pick you up. So, in winter, no-one leaves home without a length of stout rope. If you fall over, someone or two will drop a rope to you, you tie it around any convenient part of your body, and then they drag you to your door. Not only do you get a free ride home, but you clear a path for other pedestrians.

A really thick, heavy snowfall is an omen of good luck for the people of Maund. It's a perfect excuse for not going to work, your relatives from the other side of town won't come visiting, it's a free plaything for the children, food stays fresher for longer, everybody's garden achieves the same level of neatness and tidiness and the crime rate drops because the criminals can't be bothered to go out in that sort of weather.

But the main reason the people of Maund love the snow is that for many of them, it's the only fresh water they get.

~✦~

There were bodies everywhere. Face down on tables, sprawled on benches, slumped against walls, crumpled in corners, spreadeagled on the floor... everywhere. Such was the sight that greeted Rigton in the morning when, with some difficulty, he pushed open the door to the parlour, causing the body behind it to topple over.

He threaded and picked his way to the outer doors, unlocked them and pulled them open. Freshly chilled air flooded over him into the foetid atmosphere of the Lamb and Werewolf. He screamed, a sound which would have been witnessed by dozens of people on The Horse Fair had that street and the rest of Maund not been waist-high in snow. He closed and bolted the doors again, turned and leant back on them. Surveying his empire, he was saddened that his scream had disturbed not one of the alcohol-steeped squaddies who snored, farted and twitched in their sleep all over his parlour.

For the first time in his long and often bitter employment, he gave up and went back to bed.

The air in the signalling tower at Castle Guildman was as clean and sharp as the message the shuttered lamp flashed to Castle Yedder: 'Snow stops play. Assess situation tomorrow'. There was little else the respective incumbents could do, except pay people to clear snow-buried paths.

In the early afternoon Rigton rose again and dressed more warmly than before. The bodies still littered his parlour, but were groaning more than snoring. He threw open the doors to let the iciness in then retreated behind the bar to await the call. It wasn't long in coming.

'Rigton! Beer!'

Rigton walked to the bottom of the stairs and shouted.

'No beer, my lord.'

'Breakfast then!'

'No food, my lord.'

'If this is one of Yedder's jokes...'

'No joke, my lord.'

Rudolf was down the stairs and in the parlour much faster than many would have thought possible. He saw the open doors. 'Bloody hell fire!'

'Quite so, my lord,' said Rigton. 'The dray horses will be unable to get through from the brewery and the path to the baker and butcher are similarly blocked. Mrs Rigton will be quite upset if she can't get her meat.'

'I bet she will.'

'If any of us are to eat or drink today, my lord, the path must be cleared.'

An aristocrat deprived of food and drink is an ugly thing, and Rudolf kicked and slapped the men into some form of life. Trained to respond to an officer's command, despite their parlous state they were soon out in the snow, working through their hangovers.

The snow brought a sense of safety to Castle Stein. Anybody fool enough to approach in this weather would have been seen miles away and completely worn out before they even got to the moat. The only path cleared was between the kitchen and the smithy, and that was on the strict understanding that Igress could only use it to ensure the forge fire remained lit.

The household collectively decided to have an easy day of it. Gussie, Igress and Aidan built a snow Rudolf in the courtyard, and everyone had fun pelting it with all manner of objects until it was just another pile of disturbed coldness.

The frostiness made the heat of the kitchen even more welcoming and once the snow had been brushed off and wet gloves had been put by the fire to dry, Beaton's mulled wine brought an extra glow to everyone's cheeks. It was as one big happy family they all sat around the kitchen table to enjoy Mrs B's lavish roast dinner, followed by party games and silly jokes until eyelids started to droop and heads began to nod.

For the moment they were carefree; tomorrow, after all, would be another day.

Temperatures nosedived, winds moaned around the town and the few streets that had been cleared were covered again overnight by fresh snowfalls. The morning brought windblown powdery drifting, compacted by the tramp and slip of the hardy souls who ventured out, they being those who couldn't afford to stay inside and those who could afford to pay people to get them to where they wanted to go.

Yedder and Guildman stamped the snow from their feet on the already-sodden doormat in the Lamb and Werewolf.

'Your usual, my lords?' said Rigton.

'Bit nippy for beer, actually,' replied Yedder. 'Damn near slid off the road a few times, so a couple of hot toddies wouldn't go amiss today, old thing.'

Rigton bowed. 'I'll get Mrs Rigton to start heating up.'

'And call Rudolf please,' said Guildman. 'We have an important day ahead.' He and Yedder moved over towards the fireplace as Rigton left to do their bidding.

Rudolf came downstairs clasping a thick eiderdown round him. 'What the hell are you two doing here?'

'I take it you're not ready, then,' said Guildman.

'Ready for what?'

'It's your big day, old love,' Yedder reminded him. 'Taking the castle and all that?'

'In this weather? You're out of your minds.'

'It's only a bit of snow, Rude.'

'It's not "only a bit of snow", Yedder. It's a lot of snow, and a lot of ice. And if you think I'm going arse over tit out there and being carried into the castle with a broken leg, think again. I'm not setting foot out of that door until there's solid ground to walk on, so come back when it's warmer weather.'

Guildman closed his eyes and breathed very deeply.

'Warmer weather,' he said slowly, looking up with murderous intent, but Rudolf and his eiderdown had gone back to bed.

In Castle Stein, the news of Rudolf's refusal to attack in snow meant that the heightened state of alert was relaxed somewhat and everybody suddenly developed a passion for meteorology.

The weather proved both tenacious and capricious. By day, the weak winter sunlight held promise of a thaw: water trickled in downpipes, rooftop drips punched holes in the street snow and carts churned the roads into a filthy slush. But the days were short and by night, icicle daggers froze on the window ledges and the slush solidified into slithery, jagged, unyielding ice buried by frenetic blizzards. The people of Maund – rich, poor and those making their way from the one to the other in either direction – dug in for the duration, which turned out to be much longer than anyone had expected.

By the turning of the year, the green of the Timekeeper on Fran's mantelpiece had given way to a coppery amber.

'This is ridiculous,' said Fran, pacing back and forth in front of Guildman's bedroom fire. 'Six weeks! Six bloody weeks! I ask you! We're running out of time. Especially Gussie. All he's doing every day is clearing the path between Durney's and the castle. I didn't bring him back for that.'

Guildman opened his hands. 'I can't force Rudolf to launch an assault.'

Fran stopped and faced him. 'But there's no point me training Gussie to kill Rudolf if Rudolf's not going to be there for him to kill!' She put her hands on her hips. 'I suppose I could always send Gussie to the pub to kill him.'

'With all due respect, Mistress Stein, I'm not sure Gussie's a cold-blooded killer. Heat of the moment, maybe. Accidental, almost certainly. But premeditated? Hardly.'

She scowled. 'Look. I don't care how it happens just as long as it does. At this rate Rudolf's going to die of old age! Tell him you won't give him any more money unless he attacks.'

Guildman frowned. 'That would only put him beyond our control. If he's not dependent on me, he'll attack when it suits him, not when it suits us.'

'Threaten to stop paying his troop.'

'He will promise them money; they will believe him. He is their leader and they will follow him.'

'Then tell him you'll give him *more* money if he attacks.'

'He has no need of more money. He refuses to move from the Lamb and Werewolf, and all his bills there are paid to keep him under our control.'

'So we have to wait.'

Each new dawn carried fresh hope of respite from snow and ice, even if that hope had little enthusiasm and much foreboding. The townsfolk rediscovered chilblains, hot-aches and previously dormant expertise in foraging, scavenging and poaching. Benevolent aristocracy turned a blind eye to incursions on their land; heartless lords set man-traps and hired thugs. Undying loyalty, burning grudges and heavily embellished family legends were born during the bitter struggle against the elements.

Those hardy enough to stand in the street talked of the dire situation, exaggerating the paucity of their own larder lest any mention of food be construed as an invitation to be eaten out of house, home and furniture. Anything even slightly edible or combustible was taken indoors, to be either consumed by its owner or saved from consumption by someone else. The creatures of the night, who were normally accorded first scavenging rights, suddenly found themselves the prey of an increasingly fearless population who stretched the definition of 'sausage' to snapping point. And on the principle that what the ear doesn't hear the heart won't grieve over, nobody went so far as to call the pastry-wrapped savouries 'rat rolls'.

As the alleged meat ran out, vegetable soup became the order of the day, because it was the best way to make a potato and a carrot seem to last forever and no-one would object if, when huddling together for warmth, everyone smelt of onions.

All agreed that it was the best and worst winter Maund had ever experienced, and old ladies looked forward to the rash of new grandchildren that would be an inevitable consequence.

With every passing day Fran's apprehension increased as her own and Gussie's store of life diminished. A month after her visit to Guildman, she could wait no longer.

Parturicia's eyes widened. 'You lost it? You lost Twicetime?'

Fran twisted the silver Bracelet of Life around in her hands, nodded sheepishly and, for once, stayed silent.

'But – but – how?'

Fran handed her the now reddening Timekeeper. Pat closed her eyes and the vision of the lost pouch filled her mind.

'Ah.' She opened her eyes and gave the Timekeeper back. 'That was unfortunate.'

'At least we know that nobody else is using it,' offered Fran.

There was silence. Pat rested her chin on her thumb and tapped her fingers on her lips as she gazed into nowhere, lost in thought. Eventually she sighed. 'I'm sorry, Fran. I can't.'

'Oh, Pat, please. I'm desperate.'

'You've already had more than you should have done.'

'But—'

'I can't prolong life indefinitely, especially a life – no, two lives – that have already been finished once.'

Gussie was in the smithy working the bellows for Igress when Fran marched across the courtyard towards them.

'Hello, Mistress Stein,' said Igress cheerfully. 'Come for a bit of a warm, have you?'

The thunder clouding Fran's face was replaced by an over-expansive smile. She looked directly into Igress's eyes.

'It's time you had a break,' she said. 'You're very hungry.'

Igress wiped her forehead with the back of her wrist.

'It's time I had a break. I'm starving.'

'Go and see if Mrs B can make you something.'

'I'll go and see if Mrs B can make me something.'

'That's a good idea. Off you go.'

Fran's smile disappeared as Igress threw a shawl around her and walked off towards the kitchen.

'What's all that about?' asked Gussie.

'What?' said Fran coldly.

'Sending Igress away – and before you say you didn't I was standing here watching the whole thing.'

Fran slapped her Bracelet of Life on an anvil. 'I have things to do.' She took a hammer and chisel and with one blow broke the completeness of the Bracelet.

Gussie gasped as a man appeared.

'Hello...' said the man, looking at Gussie. 'Haven't we met somewhere before?'

'Oh yes,' said Gussie.

'I thought so – your face looks very familiar. Although I don't remember that body being underneath it...'

'Ahem,' coughed Fran.

'Oh, sorry,' said the man, and cleared his throat. 'Who calls on Death?'

'I do, if he's not too busy.'

Death peered at her. 'I must say, you don't look like you're about to go. Are you sure it's you?'

'Oh yes,' said Fran. 'It's me. I'm very near the end of my tether. Look.'

She held up the broken Bracelet.

'Ooh, careless,' said Death. 'Who did that?'

'I did.'

There was a strangled cry and Death's hand shot up to his mouth. 'But— but— you're of the Systerhood! You can't! It's against – well, everything! You just can't!'

Fran put the Bracelet back on the anvil, positioned the chisel and hefted the hammer.

'I just have. And I will sever it completely unless I get some more Twicetime for my friend here.'

Her calm was in stark contrast to Death's distraction.

He threw his hands in the air.

'Oh, no, I hate this. There'll be such a hoo-hah. There'll be an inquiry and that means I won't be able to do my job, and that'll create a backlog, and it'll go on and on and on and it'll take months to sort out. And then there's all the paperwork afterwards, oh no...'

'Then get me some more Twicetime.'

'What?'

'You heard.'

Death put his hands on his hips. 'Do you know who I am?'

Fran rolled her eyes. 'No – are you Billy from Bubborth? Of course I know who you are! I'm due to see you in a couple of months. I know full well who you are, and what you can do, and you can go and ask Pat for more Twicetime.'

'Are you mad?!'

'If you don't, this hammer comes down and it'll be hell for me and hell for you an' all. So what do you say? Eh? Go on, I'm sure she'll listen to you.'

Death stared at Fran.

She didn't flinch. 'Think of all that paperwork.'

He vanished.

She put the hammer on the anvil and blew out a sigh.

'I'm going to die again, aren't I?' said Gussie quietly.

Fran avoided his look. 'Not necessarily.'

He grabbed her wrist.

'Yes, necessarily. Did you think I wouldn't recognise him? I have seen him before, you know.'

'I know. I forgot.'

'Well I didn't. So talk.'

She shook her wrist free from his grasp.

'What can I say? I just wanted a bodyguard for Rosa until Rudolf was taken care of, that's all. You were supposed to come in, do the job...'

'...and die?'

Fran nodded.

Gussie sighed. 'So what's the problem?'

'We've run out of time.'

The silence that followed was broken by Gussie.

'You're not going to do this.'

'Who's going to stop me?'

'You won't leave Rosa to the mercies of Rudolf.'

Fran's eyes filled with tears. 'You don't understand. She *will* be at his mercy unless I can get you more Twicetime. I'll have failed her, and I can't live with the consequences of that.'

'That's cowardly.'

'I know. But what will that matter to me when I'm dead?'

'Don't. Don't do this. You said you'd got a couple of months left – then use them to help her. Let me... let me... die.'

The tears flowed freely. 'Gussie... I can't.'

'You can, you can. I've done it once already. I wasn't meant to be brought back.'

Fran sobbed. 'No, you weren't. Some anonymous hulk who could kill Rudolf – that's who was meant to be brought back. Not you, love. You weren't meant to be brought back and you weren't meant to become part of the family and we weren't meant to love you. But that's what happened.'

Gussie shook as he picked up her hand. His tears dropped onto the anvil and mingled with hers. 'That's... that's the most wonderful thing anybody's ever said to me.' He half-smiled. 'In this or any other life.'

Death reappeared.

Fran sniffed. 'You haven't been long.'

He shook his head. 'Sorry, she won't have it.'

'What?!'

'I tried, believe me, I tried – but she's adamant.'

'Bugger.'

'Which means one of you's got to come with me now.'

'Why?' asked Gussie.

'Why?' Death repeated, taken aback by such a question. 'Because I've been summoned and I can't go back without someone, that's why.'

The colour drained from Fran's face.

'Oh, Gussie, what have I done?'

'You've made my life mean something.'

'But that's not enough.'

'It is for me.'

'But not for me.' She hefted the hammer and repositioned the chisel. Gritting her teeth, she looked Death straight in the eye and hissed, 'I am going to cause you so much trouble.'

'Miiiiiisssssstrrrrreeeeeeeesssssssss!'

A streak of white fur shot into the smithy and leapt onto the anvil. Sooty kneaded the back of her hand as she held the chisel. 'Stop! Stop! What are you doing, mistress?! Stop it! Stop it! You can't do this – you can't break the Bracelet – you can't you can't – you can't leave me! It's not time! You can't!'

'Spirit, I bid thee silence!' she commanded.

Sooty's plaintive cries became a series of desperate sobs as Fran's words robbed him of the power of speech. She laid down the hammer, wiped her eyes on her sleeve and cupped his head in her hand. 'Spirit, I have to go.' His body shook and his tears flowed over her fingers as she looked into his eyes. 'You knew I had to – and now the time has come.'

'It doesn't have to be now,' said Death softly. 'Not for you.'

She turned her head towards him. 'Oh, I think it does. I have tried to force the hand of both the Giver and Taker of Life, and by doing so I placed myself above them.'

'Oh, I didn't see it that way,' Death cajoled. 'If I had done, I wouldn't have gone to plead on your behalf. And Pat's very forgiving. She knows why you've been driven this far.'

Fran smiled sadly. 'That's... kind of you.' She turned back to Sooty. 'But I've proven myself willing to betray my calling. The one thing that my life has served. All the training – all the instinct and knowledge – the bedrock of my existence – is nothing now.' She stroked his head. 'Spirit, I am so sorry. I have let you down so badly.'

Sooty closed his eyes and slumped on the anvil.

Deep in his heart Gussie felt a howl of anguish. He picked Sooty up and cradled him against his chest.

'But you didn't do it for you,' he said. 'You did it for Rosa.'

'Nonetheless I did it,' said Fran, 'and I've done a far, far more terrible thing.' She looked up at him. 'I've meddled with people's lives, uninvited. And worst of all, I've played with your life and your death without consulting you at all. I've messed things up so much for you, and I am truly, truly sorry.'

'Well, if you are so truly sorry, the least you can do is hand my life and my death back to me and let me decide.'

She shook her head. 'It's too late.' She leant across the anvil and stroked Sooty's head again. 'Goodbye, Spirit.'

She reached for the hammer. It wasn't there any more.

'Give me the hammer, Gussie.'

'Not on your life – or mine. Which, I believe, is the life under discussion at the moment.'

'Gussie, I won't tell you again...'

'No, you won't. Ever since I got here you've been telling me. And now it's my turn.' His voice softened. 'I had no life until you "played" as you call it. I had a... a passage of time... a purposeless marking off of the calendar. You didn't just give me life – you gave me *a* life. A life worth living. Full of friendship, and fun, and... hot meals... and purpose. I've known what it's like to be trusted, not simply tolerated. I've been depended on, needed... more than that – wanted. And you wanted me so much you're willing to give up your life for me. Do you know what that means?'

Fran's face crumpled.

'That means...' Gussie said, '...that means there's nothing greater that anybody could do for me. Nothing that happens will ever mean as much again. My life has been... fulfilled. What more could any man ask? Except now... please let me go.'

'I can't!'

'You must,' said Death as sympathetically as he could.

'No!' shouted Fran.

'You have to, gal. I was meant to die again anyway. You said so yourself. I should probably have been dead again already by now if it hadn't snowed.'

'No, not you.'

'It's my time... my turn. Rosa would miss you a lot more than she would me.'

'Listen to him,' said Death. 'You know he's right.'

'My time is due. Let him take me.'

Fran sagged, and put down the chisel.

'Oh Gussie, I'm sorry.' She walked round the anvil and hugged him. 'I'm so sorry,' she whispered. 'Forgive me.'

'Nothing to forgive.' He kissed the top of her head. 'You gave me life and love. That doesn't need forgiveness.'

She pulled away from him. 'You're a wiser man than me, love. Thank you.'

Gussie looked at Death. 'I'm ready.'

Fran spun round.

'Before you take him, will you fix my Bracelet?'

Death looked surprised. 'What?'

'Please. Before he... I need to show Gussie I'm... I'm all right, I'm... whole again. I want him to know I can go on and help Rosa. I can't do that if my Bracelet's broken, and I know you can use your energy to mend it.'

'Well...'

'Please. He needs to know I'm all right.'

Death pursed his lips. 'Very well.'

Fran held up the Bracelet. Death concentrated on it, and smoke began to rise from the broken ends. He closed his eyes to increase the power. Gussie felt a tug on his arm, the hammer was pulled from his grasp and a brilliant flash blinded him.

Mrs B twitched and whisked the teapot away abruptly.

'Oh, I'm fed up of tea, aren't you? Let's have a treat.'

Igress grinned. 'Beaton Special?'

Mrs B poured two small glasses of colourless spirit from a bottle. 'Beaton Extra.'

They clinked glasses.

'Here's to you, Mrs B,' Igress said before drinking it off.

Mrs B put the other glassful on the table so that she'd have both hands free when Igress lost consciousness.

They were in a void. Gussie was no longer holding Sooty, but a haze of purple light hovered nearby, flexing and stretching. Fran had one hand clamped as far round Gussie's wrist as her fingers would reach, and Death boggled in disbelief.

'What did you have to go and do that for?' he wailed.

'Desperate times, desperate measures,' said Fran.

'Do you know what you've gone and done?'

'I've got a fair idea.'

'Then have you any idea how long it'll take to sort out?'

'Not long.'

'Not long?!'

'Not long.'

'When you two have finished playing repeat-after-me,' Gussie said, 'could someone tell me what's going on?'

'What's going on?' said Death. 'You want to know what's going on?'

'Enough!' yelled Gussie. 'What's going on?!'

'Oi!' said Death. 'Don't you shout at me, shout at her! She's the one who's cocked things up for me good and proper.'

'Oh, don't be so melodramatic,' said Fran.

'Melodramatic?!' he shrieked, only a couple of hand gestures away from a full-blown tantrum. 'I'm Death! How much more melodramatic can it get?!'

'Blimey! If I'd known you were going to react like this—'

'Button it!' bellowed Gussie. 'The pair of you. It was a lot quieter than this last time I died.'

'That's because you're not dead this time, love,' said Fran.

'Exactly!' crowed Death.

'What do you mean I'm not dead?'

Fran tutted. 'Come on Gussie, it's not exactly difficult. You – are – not – dead.'

'Why am I not dead?'

'Well...'

'*You* aren't dead,' Death interrupted, 'because *she* has sabotaged it.'

Gussie looked puzzled. 'Sabotaged it?'

Death nodded at Fran. 'Show him. Go on, show him.'

Fran lifted one of the fingers she had clamped around Gussie's wrist. Underneath it was the Bracelet of Life, complete again, encircling his arm.

'Congratulations!' said Death testily. 'You're the only man in history ever to have three lifelines.'

'What?'

Death rubbed his hands over his face. 'Give me strength,' he said, and looked at Fran. 'Couldn't you have found somebody a bit brighter?'

'Give him a break,' she said. 'He's not of this world.'

Gussie flailed his free hand. 'No, but for one reason or

another he is stuck in it so somebody'd better explain about the three lifelines before he rips his own head off so he can't hear you talking about him as if he's not here!'

The purple light shimmered.

Death took a deep breath. 'For some reason you have a lifeline belonging to your head—'

'That's mine,' said Gussie.

'You've got another one belonging to the body—'

'That's Bill's.'

'And you have hers.'

'What? How can I have hers if she's still alive?'

'She's not. She's dead.'

'Not until I let go of this Bracelet I'm not,' Fran chipped in.

Gussie clapped his hand over hers. 'Then don't let go.'

'She has to sooner or later, or else we're stuck here for ever.'

'What?!'

'I'm afraid he's right, Gussie,' said Fran. 'Because I summoned him, he can't go back without somebody's lifeline. He can't take yours because you're protected by the Bracelet. So, he has to take mine.'

The purple light wreathed round her.

Gussie's brow furrowed. 'But he said *I'd* got your lifeline.'

'Exactly!' said Death, throwing his hands up in despair. 'Welcome to my nightmare world of inquests and inquiries and reports and form-filling and muck-raking and nit-picking and all because she decides she wants to jack it all in!'

'Oh, don't get so aerated,' Fran said. 'Honestly, you're that excitable. I don't know how you got this job in the first place.'

Death's eyes bulged and his head twitched.

'Oh, I'm sorry. This Reaper not grim enough for you?'

Fran glared at him. 'You know, for somebody with your power, you aren't half touchy.'

'Touchy? Is there any bloody wonder, considering the work you've caused me?'

'If you'd just listen for a minute instead of throwing a wobbly I'll tell you what we're going to do about it!'

She shook her head to compose herself.

'When I let go of the Bracelet, my lifeline will split. You will take the lifeline of Fran the woman, and Gussie will take the lifeline of the *power* of Fran. The power stays with the Bracelet.'

There was a short silence while Death worked through the ramifications of this.

Fran couldn't wait that long. 'You came here for a lifeline and you'll have one. Your books will balance. No inquests, no inquiries, no form-filling.'

Death pondered. 'Hmmm. That could work.'

'Oh?' said Gussie.

Death folded his arms. 'Normally, I work on an appointments system, you see. I make the appointments, I keep them. Easy. And then she comes along and nearly wrecks the damned lot by shifting the appointments.'

'Sorry?'

'She tricked me into bringing your appointment forward. Then she goes and fills your appointment.'

'Meaning?'

'Meaning I can't come back for you because your appointment's gone, and I can't come back for her at her appointed time because she's not there any more.'

'Does that mean you're going to make another appointment for me?'

Death looked at him distastefully. 'What's wrong with you? I've never met anybody so keen on dying.'

'I'm not keen, I'm... curious.'

'Well, Mr Curious, you obviously missed a vital point in our discussions. I can't make another appointment for you because you're protected by the Bracelet of Life that this fool soldered round your wrist.'

'Protected?'

'Oh, shine a friggin' light! Don't you know anything?'

'Tailoring!' retorted Gussie. 'I know tailoring! If you want a new suit making, I'm your man. But life or death after life after death – no, not so much!'

Fran put her hand on his arm. 'Gussie,' she said calmly, 'the Bracelet of Life gives you protection from Death.'

His mouth fell open and he stared at her.

'Protection from *Death*?'

She nodded.

He clamped his lips together, counted to five and then said, 'So why the hell didn't *you* wear it and save all this fuss?!'

'It doesn't work like that.'

Gussie's face said that this answer wasn't good enough, so she had to continue. 'It's complicated.'

'Take your time – I'm not going anywhere.'

'No,' said Death, 'but *I* have other appointments to keep so if you can make it snappy...'

'All right,' said Fran dismissively, 'we know you're busy. Now, Gussie, listen to me.'

'I'm listening.'

'Good. A Bracelet of Life is a very powerful thing. It can summon the Bringer of Life and the Bringer of Death. It won't protect a witch from Death, because anybody trained in magic can't be allowed to live forever in case they become too powerful, but it'll protect *you* because you're not trained. But once I've gone, it'll be trying to get back to the University of Nature and it'll keep you alive until you take it there. Got it?'

'So until I take it to the University, I'm invincible?'

'Whatever put that idea into your head? You'll be immortal, yes, but not invincible.'

'What's the difference?'

'Immortals have to pick their battles very carefully.'

Mrs B quickly assessed the three bodies slumped on the smithy floor. Gussie and Sooty appeared to be deeply asleep, but Fran's shallow breathing and the fact that her hand was clamped tight around Gussie's wrist disturbed Mrs B. She took off her shawl, folded it up and slipped it under Fran's head, then sat down next to her and clasped her free hand.

'Oh, Fran, what have you done?'

She gently stroked the witch's steel-grey hair.

'Whatever it is,' she said, 'you'll not do it alone.'

'So what happens now?' asked Gussie.

Fran swallowed hard. 'Now, I have to say goodbye.'

'Oh, no, no, no, no, no, no.'

'Yes. Gussie, I have to go. You must look after Rosa now. You must. For me.'

'I can't.'

'You can. You must. Otherwise, this will have been one huge waste of time, and I'd never forgive either of us.'

The lump in Gussie's throat was so big he could hardly speak. 'I – I'll do what you want.'

She smiled and lovingly touched his cheek. 'Good lad.'

He clasped her hand to his face. 'Thank you for my life,' he said, closing his eyes to dam the tears.

The purple light swirled around her faster and faster.

'Goodbye, Spirit – my companion, guide and truest friend. Forgive me for this sudden end, and thank you for...' – her voice cracked – '...thank you for everything.' The light condensed into a pinpoint above her head before suddenly shattering into thousands of tears of light that drenched her.

'I know,' she whispered. 'I know.'

The light wreathed around her again.

She wiped away her own tears.

'Spirit, as my last request I ask you to accept into your care this man who now wears my Bracelet of Life and carries the lifeline of my power.'

The light flickered in a state of great agitation.

'I *can't* stay. You know I can't. Now, will you accept he who wears my Bracelet and carries my power?'

The light pulsed, swelled to brilliance and faded.

'Thank you, Spirit. So, accept into your care this man I now embrace.' She put one arm around Gussie. 'Goodbye, love.'

He hugged her tightly. 'I'm going to miss you so much.'

The purple light swirled round the two of them.

'Spirit, I bid thee speak. And I bid thee goodbye.'

Fran put both arms round Gussie.

He tried to hold on to her, but found he was clasping nothing except the light that was coiling around his arms.

Fran's hand fell backwards onto the smithy floor, exposing the Bracelet around Gussie's wrist. Mrs B gathered Fran to her, and rocked backwards and forwards as she cried her heart out.

'Oh, Fran. Goodbye, love. Goodbye.'

Sooty jolted awake, stood up and looked round. His gaze rested on Fran's body; his eyes widened and he swayed. Mrs B held her hand out towards him, but he fled.

Gussie's eyes fluttered open and he slowly turned his head to one side. When he saw Mrs B holding Fran, he closed his eyes again for a few seconds before kneeling beside Fran and reaching out. 'I'll take care of her, Mrs B,' he said. 'You go and do what you have to.'

Mrs B kissed Fran's forehead, then with great care handed her to Gussie. 'Take her to... to the cold room, love,' she said, wiping her own face. 'I'll be there in a while.'

Sooty ran. He ran and ran, from the castle and into the woods, heedless of the ice and snow and oblivious to the brambles and thorns that snagged his fur and scratched his skin. He did not hear the sudden flight of birds or the startled skittering of claws on tree bark as he tore along the path. All he heard was the pounding heart of a body that he desperately wanted to shed. In the instant of Fran's death, the spirit and soul and personality that normally filled his skin to bursting had shrunk so violently that the essence of who he was no longer had any contact with the flesh and blood of him, except at that heart from which he now recoiled.

He became a mind who drove the body to the point of collapse, wearing it down as he pushed way beyond its limits, wringing every last ounce of strength from the mortal muscles. If he ran fast enough and far enough, he might run himself out of himself, leaving behind the misery and the memory. He must keep running until the exhausted body gave way under him, for if he stopped he would have to rive out the heart to end the searing pain and the gnawing despair. He wanted the body to die, to break that final bond between the spiritual and corporeal, because only then would his agony cease.

His legs buckled. He fell, rolled over and over and slammed into the cottage door before crumpling in a heap. His whole body heaved as he gasped for breath, only to choke the air out again with his sobs.

Mrs B walked slowly into the laboratory, her eyes flooded with tears and her arms held out to Rosa.

Sooty buried his head into the cushion on Durney's lap and put his paws over his ears. If he blocked out the light and the sound, maybe he could block out the fact. But as surely as the tears stained his face, the sorrow still ate away at his heart.

'Make it stop, Durney.'

Durney stroked his back. 'I can't, bud. I can't make it stop for you any more than for me. You just have to get through it.'

'I can't. I can't!'

'You have to. Now come on, head up and have a drink.'

Sooty's reply was to bury himself further in the cushion.

Durney picked him up and turned him on his back. He tried to roll over but a large, calloused hand held him still. Durney dipped his finger into a saucer of lavender-coloured milk on the table and wiped it across Sooty's mouth.

Despite the surprise Sooty instinctively licked his lips.

He shuddered. 'Ugh! What are you doing? What's that?'

'It's something you need,' said Durney softly, dipping his finger again. 'Now will you have more?'

Grudgingly, Sooty acknowledged his thirst and licked Durney's finger. Durney drip-fed him until there were no more licks because Sooty had acquiesced into a deep sleep. Durney wiped away his own tears with a hand that he could not steady.

Igress, laid on a kitchen bench, did not react when Beaton lifted and dropped her hand.

'Is she all right, Mr Beaton?' said Aidan. 'Is she—?'

'The young lady is asleep.'

'Asleep?' Aidan's voice rose as he rubbed at her hand. 'Why won't she wake up?!'

Beaton picked up the full glass from the table.

'It's not time for her to waken yet.'

Aidan was wild-eyed. 'Not time?!'

'Aidan, a footman does not panic.'

'I'm not panicking—'

'Sit!' commanded Beaton. Aidan automatically sat next to Igress on the bench. Beaton handed him the glass. 'Drink this.'

'What is it?'

'It will calm you.'

'I am c—'

'Drink!'

Aidan drank, and was soon laid out on another bench. Beaton paced up and down the kitchen until his wife returned, and her red-rimmed eyes told him what he needed to know.

'Miss Frances,' she whispered.

He put his arms round her and kissed the top of her head.

'Oh, my dear,' he said tenderly. 'I am sorry.'

She cried in his embrace for a while, then blew her nose.

'I've told milady; now we have to tell Igress and Aidan.'

'And Durney?'

Mrs B wiped her eyes. 'He'll know by now.'

The day following Fran's death dawned bright and unseasonably warm. Those outside the castle remarked on the sudden break in the weather; those inside had work of the saddest kind to do as they started to live with the realisation of Fran's loss.

Rosa spent the morning writing black-bordered letters. While Durney kept a silent vigil in the castle, Mrs B attended to the laying-out of Fran's body, ministering with a degree of care that Fran would never have lavished on herself. Igress and Gussie spent a long day sawing, nailing and staining the casket that would carry Fran to her final resting place.

Sooty disappeared from the castle early in the morning.

After a subdued evening meal, most of the household were sitting in the comforting glow of the kitchen fire when Rosa entered, carrying a white dress and Fran's small carved wooden box.

She gave the dress to Igress. 'I thought you might need some silk for the... might need some silk.'

Igress held it up; it was badly creased and there were boot prints across the skirt.

Rosa coughed. 'It's the... er... it's the dress my father made me get married in.' She looked at the ceiling briefly, as if deciding how much to tell. 'Anyway, long story short: I threw it at my father... he walked on it... it got chucked in a cupboard and it's been there ever since.' She looked at Igress. 'But it wasn't the dress's fault, and it should have some use. The petticoats should be all right, even if the top's not much good.'

Igress nodded and folded the dress up.

Rosa sighed. 'Now, I also have here Aunty Fran's Returning Wishes. Mrs B, should I wait until...?'

Mrs B shook her head slowly. 'He'll be back in his own time, milady.'

'Right, right.' Rosa sat at the kitchen table, opened the box and from it unfolded a parchment. '*I, Frances Stein, do hereby give and bequeath my worldly possessions in the following manner. Firstly, the box in which this document is found. Of all my earthly goods, this is the most precious to me, and I return it to Durney with deepest gratitude and love. May he know that not a day has passed but I have touched the box, thought of him and been comforted.*'

She put the box in Durney's hands. He ran his shaking fingers over the carvings and smiled sadly. 'I made it for her graduation, y'know. I didn't think she'd still have it.'

Mrs B put her arm round him.

Rosa swallowed.

'*Secondly, I leave all other possessions such as I have to my niece Rosa,*'

*to dispose of as she thinks fit. Thirdly, my Returning Wishes are these: if
my dear brother will allow, may I be buried and returned to Mother
Nature close by his cottage.'*

Durney nodded. 'Bring her home.'

Sooty did not return until late, and went straight up to Fran's
room. There, propped up against the pillows, was Cecil. Sooty
hugged the teddy bear, chewing his raggy ear and weeping until
sleep overtook him. The following day he was out of the castle
before anyone else had risen.

'Next week?' cried Rudolf. 'It could be snowing again by then
and I'm sick to death of being cooped up in this hovel!'

Behind the bar Rigton looked hurt, but nobody noticed.

'We will take the castle next week,' Guildman repeated.

'Next week? You know sod all about tactics, don't you?'

'I know that at Castle Stein they've been preparing their
defences for six months and they'll be expecting us to launch
an offensive at the first break in the weather. I also know not
to take troops into battle unprepared.'

'Unprepared? Un-bloody-prepared? They've been prepared
for three sodding months!'

Guildman's face hardened. 'No, the men *were* prepared
three months ago and since then – like you – they've been
sitting on their backsides getting paunchy.'

'Paunchy? I'm not bloody paunchy, I'm as fit as a lop and
raring to get off up to the castle and see to that harpy—'

In an instant Guildman shot to his feet, leant forward,
grabbed Rudolf's tunic and pulled him half-way across the

rickety table. 'You had your chance three months ago,' he spat, his eyes glittering with a fury he didn't even try to disguise, 'but you were too scared to go out in the snow. I'm paying for this army, I'm running this show and I say we attack next week.'

He threw Rudolf back onto the bench and sat down.

Rudolf straightened his tunic and thrust his chin out.

'All right, all right, have it your way. But don't blame me if you've lost the element of surprise.'

'I won't.'

Hostility simmered in the silence.

'I hear racing's starting up again tomorrow,' Yedder broke in with forced cheerfulness.

'Right then,' said Rudolf, 'we'll go.'

'Not tomorrow,' said Guildman.

Rudolf glowered. 'And why not?'

'Yedder and I will be otherwise engaged.'

'What? You're going somewhere and not taking me?'

Yedder coughed. 'We didn't think you'd want to go to Mistress Stein's funeral.'

Gussie lay on his bed, staring at the ceiling. His body was tired after the day's exertions: he and Igress had cut the silks and lined the coffin then he'd made his way to Durney's to dig the grave. His mind was wide awake, replaying the past few weeks. He kidded himself he was trying to make sense of it all, but he knew he was simply going over old ground, partly to fix Fran's image in his mind. He was angry that already the details of her face had started to fade. She had twice given him life, once at the cost of her own; the least he could do was remember her.

There was a scratching at the door.

'Gushie! Gushie!'

Gussie rose and opened the door.

Sooty padded in, leapt onto the bed and something dropped from his mouth onto the covers.

Gussie sat down next to him. 'I'm glad to see you,' he said.

'Why?'

'Because I've been worried about you, you fool. Dashing off early doors, not telling a soul where you're going—'

'Stop, stop,' said Sooty, holding up a paw. 'You're even beginning to sound like her.'

'Sorry. But I have been worried.'

Sooty pawed at the bracelet round Gussie's wrist. 'We had our arguments, y'know, me and her... but at least we understood each other. Always did, right from the start. She was... mischievous. Made me laugh. But she always knew what she was doing. Some of 'em graduate and they're... timid, unsure of themselves. Not her. She was full force, straight off. Thought she'd go on forever.' He swallowed hard. 'Anyway, I've brought you this.' He pushed something towards Gussie.

It was a lock of white fur, set in a silver clasp and hung on a silver chain.

Durney brought his cart to the castle, and Mrs B strewed its bed with yew branches, bay leaves and lavender.

Yedder, Guildman, Durney, Aidan, Beaton and Mason were the pall-bearers who carried the coffin through the castle and laid it respectfully on the cart, and then walked behind with Rosa, Mrs B and Igress as Gussie pulled the cart to Durney's cottage, Sooty leading the way. Beaton held the ropes with which they would lower the coffin into the grave, and Aidan carried a box of art supplies to decorate a memorial tablet.

There was no formal ceremony; once the coffin had been lowered, each one in turn paid their last respects, whether spoken or in the silence of their own thoughts. Mrs B had given everyone a sprig of rosemary – 'for remembrance, my dears' – which they threw into the grave with a handful of soil.

When all tributes had been paid, Gussie stepped forward.

'If nobody minds, I'd like to stay a while. I'll join you later.'

Rosa wiped her eyes, stood on tiptoe and kissed him lightly on the cheek. 'Of course. We'll see you back at the castle.'

'I'll stay as well,' said Sooty.

'And I'd like to paint the sign,' added Aidan.

Drops of rain began to fall as the others headed away from the cottage.

Gussie stood at the foot of the grave.

'Happy the bride that the sun shines on,' he said, 'and happy the corpse that the rain rains on.' He reached inside his collar and withdrew Sooty's bargain-token on its silver chain. He lifted it over his head and held it out over the grave; from his pocket he took a pair of scissors and, as carefully as his huge hands would allow, he snipped a tiny amount off the end of the fur. It drifted downwards to rest on the coffin.

Sooty's tears mingled with the rain. 'Goodbye, mistress.'

Gussie looped the bargain-token back around his neck, then picked up Sooty and carried him into the warmth of Durney's cottage.

The rest of the funeral party walked between the well-worn cart ruts back to the castle. As they approached the entrance to the kitchen tunnel, Mrs B stopped and held up her hand.

'Stay here,' she whispered to the others. 'And please – don't make a sound.'

The party did as it was bidden, because if Mrs B had heard something they hadn't, they'd rather trust her ears than their own. She tiptoed off up the tunnel, and when she returned a few minutes later, she signalled to them to turn around.

'Lord Rudolf and his men have taken the castle.'

'Right,' said Guildman. 'Yedder and I will see what we can find out, and we'll meet the rest of you later back at Durney's.'

Two burly guards with crossed pikestaffs barred the entrance to Castle Stein.

'Stand aside, chaps, would you?' said Yedder.

'Nobody gets in, sir,' said one of the guards. 'Orders of Lord Dibkiss.'

Yedder smiled at the guards. 'Then could one of you maybe pop along and tell him we're here?'

The guards looked at one another.

'Fellow commanding officers and all that?' Yedder added.

One guard nodded, and moved to the centre of the doorway as the other one went into the castle.

Yedder eyed the ramparts. 'So, this is Rude's new gaff, Gil.'

'I wish he'd told us he was moving – we could have helped.'

'Or at least brought a castle-warming gift.'

Yedder turned to the guard. 'Is everybody here?'

'No sir,' replied the guard. 'Only Lord Dibkiss's men.'

'Oh,' said Yedder. 'Surprising.'

'Not really, sir. Lord Dibkiss says he don't trust your men. No offence, sir.'

'Got the old biddy planted?' asked Rudolf.

'Mistress Stein has been buried,' replied Guildman coldly.

'So where's everybody else? Why are you on your own?'

'Funerals, Rude – family affairs and all that,' said Yedder. 'Didn't want to intrude on Roz's private grief, you know... it's hit her pretty hard.'

Rudolf grunted. 'Not as hard as I'd like to.'

Guildman's fingers tightened around the hilt of his sword.

'A little unnecessary,' he said, 'now you've got the castle.'

'Back in my rightful place,' Rudolf beamed. 'Feels *so* good.'

'As long as you're happy.'

'Oh, I am. But there's something I'd be even happier knowing.' The smile vanished and Rudolf's eyes narrowed. 'What are you two doing here on your own?'

'What *we're* doing here's irrelevant now,' said Guildman, 'since *you're* already here.'

'Irrelevant or not, Guildman, I want to know, because I think you're here to sabotage my plan.'

'We didn't know you *had* a plan,' said Yedder.

Guildman threw out his arms. 'And why would I spend vast amounts of money to get you this castle only to sabotage it?'

'Ah!' said Rudolf, pointing at him. 'But you didn't, did you?'

'Didn't what?'

'Get me this castle. I came here and got it myself.'

'So?'

'What do you mean, "so"?' said Rudolf.

Guildman turned. 'Yedder, do you understand him?'

Yedder shook his head. 'Sorry, old bean. He's lost me.'

They both looked at Rudolf in expectation.

He bared his teeth. 'Why would you come back here without that vicious viper and her cohorts?'

'Mr and Mrs B are hardly cohorts, Rude,' Yedder pointed out. 'They're staff.'

Rudolf put his arm around Yedder's shoulders.

'Yedder, I'll ask you once more and if you don't give me a straight answer I'm going to make life very painful for you.'

'All right, calm down, old thing.'

Rudolf took a deep breath. 'I am calm – at the moment. Now what's Guildman playing at by coming back here on his own? And before you say he wasn't on his own he had you with him, let me point out these guards who have sharp implements and nothing to do. Now what is Guildman's plan?'

'Why would I have a plan?' asked Guildman.

'Because Yedder's not bright enough to think of one.'

'Oh, thanks,' said Yedder.

'However,' Rudolf continued, 'he is bright enough to tell me what you are doing here.'

'We came,' said Guildman quietly, 'to unsecure the castle.'

'*Un*secure the castle? Don't you mean *secure* the castle?'

'No, I mean unsecure the castle. We were going to check on the defences and see if we could disable any precautions that may have been taken ready for our assault.'

Rudolf looked hard at Guildman.

'Our assault was going to be when, exactly?'

Guildman sighed. 'Well, it was going to be next week, but it appears you have beaten us to it.'

'Yes!' Rudolf took his arm from Yedder's shoulders and punched the air. 'I have, haven't I? For once in my life, I've beaten you, Guildman. Beaten you well and truly.'

'So it seems,' said Guildman.

'One thing still bothers me, though,' Rudolf continued. 'It would've been so much easier to bring an army and get the castle— no, let me rephrase that. It *was* so much easier to bring an army and get the castle when it was undefended because everybody was out! Why didn't you do that?'

Yedder's mouth dropped open. 'Take the castle while Roz's out at her aunty's funeral?! Hardly sporting, Rude.'

'Not the action of a gentleman,' agreed Guildman.

'"Not the action of a gentleman",' Rudolf mocked. '"Hardly sporting, Rude." That's the trouble with you two. You've no idea how to be lords. It's not hardly bloody sporting, Yedder, it's a tactical masterstroke. It's the work of genius. I've walked into this castle without lifting a sword. A clean and decisive victory, Guildman. If I'd waited for you and your men, there'd have been blood and guts all over the walls.'

Guildman was impassive. 'Even so, they wouldn't have been yours, would they?'

Rudolf slapped him across the face. Yedder reached for his sword but found several halberds pointing at his chest.

'Careful, Guildman,' said Rudolf. 'Surely it's not in your precious code of honour to insult your host in his own home?'

'Half of which will be mine anyway,' replied Guildman. 'We have a signed, legally binding agreement, remember? Once in residence, you will assign me half the castle.'

'Oh, the *agreement*,' said Rudolf, reaching into his back pocket. He brandished his copy of the contract, ripped it in two and threw it at Guildman. 'Guards! Throw them out!'

Yedder and Guildman were bundled towards the door.

'And tell my ex-wife,' called Rudolf, 'if she comes within two hundred yards of this place, she's a dead woman.'

'So, I think we know what needs to be done now,' said Guildman in a low voice as he and Yedder lay on the path where they'd been thrown.

'And quickly,' Yedder agreed.

They sat up and looked at the castle.

'How many can you see?' asked Guildman.

'The two guarding the gate... two more on the front towers watching us. I'd bank on him having two at the back as well.'

'So only the four inside.'

'Correct.'

They stood, and Guildman clapped his hand on his friend's shoulder as they turned to walk away from the castle.

'Time to put our money where Mistress Stein's mouth was.'

Yedder smiled. 'That's an awful lot of money.'

Fyer and Edley, the two guards stationed on the front towers, watched Yedder and Guildman stride along the path towards town, shake hands and go their separate ways. In a short while Yedder was as lost from sight in the higgledy-piggledy alleys of Maund as Guildman was in the depths of the forest.

There had never been so many people squeezed around the table in Durney's cottage.

'None of you has to do anything I ask of you,' said Guildman.

'Not again,' said Gussie. 'We've been through all this once with' – he gesticulated wildly at Rosa – 'madam over there. Just get on with it.' Everybody looked at him. 'My lord,' he added.

Guildman coughed. 'Right. We need spies inside the castle.'

Gussie's hand was first in the air. 'I'll go.'

'I don't think he'd let you in, Gussie.'

'What about me?' asked Sooty.

Rosa stroked his head. 'You'd be too easily recognised, Sootbags.'

'You're forgetting,' he said smugly, 'I'm a shape-shifter.'

The white cat became a tawny long-haired terrier.

'Very impressive,' said Igress.

'Thank you,' said the terrier.

'And you're forgetting,' said Gussie, 'that transforming needs a lot of concentration and you've got a very short attention span. As soon as something surprises you, you forget what you're supposed to be.'

Sooty sighed. 'Fair comment.' He slowly started to revert to a white cat from the tip of his tail, but suddenly he was completely back to normal. 'Wait a minute...'

'See what I mean?' said Gussie.

'How do you know about me and transforming?'

Gussie's eyes darted wildly round the table, but help came there none. His hand went to his mouth, and the silver bangle round his wrist glittered in the glow of the fire.

'I don't know,' he said. 'I don't know how... I just... know.'

'Nonetheless, Spirit,' said Guildman, 'if you can't keep it up, then – as Rosalind says – you'd be too easily recognised.'

'Can you disguise him, Aidan?' asked Igress. 'You painted Durney's clay heads brilliantly. Could you camouflage Sooty?'

Aidan reddened. 'Dunno. I'll give it a go.'

'Come on then,' said Sooty, leaping from Rosa's lap and walking across the table as Aidan reached for his art box. 'Time's a-wasting.'

'Good,' said Guildman. 'Now, Beaton and Mrs B.'

'Beaton'd better stay with us,' said Rosa. 'Rudolf won't have forgiven him yet for tying him to a billiard table.'

'I should still go, though, milady,' volunteered Mrs B. 'Otherwise you'll have nobody on the inside.'

'Thank you, Mrs B,' said Guildman. 'And Mason can go.'

Mason folded his arms. 'I ain't going in there to get killed.'

'You will go,' said Guildman, 'and you will not get killed.'

'Why won't I?'

'Because Rudolf has already met you and knows you've been working on the castle.'

Mason pouted. 'He thinks I'm called Basin.'

'Which is evidence that he disregards you. You pose no threat. If you were his enemy he'd know your name.'

'Besides,' added Durney, 'you're a builder, aren't you? You're there to *rebuild* the castle, not get Rudolf out of it.'

'For the which I hasn't been paid yet.'

'You hasn't finished the job yet,' Rosa reminded him.

Guildman threw two gold pieces across the table to him.

'I will pay double your original fee once the job is complete,

Mason, so you *will* be going back into the castle.'

Mrs B put her hand on Mason's arm. 'Please, Mr Mason. I'll make you a nice cup of tea when I get back in my kitchen.'

Mason's gaze rested on Mrs B's hand then travelled up her arm until he was looking directly into her eyes. Consequently it escaped him that Beaton's fists clenched, and that Rosa got up and stood next to her butler.

Mason put his hand over Mrs B's.

Rosa clamped her hand over Beaton's mouth.

'Mrs B,' said Mason, 'I'd be happy to escort you.'

The guard ushered Mrs B and Mason into the Great Hall.

'Good day to you, my lord,' said Mrs B, taking off her coat. 'How many for dinner?'

Rudolf squinted. 'Dinner?'

'Yes, sir. Milord and his troops will want some decent food inside them, won't they?'

'Well, yes, of course... but where's Beaton?'

Mrs B's face fell. 'Oh sir... after all these years... he's let me down.' She took out a hanky and her lip started to tremble. 'Says he daren't come back on account of having tied you to a billiard table, milord.'

'Oh, that. He was only following orders, wasn't he?'

'I told him that, sir, but he says you're ruthless and you don't forgive and forget.'

Rudolf put his arm around her. 'He's right. What kind of master would I be if I went around forgiving and forgetting?'

Mrs B composed herself. 'I said that, milord, but he's too much of a coward to come back and face you, so' – she took in a small, sharp breath – 'so I've left him, sir.'

Rudolf let go of her.

'You've left your husband to come back and work for me?'

Mrs B coughed. 'Begging your lordship's pardon, I serve the castle, not its owners. I was here long before yourself and I shall be here long after you've gone and if I can't cook and housekeep in this castle – well, my life's pointless, sir. This is my home. I left that... that *coward*... to come home.'

'Good for you.'

She linked her arm through Mason's and gently patted him.

'And Mr Mason's been very supportive, sir.'

Rudolf's smirked. 'I bet he has.'

Mason cleared his throat.

Mrs B brightened. 'Mr Mason's here to carry on with the building work, aren't you, dear? Once he's had a cup of tea, that is.' She giggled. 'You know what builders are like, milord. Can't do *anything* without a cup of tea.' She giggled again. 'Can I get you anything, milord?'

'Normal service, Mrs B. There's eleven of us for dinner.'

'Very good, sir. Whichever of your men is your food taster?'

'What?'

Mrs B looked surprised at his reaction.

'Your food taster, sir. I think a gentleman as important as you ought to have one and I'd feel happier knowing that if anything was to happen to you, I'd be above suspicion, sir.'

Rudolf laughed. 'Damn it, Mrs B, you're a wonderful cook, and clever enough to always have an alibi. If you weren't so ugly, and – let's face it – so old, you'd be my kind of woman.'

Durney was detailed to take the cart back up the tunnel and wait, whilst Gussie led the others – including a now ginger Sooty – along the path he'd once cleared with Fran. They stopped at the bottom of the slide.

'Here it is,' said Gussie, 'but as I told you, it's very slippery.'

'Nevertheless,' said Guildman, 'we've got to try.'

'Igress,' said Gussie, 'would you lie on the slope, please?'

Igress, carrying the coffin ropes, lay on her back on the slide. Gussie put his hands under her feet and effortlessly pushed her part way up the smooth metal surface.

'Now you, Rosalind,' said Guildman.

Rosa manoeuvred round Gussie and lay down with her head between Igress's ankles. Gussie let go of Igress, and her feet came to rest on Rosa's shoulders. Gussie put his hands under Rosa's feet and pushed again. Both Rosa and Igress travelled up the slope. Aidan shut his eyes and followed suit, as did Beaton and Guildman. Gussie gave an almighty push, propelling the human tower as far up the slope as his strength would allow.

A cry came from far away at the top. 'Ow!'

'She's made it!' cascaded down the slope from Rosa. 'But we can't see anything. It's pitch black!'

'Oh, bugger,' said Gussie. 'I forgot to bring any torches.'

'Let me help,' said Sooty.

By the time Gussie had finished saying, 'What are you going to do?' Sooty was walking up everybody, offering apologies as he went. 'Sorry... shut your eyes... pardon me... 'scuse me... oops, sorry... mind your head...'

When he got to the top, he stretched out, closed his eyes,

stuffed his front paws in his ears and breathed very deeply and evenly. Slowly, an eerie light suffused the top of the slope as he transformed into a giant glow-worm.

'Oh, well done,' cried Igress, and she stroked his back. Instantly the slope was plunged into darkness.

'Please!' he snapped. 'I'm trying to concentrate.'

Svan, the guard nominated as the food taster, put the tray down on the table. Rich aromas wafted from the steaming dinner and caressed the nose of the other guard in the room.

Rudolf lifted his knife and fork. 'Have you tasted this?'

'Oh yes, sir,' said Svan. 'Beautiful.'

'No ill effects?'

'Only despair at having finished it and an overwhelming desire for more, sir.'

Svan's guileless expression made Rudolf wonder just what they were making soldiers out of these days. He motioned to the other guard. 'You – whatever your name is—'

'Rhume, sir.'

Rudolf started on his dinner. 'Rhume, yes. Go get fed, and bring me another bottle of Beaton Special.'

Rhume saluted, salivated and marched off to the kitchen.

By Sooty's glow, Igress was able to knot the two coffin ropes into one and fasten it around the hook in the floor. Holding on to the rope with one hand, she helped Rosa up the last couple of feet then they dropped the end of the rope down to Aidan, who swarmed up it with the ease of one whose only childhood toys had been a length of hawser and a tree.

Beaton, who had been born into a butler's uniform and as a result had never needed to climb anything but steps, fashioned a basic rope cradle around him and back-pedalled up the slope, pulled by the others. Guildman adopted a military caterpillar approach on the rope, bending and stretching until he gained the top, which only left Gussie.

They dropped the rope to him, and took the strain. Before Gussie had time to think about it muscle memory took over, grasped the rope and swung his legs upwards until his feet were planted on the top of the tunnel. Hauling hand over fist on the rope, he walked up the tunnel ceiling, much to the surprise and approval of the rest of the party.

'Battling Bill,' he panted when he got to the top, 'was a bargee before he took up boxing. He used to go through canal tunnels like that.'

'Good man,' said Guildman. 'What happens now?'

'Hang on,' Gussie replied, bending down to Sooty. The light vanished and there were whispers in the dark before the light came on again, and Sooty remained as stiff as a board when Gussie pointed him upwards in the lift shaft, his light dimly illuminating a broad beam spanning the shaft. From it – and way out of reach – a rope fell away into the darkness.

'See that rope?' said Gussie. 'It goes down into a thing called a lift. If we can get to the lift, we're laughing.'

Mrs B was positioning the last kitchen chair on its individual rug as Rhume walked in. She pulled the chair from the table again and patted the back of it. 'Take a pew, love.'

Rhume sat, put his helmet on the table and his eyes tracked

the dinner coming his way. Even as Mrs B put the plate on the table, his knife and fork were swooping. By the time she'd folded her arms, his cheeks were already bulging with food.

'From a big family?' she asked.

'Fourteen,' he spluttered, spraying morsels in all directions.

'I thought so. You never see cutlery speed like that in an only child. Drink?'

Rhume nodded without breaking his seamless cycle of stab, cut, stuff in mouth.

Mrs B set a beaker of colourless spirit by his plate.

'A glass of Beaton Extra to wash it down.'

Without losing his grip on the cutlery, Rhume lifted three fingers to signify his thanks. Mrs B walked to the sink to pick up a cloth, and by the time she'd returned to the table to wipe up the crumbs, Rhume's plate was empty and he was tipping the last drops of Beaton Extra into his mouth. As he put the beaker back on the table, he wiped his mouth on his sleeve and let out a satisfied, 'Ahhh.'

'All right, love?'

'Grand, missus. Any chance of any more?'

Seconds later his plate was full again.

Full of his head as he slumped unconscious.

Guildman threw the free end of the knotted coffin ropes into the lift-shaft, and Aidan climbed down. Unfortunately, he reached the bottom of the rope before he did the top of the lift. He peered into the darkness until his eyes hurt, but darkness was all he saw.

'Right! Let's sort this place out.'

Rudolf picked up a poker from the fireplace and headed for the laboratory. His available guards dutifully followed.

Mrs B tilted Rhume back in the chair, put his helmet on his lap and dragged the chair and its load silently on its rug towards the kitchen wall. She reached into one of the cupboards, and the wall swung open.

'First one coming through,' she whispered.

'Right you are,' answered Durney from the tunnel.

Mrs B tipped Rhume out of the chair. She and Durney briskly divested him of his uniform and equipment, tied his hands and feet and dumped him in Durney's cart. Mrs B re-entered the kitchen and closed the wall. Then, having put the chair and the rug back at the table, she washed up.

Aidan lay panting on the floor by the liftshaft.

'Black as hell's kettle,' he said. 'Can't tell how far away it is. Might be two foot, might be two hundred. Sorry.'

He looked at his reddened hands. It'd be weeks before he'd be able to hold a paintbrush again.

'I've got an idea,' said Rosa. 'Gil, is there any way you could get this rope over that beam up there to make a sort of rope swing? If Aidan could use this rope to swing out to that one, he could go down that one into the lift.'

Gussie pointed Sooty upwards in the lift shaft again; the beam spanning the shaft was high above them.

'Hmm,' said Guildman. He gathered several loops of the free end of the rope, and with Gussie holding his arm for balance, leant out into the lift shaft and threw them towards the beam. They got nowhere near, simply flopping back into his hands.

'Here, let me have a go,' said Gussie and, hanging on to Beaton and Guildman for safety, he easily shot the rope over the beam, caught it as it swung past him again and gave it to Beaton, whose knotting skills were proving invaluable.

Mrs B waved a bottle of Beaton Special around the doorway.

'I've brought you another, milord,' she called over the smashing of glass, denting of crucibles and hacking of workbenches. 'I remember you like a couple of an afternoon.'

The destruction ceased while Rudolf crunched his way across the floor. 'Glad to see you've not forgotten me, Mrs B. But where's Rhume?'

'What room, sir?'

'Rhume. The guard I sent to get the beer.'

'There's been nobody in my kitchen since Mr Svan, sir.'

'Probably got lost, sir,' volunteered Svan. 'Never did seem very bright.'

'No, but he did seem hungry,' said Rudolf. 'It should have been easy enough for him to follow his nose, even with all these false doorways. Temeraire – go with Mrs B and see if you can find him.'

Aidan stood in the rope harness knotted by Beaton, waiting to be hoisted and swung out into the shaft.

'Take these,' ordered Guildman, handing over his gold-embroidered black kid funeral gauntlets to Aidan. 'All the money in the world will not buy you new hands.'

'Hang on,' said Rosa, hitching up her skirt.

Guildman and Beaton instinctively turned their backs. Gussie covered his eyes. Igress covered Aidan's.

A white cotton petticoat fell to the floor. 'If we tear a couple of strips off this,' said Rosa, stepping out of it, 'we can tie Sooty to Aidan so he's got more light. It's all right, boys – you can look now.'

Beaton took the petticoat from her. 'Allow me, milady.'

With a few sharp tugs he ripped the petticoat apart, and from the rags made a cradle. Sooty was laid in it and tied against Aidan's back.

'Ready?' said Gussie.

Aidan nodded.

Gussie hauled on the rope, lifting Aidan's feet from the floor. Guildman pulled Aidan back and then pushed him out into the shaft. Aidan grabbed the lift hawser, wrapped his legs around it, unfastened his harness and slowly descended into the blackness.

With every hand-hold of Aidan's descent, the light at the top of the shaft faded until there was nothing but velvet blackness. Everyone was quiet, and no-one made a move; not only were they listening for noises indicating Aidan's success, but a step in the wrong direction could mean plummeting downwards – one way or another.

~✦~

NOTES ON

Time

Everybody has their own definition of Time, as anyone who's ever waited for someone else knows.

Some people think that Time is money, so don't ever ask them to spare you five minutes or, with extortionate interest rates, you'll end up paying them back in a few days.

Some think that Time is an ever-flowing river, but they're the ones who fell asleep in physics and woke up in geography.

Some think that Time is a fragrant herb, but that just makes you shake your head and mutter ruefully about falling standards in education.

Some think that Time heals all wounds, but they never lost anybody to the sword or the shotgun.

And some think that Time is a constant, regulated, ordered division of the day into ever-smaller units until the units become too tiny to worry about. But that's simply Time being shorthand for knowing when things happen. It's a lot easier to say 'yesterday' than it is to say 'that space between sunrise and sunset that's not this one but the one before this one'.

Those who think that Time is elastic are almost right, but Time needs no physical intervention to stretch or shrink. Time is dynamic, which means – quite simply – that it can expand and contract at will. It's the most variable stuff around, and it obeys no known laws other than this: it will never go at the speed you want it to.

Especially when you're emotionally charged, in complete darkness, on the edge of a precipitous drop, waiting for someone to rescue you.

~•~

By Sooty's light Aidan quickly found the trapdoor on the roof of the lift and heaved it open. After climbing into the lift he soon realised what he had to do next, and he hauled on the large wheel that drove the winding mechanism.

He was about two feet away from those shouting encouragement when there was a wooden thud and the wheel refused to turn any further.

'Come on, Aidan,' called Igress. 'You can do it!'

But he couldn't.

'Release the wheel a bit and try again,' said Gussie.

Aidan wasn't particularly keen on undoing the hard work he'd just put in, and followed Gussie's advice grudgingly.

There was another wooden thud, and again the wheel came to a halt.

'I'm not sure... how much longer... I can hold this thing,' Aidan groaned.

'Hang on,' said Gussie, 'I'm coming down.'

'No! I'll never be able to hold it with you on it!'

Rosa looked out into the lift shaft which was dimly illuminated by light leaking through the open trapdoor.

'Aidan,' she soothed, 'you're doing really well. It's the trapdoor that's stuck on something and stopping you. Go back down a bit and hold it there, and I'll close the trapdoor. There'll be a loud bang, but hold on tight, all right?'

'Yes, yes, but hurry up!'

He released the wheel a little, and almost let go of it entirely when the trapdoor in the roof slammed shut. Having screamed more than he'd really have liked Igress to hear, he hauled on the wheel again, the lift rose and five faces peered in at him through the side opening.

'Now what?' said Aidan.

'We need to stop it dropping back down,' said Gussie, leaning in and putting one hand on the ceiling of the lift to support the weight. Guildman and Beaton followed suit. 'That loop of rope goes through the wheel and round this hook.'

Rosa and Igress took care of the rope and Aidan tentatively released the wheel. Realising it was secure, he let his exhausted arms flop by his side as if they were of no further use to him.

Gussie walked into the lift, took hold of the wheel and waited for the others to enter. The last one in was Igress, who pressed the tiny lever by the hook, picked up the released rope and stepped into the confined space of the lift.

Guildman and Beaton helped Gussie with the wheel and the lift began a slow, measured descent until it would go no further and they were faced with a short passageway.

'It looks like a dead end,' said Rosa.

'It's not,' said Gussie, taking the still-glowing Sooty from Aidan's back and pushing his way between Rosa and Igress. He walked into the passageway leading away from the lift, turned an iron ring on the wall, the brickwork parted and the wall swung open. He smiled and waved the others forward.

When they had all gathered on the other side of the wall, Igress hugged Aidan and gave him a smacking kiss on the cheek. 'Well done, Aidan. You were bloody brilliant.'

In the gloom of the tunnel no-one saw Aidan blush but Rosa did notice Gussie staring at the bundle of rushes and twigs that was the torch, still sitting in its holder.

'What's wrong?' she asked.

Gussie gave Sooty to Guildman then lifted the torch. A shadow fell across his heart. 'Oh, y'know... I was just thinking of the last time I was here... with... with the old gal, and...'

Rosa put her hand on his arm.

He looked at her, his eyes brimming over. 'And... she picked up this torch, and ran her hand over it like this...'

He stroked the top of the torch and it burst into flame. He yelped and dropped it.

'How on earth did you do that?' said Igress.

Everyone saw the terror written on his face. 'I don't know!'

Guildman handed Sooty to Rosa, snatched up the torch and took Gussie by the elbow, steering him ahead of the party.

'I fear we have more pressing things to worry about. Gussie, lead us out of here. You're the only one who can.'

There comes a time in everybody's life when they know what they're doing, they know they're the best person for the job and they know they should be leading the expedition if only for this one task. However, it's rare that the fool at the top recognises this, even rarer that they step aside and let the one who knows what they're doing take over, and practically unheard of that they acknowledge it publicly. But rare was becoming the norm for Gussie, so he took the torch and set off along the next tunnel. 'This way then!'

He'd only gone a few steps when he turned. 'Now we've got some light, we ought to let Sooty have a rest.'

Rosa sat down and laid Sooty on her lap. So deep was his concentration that calling him was ineffective; she had to massage his back for a while before he returned to furry, albeit ginger, normal.

'Is it over yet?' he said weakly.

She stroked his head. 'No, not yet, darling. But thanks to you, we're on the way.'

He screwed his face up as he slowly stretched himself out.

'Ow ow ow ow ow,' he said rapidly.

'Are you hurt?'

He sucked air in through his teeth. 'Pins and needles.'

Beaton took a hip flask from his pocket.

'Here you are Master Sooty, this'll buck you up a bit.'

He poured some of its liquid contents into his cupped hand and offered it to Sooty, who lapped it up.

'Thank you, Beaton,' said Sooty, after he'd licked the butler's hand clean. 'I needed that.'

Beaton took out a white handkerchief and wiped his hand dry, then replaced the top on the hip flask and put it back in his pocket.

'What? No seconds?' asked Sooty.

Rosa tweaked one of his ears. 'Don't push your luck, sunshine. You've still got a job to do, remember, and I'm not having you giving the game away by rolling round drunk.'

'Rhume, you miserable little bogslime,' Temeraire roared across the kitchen, 'come out now and I won't tear you from arse to eyeball for dereliction of duty! Oh, begging your pardon for the language, missus.' He sniffed. 'Something smells good.'

'Why, thank you – that's dinner,' smiled Mrs B. 'Oh, and here you are in the kitchen. 'You'd best have yours now before you go traipsing off looking for your friend.'

'I didn't ought to really,' he said, in a way which suggested he wasn't entirely convinced of the sentiment.

Mrs B looked shocked. 'Whatever would your poor mother say if she heard you turning down good food?'

Gussie led the others through the twisting tunnels until he came to a set of steps leading to a door. 'This takes us into the stable block,' he whispered. 'I'll see if the coast's clear.'

He turned an iron ring and pulled at the wall. Daylight shot through the opening and he peered round the brickwork.

'The smithy?!' he cried. 'We shouldn't be in the smithy!'

Rosa ran up the steps and prodded him.

'Shush! One of Rudolf's men might hear you!'

She turned to Guildman, who was walking up the steps.

'How many men does he have, Gil?'

'Ten.'

'Right. Let's see how many we can see.'

She started for the smithy but Guildman seized her arm.

'You can't go out there alone,' he said. 'It's too risky.'

'I can,' said Igress, 'it's my smithy.'

Guildman looked at her for a moment.

'All right then – but I'll go with you.'

'Begging your pardon, my lord,' Beaton broke in, 'but I fear you are too recognisable to Lord Rudolf and his men.'

'I'm not,' said Gussie. 'He doesn't know me from a smack in the chops.'

'May I suggest that Mr Gussie goes into the smithy in the guise of a blacksmith and does a reconnaissance for us?'

'Fine idea, Beaton,' said Rosa. 'Except he doesn't look much like a blacksmith in that lot.'

Gussie looked down at himself. Mr Beaton Senior's dress uniform was far too grand for a smithy.

Rosa began to undo his tie.

'Come on Gussie, let's get these off you.'

'But I don't know anything about blacksmithing,' Gussie protested as Beaton took the jacket.

'You'll look like you do if you roll your sleeves up,' said Igress, ripping a piece off her skirt and tying it on him as a neckerchief. 'Look. There's a leather pinafore draped on one of the anvils. Go put it on like you were returning to work.'

'Then what?'

'Then come back over to the forge and get the fire good and hot. It's winter and I'll need some warmth.'

'And grubby your shirt up a bit,' advised Rosa, squeezing handfuls of the white cotton to make it look less starched. 'You look very clean for a blacksmith.'

Gussie flapped his hands.

'All right, all right. Leave me alone.'

He coughed, stuck out his chin and walked into the smithy, sauntering across to the anvil with all the nonchalance of a man with a knife between his shoulder blades.

He picked up the pinafore and very deliberately put it on, smoothing it down with both hands. Then, stopping just short of the caricature of mime, he walked to the forge and raked over the embers. To his surprise, there was a lot of residual heat left in the coals from the fire Igress kept continually lit.

Sooty ambled into the smithy.

Gussie acted surprised, and both his manner and his speech were stiff and stilted as he bent down and said, 'Oh, hello, little pussy cat,' patting Sooty as though he were a wooden toy.

'It's all right, you can relax,' said Sooty, scanning the courtyard. 'Nobody's looking this way.'

Gussie sagged a little, which made him look much more like an overworked blacksmith than an undertalented actor.

Sooty yawned and stretched out his claws.

'Hello – is that Mr Mason I hear?'

Mason struggled along the ramparts with a block of stone until he was stopped by Guard Edley on the East Wing Tower.

'Where d'you think you're going with that?' asked Edley.

'The West Wing Tower.'

'Why come this way?'

'Because the West Wing Tower steps is unsafe.'

'How do you know they're unsafe?'

'How do I know?' echoed Mason, affronted as only a builder can be if you question his working practices or his estimates. 'I know, because I built 'em, that's how I know.'

A look of determination came over his face and he hefted the stone. 'Now if you've no more questions—'

'That stone,' said Edley. 'What's it for?'

'What's it for? I'll tell you what it's for, matey.' Mason nodded towards the stepped stonework on the walls of the ramparts. 'See these? These is what we in the trade calls crenellations, right? Now you stand with your back to this here crenel – this gap – and look over there towards your mate on the West Wing Tower. Now look at his crenellations compared to yours.'

'He's got bigger gaps.'

'So he has. That's because he's missing some merlons, them little walls on each side of the crenel. And that's what this stone's for – to make the merlons so's his crenellations match yours. Now if you don't mind, Lord Rudolf's very impatient for the work to be done and this stone's heavy. Here, feel.'

Mason heaved the stone towards Edley whose rugby instincts overtook him. He dropped his pikestaff and caught the stone – just in time to carry it over the side and into the moat as Mason pushed him.

With a deft flick of flags, one of Yedder's boat crews was detailed to pick up their erstwhile comrade.

'We're going to need more rags,' said Rosa, 'to tie people up and keep them quiet.' She hitched up her skirt and dropped another petticoat. 'Beaton, you know what to do.'

The butler began tearing the petticoat into strips.

'Milady,' said Aidan, 'your coat's got braid round the edge. We could use that as rope.'

'Oh, well spotted, Aidan,' said Rosa. 'Never occurred to me at all.' She gave him her coat and, using Beaton's pocket knife, Aidan set to work separating the braid from the fabric.

Igress took off her cloak and handed it to Guildman. She looked into his eyes as she unpinned her hair and shook it, ruffling it with her hands. Still keeping his gaze, she lifted her blouse from the waistband of her skirt and let it hang carelessly. When she started to undo the buttons, he lifted his eyes and stared above her head.

'Stay here and keep quiet,' she warned them all, before adjusting her blouse to reveal bare shoulders. She took her cloak back from Guildman, folded it a few times and swaggered off with it.

Aidan gulped. 'W— what's she doing?'

'I don't know,' said Guildman. 'But *she* seems to.'

Igress sauntered provocatively across the smithy to Gussie.

'Pump the bellows,' she whispered. 'Keep the fire going.'

'You look like you're hot enough already,' Gussie shot.

'Cheeky. Now when I say so, go into the wood workshop. There's a piece of wood clamped in a vice. Start planing it. Keep your back to the door and don't come out. Got it?'

'Wood, vice, plane. All right.' He paused for a moment. 'What are you going to do?'

'Work a little vice of my own.'

'What?'

'Never you mind. Just keep the fire hot, do as I tell you and don't worry.'

'Ooh, little miss bossy boots.'

She grinned and slapped him on the arm.

He pumped the bellows as she sat on her folded cloak on the floor, knees bent, feet flat on the stone flags. Her legs were parted, the dip of her skirt offering a tantalising glimpse of her assets, holding promise of further delights.

'Meeeee-owwww!' said Sooty, padding over to her. 'A girl like you could start a fight, you know.'

'I do hope so,' she said. She patted her skirt, and he needed no further encouragement to nestle comfortably in the warmth between her thighs.

'Who are you?' asked Fyer, the guard on the West Wing Tower.

'Mason,' the builder replied, picking up one of the loose blocks of stone that still littered the ramparts.

'And where are you going with that?'

'Flippin' 'eck, not you an' all. Nogginhead's just asked me the same question.'

'Who?'

'Your mate over on the East Wing Tower,' said Mason. He turned and pointed. 'Him over the— hell's bells, where is he? You're supposed to be guarding this place, aren't you?'

'We *are* guarding it.'

Mason's foot tapped, his brow furrowed and he spoke rapidly. '*He's* not. He's not even there, is he? What if one of these blokes in these boats decides to scale the walls and he's not there to stop him? Eh? Eh? Then where will you be? Up to your armpits in infidels, let me tell you. Oh no, this is not good. This is not good at all.'

'But—' said Fyer.

'But? There's no buts about it, my lad. I'm going to report this to Lord Rudolf. He's paying you good money to guard this castle. I'm disgusted, and I'm going to tell him. Here, hold this.'

He pushed the stone into Fyer's hands, and kept on pushing until Fyer had overbalanced and pitched backwards over the broken crenellations.

'Excuse me, sir!' shouted Svan.

'What?!' Rudolf shouted back, not looking up from reducing the laboratory equipment to shards. 'What is it?'

'What's that noise sir?'

Rudolf stopped hacking. 'Noise?'

'Rumbling noise, sir. Heard it about three times now.'

'Oh, it's probably only Durney bringing wood for— Durney! The tunnel!'

Mrs B tilted her head towards the kitchen door and listened, then went into the tunnel and closed the wall.

'Time to go, Durney,' she said, and soon the cart containing the comatose Rhume and Temeraire was rumbling away down the tunnel.

Rudolf and his remaining house guards ran into the kitchen, but all they found was a dirty plate and an empty glass.

Rudolf hammered on the wall, but it wouldn't open.

'Now Gussie,' whispered Igress, 'go to the wood workshop.'

He went, and shortly the sound of planing for no purpose floated through the smithy as the guard strolled over.

'Afternoon, sergeant,' Igress purred.

'I'm not a sergeant, I'm only a guard.'

She leant forward, gravity straining her buttons.

'Don't matter,' she said. 'I love a man in uniform. What's your name, guard?'

'Rale. And yours?'

'Igress. We're servants.' She tilted her head towards the wood workshop. 'There's him in there, me and' – she looked down and stroked Sooty – 'pussy here.'

Sooty turned his snigger into a sneeze. He screwed his eyes tight shut, but the laughter was rising and he started to shake.

'There, there,' soothed Igress. 'I think pussy's getting cold.'

Rale knelt on one knee to stroke him, but Sooty shot between his legs and streaked across the courtyard. The surprised guard overbalanced and landed on Igress, pulling her blouse even further down.

'Sorry,' she breathed, 'he's a bit shy around men.'

'Not like you, then.'

The sound of a plane shushing on wood reminded Rale there was someone else nearby. He nodded in the direction of the sound. 'Who's that?'

'Husband.'

Rale tried to get up. 'Husband?'

Igress draped a leg across his body.

'Not a proper husband,' she pouted, 'if you know what I mean. Not since the accident.'

'Accident?'

'Oh, a terrible blacksmithing accident. Hammer, anvil, not looking what he was doing... bang!' She sighed as deeply as her chest would allow, swaying slightly from side to side. 'Since then, you might say we've... gone short.'

'But not for much longer,' Rale leered.

Igress began a deep throaty laugh.

'Shhh!' hissed Rale. 'He'll hear you!'

Igress shook her head, a movement which somehow managed to involve her bosom.

'His hearing's shot. Years of banging in the smithy. Deaf as a post.' She stopped. 'Mind you, he's not blind. Stand up.'

The guard did as she said, somewhat reluctantly as Igress swung her leg wide to release him and in the process rucked her skirt up even higher.

'Give us a hand,' she said.

Rale pulled her to her feet and his chest. She steadied herself by leaning on him; he stopped her from falling by clasping her backside and biting her shoulder.

Igress grabbed his hand. 'Come on – there's an empty room over here we can use.' She dragged him towards the secret passageway and pushed him in.

In a matter of seconds he was bound and gagged.

'Well done, Igress!' said Rosa. 'That was very impressive.'

'Yes, thank you,' said Guildman. 'An object lesson in... erm... outflanking the enemy by... ah... by any means possible.'

Igress blushed. Aidan stared at her. Beaton chuckled.

'Now we must split Rudolf's men up further,' said Guildman. 'Leave him isolated. We need a distraction – something he can't ignore. Something he'll have to send men to deal with.'

'A fire?' said Rosa. 'I'd rather burn the place to the ground than let him have it. And there's a fire in the smithy already. What if it got out of hand?'

'Good idea,' said Guildman, turning to go.

Igress pulled him back. 'I'll do it!' she said. 'I'll set fire to the stables. That thatched roof should go up dead easy.'

She walked towards the fire.

'Nobody's burning down *my* smithy.'

Mason was walking smartly along the ramparts towards the East Wing Tower when Rudolf and two men reached the top of the stairs and burst out into the daylight. Mason did a swift about-turn and subtly speeded up.

'Get him!' ordered Rudolf.

Mason was fast running out of rampart when one of the guards gripped his collar. However, had the guard known that Mason would keep going and jump off the tower, he might have let go earlier rather than let gravity pull Mason from his grasp. He crashed into the stonework to stop himself going over the side. Being Mason's handiwork, it went over with him.

Rudolf looked down to see both men and stonework smash into the moat. He also saw a flotilla of small boats surrounding the castle and Yedder standing on the opposite bank.

Yedder waved his flags in a variety of signals.

Rudolf looked at Svan.

'What's he saying?'

'Hope – you – don't – mind,' Svan translated. 'Brought – chaps – for – rowing – practice.'

Rudolf shook his head and turned his back on Yedder, only to see smoke and flames rising from the stables. His face and his hands contorted with hate.

'Oh, you spiteful baggage!' he spat. 'She's torching my castle! Svan, Coest – put that fire out! You two – follow me. She's gonna die for this!'

Svan and Coest proved particularly ineffectual at firefighting, partly because they didn't know where to get water from, but chiefly because they ran into Guildman and Gussie.

After a brief but conclusive skirmish, Gussie and Beaton

had Svan secured in the wood workshop, and Aidan and Guildman had Coest at sword point in the foundry.

'A soldier does not betray his regiment,' stated Coest.

Guildman pulled open Coest's tunic and poured a bag of coins inside it.

'I ask again – how many men are left inside?'

Coest smiled. 'Two, my lord.'

In the wood workshop, Beaton was pedalling away on a treadle. A series of ropes and cogs transferred the power from the treadle along a hinged wooden arm to a circular saw. The faster Beaton pedalled, the faster the saw spun and the more effective it became at cutting through the bench on which Svan was tied.

'Surely you don't expect me to talk,' said Svan.

'Yes, Mr Svan,' replied Gussie. 'That's *exactly* what I expect you to do.'

Beaton pedalled faster.

Between Svan's legs, the blade chewed its way through the bench, rapidly approaching the point of no return.

'All right!' Svan shrieked. 'I'll talk.'

Soon both guards lay trussed up in the secret passageway alongside their already fallen comrade.

'Svan said there's two left inside,' Gussie told Guildman.

'Good.' Guildman turned to the others. 'You stay here and stop the fire spreading; Gussie and I will go for Rudolf.'

'I'm coming with you,' said Rosa.

'No.'

'It's my castle, and I'm coming with you.'

Rudolf and his last two guards burst into the kitchen through one door as Guildman, Gussie and Rosa ran in from the courtyard. Rudolf immediately retreated behind his men, sheathed his sword and drew a dagger.

'Kill the men!' he ordered. 'The bitch is mine!'

The guards charged.

As Guildman and Gussie reacted, Rudolf dodged round them, slashing at Guildman's free arm before dragging Rosa out of the kitchen by the hair.

Gussie's head may have been pacifist but his body had spent most of its life fighting. He snatched up the lid from Mrs B's enormous jam pan and used it as a shield to deflect sword-thrusts while jabbing at the guard with a carving knife, even managing to get one or two cuts in before a well-aimed kick sent the knife spinning from his hand. The guard's sword clanged onto his makeshift shield; Gussie forced his opponent's arm upwards and delivered a punch to the stomach. The blow winded the guard, who staggered backwards, giving Gussie just enough time to smash the pan lid into the side of the guard's head, knocking him to the floor, stunning him temporarily and breaking the knob off.

Many years of swordsmanship ensured Guildman was faster on his feet than his opponent, but he wasn't used to fighting someone who shrugged off injury like rain and relentlessly came back for more. He knew he was tiring; his sword got heavier with every strike against his opponent's weapon, and the exertion was increasing the blood loss from the gash on his arm. Desperation drove him on: he must go after Rudolf and save Rosalind, but he couldn't leave Gussie to fight two men on his own, especially when one of them seemed impervious to pain.

Suddenly he saw his opponent pinned to the wall thanks to the end of a kitchen bench wielded by Gussie.

'Hit him!' Gussie yelled. 'Hit him hard!'

Guildman reached for the nearest pan and swung it with as much force as he could muster against the guard's helmet. The clash of metal against metal sent shock waves up his arm, but that was nothing compared to the effect on the guard, who slumped unconscious.

Guildman turned. 'Behind you!' he called.

Without looking, Gussie stabbed the bench backwards, catching the other guard in the very place guaranteed to bend a man double. As the guard tried to stand up, Gussie's punch told him he shouldn't and he hit the deck for the last time.

Gussie turned back to Guildman, but he had already gone.

'Psst! Psst! Gussie!'

Gussie spun round.

A small ginger head poked round the side of a bread crock.

'Can I come out now?'

Relief swept over Gussie.

'Yes, yes, come out. And go for help!'

Sooty bolted through the castle as fast as he could, bounding up the stairs of the East Wing Tower and skidding across the flagstones when he reached the open air. He stood up against the stonework of the battlements, but was too short to see over the top.

'Yedder!' he shrieked.

Yedder looked up.

A golden eagle took off from behind the battlements and glided to earth in a sweeping arc, coming to rest on the ground beside him.

'Help, Yedder!' it croaked. 'We need help!'

Guildman ran into the Great Hall, his sword in his right hand, his left arm hanging limply at his side. Rudolf was waiting, the blade of a dagger across Rosa's throat.

'Drop your sword, Guildman,' commanded Rudolf.

Guildman walked towards him.

'Drop it!'

Guildman carried on walking.

'Drop your sword or I kill her!'

Guildman's sword clattered on the stone floor.

'Let her go, Rudolf.'

'No. She'll only come after me, scratching and gouging and kicking and biting.'

'More than that, you bastard!' Rosa hissed.

'Mind you, it'd be the first time in our marriage she'd wanted to get near me, wouldn't it, darling?' He kissed her on the cheek.

She gritted her teeth and pulled her face away from his. The skin on her neck tightened under the pressure of the blade.

'Let her go,' said Guildman. 'Kill me.'

'Oh, now we're getting somewhere,' Rudolf smiled. 'Somebody finally understands what's going to happen.'

'Chaaaaaarge!' Gussie hollered, hurtling into the room brandishing one of the guards' swords.

419

Rudolf instinctively swung the dagger towards him.

Rosa elbowed Rudolf in the stomach and as he folded, Guildman kicked the blade from his hand and picked up his own sword.

Rudolf fled into the laboratory and slammed the door.

'Leave him, Gussie,' called Guildman. 'He's mine.'

Gussie stopped outside the door.

'I am supposed to be the bodyguard.'

Guildman walked towards him.

'Which is why she'll need you when this is over.'

'And you? Won't she need you?'

'Excuse me,' Rosa butted in, '*she's* still here. Doesn't *she* get a say in what happens?'

They both looked at her.

'Not this time,' said Gussie. He turned to Guildman. 'This is the job I was created for.'

Guildman shook his head. 'This job was mine long before you were even thought of. I should have done it years ago.'

'But?'

Guildman sighed. 'But I didn't. And now I am. So, turn the handle and stand aside.'

Gussie did as he was bidden. Guildman hefted his sword, and with his foot gently pushed the door. It creaked slowly open to reveal Rudolf, pointing the shotgun straight at him.

Guildman backed slowly across the hall as Rudolf came out of the laboratory.

'No!' shouted Rosa, and ran towards them. She was stopped by Gussie, who held her fast despite her kicking and struggling.

'Good boy,' said Rudolf. 'Now bring her over here to stand next to him.'

Gussie did so.

'That's it,' said Rudolf. 'I want her to get the full effect.'

'Don't,' said Guildman calmly.

'Don't what? Don't hurt her? I'm not going to hurt her; you are. You're going to hurt her, because you're going to die. Your death will destroy her, so I don't have to.'

Rosa howled in torment.

Rudolf laughed. 'Listen to that pain, Guildman. Exquisite, isn't it? You've no idea how good that sounds.'

'You bastard!' yelled Rosa. 'You harm one hair on his head—'

'I won't,' said Rudolf, jabbing the end of the shotgun into Guildman's chest, pushing him back a step. 'I'm going straight through his heart.'

Rosa's rage turned to body-wracking sobs. 'No! No!'

She slumped against Gussie.

Rudolf's lip curled. 'That's all you've ever said to me, isn't it? Always no, no, no. What's wrong with you? Haven't you always wanted a man who'll pour his heart out to you? I'm giving you what you want, Rosa. I'm going to open his heart and all his love will come pouring out – just for you.' His face fell. 'You could look happy about it.'

'I will kill you!' she screamed.

'First things first, dear. Guildman, throw the sword away – you won't be needing it.'

Guildman dropped the weapon.

Rudolf smirked.

'What a disappointment you've been,' he sneered. 'Such a gentleman when you could have been a proper lord. So, like a gentleman, I'm going to allow you some last words. And then like a lord, I'm going to kill you.'

Guildman was silent.

'No last words, Guildman? No professions of love for another man's wife, perhaps? Oh, no, that'd be ungentlemanly, wouldn't it?'

Guildman took Rosa's hand and cupped her palm under his left elbow. He breathed deeply, closed his eyes and raised his bloodstained left hand to his shoulder. Pain scored his face as he formed a fist, sending fresh blood running from his wound and dropping into her hand. He stared through her eyes into the depths of her heart.

'By this blood,' he whispered, 'remember: for all the years gone by, and for all the years to come, you are my love. You are the flame that fires my life. Without you there is nothing.'

She pressed the precious blood to her chest. Trembling, she lifted the silver chain around her neck; the button Guildman had ripped from his sleeve hung there. She scraped the embossed crest across her palm, raising pinpricks of crimson.

'By this blood I will remember.'

Guildman pressed his lips hard on her fingers.

'Oh, very touching,' said Rudolf. 'Anything else?'

Guildman dropped his arms, took a deep breath and raised his head. The pain left his face, as if he had drawn new strength from his love, and his voice was steady.

'Yes. The difference between right and wrong.'

'What?' snapped Rudolf. 'What about it?'

Guildman concentrated on Rudolf's eyes.

'I ask that Rosalind teaches this to our child.'

Rudolf waved one hand around.

'Yes, yes, yes, all very noble and honourable I'm—'

He stopped, his eyes deadening as he replayed the conversation in his mind. By the time he'd squealed 'What?!' Gussie had pushed Guildman and Rosa out of the way and stuck two fat fingers in the gun barrels.

'What the hell are you doing?!' blazed Rudolf.

'Oh, come on now,' said Gussie amiably, 'you can't deprive a child of its father, can you?'

'I can after I've blown your bloody hand off.'

'Waste of time, ducky. She'll only sew me another one on.'

'Are you mad?!'

'Hark who's talking.'

Gussie grasped the gun barrel with his free hand and pulled it towards his chest.

'Go on, then,' he said. 'Oh, no, you can't, can you? You pull that trigger and you'll blow us both to smithereens, and who'll be the loser then, eh? Not me; I'm a dead man already. Hell, I'm two dead men already.'

Rudolf dropped the gun and drew his sword with a wide sweep of his arm. The blade slashed across Gussie's chest.

Gussie roared, and the air thickened.

Revelations blasted through his mind, heart and soul in a surging eruption: lost cities, primeval forests, books of enchantment, colours beyond imagining; people he couldn't have known yet half-recognised; sounds, smells and tastes that awakened in him memories of a childhood he'd never had, horrors he'd never experienced and joys never gifted to him.

And forcing into every pore and cell of his being, driving this torrent, drenching him with the intensity of obsession, was the power. The power of every root, fin, wing, claw and hand, the power to sunder continents and rend civilisations, the power of glaciers and volcanoes and tidal waves, the very power of life and death, magnificent, majestic, unfettered, unstoppable, unceasing.

The all-consuming, cataclysmic power of the world.

He had once more irrevocably changed. Someone, or something, had blasted away the dark cell of his existence and thrust him into the sunlight of life. Every nerve-ending had reawakened, every emotion seared him. In what, to him, took an age, he looked down at the blood soaking into his shirt from the laceration across his chest. The pain gave birth to rage and he drew back a clenched fist, hatred narrowing his eyes.

'Gussie!' screamed Rosa. 'Stop!'

Guildman threw himself in front of Rudolf, and his shoulder took the full force of Gussie's fist.

Gussie shuddered as Guildman hit the floor. 'What the—'

Rosa ran to Guildman, lying crumpled at Rudolf's feet.

Rudolf did not move.

Gussie stared at him, then leant over and knocked on Rudolf's forehead.

It was as cold and hard as a marble statue should be.

A voice from the doorway startled him.

'I say,' called Yedder. 'Are we too late for the scrap?'

After a bit of wincing and stiff-bodied manoeuvring, Gussie lay back on his pillows. Mrs B sat on the bed and fed him home-made soup; it warmed and comforted him and took some of the physical pain away, if not the mental turmoil.

'Does this mean I'm a witch then?' he asked.

Mrs B chuckled as she lifted the tray from the bed and put it on a side table.

'Oh no, love. You have the power, but not the training.'

He pulled idly at the bedcover. 'Is that why I didn't kill Rudolf? Because I don't have the training?'

'You marbleised him – how dead do you want him to be?'

She started to stand, but Gussie caught hold of her arm.

'*She* could have killed him, couldn't she?'

Mrs B took a sharp breath through her teeth and grimaced. 'Yes... and no.'

'She didn't need me to do it – she had the power.'

'But not the reason.'

'What?'

'It's not right to go round killing people for no reason at all – people end up dead.'

'But what about her ladyship?'

Mrs B smiled. 'Oh, yes, she'd have killed him.'

Gussie tutted. 'No... I mean – wasn't her ladyship's safety a good reason?'

Mrs B shook her head. 'The only way Miss Frances could have killed Lord Rudolf was if he'd put someone's life in immediate danger. She knew he would sooner or later, but he hadn't actually done it.'

'He'd threatened often enough.'

'Ah, but that's potential danger, not immediate. You can't go acting on potential dangers, because they have a habit of going away and then you'll have killed somebody for nothing. If we all went round acting on potential dangers, we'd never set foot out of bed.'

Gussie looked glum.

'You said she knew he would sooner or later...'

'But he didn't. Not while she was still alive.'

'But I thought she could make anybody do what she wanted. Couldn't she have forced him to do it?'

Mrs B's face clouded over. She stood up and began to straighten the bedcovers. 'Oh, Gussie, that's a dangerous path to tread. She was sailing close enough to the wind as it was.'

'What do you mean?'

'It was bad enough her even tempting him into a position where he might be killed; she couldn't have forced him into it. That would've been manipulating him for her own purposes.'

'So? Doesn't everybody do that to somebody or other? Isn't that just life?'

'Not when it involves death. And not in the Systerhood. You can't go round creating your own need.'

Gussie's face was a blank.

Mrs B softened a little, and sat on the bed again. 'If Rudolf attacked, Miss Frances would need to kill him, right?'

Gussie nodded. 'Right.'

'If he attacks voluntarily, he's creating that need. But if she forces him to attack, she's creating that need. Do you see the difference?'

'Yes...'

'Well, for her to create that need goes against all the teachings of the Systerhood. Witches exist to fulfil needs, not to create them. Do you understand?'

Gussie furrowed his brow. 'I think so.'

'Good. Because this is vital and you must understand it: to create a need for the power is to serve the power and that's not right. The power is there to serve, not to be served. Unchecked, power corrupts. And if the Systers create a need for their own existence, then they and the power they possess are out of control.'

'Mrs B, how do you know all this? Are you a witch?'

Mrs B smiled. 'No, love. I did train, but I didn't graduate.'

'Why not?'

'Let's just say there was a man and a different kind of magic involved.'

Fran's wake never took place as planned because of the battle for the castle, but Rosa knew that at some point there had to be a celebration of Fran's life at which memories of her could be shared and cherished and her sacrifice truly appreciated. However, she waited until Rudolf's condition could be considered permanent, as she was mindful of the effect that a surprise guest turning up can have on a party.

And that brought them to the first anniversary of Gussie's arrival in the castle.

The feast was magnificent and so plentiful that everyone had to help serve it before they could help eat it. Mrs B had pulled out all the stops to honour the woman she'd known and loved since the day an attentive and intelligent baby arrived in the world and was given the name Lady Frances Stein.

As the small talk got bigger and the fond smiles turned to laughter, Mrs B topped up everybody's glass and handed Rosa a teaspoon. Rosa looked up at her; Mrs B nodded her approval.

Rosa stood up and knocked the teaspoon on the side of her glass.

The hubbub subsided.

'Friends,' she said, 'if I might take a moment of your time. Funny thing, time. How much can change in a year; how much can change in an instant. This has been a grand celebration of Aunty Fran's life, but – with your permission, Durney and Sootbags – I'd now like to make it a celebration of all our lives.'

Sooty and Durney conferred.

'Permission granted,' said Sooty. 'It's what she would have wanted.'

'Thank you. So let's make it an anniversary party for Igress and Aidan, who came here just over a year ago. Let's make it a sort of rebirthday party for Gussie, who underwent the biggest change of his life – or lives – a year ago. Let's make it a thank-you celebration for all of you for helping me to be rid of Rudolf and safe in my own home. I'm immensely grateful to each and every one of you. Yes, even you, Mason. If you hadn't been such a slow builder, you wouldn't have been around to deal with a couple of guards on the battlements.'

A ripple of laughter went round the table and Yedder clapped Mason on the back. Mason managed to look both proud and insulted.

Rosa picked up her glass.

'Ladies and gentlemen, friends who have become family,

please join me in raising your glasses. To life: may we never be afraid to live it.'

All glasses were duly raised. 'To life.'

'And if I might just add one more thing,' Rosa went on, taking Guildman's hand. 'Gil. I owe you more than I'll ever know. Thank you for keeping Rudolf at bay, and thank you for the knowledge that you would always be there for me. You were done a great wrong many years ago, and now is the time to put that right, so I ask you this: will you come here to Castle Stein and live with me – as my husband? Lord Guildman, will you marry me?'

His answer was lost in the cheering, but no man ever looked happier.

As the hangovers faded the following day, Beaton showed a guest into the drawing room at Castle Stein. Gussie and Guildman stood until the lady with the long coat and flat shoes had sat down.

'Millie,' said Rosa. 'I have a proposition for you.'

'Oh?'

'I'd like my ex-husband to live with you.'

Millie's face fell. 'Oh.'

'We know how fond you are of him...'

'With all due respect, Lady Stein, I've learnt that Rudolf is not a man to be fond of. He is to be tolerated – and only for the income that he brings.'

'Which could be considerable,' said Guildman.

'Which could be non-existent, knowing Rudolf.'

Gussie laughed. Millie stared at him.

Guildman spoke again.

'I will ensure the income is considerable, madam.'

'I don't doubt my lord's generosity,' said Millie, 'but experience has taught me that Rudolf is not husband material.'

'Oh, you don't have to marry him,' said Rosa.

'You couldn't,' chirped Gussie.

Millie studied him. 'Couldn't?'

'He is no longer the man he was,' said Guildman.

'Not dead,' added Gussie, 'but not exactly alive either.'

Her gaze lingered on Gussie.

'I've no desire to be a nursemaid,' she said.

Guildman chuckled.

'Nor will you be, madam. Rudolf will simply live with you, and I will pay you a generous rent for the room he occupies.'

'But I'd have to look after him.'

Rosa stood up. 'It might help if you saw him.'

'Is something wrong?' asked Gussie. 'You're staring at me.'

Millie blushed. 'Forgive me. You remind me of someone, that's all.' She walked over to him and rubbed her hands down his arms. 'You've got a body very much like someone I knew.'

Gussie opened his shirt.

'Was it Battling Bill Baldicott, the Peripatetic Prize-Fighter?' he asked.

Millie took a sharp breath and put her hand to her mouth.

'Oh! Is it...? Are you...?'

Gussie nodded.

As tears came to her eyes she slowly reached out and gently touched his chest, avoiding the scar made by Rudolf's sword.

'The spread eagle. He had that done for me, you know.'

'Really?'

She smiled wistfully.

'Yes... in honour of something he used to like.'

'Oh,' Gussie beamed, then his expression changed entirely. 'Oh. Ahem. Yes, well.'

'To be honest, I was a bit confused. I didn't recognise your face, but I never forget a body.'

She touched Gussie's chest again.

'Would you... would you come and see me sometime? For old times' sake?'

This time Gussie blushed. 'I'm afraid that's all it'd be for.'

'Here he is,' Rosa broke in, taking dust-sheets off Rudolf.

Millie turned. 'Ah... Is that...?'

Rosa nodded and knocked on his arm.

'Marble. And it is him. Not a carving.'

'And you want me to take him?'

'He won't be any trouble.'

Gussie snorted. 'That'll make a change.'

'He doesn't belong here,' explained Guildman, 'and he spent so many happy hours with you.'

Millie sighed. 'I suppose I could use him as a whip stand.'

Rosa beamed. 'I'll have him sent round tomorrow.'

'And I'd like payment in advance, milord, if you please. Nothing personal, but I like to be certain.'

'Of course,' said Guildman. 'Although it is said that nothing is certain except death and taxes.'

The non-taxpaying Gussie grinned.

'They're wrong. On both counts.'

Thanks

The biggest thanks again go to my husband Martin, without whom this book would never have been written.

Thanks also to: the very talented Lisa-Marie Damant once more for her marvellous illustrations; David V Barrett for much-needed and invaluable advice; the Inspector and Sarge for long-time support and more; Paul Kerensa for education, encouragement and kind words; Katie Prickett, Niki Devine and Gill Anderton for honest and heartening feedback (sorry about the bread, Niki); Pam Mungroo for enlightenment and guidance; the readers of *Gingerbread Children* for asking for another book; and to you, for having a look at this one.

And to Tony. I didn't get to choose you as my brother, but I would have.

About the author

Carol Carman is a former shop assistant, computer programmer, systems analyst, house doer-upper, fog-knitter, treacle-weaver and BBC journalist and radio presenter.

She edits and illustrates the *Grunty Fen* series of books by Christopher South (dennisofgruntyfen.co.uk), she's written fiction and poetry for the website *The Reaper* and just for her own amusement she leads a double life as the poet Fifi Fanshawe (fififanshawe.co.uk).

If you've enjoyed this book, please tell your friends and do leave a review wherever you can – Amazon, Facebook, Goodreads or wherever – they really do help an author.

And if you haven't read Carol's first novel, *Gingerbread Children*, what are you waiting for?

You can follow Carol on Twitter @CarolCarman.

If you'd like to get in touch, please email:

info@mccawmedia.co.uk